Coast on Fire

An Apocalyptic LitRPG
Book 5 of the System Apocalypse

By

Tao Wong

Copyright

This is a work of fiction. Names, characters, businesses, places, events and incidents are either the products of the author's imagination or used in a fictitious manner. Any resemblance to actual persons, living or dead, or actual events is purely coincidental.

This book is licensed for your personal enjoyment only. This book may not be re-sold or given away to other people. If you would like to share this book with another person, please purchase an additional copy for each recipient. If you're reading this book and did not purchase it, or it was not purchased for your use only, then please return to your favorite book retailer and purchase your own copy. Thank you for respecting the hard work of this author.

A Starlit Publishing Book
Published by Starlit Publishing
69 Teslin Rd
Whitehorse, YT
Y1A 3M5
Canada

www.starlitpublishing.com

Ebook ISBN: 9781775380931
Paperback ISBN: 9781775380948
Hardcover ISBN: 9781989458501

Books in The System Apocalypse series

Main Storyline

Life in the North

Redeemer of the Dead

The Cost of Survival

Cities in Chains

Coast on Fire

World Unbound

Stars Awoken

Rebel Star

Stars Asunder

Anthologies

System Apocalypse Short Story Anthology Volume 1

Comic Series

The System Apocalypse (On-going)

Contents

What Has Gone Before

Nearly two years have passed since the System came to Earth, bringing with it monsters, aliens and glowing blue boxes of notifications that detailed their lives in this new Galactic System. Humanity was forced to evolve, their lives dictated by statistic screens, Classes and Skills that gave them strength and abilities beyond the norm, providing them a fighting chance to survive. Still, the apocalypse saw the death of nearly 90% of humanity, the malfunctioning of everything electronic and a new, blood-filled existence.

John Lee was camping in the Yukon when the change occurred. Gifted with perks beyond the normal, he journeyed to Whitehorse and aided in the establishment of the city under the rule of the alien Truinnar, Lord Graxan Roxley. With the help of other survivors, the Village of Whitehorse was quickly established to provide a stable environment for growth, battling rampant dungeons, monster hordes and crazed humans in equal measure.

As Whitehorse was now firmly under the control of the Truinnar, John and his teammates left for British Columbia to aid the surviving members of humanity. There, they found a mixed bag of survivors and settlements. Some cities were ravaged, destroyed in infrastructure, population and hope. Others struggled on, under the control of other aliens and human control. Working together, the survivors and John battled the aggressive Thirteen Moon Sect in their attempts to take over British Columbia, eventually winning against the larger, more powerful alien organisation.

Now the owner of numerous settlements in British Columbia including Vancouver, Kamloops and Kelowna, John must deal with the politics of the settlements and continue with his plans of liberating as much of humanity as possible.

Chapter 1

I've kited a Salamander over forty Levels above me. Had a Master Level Psychic fry my brain. Hell, I've even faced down a Dragon. I've faced calamities and crises, fought and bled, nearly died more times than I care to admit. For all that, I'd rather go back to any of those times than stay a single minute longer in this meeting room.

"Electronic voting is a farce! We cannot trust his AI to count the votes!" Christian Hecker, Level 38 Infantry Soldier and ex-CEO of a gold mining corporation, says as he leans forward. The mid-60s, brown-eyed, greying Caucasian gentleman is bereft of his rifle today, though he has his sword slung over his back and a pistol on his hip.

I regard the boomer as he besmirches Kim—my AI's—honor, wondering what his angle is. As one side of the split Combat Classers, I've quickly learned that Christian always has an angle.

"We're not doing a straight democratic election," snaps Damian. The Level 22 Appraiser is spinning a pen around his fingers, obviously uneasy in our company. He's got the lowest Level of everyone here, even if it is rising faster now that the Thirteen Moon Sect isn't around. Still, as the voice of the scavengers, he has the moral right to be here. One that I'd had to enforce by dismissing an earlier meeting when he had been "unavoidably delayed." "That'd just let you people load up all the seats with your friends."

"You people?" Anika arches a graceful, plucked eyebrow. Ms. Kapoor, the Level 39 Summoner, is one of the few non-Caucasians in this room.

"I believe he means the non-Delvers," I answer Anika, smiling slightly in amusement at Damian's poor phrasing.

She inclines her head to me, appearing somewhat mollified. Truthfully, I figure getting annoyed over bad phrasing shows how uptight she is, but my role isn't to judge, just pacify.

"Rationed seats are wrong," Tsien Wuji says. He's a Level 39 Engineer specializing in infrastructure construction. He's also an influential member of the non-Combat Classers, Damien's counterpart, and the other of the pair of their representatives, the more talkative of the two.

"Allocated," Leo Brand says with a sigh, covering his face with his hand.

There are a few quick smiles around the room as Leo once again corrects Wuji's malapropism. Leo's an ex-ER doctor, now a Doctor who finds most of his life's work superfluous. After all, with the System, if you're not dead, you'll heal. And since he's a self-professed coward who refuses to enter the city dungeon, he's been at a bit of a loss as to what to do with himself.

"Will you finally buy a Language upgrade in the Shop? I'll even pay for it," Anika says once again with a roll of her eyes.

"No need. Waste money," Wuji denies her offer once again.

"We cannot continue this farce of a government any longer. My people want results!" Christian says, ignoring the byplay as he pushes ahead with his agenda. "They are sick and tired of being locked out of decisions about their city."

"Farce?" Ali says, floating visible beside me. The two-foot-tall Spirit chuckles softly, his olive skin beautifully off-set by the dark suit and cream shirt he wears. "Did you call boy-o a farce?"

"Farce?" Wuji whispers to Leo. His friend leans over to explain the word.

"I consider this unelected government, this tyrannical rule of your *boy-o* a farce," Christian says.

When we first met, Christian had been the less combative of the pair of combat Classer leaders. The last week of dealing with me has worn away the false warmth he showcased before I rejected his subtle manipulation and, later on, bribes.

"It's certainly better than what we had with the Thirteen Moons," Anika says, waving around the noisy conference room. The wave also encompasses my only direct support in the room—Lana, my girlfriend and the more politically inclined part of my team. Though, by common agreement, she stays silent during these meetings, letting me take the brunt of criticism and allowing her to work her charm during the breaks. "We're at least having a meeting. Even if someone doesn't listen to us."

Finally fed up with the various barbs, I speak up. "I'd listen if you people ever came to an agreement."

"We would, but your irrational requirements are impossible to meet!" Christian snaps.

"Oh? All I'm asking is that you all come to a reasonable agreement on what the government would look like," I say. "I'm only here today because you promised me that you would have an agreement by today."

"We promised that we'd have something to discuss with you," Anika says, eyes dancing with humor. "I'll admit, we haven't gotten that far though."

"Fine. Since I'm here, someone sum up the sticking points."

Silence takes hold of the conference room at those words. The various "council" members suddenly find anywhere to look but at me. Wuji opens his mouth to speak, but Leo puts his hand on the man's arm, shaking his head. The older Chinese man subsides, allowing Damian to clear his throat.

"Well, we're currently facing a problem of deciding both the number of seats on the council and the method of election. The Delvers and ummm… my people, are looking for a guarantee that our voices will be heard. We refuse to continue to risk our lives, bringing in more revenue and goods than the ummm…" Damian stops there.

"You can call them civilians. Or crafters if you want," Ali offers. "The closest translation to the Galactic term is Artisan. Feel free to use it or not."

Damian nods in gratitude to Ali before he continues more confidently. "The Artisans want a straight election, but because of the ratio of combat Classers and Artisans—"

"Are you sure you want to base your argument on revenue?" Anika says wryly. "They'll eventually beat us, you know. In fact, I wouldn't be surprised if their generated revenues are already greater than ours if you include the other cities."

"That's not the point!" Christian says. "We are just trying to ensure we are not sent into battle and forced to guard people, without a say!"

Damian sighs and looks at me, his gaze serious. "I must admit my people have that concern too. Scavenging is growing more and more difficult with returns growing smaller. Sooner or later, I expect that most of my people will turn into hunters or delvers. And at that point, well…"

"We don't want the *Artisans* sending us into dangerous zones just so they can get better crafting material. Or under-paying for those items," Anika says.

"We not do that. The Shop set ceiling. Floor. Stopping place," Wuji says. "We pay good price. Get materials from you."

"A good price because you want the city to subsidize the purchases!" Christian snaps. "Otherwise, there's no way you'd be able to afford the Galactic price for most of our better material."

I sigh, listening to the argument devolve. No real surprise here. I've had Lana explain this discussion before, since it's similar to the one we had in Whitehorse. Simply put, low-cost materials almost always receive a better price locally. The cost of transportation often makes it possible for local Artisans to purchase those materials at a similar, if not slightly higher, price than what Galactic buyers would pay. However, and this is a big however, high Level materials aren't the same. The cost of transportation for high-Level materials is significantly lower as a percentage of price, which means Galactic buyers, who are both more numerous and better funded, can often offer a higher price than locals. Part of the reason is that for Artisans to gain Levels, they need to constantly challenge themselves with better materials. It's also one of the reasons why the cost of high Level enchantments and equipment climbs steeply.

It doesn't help that since we're on a Dungeon World with a consummate increase in Mana flow, we actually have a larger number of spawnings. That means that the volume of low-to-medium quality crafting material is higher, which of course results in greater efficiencies in transportation since Galactic corps can do larger mass teleportations or send bigger transport ships. All in all, it means that our crafters are in a bad competitive situation.

"We must Level!" Wuji insists.

"But taxing our purchases and sales puts our lives at risk," Anika says softly. "We need that equipment, those Class Skills. You don't put your lives at risk every time you try to Level."

"So we're not as important?" Leo says without heat. "Our lives don't matter?"

"You're not risking yours," Christian snaps.

I groan, watching them start up again. That barely attracts any attention, so I smack my hand on the table, grabbing everyone's attention. "All right, people. I've got another meeting to go to, so you guys keep talking. We'll talk again in another week."

"That's—"

"No, we need to—"

"These delays are unacceptable!" Christian says, standing.

"That's nice," I say with a smile to everyone, ignoring the various protests as I open a Portal.

Lana and Roland, her pet tiger, duck into the Portal first. The pitch-black hole in space swallows them without a ripple. Three quick steps, even while the council calls for me to come back, and a closed Portal later, I'm free.

***

A grin splits my face as I draw a deep breath of the sweet, sweet air of freedom.

"Ack!" I cough, a burning pain in my throat and lungs.

You are Poisoned

-3 HP per second

Duration: (Continuous till you are out of the cloud)

"Where did you bring us?" Lana says, her voice muffled by the helmet she's put on.

A moment later, my helmet expands from the collar around my neck, covering my face and clearing the air. I'm still poisoned, but it's no longer dangerous as my System-assisted healing fights the toxin.

"Just outside of Kelowna actually," I say with a frown, sword in hand as I survey our surroundings. Poison clouds aren't normal, as far as I know. I have to admit, I've only been here thrice since the change.

"Floating Poisonous Cloud. Not sure why, but it seems to be directed by the wind. Kim's telling me that wisps of this have hit the city, but nothing major. They're keeping the kids and other vulnerables inside, but prevailing winds will have the cloud gone in an hour," Ali says as he stares at notifications only he can see.

"Ali says it's natural. Sort of. Nothing to be concerned about," I tell Lana. She nods firmly, and we walk toward to the city. After a moment, I realize something. "Where's Roland?"

"He's already left."

"Ah… good." I nod and keep walking. Ever since she picked up the tiger, he's become her constant companion, even more than the puppies. "Wanted to ask you something. You've been hovering at Level 49 for a while now. Is something going on?"

"Nothing major. I've been channeling my experience to Roland to upgrade his Level. You remember, he was a bit on the lower end when we found him."

"You can do that?"

"It's a benefit of being a Linked companion for me. Makes it easier to find new companions and upgrade them. It only works until he hits my Level, then we'll upgrade at the same time."

"Are you going to continue that till he hits Level 49?" I say, trying to recall Roland's Level now—32 or something like that?

"Not sure yet," Lana says.

I nod, and we continue the walk in silence through the invisible cloud of poison, enjoying the beautiful, sunshine-lit valley, verdant plains with the occasional pine trees, and the river beside us, glittering with blue.

"Why did you drop us out so far?"

"Oh… umm…" I stutter. "Well…"

Lana arches an eyebrow at me before the buxom redhead takes my arm and squeezes her bountiful treasures into me. "Were you thinking of taking me for a walk?"

"Well… yeah. It's beautiful out here. Except for the cloud…" I sigh, shaking my head. "We haven't… well…" I fall silent, still uncomfortable talking about things like this.

Lana smiles, bonking her helmeted head against mine with a friendly nudge. "You couldn't have known. It was very sweet, and it is still beautiful."

I smile at that, relaxing slightly and giving the arm that holds mine a squeeze. For the next while, I can afford to just be a man walking his lady, talking about our days. For a while, I can put aside the niggling questions of what the Sect is doing, if the Duchess intends to expand south, and what, if anything, I'll do about the Americans.

For a little while.

***

Kelowna has seen better days. The once-picturesque town beside the river is still beautiful from a distance, but if you get closer, you notice the burnt-out buildings, abandoned vehicles, and occasional brown lawn. There's a desolate feeling to the city, which is significantly magnified in the abandoned outskirts.

Luckily, it takes us a while to receive the "entering Town" notification. The Sect was kind enough to actually decrease the settlement boundary to just East Kelowna, and even then, only the downtown region near the river and a bit east of that is considered Town. I'm grateful for them spending their funds on that, because otherwise, the settlement itself would still be in the Village stage, unable to reach the minimum land-owned threshold.

I still find it amusing that somehow, the town's City Center is the Benvoulin Church, rather than a more central location. I'm sure there's a study with a complex mathematical analysis of why each location is picked, especially for Dungeon Worlds, but that's a book even I refuse to read. I'm still debating if I should pay to shift the city center orb somewhere safer and more central, but for now, the church works.

As we walk into the historical, picturesque steepled place of worship, we're greeted by the titular overseer of the city. The older gentleman waves his show cane at me, no longer needing it thanks to the System, and greets me with a smile.

"John!" Kyle says. "Didn't expect you till later."

Kyle Reimer (Level 18 Vintner)
HP: 130/130
MP: 240/240
Conditions: None

"Afternoon, Kyle," I say, smiling. "I cut my other meeting short. They—" I glare at Lana after she elbows me, shooting me a warning glance. After a second, I realize her point and turn back to Kyle. "Well, here I am. Shall we go in?"

Kyle smiles slightly, seeing the interplay and probably reading a lot more into what I didn't say than he should have had the opportunity to. I'm still not used to this entire "being a leader" thing, but Lana is right. Bitching about one settlement to another is probably not a good idea.

"No need. I understand you upgraded your AI to allow you to upgrade any of your settlements without touching the core?" Kyle says.

"Yup, bits-for-brains is good to go," Ali says, making himself visible as he floats upside down, watching a System-generated TV screen the right way around. The fact that I can see his screen means Ali's messing with me. Again.

"Good. Then I've got a few things to show you," Kyle says with a wave.

I nod, glancing at the building and absently offering a nod to the god who's supposed to be inside. Not that I believe in Him, but my father ground respect into me. And if He is real, well... a little respect won't hurt.

"To begin, I thought you'd like to see the mall? It's our main trade hub for now..."

Lana and I nod, and the trio of us take off, walking through the streets to the mall. Kyle prattles on, filling us in on the town and how things have gone. Kelowna was an interesting case in the settlements I own. Due to its number of surrounding vineyards, it had seen a significant immigration of Alchemists, Chemists, Biologists, and other alien Artisans intent on studying the change the System has brought about. And exploiting it of course.

"So everyone is happy about the Sect leaving, including the aliens," Kyle finishes. "Seems like they were trying to drive away a number of our earliest immigrants. The only big issue we have is that we're struggling to work out the legal aspects of having so many different alien groups in the city. Our Lawyers and Accountants are struggling to understand the differences in the various corporations and organizations that have purchased land in the city, especially because many of them are claiming specific tax exemptions that we've never heard of."

"Capital L and A? Or just old time professionals?" I say, curious.

"Mostly. A few took up other Classes but have gone back to their original professions, but most of those have dual-Classed," Kyle explains.

"Getting that first Level took a while, but at least they don't have to discard their combat Classes. Some are just doing the job without the Class."

I grunt in acknowledgement. I wouldn't want to discard my combat Class to become a Lawyer either. In this world, being able to kick ass makes a lot of difference. As things settle down, more and more knowledge about the System keeps cropping up. The fact that it's not only possible but relatively easy to dual-Class is something those in Kelowna learned early on and disseminated to the other settlements. Not that I'm intending to change my Class.

"Did they buy the Skill to divvy up their experience?" Ali asks and, at the puzzled glances all around, rolls his eyes. "There's a Class Skill called... ummm…"

"PORTION CONTROL."

"Right, Portion… wait, that's not what it's called," Ali says, glaring at the notification window created by Kim, my AI. Sniggers abound at the Spirit's grumpy response. "Anyway, it's a Skill similar to Lana's, except you can only use it on yourself. You can portion out part or all of your experience to a specific Class rather than having an even split. Makes it possible to Level both, unlike a complete changeover."

"I still think that keeping your first Class is a much better idea," Lana says, shaking her head. "Especially if it's a combat Class. Hard enough Leveling one Class, but having to switchover midway? That's insane, especially with the increased experience gain requirements."

"Not everyone wants to be a fighter, my dear," Kyle says with a smile. "In fact, most of us are happy that things are settling down. It's why we want your boy to grant the Adventurer's Guild's request as soon as possible. Once they're established, we can seriously work on getting our fields back."

"And you're happy with the fact that so many of your fields have been bought by others?" I say with a frown.

"Happy isn't the right word. Maybe resigned? It's better than having the land become a spawning ground. And you might have noticed we lost a lot more people than most. Most of the original landowners are either absent or dead, and what we have is a large number of Galactic aliens and temporary workers," Kyle says with a shrug and a small smile. "The few who are around… well, let's just say some people have upgraded their places."

I snort but take his word for it. Not my place to handle the day-to-day operations. It's why I hired the older gentleman. In fact… "Have you looked at gene editing?"

"Looked at it," Kyle says evasively.

"Kyle…?"

"Look, young man, when you've reached the age I have, well, adding a few extra years isn't as attractive as you might think. All my friends are dead. Most of my family is too." At our wince, he adds, "Long before this. My wife succumbed to cancer a few years ago, and we never had kids. My brother died from a stroke a week before the change. This new world, it's interesting. I want to help, but I'm tired. At a certain point… well, it'd be nice to have a rest."

I grunt and drop the topic unhappily. Maybe I'll bug him later, but for now, I leave it. I find it hard to believe that any man who's managed to survive an entire year plus in this post-System world is the kind to roll over and die because he's "tired." Now it's just a matter of making Kyle see that too.

"Anyway, we were talking about that Adventurer's Guild. We've got four applications, each with their own people in town already…" Kyle says, changing the topic.

I stay silent, listening to Kyle and his opinions. It is, after all, why I came. The Settlement Screen might give me numbers and facts, but the in-person reports give me context.

***

Exhausted, I collapse onto my couch, grateful that the System continues to keep my Whitehorse residence in good shape. Early summer in Whitehorse means that at eight o'clock at night, the sun is still shining brightly, bringing the bright greens and blues to life. The transition from somewhat setting sun in Kelowna to bright light in Whitehorse had been slightly disorienting the first time I'd done it, but this time around, it seems natural. The only pity is that Lana decided to stay in Kamloops with her pets to spend more time with Mikito. Making multiple jumps to get home is annoying, but it seems to affect others more than me.

Silence. Blessed silence. Which is interrupted by a knocking on my door. I frown, then frown even more when I see who it is on my minimap. Resolutely, I ignore the knocking.

"John, I know you're in there." Roxley's voice is authoritative and commanding. Not because he's trying to order me around but because that's just the way he is. Even so, I have to admit that voice does things to me that wouldn't be polite to mention in company.

Lord Graxan Roxley. Duke of the Yukon. The Duchess of the Pourquoi States's errand boy on Earth. A tall, dark drink of muscle, nobility, and charisma. Someone I flirted with for a time—before the son of a bitch betrayed me and the city of Whitehorse by joining the Duchess. For all that, I can't help but be slightly interested in seeing him again…

"I'm coming in. Don't shoot."

I growl softly, deciding that I won't shoot him or even deign to stand. Instead, I put my elbow and arm over my eyes and stay flopped on my couch. It's only when an uncomfortable amount of time has passed that I move my hand away to see Roxley leaning against the doorjamb, staring at me with a look that dries my throat.

Down, boy. I've got a girlfriend.

Even if she's hinted that she's not entirely opposed to…

Down, boy.

Down.

I clear my throat and subtly shift my position by sitting up. Damn pretty dark elf. "What are you doing here?"

Roxley smirks before he straightens up, his face falling into a more serious expression. "As Her Grace's representative on Earth, I am here to greet the Redeemer of the Dead upon his entrance to her city and inquire about his intentions."

"I'm here to sleep," I state tersely. "Do you know how hard it is to not be bothered when I'm in my cities? Everyone wants a word with me. All. The. Damn. Time. I've got people literally walking into my house, demanding to talk to me about their latest pet project. Droids for recycling plastic, refurbishment of the kids' playgrounds, a grant for Galactic languages, and on and on."

"I keep telling boy-o if he shoots the first few, they'll stop bothering him," Ali says, waving hi to Roxley.

"Ali. I believe someone is awaiting you…?" Roxley says leadingly, getting a big grin from the Spirit who flickers then disappears. If I'm not wrong, the damn Spirit has gone to visit Roxley's AI to gossip once more. I'm still a little perturbed by what goes on on the backend between the two, but interrogating Ali has offered little answers.

Damn traitor. Then again, Ali has never seen my problem with Roxley and his actions.

"Ah. And you have no intentions of expanding your territory?" Roxley continues once we're alone.

"Not up north, no," I say, eyes narrowing. "And you?"

"The Duchess has stated that she has no intentions of expanding beyond your Watson Lake. Our intentions involve the north and the resource fields and zones therein," Roxley says, waving. "Our main point of focus is expanding the Towns of Whitehorse, Anchorage, and Fairbanks to Cities, thus increasing their respective zones of control."

"I see…" My eyes narrow as I try to decide how much I believe him. In the end, I decide to do so, mostly because I understand how much work Roxley has ahead of him. It makes no sense for the Duchess to take control of a bunch of lower Level zones when she hasn't completely controlled the areas she already "owns." Higher Level zones provide higher Level goods, which mean more money—never mind the Level-tourism revenue she stands to earn.

"On a personal basis, I am surprised to see you back. Are you not concerned about the Weapon Master?" Roxley says with a raised eyebrow.

"That's why I sent Ali through first." I grin then shrug. "I'm done running. I've gotten a few Levels since we last danced. And anyway, way I understand it, he's gone for now. I doubt he'll be back so soon."

"Risky." Roxley sighs, giving up on admonishing me. "And is that all the reason for returning? Nothing personal?" At my flat stare, Roxley sighs again. "Well then, as Her Grace's representative, I do extend my offer of aid in any matters of administration."

"Why?"

Pain and regret at my brusque attitude flicker across his face before he resumes a neutral expression. "Your presence south of our holdings is considered a benefit to Her Grace. You are much less likely to be combative than the Sect or any other, hmmm, foreign interests that may appear. As such, the stronger your government, the greater the benefit."

"Great…" I drawl as I assess the sincerity of his, and her, offer. "And what does this offer amount to? Credits? Technology? Maybe some Skill orbs?"

"None of the above, I fear," Roxley says. "While we do wish to aid you, the aid must be proportional. Advice, at this time, is the best we can offer."

"Advice," I say, sarcasm dripping from my voice. "Right, I'll make sure to ask for it. Now, I was here to sleep…"

"John…"

But I've already slumped back on the couch, arm thrown over my face in a copy of the same pose from before. Except this one radiates anger.

"Ms. Olmstead is doing well with treatment. I expect she will be on her feet within the next few days."

Sensing that I won't say anything, Roxley sighs, after which I hear the stomp of his feet leaving the house. I grunt in mild happiness, glad to be left alone and for the news he imparted.

Here to help. Har! Advice my ass.

***

It's much later, when I've finished stewing, that I manage to actually calm down enough to do what I had Portalled all the way north for. Since I'm currently limited to 1,000 KM per jump, I actually had to cast it thrice—once to Kamloops, then again into the middle of nowhere before arriving. I did kind of feel bad that I didn't spend more time in Kamloops visiting Lana and Mikito, but needs must come first. At the thought of the little Japanese Samurai, I made myself a promise to visit with her. Losing her apprentice, then Mel, in short order has resulted in Mikito withdrawing once again. While she isn't suicidal, she has grown quieter and more subdued. It's why Lana left the puppies behind with her—their furry presence is a good healing aid. Anna, on the other hand, is just getting lazy, preferring to sleep than go gallivanting with us on our errands.

Too many damn things to do and not enough time. I've been so busy, I haven't even dealt with the numerous notifications I received from the knockdown, drag-out fight with the Sect. Including that most important of ones—my Level Up. With a mental command, my Status Screen populates.

Status Screen			
Name	John Lee	Class	Erethran Honor Guard
Race	Human (Male)	Level	43
Titles			
Monster's Bane, Redeemer of the Dead, Duelist			
Health	1970	Stamina	1970
Mana	1510	Mana Regeneration	111 / minute
Attributes			
Strength	106	Agility	187
Constitution	197	Perception	61
Intelligence	151	Willpower	151
Charisma	16	Luck	32

Class Skills			
Mana Imbue	2	Blade Strike	2
Thousand Steps	1	Altered Space	2
Two are One	1	The Body's Resolve	3
Greater Detection	1	A Thousand blades	1
Soul Shield	2	Blink Step	2
Portal	3	Instantaneous Inventory*	1
Cleave*	2	Frenzy*	1
Elemental Strike*	1 (Ice)	Shrunken Footprints*	1
Tech Link*	2		

Combat Spells	
Improved Minor Healing (II)	Greater Regeneration
Greater Healing	Mana Drip
Improved Mana Dart (IV)	Enhanced Lightning Strike
Fireball	Polar Zone
Freezing Blade	

Being part of such an insane battle did wonders for my experience. Killing the Sect Enforcer pretty much by myself pushed me most of the way to the top of Level 40. After that, the numerous small fry and the Blood Warrior I dealt with pushed me two-thirds of the way through Level 41.

Ending the Master Level Psychic was enough to push me to Level 42 and netted me my third Title, as well as bonus experience for the kill.

Title Gained

For winning in a battle against a Combat Classer two Class Advancements above yours, you have earned the title **Duelist***. Others will fear your prowess from now on. Increased reputation in certain circles. +10% chance effect of social Skills in appropriate situations. +5% increase in damage against those with higher Class Advancements*

I whistle slightly, noting the Title's effects. Damn, but that's nice. Of course, I cheated. For one thing, that Psychic was a Level 1 Master Class. For another thing, he was only one Advancement Level higher than mine, though technically the System still reads me as a Basic Class since I'm still in my first tier. It's why my Monster's Bane Title is still so effective. I cheat.

After that, I learned another little secret of being the owner of a Settlement. Any battle conducted during a declared war actually nets the owners of those Settlements a small experience gain for the entire battle. Of course, since it's based off everyone killed, it was more than sufficient to push me up to Level 43, which is where I'm seated right now. It almost makes up for the fact that I currently have an "On-going War" declaration on the settlements, limiting some of the things I can purchase.

All those sudden experience gains mean that I have nine free attributes and two free Class Skill points. Now that I don't need Portal as desperately, I actually have a chance to consider what to do with these Class Skill points. Though first, I want to look at what I can do to shore up my attributes.

Charisma continues to be my "dump" stat, as per Jason's terminology. Though considering how I was—reluctantly—drawn into the world of politics, I might want to up it a little. Not that I have the Skills for it, but… yeah. Then we have my mainstays—my combat stats. I still feel as though my ability to perceive what the hell is going on lags behind what I am doing, especially when I am moving at the maximum speeds that my body can handle. It isn't a huge difference, but it is there. There is something to be said about putting more points into Perception, especially since Agility and Strength go up by themselves anyway. Unfortunately, there's no guarantee that the next few points will alter it in the way I need it to, rather than widening my hearing range or something less useful.

My Constitution is the bedrock of my survival, though more than once, I've noticed a distinct lack of Mana during my fights. Even with the ridiculous amount of regeneration I receive, once we start getting involved in these long, drawn-out battles, I realize exactly how hampered I can be by my Mana. It doesn't help that so many of my Spells were Mana hogs.

I'll admit, Luck is tempting as well. Even if I'm not adventuring as much, the bonus in loot drops is always nice, though harder to quantify. And having someone, something, with its finger on the scale seems like a nice idea. The gods know that I've seen enough of how fate can take a crap on you.

In the end, I discard Luck, Agility, and Strength. I'd increased Agility and Strength the last time around and Luck had a slight bump a few Levels back. With it being so nebulous, I can't justify using my points on it all the time. Better to go for something more tangible.

While Willpower upped my on-going Mana regeneration, I am leaning toward increasing Intelligence since it gives me a higher starting point. A single point of Intelligence is worth 10 Mana, which doesn't seem much but is worth 1/10th of a Blink Step, probably one of my most used Skills.

Constitution still continues to be a no-brainer. After all, I am pretty much the "Tank" of the group, which meant I get shot. A lot. On top of that, while I hate to "waste" points on Charisma, it is clear that I am going to be in social situations a lot more often. Still, I refuse to dedicate a full Level's worth to it, so Perception is getting at least a point. If Jason were here, he'd probably bitch me out about deviating from my build or being a generalist, but thus far, it's worked.

Having made my decision, I dump three points into Intelligence and Constitution, two into Charisma, and one in Perception, wiping out my free attributes. The next Level, I might put another point into Luck and Perception then rotate over to Charisma if I see some benefit in my interactions with others.

Figuring out what I intend to do with my Class Skills, on the other hand, is much simpler. I've wanted Sanctum and Army of One for a while now, and I can buy them. So I do.

Sanctum

An Erethran Honor Guard's ultimate trump card in safeguarding their target, Sanctum creates a flexible shield that blocks all incoming attacks, hostile teleportations, and Skills. At this Level of Skill, the user must specify dimensions of the Sanctum upon use of the Skill. The Sanctum cannot be moved while the Skill is activated.

Dimensions: Maximum 10 cubic meters.

Cost: 1,000 Mana

Duration: 1 minute and three seconds

"Whoa." I blink, staring at the Mana cost. A thousand Mana. That's insane. Even with my frankly ridiculous Stats, I can only cast this once.

A proper Erethran Honor Guard who'd advanced the normal way could probably cast this twice at best. And the duration isn't even that great.

"Boy-o, just to clarify, since I'm summarizing the actual System description as always, this Skill blocks everything. Someone could drop an orbital strike backed up by a dragon's curse on you and nothing would get through," Ali says.

"Everything?"

"Everything."

"Damn…" I say, staring at the description. "What's with the three seconds?"

"Figured on this one, we need a little precision," Ali says pointedly.

I consider the matter and nod. Yeah, I can see how knowing exactly how long my ability to be invincible lasts would require exactness. Most other times, it matters a lot less.

Army of One

The Honor Guard's feared penultimate combat ability, Army of One builds upon previous Skills, allowing the user to unleash an awe-inspiring attack to deal with their enemies.

*Effect: Army of One allows the projection of (Number of Thousand Blades conjured weapons * 3) Blade Strike attacks up to 200 meters away from user. Each attack deals 2 * Blade Strike Level damage (inclusive of Mana Imbue and Soulbound weapon bonus)*

Cost: 750 Mana

I admit, it takes me a bit to figure out the math on this. Basically, it works out to three conjured Thousand Blades multiplied by three—nine— attacks that each deal twice the equivalent of my Soulbound weapon's attack.

Which, at the present moment, is slightly over a hundred points of damage. That works out to ten attacks—including the original strike from my sword—each dealing about two hundred points of damage, which I can use as an area-of-effect or targeted strike. Put another way, I could almost one-shot myself with just base damage, which doesn't include external effects like armor or targeting. And this is only the first Level.

"Jesus…" I swear. If I'd had this during our most recent battle… then again, without Portal at Level 3, I wouldn't have been able to bring my friends. Well, not easily at least, since my range would have been shortened significantly.

Truthfully, the next Level up in Portal is tempting too. It adds approximately 4,000 kilometers to my range, which is significant. I could easily jump from Whitehorse to LA—if I ever traveled that far first.

"These Skills are over-powered," I mutter.

"Eh… you should see Mike's penultimate Skills. Hell, you saw his Sphere of Protection. It gave all friendlies within its bubble a 30% bonus to their resistances," Ali says.

That's when I realize. "You're back?"

"We don't actually need to take as long as you meatbags to talk, boy-o."

I sigh and shut up, letting myself sink into the couch. "Asshole."

Sleep. I'm here for sleep.

Chapter 2

I find Aiden standing outside my house early the next day, as I return from a hunting session. A quick check with Ali had indicated that the Kapre had been having issues with an Alpha monster a short jog from town, and after accepting their quest, I proceeded to apply a judicious amount of fire to the problem. And then a lot of Polar Zones. Look, you tell me how else I'm supposed to deal with a sentient moss monster.

Soot covered, with the taste of ash in my mouth, all I wanted was a hot shower and breakfast. Cleanse might clean me, but it never felt *right*. Which meant that my visitor, manbun and all, is an unpleasant surprise.

"Aiden," I greet my ex-party member and teacher.

An extremely talented Mage who mixes his esoteric, mangled Eastern philosophy with an analytical mind to advance his magic, Aiden is also a minor coward. After a number of harrowing experiences with us, he no longer journeys out of the city. I disagree—passionately—with his decision, but I understand it. It makes our relationship weird since I desperately try not to judge his actions and fail, then I spiral into mental admonishment of myself over it.

"John. I was hoping I could catch a ride?" Aiden says.

"Ride?"

"To Kaloomps. Lana mentioned in a message that you purchased a Mana field enhancement in the city. I was hoping to study it, perhaps improve the core formula, and well, bring it back," Aiden explains.

"Of course. I need a shower, but we'll go after that." I pause after stepping into the door, curious. "How'd you know I was back? And when to see me?"

"Ah…" Aiden shifts uncomfortably.

"Roxley."

"Yes."

I leave before I say anything I would regret. Being on Roxley's good side is smart, especially if you're living in Whitehorse. The man did nothing wrong. Just because that devious, back-alley scoundrel...

Exhale. Shower. Portal. Breakfast.

***

Breakfast is in Kaloomps, a simple series of Portals away. Aiden and I joined the team—or the portion of it that's here—which includes Sam, our Level 39 Technomancer; Lana; and Mikito. Ingrid, our Assassin / Thief / general sneaky body is still in Seattle, making nice with the Americans. With the Sect pulling back entirely, the Americans have devolved into a series of skirmishes with one another as they scramble for control in the city.

After I made the necessary introductions, most everyone left me alone to enjoy my breakfast while the girls caught up with Aiden and Sam stayed his taciturn self. Sam rarely gets involved in our private conversations, a factor I enjoy about the older gentleman.

"Did John make arrangements for where you'll be staying?" Lana asks Aiden after they've finished discussing the latest gossip from Whitehorse, the majority of breakfast finally finished.

"No..."

At Lana's look, I protest, "I didn't even know he was coming till this morning!"

"Don't worry about it. We've got an apartment where we can put you up," Lana says with a sniff at me.

"We've got an apartment?" I say, surprised.

"Not all of us enjoy sleeping on the floor of the nearest abandoned room," Lana teases, making Mikito smile.

Even Sam snorts a little. Then again, that man set up his little house-cum-workshop almost immediately. As far as I know, Sam has a workshop in every major settlement he's visited and spent more than a week in.

"It's convenient," I mutter. Between my high Constitution and resistances, sleeping on the floor isn't really that uncomfortable. In fact, with System-aided healing, I don't even wake up with sore muscles. I'll admit though, I do enjoy sleeping in a real bed sometimes, but that's what my house in Whitehorse is for. After all the upgrades we've done for the building, even with the massive swarms, it stays in good shape.

"Thank you. If you show me where it is, I'd love to get started on the enchantment immediately," Aiden says. "I can already feel the difference in my regeneration rate."

Lana nods, getting up and setting her plates aside, shortly followed by Aiden. Sam takes his leave at the same time, off to continue working on his latest project—an analysis and dismantling of Sabre. With my Personal Assault Vehicle badly damaged during our last encounter, it's still in the process of fixing itself, which makes it the perfect time for Sam to analyze the changes. While he doesn't expect to actually replicate the machine, the knowledge he's gaining is supposedly increasing his skills significantly.

That leaves Mikito, who I gesture to stay when she gets up. The dark-haired lady sits down quietly, hands folded all prim and proper. Hard to imagine that this sophisticated, well-mannered young lady is also one of the deadliest—if not the deadliest—melee duelist I know. Well, excepting a certain frustrating Truinnar.

I break the silence with a prosaic question. "How are you doing?"

"Well."

"Well, as in good or well as in well, things could be worse?"

"I am doing fine," Mikito says. "Lana already spoke to me last night. Your concern is touching but unnecessary."

I grimace at my friend. This… well, this is an area I don't know how to handle. She's hurting a bit, but if she says she's good, what am I supposed to do? Tell her she isn't? The fact stands that we all have our own pain, our own emotional scars. This world isn't one where you can spend years in therapy, talking about your feelings till you get better. The next crisis is always just around the corner.

"Okay," I say, slumping back. After a moment, I meet her gaze and change the topic. "We've been missing our morning training sessions."

"You've not been around," Mikito says.

"Yeah. Whitehorse or Vancouver's fast becoming my base of operations. Simpler that way. I could use your evaluation on the delvers in Vancouver. And I've been meaning to test out their dungeon."

"Lana says it's only a gradated dungeon? It gets harder the farther you go?" Mikito says quietly. "Doesn't seem like you need me for that."

"Well, no one knows how strong it is anymore. At least, none of the delvers, though they believe the Sect did. Be nice to understand that," I say, shrugging. "Furthest the teams have gotten is to a Level 40 plus building zone, and they barely made it out at that."

"When?"

"Pardon?"

"When do you want me there?" Mikito clarifies.

"When can you get up?" I pause. "Down."

Mikito bites her lip as she thinks things through. "We still need to work out who is going to replace Mel. None of the… the…" She clears her throat.

"No one is shining through right now. And I'd like to get their average Level up a little more."

I stay silent, letting her work things through herself. I know part of the reason why she's taking so long to leave here is a reluctance to let go, a need to do good by Mel and her apprentice. Who, I have to admit, I can't even remember the name of. I know I could if I wanted to, but I don't. Dwelling on the past, the many people lost, is just a road to further pain.

"Two weeks. Maybe three," Mikito finally says.

"All right." I nod, accepting her word. It's not great, but I'm sure I can figure out something to do in the meantime. If nothing else, my goal of basically visiting every village, town, and other settlement in BC will be mostly done by then.

***

Routine. I'm falling into a routine, even after a few days of peace and quiet. Training, breakfast, Portal to the last town I was at before exploring further to map and add the new locations to my map of explored places. Spend a couple of hours of exploring, then Portal again back to Vancouver and my office on the top floor of the central library and thus the City Center. Depending on how far and which direction I'm going, it sometimes requires multiple Portals, but that doesn't matter. It's all the same.

Routine. That is how she finds me. By the time I'm fully cognizant of my actions, I've dropped the Portal, cast a Soul Shield, and have my sword at the lady's neck. She raises an eyebrow, seated as she is at a desk—a new desk, set perpendicular to mine—all coiffed and put together.

"Mr. Lee," she says. "Or do you prefer your Galactic titles?"

"Who the hell are you? What are you doing here?" I snarl.

Ali floats above me as he updates my minimap with more information. Lots of dots right outside my door. At least a dozen, though they're all coded grey for non-aggressive. At least for now.

"My name is Katherine Ward. I'm your new personal assistant," the woman says, meeting my gaze without fear.

Seeing that there's no direct physical threat at the moment, I pull my sword back while regarding the older lady. Late or mid 50s probably, with smooth skin, minimal natural makeup, a pixie-cut hairstyle that frames piercing brown eyes, and a form-fitting, classic business suit. In other words, the perfect secretary.

Katherine Ward (Level 21 Assistant)

HP: 120/120

MP: 240/240

Conditions: None

"What? The male secretaries go on strike?" I say wryly, walking to sit on my desk as I stare at the woman. She's no physical threat to me.

"There were few men doing this job even before the incident," Katherine says. "There are even fewer now. And as you might note, none of them are here."

"What makes you think I'd hire you?" I say, shaking my head. "You just walked into my office and set up."

"Well, for one thing, your AI has agreed to the need for me," Katherine says. "For another, the fact that I could just walk into your office speaks of a lack of organization on your part."

I grunt. She's not wrong. Being accosted by random individuals with their own agendas has been driving me slightly insane. That I've been using

Portal and Blink Step to get away from them is less than dignified. Though effective. But dodging the problem can hold only for so long…

"Kim?"

"WE HAVE CONDUCTED EXTENSIVE INVESTIGATION INTO MS. WARD'S PRIOR EXPERIENCE. HER RESUME IS EXTREMELY IMPRESSIVE, WITH PRIOR WORK EXPERIENCE INCLUDING CEOS OF YOUR WORLD. PRIOR TO YOUR APPEARANCE, MS. WARD WAS ONE OF THE MAIN ORGANIZERS OF THE EASTSIDE ASSOCIATION."

"The what?"

"EASTSIDE ASSOCIATION—A GROUP OF LIKE-MINDED ARTISANS WHO WORKED AS A CO-OPERATIVE ASSOCIATION TO MANUFACTURE COMPLEX EQUIPMENT FOR RESALE. THE ASSOCIATION USED PROFITS TO PROVIDE ASSISTED HOUSING AND LOAN REPAYMENTS."

"What bits-for-brains means is that she's a do-gooder with skills. And diplomacy. After the art restoration incident, we decided you needed some help. Bits and I did some research and reached out to a few candidates. Unfortunately, she's the only one not majorly compromised. So far," Ali says.

"And the ambush?" I growl softly to him while I stare at Katherine. She hasn't flinched, just sitting there waiting.

"Her doing. We were actually going to talk to you about her tonight."

"What's with the ambush?" I say out loud.

"After the limited information provided by Kim, I conducted some research myself. It was soon clear"—and at that, she looks at the door leading out of my office—"that you require help in organizing your day. While you desire to not be 'bothered' by such incidents, you do need to deal with them. Or at least arrange for others to deal with them."

"And you can help with that," I state flatly.

"Yes."

"How do I know you don't have your own agenda? People you'll sneak into places of power?"

"You are asking how you'd expect to trust me and that is an impossible question. Trust must be built and we currently are strangers. However, be assured that your AI is watching what I do," Katherine says.

"*As am I.*"

"If we are finished with the interrogation, I have a recommended schedule for the day. I have set aside an hour for you to meet with petitioners—fifty-five minutes now—after which we have an hour for hiring. And then—"

"Why not the other way around?" I interrupt.

"At this time, we do not have a full grasp of your responsibilities. Also, as evidenced, you have certain trust issues. It is better for you to gain some first-hand experience with your petitioners. I would even recommend that you randomly select some to speak with on an on-going basis even after hiring and delegation is complete."

"I…" I consider what she said and wave her to continue. Fine. Let's see how this plays out. If there's a trap here, I'm not experienced enough to see it. Or I am, but I want to see how it plays out. Because she's right—avoiding running the city isn't going to work. And the council is too busy fighting about how they're going to run it to actually do it. But… "Tomorrow morning, I want it free."

"For…?"

I smile, waving her to continue.

***

Hours later, after a number of meetings with petitioners and job applicants, I'm finally alone. One thing I'm grateful for is Katherine having the foresight to order in lunch. When lunch is served, Lana saunters in, glancing at Katherine with narrowed eyes. After a few minutes of soft-spoken conversation, the initial wariness slips away from my girlfriend as she drops into a chair next to me.

"How'd you make it here?" I say, frowning. One of the more significant purchases I intend to make is the installation of communication arrays in each settlement. Once set up, they will allow for long-distance transmissions between each settlement. "And how'd you find me?"

"Mmm… your new assistant contacted me," Lana says around a mouthful of crab. "And I took the boys out for a run."

I grunt, wanting to chide her for risking her neck, but decide against it. Lana's a survivor like me and can handle herself. Anyway, with her pets, in many ways, she is a lot tougher than she should be for her Level. Especially since she's been focusing on Leveling them lately. Especially Roland. Roland is scary.

"Katherine?" I say with a frown. I'm really curious how my new assistant knows enough to contact Lana already so quickly.

"My Class provides me with a number of Skills. A minor Skill in communication called 'Contact List' allows me to contact a certain number of individuals within my sphere of influence. Normally I'd need to designate them individually, but with another Skill of mine—Intuit—I am able to access a portion of what would be your contact list. It was a simple matter then to mark Ms. Pearson as a priority individual," Katherine says. Interestingly enough, she's also pulled a plate of food to her, though she's eating with significantly more decorum. I guess the lady has no problem eating in front of her boss. "Now, we were going to speak about your most recent interviews…"

I sigh, but considering Lana's here, I might as well make use of her skills and knowledge. At this point, I get a nice surprise as Ali uses his gifts as my companion to flash up images of each applicant as we speak, allowing Lana to view them and, in some cases, watch certain portions of the interview.

While we don't have a broad-based idea of the government system that we want in place, we do have the roughest of sketches. Security, legal, education, and city management are the highlights. The last encompasses a lot of things, from city planning for new System-registered buildings to working with petitioners who have their own ideas about what the city needs. We already have a burgeoning homeless problem—System-homeless that is—which needs to be resolved. With pre-System infrastructure slowly falling apart, staying in non-registered homes is fast becoming less and less comfortable for many.

We talk, debate, and weigh the pros and cons of the applicants for our budding bureaucracy. Of the eight who arrived and passed Kim's background checks, three are removed from the list for being too skeezy. Another two are put on hold till we can find a proper task for them. And the last three are hired to begin the process of actually putting together a working bureaucracy. Thankfully, with the System and the various Skills involved, the numbers we would require should be significantly lower than pre-System. Never mind that we've also got a much lower population. Unfortunately, Security continues to be a crucial gap. Everyone who could do the job has either been deported by the Sect or is a delver and thus tied to the vying political groups.

"I approve," Lana says, stretching in her chair as silence finally finds us. "Roxley mentioned that you'd need an assistant soon unless I wanted to be stuck with the job. It was part of the reason why I came down today actually. But Katherine seems to have things well in hand."

"Never said I've hired her," I say.

Katherine doesn't rise to my provocation, continuing to eat calmly, having already informed the successful applicants. I'll have to give them their brief tomorrow and get them working on hiring others, but at least this should sort out some of the pressing applications. And perhaps get the city back up and running. Not surprisingly, the Sect took their own form of organization with them, and in any case, the Sect had very different objectives than us—for one thing, we have the entire downtown now available for reallocation.

"She seems to be doing a good job," Lana says.

"Yeah, yeah." I wave, indicating Lana is correct. Good job or not, I don't like the feeling of being rushed, even if I can admit that we're getting a lot done.

"Lana says to stop being so paranoid. You need the help and we'll keep an eye on her."

"What's next on the agenda?" I ask, deciding to change the subject.

"Upgrades," Lana says.

"Fair enough," I say.

The moment I do, Kim displays the summarized Settlement Management Screen.

__Summarized Settlement Status__

Current Population: 129,308

Combined Settlement Treasury: 98.93 Million Credits (+157k per day)

Combined City Mana: 13,309 Mana Points (+298 Mana per day)

Taxes: 10% Sales Tax on Shop

Facilities of Note: City Dungeon (1), Mega Farms (3)

Enchantments of Note: Mana Collection Field

*Defenses of Note: Settlement Shields (III * 1 & IV * 2)*

While it is a summarized information screen about the major areas of concern for the settlements under my control, it obviously misses a lot. Still, considering I need to know the basics, it is a good starting point. Interestingly enough, while Credits could be transferred between settlements without any issue, transferring Mana is actually much more expensive and ends up being a 5-to-1 ratio. The summarized amount shows the Mana we have available if we use it in Vancouver, which would obviously change depending on where we want to trigger the Mana usage. Considering Mana usage is mainly linked to upgrading or changing higher-tiered buildings, it isn't as much of an issue. Yet.

One thing I don't like is the way the defensive notes don't list the full defenses of each settlement. Then again, as I've noticed in Kamloops, anything that isn't stupidly powerful is pitiful when stacked up against a real assault. Which I guess split defenses into two kinds: those useful against monsters and those that are needed against other sentients.

"Not sure I'm that confident in spending our Credits on upgrades yet," I say, frowning at the information. "I know Kyle has specific goals—especially with the Adventurers Guild, whose reps I should meet—but I'm sure the Kelowna council have ideas too now that we're not on a war footing."

"Might be an idea to throw the question at your Vancouver council too," Lana adds. "There's nothing that the city needs desperately, so we can let them argue it out and offer their suggestions."

"That's… not a bad idea." At the worst, it'd give them something else to argue about while I deal with the actual work of running the city. But I'd invited everyone onto the council—or well, acceded to their demands to be included—because they were parties of import in the city and could provide me more information about it. Which meant they might actually be able to provide some real information. "Katherine…"

"I'll message the council members and let them know you'd like their feedback on the priorities for improvements to the city at the next scheduled meeting," Katherine says.

"Thanks," I mutter, staring at the screen.

Perhaps the most interesting thing we have is the City Dungeon. We actually have a natural dungeon forming on the grounds of Simon Fraser University, but thankfully, it's high up in the mountains and currently still growing. It's still something that needs to be dealt with, but for now, I focus my attention on the City Dungeon.

Over the time I spent reading about the System, I'd learnt a little about City Dungeons. City Dungeons are different from natural dungeons. Natural dungeons form from an overabundance of Mana and the fortitudinous encounter with a monster. Or vice versa—an Alpha monster can, through its continued presence, potentially develop a natural dungeon. Depending on the type and volume of Mana, the natural dungeon can be a single-clear dungeon or a multiple-clear dungeon where the System actually forms the monsters from "memory." In both cases though, these natural dungeons often have a specific difficulty level that permeates the entire dungeon—mostly due to the monster type(s) that inhabit them.

City Dungeons, on the other hand, are always multiple-clear dungeons. They are formed through the conscious redirection of Mana flow into a specific area, with enchantments, rituals, and Mana engines directed to contain and form the dungeon. City Dungeons are generally structured, with upper levels being the lowest available zone and growing in difficulty as you journey deeper. The most common City Dungeon type is an underground dungeon with each level a new, more difficult zone. The larger the city, the more settlements that feed the dungeon structure, the more powerful and greater the potential difficulty the dungeon will have.

However, our City Dungeon is slightly different. Rather than an entrance to an actual dungeon, it is spread out across what used to be the University of British Columbia. The grounds are generally considered the basic zone meant for beginners. Faculty buildings and residences are where the actual dungeon levels are located, with certain faculties being more dangerous than others.

All that information gives me some context when I review the City Dungeon management screen.

City Dungeon

Location: Vancouver

Dungeon Level: Tier III

Mana Consumption: 218 per day

Known Spawns: Jackalopes, Evolved Canada Geese, Wolpertinger, Spirits, Kmi Leeches, Medusa, Tikbalang, Mngwa

Known Loot: Hide (of Known Spawns), Trivial, Minor, Major Healing & Mana Potions, Tier V Beam & Projectile Weapons, Tier IV & V Bladed Weapons, Tier V Explosives, more...

"Hey, Ali, can you explain the Tier system again? I'm a bit confused here," I mutter, waving at the Dungeon Level. "We've talked about how each Tier V is basically beginner equipment, and Tier IV is up to Level 20 or so. And how the Tiers work on a logarithmic process, so Tier III is roughly what? Up to Level 50? That doesn't seem to work right, because then Tier II would be the entire Advanced Class."

"The Tiers are for tech items mostly. Basically, any replicable that can be mass produced," Ali says. "Tier I and II items are generally high-level military items, things that are reserved for their use when taken in the larger context. Obviously anyone can buy them, but you get a lot of raised eyebrows when you buy a Tier II spaceship.

"In terms of Levels, you could consider the tech tiers to cover most of the Advanced Class with Tier II weaponry being basically powerful enough to seriously injure a high Level Advanced Class combatant. As an example, you've probably noticed that Sabre isn't really up to your standards anymore. Mikito certainly doesn't bother using her PAV half the time. In general, you'd be looking for things in the next section—the enchanted, unique, and legendary items which all have their own tiers."

I frown. "So you're saying most equipment doesn't really work for Master Level Classes?"

"No, I'm saying that at that level, they're playing on a different field. They're getting unique items custom-made for them rather than picking things up from the Shop or Dungeons. Rather than relying on random drops to augment their abilities, they want equipment that will either buff up specific advantages or deal with certain disadvantages. Once you're a Master Class individual, specialization matters," Ali says. "Also, they'll probably have a couple of sets of equipment to swap around, for social and combat situations at the very least."

"And the dungeon tier?"

"A Tier III dungeon isn't exactly the same. It's more an expression of how many Adventurers and the number and types of monsters that the dungeon has than the Level of loot. Tier III means that it's suitable for Adventurers up to the mid-to-high Advanced Classes, potentially higher if you consider bosses. As a group, that is. It's rare to see a City Dungeon above Tier III. In fact, if you weren't on a Dungeon World, it's unlikely your city would have anything above a Tier IV. But with the excess Mana you guys have…"

"It's easier," I say.

"It's almost a given. See your SFU."

I grunt in acknowledgement and sigh. "And the list of loot?"

"Just what's known. City Dungeons create loot slightly differently. Obviously monster drops are the same, if less, than what you'd get naturally. But you also get equipment from drops in a city dungeon. Just realize that they can be occasionally… umm… quirky."

"THE COMMON ADVENTURER TERMINOLOGY IS CURSED."

"Yeah…" Ali opens his hands slightly. "There are rules involved. The dungeon owner feeds the schematics for such items—or the actual items, though that's less effective—into the City Dungeon via your management screen. The System can then generate these items. Depending on the complexity of the item, occasional 'curses' can happen. It's unlikely you'll get cursed gold for example—very simple to reproduce basic minerals. But an enchanted blade? Yeah, it's complicated."

I frown, tapping my fingers. "There are ways of knowing what might or might not be cursed?"

"THE DUNGEON MANAGEMENT SCREEN PROVIDES DETAILED BREAKDOWN ON THE LEVEL OF ASSIMILATION AND THE PROBABILITY OF CURSED ITEM PRODUCTION."

Lana leans over, tapping on my screen. Obviously it doesn't do anything until Ali wills it to, but he knows me well enough to let Lana play around with my views. In a second, the dungeon management screen blooms, expanding rapidly. The summarized information disappears as even more information appears. Everything gets more detailed, including data that was hidden before, like the number of visitors, the declared drop rate of various items, which items have been released, and the like. While Lana browses with Ali's help, I'm doing my own investigation.

"As the dungeon owner, shouldn't I have a proper map of it?" I grumble.

"CURRENT MAPPED INFORMATION IS PROVIDED BY YOUR DELVERS."

"I know, but shouldn't I get more details? I own the damn dungeon."

"YOU ARE THE ADMINISTRATOR OF THE DUNGEON. THIS DOES NOT PROVIDE ACCESS TO THE DATA YOU ARE SEARCHING FOR BY DEFAULT. WE MAY PURCHASE SAID INFORMATION IN THE STORE."

I groan. Freaking scam of a System.

"Boy-o, you need to realize that growing a dungeon is more akin to growing a forest than building a house. You throw down some seeds, water the plants with Mana, maybe prune or cut down a tree or two. But you don't get much say in how the forest really grows."

"That's… insane," I mutter. "It's a freaking dungeon and I don't get any real information on it?"

"Nope. And you shouldn't be calling others insane. Your people used to capture predatory animals and make them pets," Ali says, staring at the quiet, striped orange cat lounging in the corner.

"Yeah, but those people are crazy."

"As are city owners," Ali says. "Also, you're forgetting the lure of greed. Mining a City Dungeon is a very, very good way of getting low-tier goods. It's a stable source of income and attracts a ton of beginner adventurers since it's a lot safer. In non-Dungeon Worlds, it also helps manage Mana buildup and keeps the zones around a city much lower. Here, it does the same. With, you know, less effect."

I sigh, rubbing my head. Lana finally stops swinging the notification screens about and looks at me with a pensive expression.

"What?"

"Managing the dungeon's similar to managing a business, just weird. There's a ton of things in here, most of which could bear watching. Where the Mana is going, how much Mana should be going in, what rate the dungeon is growing at…" Lana shakes her head. "And we've not even gotten to that entire loot generation section. You need to find someone to manage this."

"Great. I'll add it to the task list," I say sarcastically.

After a moment, I look over and see Katherine finish moving her fingers before offering me a knowing nod. Great. I guess I really do have a task list now. Next I'll be getting a bell around my neck.

After that, Lana and I get back to talk about upgrades. She's got her own ideas, from her time in Whitehorse as well as Kamloops, and isn't shy about pushing for them. I can't blame her, and unlike the councillors, she's got an in to get her own views heard. After all, I'm not sleeping with any of the others.

Yay nepotism.

Chapter 3

Wandering the stacks of the library, I find myself running my finger along the spines of abandoned books later that evening. I'm waiting for Lana, who has gone for a "dinner" with Katherine, one that I was pointedly not invited to. So I'm wandering my domain, staring at tomes of knowledge that have been discarded, much like our prior civilization.

"You're a morose bastard," Ali says, floating beside me.

"Yup," I agree absently before looking around.

Where am I? Biology? Rows and rows of books about the biological world that now matters not a whit. After all, the System has replaced and altered our bodies so significantly that I doubt even half of what is in these books matters now. Furthermore, for the low, low price of a few hundred Credits, all this painstaking knowledge could be bought and downloaded directly into our brains.

"What's got you down now?"

"Just the futility of life," I murmur, shaking my head. All the time, all the expertise denoted in these books, gone. A wave of the System, a snarling face, and poof. All gone.

"Uh huh," Ali says, leaning back in mid-air as he floats beside me.

"Nothing futile about these books," an older man says as he walks around the corner. Scraggly hair down to his collar, he's dressed in a dress shirt and a pair of jeans, a pile of books waiting to be reshelved in his hands.

"Eric," I greet the Librarian.

One of the first people to accost me once things had settled, he literally demanded to be allowed the run of the library again. As a former employee—admittedly from the Marpole branch—he was intent on collecting and returning all the books he could find. I'm not entirely sure if it's a matter of Leveling or a complex, but rather than argue, I agreed to his request with some stipulations. No approaching my City Core for one.

"What is contained within might not be useful now, but knowledge, any knowledge, is precious. And while your System might provide fast and easy gains in knowledge, have you not noticed that the learning process itself has certain advantages?" Eric says as he shelves a book.

"Uhh…"

"Your training with Mikito?" Ali points out helpfully.

"Right…" The difference between knowing something and understanding it.

"What is contained here might be of use in the future as well. In fact, there are certain skills that may be gained and Titles for those who choose to proceed the hard way," Eric says, looking at me. "It is why I strongly recommend that we re-open the library. And of course, begin the process of updating our inventory."

I raise my hand, cutting off any further pitch. Eric's lips thin, but he inclines his head in acknowledgement before walking away to continue his task. For a moment, I stare at his retreating back.

"He's creepy."

"Really? He doesn't seem any stranger than most humans to me."

Sometimes, I'm not entirely sure whether Ali is kidding or not when he says things like that. With a sigh, I continue to walk, shifting my thoughts to something more productive.

Maybe a half hour later, Lana finds me, Roland accompanying her while Howard and Shadow chase one another outside.

"John," Lana greets me after kissing me, leaning backward to stare into my eyes. "What are you thinking about?"

"Government. Or a corporation. I've been thinking about how I'm the sole owner of these settlements and it's not a good idea," I say.

"And you don't intend to relinquish control," Lana states, knowing my reasons for keeping control.

"Exactly. So I need an organization of sorts that both keeps me in control when necessary but also allows people like Ken or the city council to run things and that is flexible enough to keep expanding," I say. "And, of course, has a decent backup to ensure we don't actually lose the city if I die."

A flicker of something crosses Lana's face. "Where were you thinking?"

"Closest thing I can think of is a constitutional monarchy of sorts. But that brings its own problems," I say with a grimace.

"Lines of succession, intrigue, and backstabbing?"

"Exactly."

Lana turns to the floating Spirit. "Ali, aren't there more Galactic options?"

"Tons. But I'm not exactly an expert on this. The Erethrans use a stratocracy, with citizenship varying based on Levels and time served with the armed forces. Their Emperor is actually just the most powerful Erethran citizen who is then guarded by the Honor Guard. He and his family, along with their advisors, make up both the Erethrans' reserves and their ruling body. Of course, the fact that the Emperor is able to buy Skills and equipment for his children and put them out for safe training tilts things in his favor, but it's still technically a stratocracy.

"The Truinnar and the Xylarghs are both monarchies. The Truinnar use what you'd call a pure monarchy, with their Emperor ruling over all and having direct oaths of servitude from his subjects. He even has the Class. The Xylarghs are closer to a constitutional monarchy, with the monarchy and the Dragon Knights making up one bloc of power and the Artisans another.

Democracy is a lot less common. The closest examples I can think of that you'd be familiar with are the Kapre. But they're weird—while they don't exactly have a hive mind, they've got an empathic mind backed by racial Skills in empathy."

I grunt, recalling our conversations about the tree-like creatures that make up the Kapre. Talking and dealing with them always felt strange due to the long pauses and the feeling that you're talking to more than one at a time. Which, in a way, you are.

"Well, we're not interested in a democracy," Lana says, eyes dancing with humor. "I doubt John wants to hear the 'will of the people.'"

"People are stupid," I grumble then amend my note. "But they should have a voice. Just not direct to me."

"Well, if you're keeping final say, you should probably be a monarchy of some sort," Ali says.

"Nope. Not going to get called King John," I say sternly. I can see Lana's eyes dancing with humor as I state that. "Anyway, that'd make you the fool."

"Yeah well, I'd pity the fool who called me one," Ali says. "We could potentially call it a dictatorship of some form…"

I grunt in annoyance, drawing another shrug from Ali.

"Perhaps a corporation?" Lana says.

"Like a Guild?"

"Can't be a Guild, remember? No land ownership." Ali corrects me.

"I never did understand that. What's the difference between a Sect and a Guild? And how do corporations fit in there?" I growl.

"Right…" Ali says. "Well, corporations can be Guilds and vice versa. A Guild is basically a co-operative of Adventurers. The main difference between a Guild or a Sect is that a Guild can't hold land. Because they can't hold land—specifically, they can't hold settlements—they are allowed to have their Guild branches in numerous cities. Which gives them a significant amount of power.

"Sects, on the other hand, can't—or well, generally don't—hold land in cities they don't control. If they do, that land is considered part of their territory. It's why other groups won't let them own land in their cities."

"Part of their territory?" I say with a frown.

"Think of it like an embassy." At my puzzled frown, Lana shakes her head. "Embassies are considered the land of their countries. So a Canadian embassy in Saudi Arabia is part of Canada and people within the embassy aren't required to follow Saudi law."

"Ah…" I exclaim, realizing what she means. I recall that movie. The one with Ben Affleck. It had something to do with that entire rule of law. I have to admit, I fell asleep while watching it.

"Sects also don't let their people join Guilds, and their people have to renounce their ties with other kingdoms. Guilds, on the other hand, don't care—so long as you serve the guild and do their work, you're welcome to have diverging interests."

"So how do corporations work in all this?' I ask, figuring I've got a rough handle between Sects and Guilds.

"Corporations can't be Sects, because Sects require oaths of loyalty. They're more loosely formed, with stakeholders who own and sometimes run the organization and employees. They can own land too, but unlike Sects, whatever they purchase outside of settlements doesn't come under their own laws. Like Guilds, they often have widespread interests, but unlike Guilds, they can own land. But… there's a lot of unhappiness about them in the Galactic core. In fact, many corporations are barred from some of the largest empires and blocked entirely from owning land or operations in certain kingdoms."

"So my options are a soulless corporation or being called King for the rest of my life," I mutter. "Not acceptable."

"I'm sure we can figure out something better. Now that we've got an idea what you're looking for," Lana says when she realizes I'm not really joking.

"Let's." I stare at Ali, who sighs and nods. Grateful to have given the Spirit a task he can deal with, I send him off while I turn to Lana. The redhead raises an eyebrow, and I shake my head. "No more work."

She smiles and takes my hand, guiding me to walk along the stacks once again. For a few hours at least, I'm going to take a break. Especially considering what I've got on the agenda tomorrow morning.

***

Morning. Early morning. Even in the summer, the sun has barely risen as we stand at the foot of the mountain, staring at the rolling mist ahead of us. Wisps of it exit the barrier, its presence significantly denser a few feet ahead. It's Lana, her pets, and me. Ingrid isn't back from the US, Mikito is still in Kamloops, and this isn't Sam's scene. Mostly.

"Should we have invited Sam?" I mutter, staring at the foreboding mist. If mist can look treacherous and dangerous, this mist would definitely qualify.

"You barely invited me," Lana says grumpily, a travel mug of coffee in her hands.

"Didn't want to share the experience," I say teasingly before sobering. "Truthfully, didn't know you'd be here. And I figured I should know what the dungeon is like. Maybe even clear it before the delvers actually get it done."

"What is it anyway?" Lana says, tilting her head as she stares inside.

"Yurks," Ali says, grimacing. "Semi-sentient, reptilian-frog hybrid creatures in your parlance. They're mildly humanoid."

Lana frowns at the mist, which doesn't seem to be intent on leaving. "Is the mist part of the dungeon?"

"Yes."

Outside of the dungeon bounds, my minimap cuts out completely, giving me no further information. Frustrating. I turn my head, staring at the two roads that lead farther up the mountain and toward the university that stretches out ahead and to the right of us. Even without the mist, I wouldn't expect to see much beyond the untamed forests and roads, but I could always hope.

"Well, what are we waiting for?" Lana says before downing the last of her coffee and making the mug disappear.

Without an audible cue, the puppies spread out ahead of us, Roland joining the group while Anna stays by our side as we walk ahead.

The moment we enter the mists, we get a notification.

Dungeon Located!

You have entered a Level 50+ Dungeon.

Warning! The current dungeon has not been fully cleared. Successful completion of the dungeon by a System-registered individual will generate increased rewards.

As expected. It's one of the reasons why it's yet to be cleared by the delvers. None of the teams are at the point where they can comfortably deal with the problem. This might be a touch much for just the two of us as well—even if I over-Level it. Sort of. Never having had a Basic Class always makes these estimations tricky.

Once again, I note that the double experience reward, as well as the System limitation notification, is gone. Ever since the System fully integrated, we no longer get those, since the System can at least provide the basics of a warning about any dungeons we enter. Annoying, but at least the first clear bonus is still around.

Even if we can't clear it today, I should be able to open a Portal and pop out. Maybe we can pull Mikito in the next time and deal with it then. But I have to admit, I'm kind of looking forward to the challenge today.

"Don't forget, you have meetings this afternoon. So no going crazy in there," Lana warns as we walk up the road.

The mist wraps around us, reducing visibility and muffling her voice. In answer, I grunt, my sword held idly. No point using a rifle if I can't see what I'm shooting. Indicators on the helmet HUD show that the external atmosphere isn't poisoned, so the mist itself is benign.

Ting

What the heck? I tilt my head to the side, catching a glimpse of something white falling as it deflects off my Soul Shield. Lana beats me to it, bending and picking up the needle-thin, plastic-looking item with purple liquid dripping from its tip.

As she begins to speak, she slaps a hand to her arm, growling in pain. "Poison!"

I flick my hand quickly, placing Soul Shield on Lana. For good measure, I add Two are One. Lana's rubbing her hand now, eyes slightly unfocused.

"How bad?" I ask.

"Not too bad. It's reducing my Mana regeneration a bit for the next few hours."

Even as she speaks, another plink signifies another attack failing to penetrate. The attacks themselves are so weak they barely even move the health gauge of the Soul Shield. I debate throwing the rest of my buffs on us but decide against it. Better to keep my Mana for now.

"Attacks like these are stackable," Ali says. Perhaps because he feels like taunting them, he's fully visible, their shots passing through his body.

"Still nothing on the minimap?" I debate throwing a Blade Strike along the line of where the attacks originate. I hold back for the moment since striking out randomly isn't likely to do anything but damage fauna. Though if we don't get results soon, I might just use an area effect attack and see if I get lucky.

"The boys are on it," Lana says softly, her shotgun held casually now.

A moment later, I see a notification pop up that I've gained a small smattering of experience. "Who was that?"

"Roland. And that's Shadow." As she speaks, another notification flashes, the experience gain the only information clue that anything is happening. "Howard's having a little harder time." Lana shakes her head. "Might call him back actually. He doesn't have the other two's advantages. In fact..."

A few minutes later, Howard trots out of the undergrowth, a limp corpse held in his mouth. The creature he deposits at our feet is, as advertised, a green, reptilian-frog hybrid on two floppy feet wearing a leather sash from which a series of needles hang. In addition, a small bottle swings on a string from the belt, unstoppered and slowly dripping out its poisonous contents.

"Good boy." Lana rubs the puppy's giant head as the husky shifts to stand guard over us. A low growl is drawn from it a second later when a fast-moving projectile strikes its paw. "John…?"

"On it." I cast the Soul Shield over the puppy and make a mental note to refresh the protection when it runs out. That's a significant negative I've noticed—in higher Mana zones like a dungeon, the Skill drains away faster. Once that's cast, I eye the body.

Yurk Scout (Level 20)
_HP: 0/224_
_MP: 0/130_
Condition: Dead

"Scouts?" I frown. The attack didn't seem to do much damage to either Howard or Lana. Harassing and annoying, but not dangerous.

"Probably meant to wear you down," Ali says. "The scouts will poison you, reduce your regeneration now. When you're in the thick of it, you'll find the Mana regeneration debuff a crucial issue."

"Ah…" I nod. One of those dungeons.

We keep walking, letting Lana's pets deal with the Scouts. Since they can't really hurt us through the Soul Shield, it's good experience for her. That being said, I keep an eye out. This is the first trip through.

***

"Think they're edible?" Lana says, eyeing a fleeing Yurk Warrior and the burnt corpses strewn around us.

Once we actually enter the campus grounds, we are met by a group of Yurk Warriors. A large group of them, each Level 30 plus. Unfortunately for them, they decide to group up. The moment my Fireball impacts, Lana throws on her Aura of the Red Queen, forcing them to run.

"Maybe. Probably tastes like fishy chicken," I say.

Lana tilts her head toward me.

"I'm Chinese. My dad introduced me to some different culinary experiences," I say. "Frog legs are okay. Taste like slightly slimy chicken."

"Oh. Wow…" Lana says, staring at the corpses around us.

It's weird eating sentients. Or semi-sentients. Not something we've done much of even with the System. On the other hand, they do smell kind of nice.

"Go ahead. I won't tell," I say.

She flashes me a look but still steps forward. A few seconds later, she's wiping her fingers on her one-piece. "You're right."

A quick wave of my hand pulls the bodies into my Altered Space, dumping them away for later sale. A part of me wonders how casually eating the meat of our fallen enemies is even a thing. How callous could we have gotten? Considering how sharp their teeth are, I'm pretty sure that's what they were going to do to us though.

"You never told me how you learnt to cook."

"Oh? Not much of a story to tell," I say, sweeping my gaze around the buildings again.

Taking the right roadway, we swing into what used to be the International College building, a stand-alone facility that is a short distance from the main campus. The red brick building with grey concrete appears and disappears as the mist obscures our vision. I nod toward the entrance, and we saunter over and stop at the opaque entrance.

"Grenades?" I ask.

"Just one."

A minute of hard work later, we're walking down the next hallway, slightly charred and with refreshed Soul Shields.

"You know I grew up without my mom, right? Well, my dad wasn't much for cooking. So I had to learn to do it myself. After I grew tired of instant noodles—and a few complaints from my dad—I started watching cooking shows."

"Cooking shows?"

"Ramsay, *Iron Chef*, Ray, some road shows too," I say, shrugging. "Picked up a few tips here and there while watching and read a few books. It was just one of those things I had to learn, and later on, I found it comforting. Something I could control."

Before Lana can continue the conversation, I hold up my hand. My map is showing that each of the classrooms ahead of us is filled, and this time, it looks as though we'll have to get serious. Howard hunkers down while Anna burns more brightly. Roland slides into place next to the first door, waiting quietly in gathered shadows.

"Ali?" I frown, staring at the semi-circular series of dots ahead of us. It looks almost like a trap...

"Can't go through," Ali says, floating up to tap the walls. "They're Mana-imbued to prevent me from floating in. I'd have to go through an open door."

"Grenades?" Lana says, turning her hand over to show me a concussion grenade. Less damage, more shock and distraction. Not a bad choice.

"On three," I say, moving to the other side of the door.

We stack up on the door in an amateur approximation of good tactics. When I push the door open, Lana tosses the grenade inside and I shut the door again, getting only the barest glimpse of the Yurks all curled up behind solid barriers. An arrow bounces off my shield even as I close the door. The light rumble from the explosion comes a second later.

Flinging the door open, I Blink Step slightly behind one of the barriers, appearing a few feet in the air even as Roland bounces in, unleashing a loud roar as he jumps over the blockade on the opposite side of the room. Anna and Howard rush in a few seconds later while Lana and Shadow keep an eye on the hallway. Even as I land and spin, my swords in both hands, I only catch one across its chest as the Yurks scramble away.

Yurk Elite Warriors (Level 40)

HP: 378/413

MP: 188/201

Conditions: Mild Stun

Mildly stunned or not, the damn Yurk is still moving. Nine Yurks, scattered around the room, are taking us on. None of my AOEs will work—the classroom too small for their attacks. My only other spell is Mana Dart which, while great for Mana conservation, isn't powerful enough to do real damage. That pretty much leaves my Skills and Freezing Blade.

Considering their health, I ignore using my spell for now and just get on with the killing. They might be fast and skilled, but they're smaller than me and in a retreat. I catch up with one of them fast. Behind me, I feel the impact of blades against the Soul Shield as his friends rally. Dismissing a sword, I block the Yurk's cut and grab my target by the neck to spin and throw the smaller Yurk at his friends. Legs and hands flopping in the air, the Yurk bowls over his friends, tangling the group up long enough for me to send in a pair of Blade Strikes. A second later, I'm rushing over to the next in line, intent on finishing up my group.

Lana steps into the room while I deal with the trio on my side, sending a widespread blast of pellets to finish them off before she twists to attack Roland's and Howard's targets. Anna has one of the Yurks on the ground, her jaw closed around its shoulder as her flames lick across its body while it thrashes around in pain. Howard's worrying and backing off another two.

I block a Cleave from one of the Yurks, pushed back a little by the sudden attack. Even as the Yurk tries to entangle my sword, its friend creeps around its side, ready to plunge a blade into me. Stepping sideways at the same time as I dismiss my blade, I use the momentum to complete a spinning back kick, sending the flanking frog into a nearby wall. As I land and recover, I slap the initial attacker's glowing blade aside with my hand, my Soul Shield glowing as the sabre leaves a light line of red along my arm. Recalling my sword, I plunge it into the Yurk's body before bull-rushing the Yurk attempting to pull itself out of the wall.

With the added firepower from the redhead, the battle comes to a close soon enough. Battle over, I dismiss the blade and grimace as the blood on it, no longer having a place to grip, falls, splattering over my hand. Thankfully the Soul Shield actually protects me, allowing me to shake my hand clear of the gunk. While I'm doing so, Ali is looting and storing the corpses. After a second, I refresh the Soul Shields on myself and Lana, surprised by how low the shields have gotten. Even now, I can see the injuries on the pets slowly healing, the minor scrapes and cuts sewing back together as the puppies lick their wounds.

"Nine Level 40s. Not bad, but nothing surprising," I say.

"Eleven," Ali says, pointing at the additions.

"Eleven…?" I frown, staring.

He's right. There were nine on the minimap, but in the heat of the battle, I hadn't realized there were two adds. I stare at the additions, noting the slightly different equipment loadout and information screen.

Yurk Rogues (Level 36)
_HP: 0/274_
_MP: 0/347_
Condition: Dead

"Bastard snuck up on me," Lana says, kicking one body.

"You know, if they're frogs, they lay eggs in groups. So, not sure if they actually have a family structure like ours," I say, shrugging. "Never mind the fact that they're aliens."

"It's just a saying," Lana says.

I cock my head to the side, curious to see if Ali has any information.

"Don't look at me. I'm not interested in learning about the mating habits of Yurks. Or, you know, any of you meaties."

"Meaties?"

"Trying out a new descriptor."

"Don't."

Ali sniffs, floating into the hallway as we gather at the door to the next classroom. We stack up again, ready to repeat the process. Interesting that they don't come out. I debate if it's a matter of tactics, stupidity, or just the dungeon and then give up. Not my problem if they want to make this easy.

***

"Well, that was anticlimactic," I mutter to Lana an hour later.

We swept through the building without a problem, the small battles not an issue for the pair of us. Frankly, by myself, I out-Leveled our attackers. With Lana's pets harrying and dealing with the others, it was a simple matter to clear each room.

"Getting cocky, aren't you?" Lana says.

"Actually, I'm thinking there should be more to this," I say, waving us forward and up the hill once again. We'll reach the main campus soon, which is where the roads and dungeon square should show up.

"We're nearly out of time, boy-o," Ali reminds me.

"I know. I just want to see the square. We can pop right in there next time," I say as we continue to walk forward.

Occasionally, the plink of an attack reminds me that the damn scouts are still out there. That, and the strangled yelps or a sudden crunch as Roland and Shadow get to work on our flanks.

"I should bring the boys up here more often," Lana says with a slight smile. "They seem to be having fun."

"I can tell." Rather than spend more time exploring the outer layer of buildings, I swing us toward the main parking lot and the campus's town square.

We're just passing another grey, boring building on our left, the parking lot on our right, when we hear a slow, thudding drum beat.

"Boy-o…" Ali says, frowning.

In front of us, slowly appearing on the map and disappearing as the mists continue to envelop us, is a large cluster of monsters. There's nearly a hundred or so, many in the Level 30s or higher.

"I think they were delaying us," Lana says softly, eyes wide as she stares at the shared minimap.

Glimpsed through the mists, the front ranks are slowly marching forward, shields held in front of them.

"Yeah…" I stare at my Mana pool and sigh, popping a bottle of Mana restoration and swigging it down. Between that and my regeneration, I'm back up to two-thirds full, which should do. "I want to try something, then we can go."

Lana nods, face grim as she engages her aura once more. It bursts forth, making the front group stagger before they seem revitalized by the continued drumming.

I step forward, crouching and whisper the command. "Army of One."

Around me, six identical copies of my sword pop into existence, tripling the total number that I get from Thousand Blades. I grunt, swinging my hand down, and the blades shoot forward rather than projecting a strike like Blade Strike. The glowing red-and-blue blades strike the front ranks, boring through the monsters and continuing onward, shattering their careful formation.

"Nice," Lana says as she unloads her shotgun into the group.

Anna helps, flames stretching from her body to run across the group like long tendrils. But for all that, for how impressive it looks, the Yurks stagger back up to their feet and reform their lines.

I sigh. I guess I know where I'm putting more Class Skill points next time. I need more blades and more damage. While the damage will get better as I grow in strength and my blade does as well, the number of blades is a matter of another Skill.

Once they've reset the line, harried by Anna's and Lana's attacks, the group continues their slow and steady march. A low growl from Howard behind us alerts us to the troops that have flanked us, pinning us in place and forcing both Shadow and Roland out of hiding.

"John…" Lana's voice grows concerned as the group gets within thirty meters.

A shift in their positioning shows that they're ready to charge. My wordless answer is to pop open the Portal, and the puppies and Roland dart in without a word. Lana and Anna follow even as arrows and spears fly, raining down around us. I follow her through the Portal.

"Well, that was disappointing," I say, grabbing one of the spears flying through the fast-closing Portal before it pins Anna.

"Disappointing?" Lana says.

"My Skill," I say, shaking my head. "It's really reliant on my other Skills and I just don't have the points for it all. I'm going to need to put more points into it for it to get useful."

A cough drags our attention back to Katherine, who has stood up from behind my desk to extract a few arrows and spears that have embedded themselves on it and around the walls. "Perhaps another location would be better for you to teleport to whilst in combat?"

"Sorry!" I say, watching as the prim and proper woman stacks the weapons aside.

"You know she's going to make you pay for that, right?" Lana whispers to me.

"Nah, she wouldn't do that," I say, confident in Katherine's professionalism. I purposely ignore Lana's and Ali's looks, content to bask in my naiveté. Though if you know you're fooling yourself, is it really naiveté?

"So what's on the agenda?"

Lana waves goodbye, off to deal with her own chores. Behind her desk, Katherine pulls up her status screens and rattles off the agenda for the day. More meetings of course. It's always more meetings.

***

"The Adventurer Guilds are here," Katherine announces with slight disapproval as I lounge in my chair.

Since there's no paperwork, I've pulled my chair out from behind the desk. I'm in a nice, comfortable lounge chair taken from below, rather than the uncomfortable office chairs that used to fill this corner office. Katherine, for reasons of her own, is behind a desk.

"Send them in."

A few minutes later, a tall humanoid elf walks in, a smile on his lips. Tall, blond, and pretty, he could have walked off the set of a *Lord of the Rings* movie if it weren't for the futuristic sci-fi jumpsuit and beam rifle slung over his shoulder. I stand, offering a hand and shaking his before I flop back down in my chair, gesturing for him to choose his poison. After glancing at the options—office chairs, another lounger, and the couch—he takes an office chair and rolls it over to me. I note how he dismisses Katherine's presence almost immediately, his focus on me.

Mental Effect Resisted

"I'm John Lee."

"Kryl a Sharra. I'm the Guild liaison of the Burning Leaves, a Tier II Guild," Kryl says.

I'm a bit impressed by the fact that he's from a Tier II Guild—those represent deep pockets, according to Ali, with Guild Halls in over five hundred settled worlds and a deep roster of dedicated Adventurers. Among other things, Guilds have to meet a certain number of Galactic Council quests and hit certain taxation numbers to qualify for each level. All things considered, there's just over a hundred Tier II Guilds in the entire Galactic System.

Kryl a Sharra (Level 18 Fell Ranger)

HP: 740/740

MP: 485/520

Conditions: Aura of Command

I don't mention the Aura or the fact that he's still using it. A glance at Katherine shows that her conditions still list as none, a rather surprising matter. Then again, I don't know what kind of Skills she has, but being an Assistant who can be easily swayed probably wouldn't be great. Something worth noting at least.

"What can I do for you, Kryl?"

"The Movana designate their Nobles by adding an a in between their names. So Kryl should, if you were feeling polite, be called a Sharra."

A flash of annoyance shows on Kryl's face before he stamps it out. "We would like to know when our application for a Guild Hall in your settlements would be approved."

"You've got applications for places outside of Kamloops?" I say with a frown.

"Yes. They were added a few days ago," Kryl says smoothly.

"Huh." I consider what else to say then make the decision. "Get out."

"What?" Kryl exclaims, eyes widening.

"Get. Out. You're not welcome in this office anymore. If your Guild wants to continue talking, they can send someone else."

Kryl narrows his eyes in thought then nods before walking out in silence. Rude and manipulative as he might be, at least he's smart enough to realize what he did wrong. Using his aura to attempt to manipulate the negotiation and force us to take his Guild is idiotic. Sure, it might work with some, but that's no way to build a lasting relationship. When he walks out, Katherine lets out a little snort that I assume to be one of approval. Ass.

"Next."

***

"Brommax's Raiders are a Tier III Guild. We'll be able to not only provide a wider market for your goods through our Guild Shops, but we also have a deep bench of Adventurers to fulfill any of your requests and we are willing—and able—to staff all three of your settlements," the big yellow Yerrick says. I forget his name, having seen so many for now. I could look, but that's what Katherine's for.

"Raiders?"

"It's a translation imprecision."

"He's telling the truth. An English translation thing. Maybe those US Rangers might be a better translation."

"I'm really only interested in discussing one town at a time," I say. "Kelowna in particular."

"Of course. We're willing to negotiate on the monthly Credit fee, as well as any additional settlement security requirements you might have."

"Keep talking," I say, leaning forward. Finally. The Yerrick is the third in line, and the first I'm actually interested in.

***

"I represent the Platinum Pixies, a Tier IV Guild. Our Guild might not be the biggest, but we punch above our weight class," the pixie says, hovering in front of me with a grin.

"You guys allow non-pixies in?"

An uncomfortable silence later, I watch her tiny form flit out.

***

"Crystal Clans isn't your typical Guild. We're a Tier III Guild, but we're more focused on Artisan work. Our people are looking for stable and plentiful sources of materials, which is why a Guild Hall in a Dungeon World is perfect for us," the dwarf states, offering me a grin and launching into his spiel the moment he sits down.

"Sounds like a lot of great things for you—"

"What? A stable market that buys at a higher price than the Shop doesn't sound good to you? How about Advanced and Master Artisans who can guide some of your people? We can work in class schedules."

"That's nice, but we're a bit worried about our security..." I say leadingly.

"We aren't all Artisans. A significant minority are fighters—we do need guards for some of our rarer materials. And a number of Adventurers see the advantage of having access to Master Level Artisans," Wrox says, beard waggling. "We'll have a number of those people in your towns."

"And a security agreement?"

"Can be negotiated."

"Good. Now, about the rent…"

***

"No."

"But with the number of fallen in the transition, we will be able to raise—"

"No."

"You don't understand—"

"Get out. Before I throw you out."

"Simpletons."

I watch the multi-legged heptadon walk out of the room, almost flouncing out. A hand held out to Katherine puts guests on hold while I keep my breathing deep and steady to get my temper back in control. Asshole necromancers.

***

"Labashi." I blink, standing and shaking the Hakarta's hand.

He's still as big, green-grey, and tusky as ever. However, I'm surprised to see him here in Vancouver. Last I knew, he was up in Whitehorse, finishing his initial contract with the Duchess.

"Redeemer." He inclines his head and sits down. A hand comes up, offering me a small, red-wrapped piece of heaven. "Chocolate?"

"Don't mind if I do," I say, grabbing the chocolate and popping the piece in my mouth. I blink when the chocolate melts in my mouth on contact, the liquid delight a surprise. Even as I sit, quietly enjoying the expensive treat, Labashi offers a piece to Katherine while introducing himself. "Good chocolate."

"Yes," Labashi says, leaning forward. "A great export."

My mind shifts for a second to Adventurers fighting through hordes of monsters, risking life and limb, only to loot their corpses and exclaim in delight at finding a Toblerone. I chuckle, making Labashi stare at me with concern.

I wave away his questioning look, continuing. "What are you doing here, Major?"

"Visiting an ally. And pitching my Corp as an option."

"You can do that?"

"It is not the most common use of that building slot, but is possible," Labashi says.

"MERCENARY CORPS ARE UNDER THE SAME CLASSIFICATION AS ADVENTURERS GUILDS. AS SUCH, A SINGLE COMPANY MAY BE ADDED TO ANY SINGLE TOWN."

"What else is covered under that classification?" I send the thought to Kim and Ali, grumpy about missing another thing. Between a lack of interest on my part and the sheer volume of information, I'm missing a lot about running a settlement.

"Assassin's Guilds and Thief Circles fall under the same categories. Also Spy centers, but you need to build up the requirements internally."

I sit in silence for a moment, listening to my companions while Labashi enjoys his tea. When my eyes refocus, Labashi shifts his attention back to me fully.

"Why a merc group?"

"We prefer mercenary corps," Labashi says easily. "Most Adventuring Guilds will promise protection, but they're not good at it. That's what we do. We can provide a higher number of individuals with better Classes and training. While we might not provide the same level of business contacts or a Guild Shop, we can provide training. For our needs, we'll also need a much larger base of operations, which will aid you in developing to the next level of Small City. And lastly, we're willing to pay a much higher base rental than any Guild."

He's not wrong. One of the requirements, over and above the basic population requirements, of a Small City is a 98% land ownership requirement. Except it isn't just any land ownership; it designated the amount of physical land too, so you couldn't just shrink your settlement down to beat the System.

Still, I frown, drumming my fingers on my legs. "Why do you need a location?"

"Because we have none yet. A Headquarters building will allow us to set up long-range teleportation arrays and cheaper housing for our people. We expect to have significant work on your world. Having a permanent base will keep our overall cost down and allow for further training opportunities. That you have a City Dungeon is already a significant bonus," Labashi says.

I'm a bit surprised he's laying all his cards out like that, which makes me slightly suspicious about what he's hiding.

"Why not further north with the Duchess and her people?" I ask, frowning. After all, Roxley probably wouldn't mind their presence. And while the Truinnar might be willing to help us out, I know he wouldn't do it by harming his interest—or his mistress's.

"All her current allocations are earmarked for others. Our Contract includes a headquarters, but only at a later date. We prefer to have one sooner," Labashi says.

Right. So that means he'd be willing to pay more, but not outrageously. Thus, while the deal might be good, it won't be great.

"All right, let's talk details. Call me tentatively interested," I say, leaning forward. Best to hear what he has to say. Maybe I can garner a little more information that way. And I have to admit, a company of Hakarta in town could provide some really outstanding protection.

***

"That all of them?" I say, watching the swaying form of the duck-like creature walk out.

Weird. So weird. Think Howard the Duck crossed with a cross-dresser. I have to admit, for most of the meeting, I was battling my sense of incredulity.

"Yes. For today," Katherine answers.

"Huh." I tilt my head toward the exit. "You know, no one's barged in since you started. And everyone seems to know when to come in, even if we end up chatting a bit."

"Ah, a simple matter with a Skill of mine."

When she refuses to elaborate, even after a long silence, I push ahead. "You said for today."

"Yes. A few more requests have come in since the schedule was created. I plan to have another bloc of such meetings in a few days. At which point, I believe, we should have a clear idea of who and what might be offered," Katherine elaborates.

"Nice." I sigh and lean back. Good. I don't have to make a damn decision just yet. Even if I know that I can't push things off too long.

Chapter 4

Early morning drives on the West Coast are always beautiful, even if it's on forest-lined, battered highways leading to industrial wastelands. Fighting back a yawn—drawn forth from boredom more than physical cues—I swing Sabre around the mangled corpse of a deer on my way to the meeting.

Weeks after we've taken the cities, things have finally begun to settle down. I'm still hesitating on approving any single Adventuring Guild, even the ones who have dropped by a few times to press their cases. Truth be told, I'm not entirely sure who or how to set up the deal, so I'm procrastinating till a better idea comes along. Luckily, I've got Peter, one of my new city managers, researching previous deals made both on Earth and other worlds. It's as good an excuse as any for delaying.

Katherine's recommendation to build out the bureaucracy to run the cities has developed quite well. Kamloops and Kelowna have shaken themselves out pretty fast—an advantage of their tiny populations. There have been few arguments involved, and if anyone does want to bitch about management, they only need to walk down the street. It makes me think about life in small towns and villages, before the industrialization of the world. It makes me think of Whitehorse too, if less political. Don't get me wrong, I'm not yearning for a time before proper plumbing and professional entertainment, but there's something to be said about being able to punch in the face the asshole who raised your taxes. Or having your neighbor lend you a gun because it's the right thing to do.

"How much farther?" I ask Ali, mostly rhetorically.

"Uhhh…" Ali blinks, turning his head to the side.

I look up and blink. "And why are you wearing a turban and a robe?"

"Seriously?" Ali glares at me, the white robe floating around his feet as he sits. "You know better, boy-o."

"Fine. I know it's not a turban—that's for Sikhs. I just don't know the term, at least for men," I point out.

"If it's white, it's called a keffiyeh and thawb." A shit-eating grin splits his darkly tanned face. "And I figure we're meeting Americans, right? Might as well play to their delusions."

I sigh and shake my head. I guess he's going to make himself known then. A part of me considers ordering the Spirit to stay hidden so he can be another card up my sleeve. I recall doing that when I first entered Whitehorse, scared of what I'd find. But considering what we're about to do, I have a feeling that hiding him could be futile and potentially lead to accusations of deception.

"We're trying for a peaceful, productive meeting," I say without much hope in my tone. Still, a man has to try.

"This better?"

After I pick myself and Sabre off the asphalt and brush down my now-dirty armored jumpsuit, I resolutely refuse to look at the Spirit while speaking to him. "Why are you wearing a *Borat* swimsuit?"

"What? Everyone loves that movie."

"Your definition of everyone needs readjusting. And I repeat, we want a peaceful, productive meeting. So for all our sakes, control yourself. Or else I'll banish you," I say.

Ali sniffs, and I risk a quick glance out of the corner of my eyes to see him in a simple black shirt and blue jeans. I exhale softly, catching the grin on Ali's face, and I realize the ass was messing with me. Still, it worked. I'm a lot less tense.

As we roll along the 5 into the outskirts of Everett, I eye my surroundings with a little more care. All I really know of this satellite town is that it's mostly industrial buildings and bikini-barista coffee shacks. As I drive past one such shack, tucked in the corner of a gas station, I'm surprised to see movement within. A moment later, I realize it's an evolved cat, not a human. I'm a bit disappointed. Those bikini-barista girls are weird, a strange intersection of the West Coast caffeine obsession and male lust. I blink after a moment—Ali's most recent game crossed my mind as it free-associated around bikinis.

"What did you say?" Ali asks, cocking his head in my direction.

"Kittens. Cute, fluffy kittens," I remind myself aloud, trying to bleach my brain.

Thankfully, we're going to be meeting outside downtown Everett at Spencer Island Park. It's not anyone's choice location, too far out of Seattle proper for the groups based in the city, not inside Everett itself or any other satellite town for the suburb groups. No one's happy, which makes it the perfect meeting spot.

Ali fills in my minimap long before I arrive at the meeting space, showcasing the wide variety of Classes and individuals awaiting me. There are Scouts, Hunters, Sneaks, and Rogues galore on the outside, keeping away the monsters that might disturb the meeting. And within, we've got an even wider variety of Classes—but as always, almost all of them are Combat Classers. Damn it.

When I glide into the parking lot on Sabre, I attract some attention. When they realize I'm alone, I attract even more. And by the time I take my place off to the side, without joining any of the other groups, everyone is looking at me. Tapping the side of my helmet, I let it slide down to let everyone see me properly while I regard the groups.

In one corner is a group predominantly made up of Mages of one form or another, all Advanced Classes, all of them within five Levels of each other, most leaning toward an Asian / South-Asian mix. They've got specializations from Ice Elementalists to Conjurers to Metamagician and more. Almost all of them have decent Constitutions, but few seem to have put anything into Strength or Agility. In addition to the Mages, I spot a couple of what must be tanks, one of them still in his security guard uniform. A single girl stands out in the crowd of men, alone. At a guess, those would be the programmers from Microsoft.

In another corner are the Sons of Odin, who are shooting dismissive and angry looks at me and the Mage group. No surprise in their makeup, though there's a few more women among the long-haired, biker-styled idiots than I'd expect. Lots of yellow hair there, some obviously bottle blond. I check out their Levels and their Classes, noting a decent mix that leans toward melee fighting with a wider range than the Mages. Their leader is obvious, a tattooed monster of a man, nearly seven feet tall with a ponytail and biker leathers, a monster of a pistol strapped to his leg. Quick verification from Ali shows that it's likely enchanted leather, offering more than just aesthetic appeal.

Sweeping my eyes along, I assess the other groups. A multi-national group leaning toward Latinos in one corner. An all-female group in another. A couple of groups almost exclusively made of African Americans. Another pair that I could swear is made up of the criminal elements. The baristas— one of the few non-Combatant groups here—have their own corner with a table laid out, doing brisk business selling cups of joe and bottles of their pre-made coffee.

My gaze is drawn to the large group of individuals in military uniform. Or are those army fatigues? My enhanced memory absently points out that a uniform is just a mode of dress and fatigues are just combat uniform. Or at least, that's what those books alluded to. When my eyes lock on the group, my stare is met by a gentleman in his late forties. Flanking him is a group that is obviously his security detail and the person I assume is his aide. I'm sure the things on their uniforms have something interesting to say, but I don't read military. Perhaps I should have paid more attention to those rank insignias in those first-person shooters I used to play. That is, if fictional space marine insignia translates to the real world.

"Coffee?" A soft whisper of a voice to my left almost makes me jump. Even if I knew she was going to try it, Ingrid almost has me levitating off the ground.

"Sure," I keep my tone cool as I take the cup. Even the faintest whiff is enough to make me salivate. The taste itself is incredible—perfectly mellow, with strong hints of cinnamon and an aftertaste that disappears before I sip again. I've finished half the cup before I realize it. "Damn…"

Superior Cold Coffee Ingested

+8% to Regeneration Rates

Duration: 1 hour

"Told you," Ingrid says with a smirk. "So where's everyone else?"

"They'll be here."

Ingrid rolls her eyes. "Well, don't screw it up. It took me quite a bit to get everyone to show up."

"You did good," I say. A glance at the clock in the upper right tells me we've got another five minutes before we're supposed to start.

"Let's get this started," the blond biker says, stomping forward. I mentally tag him as BB—a childish toy wanting to be grown up. "We're wasting time and kills here."

A glance around shows that while he might be impatient, no one seems to be gainsaying his words. Grunting, I walk forward, a slight queasiness in my stomach that I push aside. Public speaking was never my forte, but after all I've gone through, that fear is easy enough to deal with.

"Afternoon. Thank you all for coming," I say. Blondie shifts in impatience, but I ignore him as I let my gaze wander around. "My name is John Lee. I'm the current owner of Vancouver and the settlements around it. Since you guys are our closest neighbors, I figured it's time for us to meet and talk. Especially before the Sect returns."

"Sect?" a voice calls from one of the groups.

"The aliens," BB replies. "Invading our territory, claiming it for their own."

"Are they expected to return? Your friend indicated that they had retreated from their holdings in Vancouver," the soldier says. Well, Officer, to be exact for his Class.

For now, I ignore their names since I can fix their characteristics in my mind easier this way. Also, I hate remembering names and I have more important things to deal with. "Not soon. We've done enough damage to them here that they're going to consolidate before they come back. But they'll be back. If not them, someone else."

The Officer inclines his head slightly, accepting my words. Murmurs rise as others talk.

One of the Mages steps forward. A Blue Mage, whatever that is. "So what do you want? You didn't call this meeting to just say hi."

"Yeah, what do you want, eh?" BB mocks.

"No. I didn't," I say, replying to the Blue Mage and ignoring BB. "How much do you people know of the world around us? Of the state of your nation and the world?" I ask rhetorically. "We're lucky here, mostly. We've got our cities back under human control. There are other cities, other countries where humans are desperately fighting for any space they can find.

There are a lot of places where humans are what the Sect would have us be—Serfs and servants, landless peasants without a say." I pause before I take my next gamble. "If you'll allow me, there's someone I think you should all hear from."

"Someone…?"

There're more than a few looks around me, obviously not seeing anyone. But more than a few nod and a few shrug, figuring I've got whoever I want farther out. Which means when the glowing black and gold Portal opens up, there are a few exclamations of shock.

"That's sweet."

"Nice. Dimension Door?"

"Long-range teleport," his friend mutters.

The Mages whisper among themselves.

"A Skill," I answer everyone.

Lana comes out first, followed soon after by her pets. The animals get a few looks but no exclamations since they're obviously under control. That, and the seven-foot-tall brute of a minotaur clad in modern combat armor draws all the attention, such that Mikito is barely even seen.

"Monster!"

A targeted beam attack splashes against Capstan's portable shield. The Yerrick growls as he drops a hand to his combat axe. Lana steps forward quickly, blocking the attacks as best she can while I throw a Soul Shield on her and the pets spread out, letting out low growls. Another second and a twist of my hand has me layering a Soul Shield on top of Ulrick as well.

"Stop that!" I snap.

"He's a monster. A… bull-thing!" The first attacker still has his beam rifle pointed at Ulrick, though he's not shooting. His friends have all pulled weapons as well, ready to attack the Yerrick.

"Minotaur," one of the Mages mutters pedantically.

"I'd drop that," Ingrid says, whispering into the attacker's ear. A knife is at his throat, the young First Nations woman magically appearing next to the man.

A part of me wonders when she disappeared, but I dismiss that question for more important things. Like the rising tension as BB pulls and points his pistol at her head.

"Chill it," I snarl.

"Calm," Lana states, the Aura of the Red Queen flaring again. Her hair seems to darken, becoming a blood red that is not entirely natural. Those violet eyes shift to a brilliant purple as her skin becomes fairer and closer to marble. More, a palpable sense of danger comes from her now.

The attacking group, bearing the brunt of her attention, whitens, a few stepping backward and lowering their guns, others clenching their fists.

"So. Hot," a hipster kid manning the barista bar, the same one who exclaimed how "sweet" my portal was, says, his tongue almost hanging out. Probably not the effect Lana's Aura was meant for.

"Charisma effect. Not always going to work the way you think it will," Ali mentions. *"But I got to agree, damn but the lady's quite edible."*

"I hope this isn't how you mean to treat us. Threats are not the basis of a good working relationship," the Officer says, his legs spread as he stands at ease, hands behind his back. Still, I can see the slight tightness around his eyes, the tension in his shoulders as he wills himself to ignore Lana's aura.

BB keeps his gun pointed at Ingrid, fingers white around the pistol hilt.

"Capstan Ulrick is our friend and a guest. Attacking him is an attack on us," I say firmly. "But we're willing to set the violence aside and talk if everyone else is."

"Fuck that. I ain't listening to no alien," snarls BB.

"Then leave," I say.

"You…" BB growls, shifting his gaze and pistol to point at me.

I ignore his provocations, watching as the others edge away from fighting. Repressed by Lana's aura and without additional violence or any hostile action by Capstan, the initial impetus fades. Lana, sensing the mood change, drops her Aura. Yet the pets don't move from their positions around the Yerrick.

It's then, and only then, that I dismiss the Portal. My Mana is nearly half gone, between all the casting and Skill usage, but there's more than enough to get us out of here again. The way the Officer is eyeing me and the location where the Portal is, I can see his mind churning.

Until Capstan speaks. "My name is Capstan Ulrick, First Fist of my tribe. The Redeemer has requested that I speak of my people's history to you, to explain a little of what you must understand. The dangers that lie ahead." Capstan's eyes sweep over the group. "The Yerrick are a displaced people. Our home world was integrated into the System without warning, like yours. Unlike you, we integrated into the greater Galactic System as one of their many worlds. What we did not understand was the meaning of this. We did not understand that a settlement, once sold, cannot be rebought. That land, once taken by the larger groups, could never be retrieved. Not without war.

"We were lied to, tricked, and threatened. We lost our lands, our settlements, and eventually, our world. Now the Yerrick serve under others. My people are scattered through the Galaxy as they attempt to earn enough Credits to survive."

"Boo hoo hoo. One set of aliens taking advantage of another," one of the Sons of Odin interjects.

Capstan stares at the interrupter, the look he gives him priceless—it's the kind of look you give a particularly hairy bug and you're trying to decide if killing it or smacking it away is the better choice. Once the Son of Odin quiets down, Capstan speaks in detail. For the next hour, he talks. At first explaining the process and their history, later diverting to specific questions.

I keep quiet, listening with half my attention. I know most of this already, having spoken with him before. But the information is a revelation to most others.

So much of it is familiar though—to anyone who studies history anyway. Find a few groups that are at odds, pit them against each other while you pay pennies on the dollar for goods—land—that you want while selling your goods at a huge markup. Control the information, control access to the Shops, bring in secondary or tertiary groups to "rule." Never, ever keep a promise that is bad for you, breaking contracts and rules where you can. After all, a Contract might hold you and the other party to it, but if you word it right, the Contract can affect an entire settlement on one end and a disposable corporation on the other.

And always, always, keep control of what's important—the City Core and the people.

"Thanks, First Fist," I say to Capstan after an hour, when the crowd is getting bored, other than a few notable individuals. "Now, the reason I wanted you to hear that is for you guys to start figuring out what the hell you're doing. From what I understand, you've left the Sect in control of various City Cores because none of you can agree on who gets to control them. Or hell, which form of government you intend to take."

"There shouldn't be any real argument. We're still part of the US of A. We should be having an election," a rather tubby gentleman mutters, his arms crossed in front of him.

His friends are all nodding firmly, as are a few groups.

"We are in a national emergency. In such a circumstance, the United States Army should take control of the city till we are in contact with a legitimate authority," the Officer says, shaking his head. "If an election is decided upon, we can help conduct such an event in a fair and impartial manner."

"Oh, like we're going to let you army boys take over," growls an African American man. I'm a bit jealous really—he's wearing the System-equivalent of a leather hoodie and it's styling. "Like you guys are actually supposed to be acting on US soil."

"This is a unique situation," the Officer says, turning to the man. "And there are specific protocols that have been put in place—"

"Yeah, and you still won't tell us about what's happened with your nukes," one of the baristas says, glaring.

"We've already said there is an SOP involved in such a situation. Suffice it to say that there are plans in place for a catastrophic event like this."

"Oh really, you guys got *protocols* for the end of the world and the introduction of humanity to a *gaming* system?" scoffs the Blue Mage.

"Not exactly, but—"

"Ahem," I cough, quite loudly. "Look, I get it. You all have questions, and you've got your own things to deal with. But the longer you argue, the more people—your people—die. You need to get yourselves a city, which means putting together a real organization that all your city cores are tied to."

"And how did you do that?" the Latino spokesperson asks, eyeing me.

"I own it. All of it," I say, seeing no point in lying. "We're working on a better government system, but Vancouver and its surrounding cities are now tied together."

"You're a Canadian dictator?" the African American says, choking on a laugh.

"Free maple syrup for all!" the Son of Odin heckler speaks up. This time, he does get a few laughs. "Watch out for the giant beavers!"

That last one gets less of a laugh as they stare at the giant red fox and Lana's puppies.

"For now," I say with a shrug, ignoring the heckling. "Speed is important, if you guys haven't understood Capstan's point. Once the big boys start moving—and some already have—we're screwed. As it is, Texas is wholly owned by the Inlin Corporation. Alaska and the Yukon by the Duchess. Europe's a battleground between five different groups, two of which are backed by the Movana. We need to establish a foothold and take out the smaller groups if we want any say in our lives."

"And you want our help," the Officer says, eyes narrowed.

"Aye. My people are good. But there aren't enough of us. If we're going to be expanding, we're going to need help," I say.

"And there we have it. The real reason you came down," BB says before spitting to the side. "I knew you people had an agenda. We ain't going to die for you."

"I'm not—" I protest.

"And who's going to take control of those cities, dictator?" the Latino calls out, hands crossed in front of him.

"That's up to discussion."

A roar of disapproval explodes when I say that. More questions are shouted, BB smirking as he watches the entire meeting break down. Lana shoots me a look, but I shake my head, instinct telling me that using her ability now would be seen as a provocation.

***

Forty minutes later, we stand around, staring at the few groups that have stayed after the others dispersed. I did my best, as did Lana, but the meeting went out of our control, egged on by BB and a few other malcontents. I couldn't exactly blame them—having a stranger come in and tell them they sucked was never going to work out well. But someone had to say it.

"That could have gone better," I mutter.

"*No shit, boy-o. Told you you should have let Lana talk,*" Ali says.

I end up rolling my eyes slightly while Lana flashes me a sympathetic smile.

"From what you said, I understand you have certain plans concerning liberating more cities?" the Officer says as he walks toward our group.

With the meeting over, I'd popped open a Portal for Capstan to head back to Vancouver with a promise to port him the rest of the way home soon.

"Aye," I say, glancing at the few interested groups.

The all-women group clad in Adventurer chic, a weirdo group who looks as if they took their dress code inspiration from superheroes, the Mages, Barista group, and a few more "normal" groups standby. About a third of everyone who came.

"Well?" the Blue Mage barks, the East Indian almost bouncing in impatience. I absently note that he's not gotten a genetic cleanse—or if he did, he opted out of getting more height, being a not-so-impressive 5'6".

"Calgary," I answer. "I'll need to visit Edmonton first, which is human-controlled, and see what they want, but after that, we're looking at Calgary. That's currently controlled by two different factions—the Kingdom of Pewsin and Uvrik Corp. The first is a side kingdom of, hmmm, halflings I guess is the closest term. Not hobbits. These guys are vicious bastards. Uvrik Corp is a 'small' Galactic corporation with a focus mostly on fortifying foodstuff."

"Halflings and a food corporation," one of the Mages mutters. "I swear there's a joke in there somewhere."

"If you look hard enough, there's a joke all around you," Lana says.

"Joke or not, between those two groups, they've got over twenty Advanced Class in play, with three of them in the high Levels. Even a single high Level Advanced Classer can do a lot of damage. We'd need at least three or four of our guys to contain one of them," I say firmly.

"Our guys?"

"Well, if you all agree," I say.

"You're asking us to free a Canadian city," one of the ladies says, eyeing the three of us.

"I'm asking you to free a city full of humans. Yes," I say, meeting her eyes.

"She is correct that you are asking for much..." the Officer says leadingly.

I sigh quietly, knowing that there's going to be politics. Always damn politics. "What do you want?"

"Your help. Your Skill."

I cock my head to the side, waiting for more. As the Officer continues. "Your actions in taking Vancouver from the Thirteen Moon Sect helped Seattle greatly. Your Class, your Skill, and your people could do the same for our other cities."

"Yeah, but what do we get out of it?" I say softly, angling for some advantage here. Truth be told, coming down here to get help was part of the goal, so I'm not exactly bargaining from a position of power. But at least, the need is mutual.

"That depends on how that Skill of yours works," the Officer says, skin around his grey eyes crinkling as he smiles.

"Right…" I narrow my eyes as I finally get around to reading his Status. Octavian Wier, Level 7 Officer. "Octavian. Well, that's something we can certainly discuss."

"I prefer my middle name, but it's Colonel Wier to you. Acting commander of the 7th Infantry Division out of Fort Lewis," Wier says, seemingly nonplussed by my use of his name. I see a few looks shared around, but not much.

"Acting, sure. You're all that's left after the hydra rolled over your base," one of the Mages says with a snort. "That damn monster made its way halfway up the city before we ended it."

I glare at the man, shutting him up as the soldiers stiffen. Taunting people whose job is to protect others with the deaths of their friends doesn't seem either charitable or smart.

Once I get my silence, I look back at the colonel. "Well, I don't have much information on the state your country is in, so I'm going to need data at the very least. But if we do this, we're really going to need your support on our end as well. All of you."

I see more than a few pauses, a few looks around, and I sigh. Convincing these people, even the ones who stayed to help, seems as if it's going to take a bit. Or, on seeing the avarice in some eyes, some bribing. Rather than convincing everyone to get involved here and now, we take names and information with promises of meeting up personally to discuss the levels of their support. Better to do the discussions in person.

***

Octavian's is the first group we speak with. Rather than going back to his base, we end up at the discarded remnants of a local coffee store. It's not the best option, but it has chairs and we've all got travel mugs of Barista-made coffee, so it seems mildly appropriate. We get there after I've sent most of the team home, rather than dragging everyone about. Outside, the pets and most of Wier's soldiers stand guard, including an interesting pair of Rangers. I'm slightly amused that the older aide keeps staring at me with what I assume is disapproval, but at least he hasn't voiced it. Either way, I send a note to Ali to dig into the soldiers' Status information while we talk, curious what kind of goodies they might have picked up.

"So. Retaking the USA," I say, starting us off.

"Yes. Currently, remnants of our chain of command are gathered around Fort Belvoir, where there is a Shop. We're in contact with them," Colonel Wier says, a fact that startles me. Long-range communication is one of the things that we all lost, and while it's possible to replace it, it's expensive. That he—and the Fort—chose to get it up is startling at first. Then, it's kind of obvious. "There are three other alien groups in Washington: one Corporation and a pair of alien governments—one a Kingdom consisting of half-giants, and one an Empire of kobolds."

"What kind of kobolds?" Ali asks with a frown.

"Kind?"

"You humans seem to mix up three different races. Are they draconic, dog-like, or like short, skinny humans?"

"Uhhh… dog-like."

"Pooskeens. From the planet Pos."

"Won't that make them Poskeens?"

Ali stares at me, hands on his hips.

"Sorry. Right. Alien grammar," I mutter, shaking my head.

"What I'm going to say, I hope you will keep to yourself for now," The Colonel says softly, visibly bracing himself before he continues. "In Fort Belvoir, we have the current Secretary of Agriculture, the highest elected authority we are in contact with. Along with him, we have a number of congressmen and senators. We have confirmed the death of most of the others in the chain of command including the vice president. Others are believed to be compromised.

"As such, the Secretary has—legitimately—assumed power. However, a number of army and national guard groups don't have contact with us or him or are refusing to take orders from us. Some refuse to act on US soil. Others have gone rogue. We've got rebel groups, independent operating groups, and a few cities all working by themselves throughout the country."

"No one knows who to trust, so everyone's doing their own thing?" Lana interjects, her brows drawn together.

"In essence, yes. There are police forces and national guard members working independently," Wier says finally. "We need to put an end to this as quickly as possible, which is why I'm looking for your help. If you can open those Portals of yours, we can shift our men to bolster allied forces and begin negotiations with those on the fence."

"It doesn't work that way," I say with a sigh. I ponder for a moment keeping the details of my power back, but in this case, I realize I'm going to have to tell him something. "I can only Portal to places I've been to before. And keeping the Portals open are extremely Mana intensive."

Wier nods slowly, rubbing his chin. "We can work with that. If we allocate specific teams, my men can still provide force multipliers and specialized help. We could even provide you guards and aides now."

"No thanks," I say with a shake of my head. "No offence, but I work better alone."

Wier just shoots a look at my team but I refuse to back down from that statement. For one thing, it's the truth, damn it. For another thing, anyone he sends with me is just going to act as a spy and nanny, and I neither want or need either.

"If we help you, you and your people will help us free the Canadian cities. All of them," I say.

Wier cracks a slight smile, leaning forward. Now that I'm actually negotiating, he knows he has me. The rest of this is just a matter of numbers and plans, of how we're going to do this rather than if. And really, I never was going to turn him down. For the next hour or so, we negotiate men and numbers, timelines, and other details. We leave a lot unsaid or to be confirmed, a lot to be determined later or open for amendments because we both understand how Murphy can be a bastard. But in the end, we have a rough agreement, one that starts with him helping us first before we shift to some American cities. When we're done, we shake hands as you do. And that's when we get a surprise.

Settlement Agreement Reached

Would you like to confirm the agreement (see attached)? There are significant penalties to reputation for breaching such an agreement. Additional penalties may apply (see agreement).

(Y/N)

I blink, staring at the new notification. Wier shows surprise too, obviously getting a similar screen.

"*Well, that's interesting,*" Ali says, staring at the screen as well.

"You didn't know about this?"

"Never had a Companion who was a settlement owner, so no."

"How do I add penalties to this then?"

"You can't. Looks like you need the Skills or an upgrade to your City."

"So no penalties. Huh."

"This is interesting. But I don't need a System to keep my word," Wier says.

Even if he does say that, I note he acknowledges and accepts the System agreement. I do too a moment later.

"Nice. Now for the next conversation," I say, smiling. "Not to be rude, but…"

"I understand. It's a pleasure doing business with you. We'll be in touch for further details."

"I'll need to visit your base at some point."

"Of course," Wier agrees readily. One of the things we had to cover in our discussion was the limits of my Portal Skill. "Just let us know."

"I will." I flash him a grin, making a note to get work on a communications array sorted.

Interestingly enough, what Wier did wasn't purchase the array from the System but the plans. He shared that with us, so now all we had to do was get some high Level Mechanics and Engineers on it and we'd finally have a communications array stretching across the province.

***

"Who's next?" I ask Lana and Ingrid after we leave, the young ladies on Lana's overgrown, pony-sized puppies. Ingrid knows where we'll have to go, and Lana was the one who set up the meetings.

"Mages."

"Ah…" I can't help but grin at that.

Look, the Microsoft campus was the kind of place where any programmer would have loved to have worked. Just short of the Google campus really. But that was a fairy tale dream for someone of my talents. Don't get me wrong, I wasn't bad, but 'not bad' doesn't get you into the big leagues.

"Down, boy," Lana says, shaking her head. "Try not to get a nerd boner while talking to them, will you?"

"Funny." I consider the meeting. Obviously Gates won't be there, or Balmer. If they were, we'd have seen them at the meeting, but… "I didn't recognize most of those Mages at the meeting."

Ingrid nods. "No surprise. They lost a lot of people when the System came along. These days, the team you saw, they're the front. I hear their real leadership team is out there, but I've yet to see them. Way I understand it, they're busy Leveling."

Under that somber spell, we make our way to their headquarters and are met just before we enter. The same group we saw at the meeting greets us. Now that I've got a bit more time, I look over the mixed race group and spot someone who's likely of Vietnamese / Laos descent, a couple of Indians, and a few Caucasians.

"Mr. Lee," the Blue Mage says, offering me his hand.

Realizing I might actually have to talk to him significantly more, I spend the time analyzing his status as I get off Sabre and set it to follow me along.

Charles Cutler (Blue Mage Level 6)

HP: 560/560

MP: 1840/1840

Conditions: None

"Nice to meet you." I glance around. "Are we not being invited in?"

"No, no, nothing like that. We just wanted to make sure you had a proper escort," Charles says, rubbing the top of his bald crown. For all that he might be folliclely challenged, the fortyish man seems to be in good health, with no sign of a gut and even some definition around his arms. "We've already voted and decided to give you all the help you need."

"Pardon…?" I freeze, staring at Charles.

"You owe me fifty," someone says in a thick Indian accent, but I'm still staring at Charles, waiting for his explanation.

"We'll help you. There are limitations—we won't reduce our guard below what's safe for us—but if you need it, we'll throw whatever help we can. You can consider us Allies," Charles says again.

Settlement Alliance Offered (John Lee & the Mages of Seattle)

An offer of alliance has been offered. An alliance will automatically classify all trade between settlements as alliance trades for the purposes of taxes, tariffs, and duties. In addition, this open alliance offer includes a mutual defense treaty. Failures to uphold this alliance will result in penalties to reputation. Additional penalties may apply (see details).

Note: As you are in a State of War with the Thirteen Moon Sect, the Mages of Seattle will automatically be considered at War upon agreement to this alliance.

Agree? (Y/N)

"Ali? The details?" I say, my eyes wide as I scan the information. I absently note that Charles has already read and dismissed his notification, a glowing little mark indicating that they've accepted their side of the agreement showing up on my own blue screen.

"One second. It's lengthy. Damn, but I wish Kim was here," Ali says, his eyes darting over the information.

After a moment, I share the screen with Lana, whose eyebrows rise then furrow as she reads. The lady has a business degree, so she might catch something Ali or I don't.

"This is generous." I stare at Charles. "Why?"

"Simply put? We understand your motivations."

"My what…?" I stop, realizing what he means. "You've been buying information on me from the Shop."

"Yes. Ever since your friend"—he waves at Ingrid, who is busy chatting with another young lady in the group—"came to us about you and your plans, we've been researching you. It's been entertaining and enlightening. We understand your goals, and we agree with them."

I open my mouth to ask why again but stop, realizing that's probably rather insulting. Why can't other people want to do good? Yet a cynical part of me really questions their ready agreement.

"We also think you and the Colonel will need our help. We have a number of Seers and Diviners who can fix some of your problems, guide you around potential issues," Charles continues as we walk into the campus, a slight twitch of his lips as he notes my expression of surprise.

I'm getting a little annoyed at being tracked so much, but I push it down. "That's good."

"Now, I understand you were a programmer before? Have you ever been to our campus? It's not what it was, but we'd like to think it's still pretty amazing," Charles says, waving. "In that building, we've got our Alchemists, Potionoligists, and…"

I shut up, listening to him while Ali and Lana go over the documents. We'll probably agree if they don't see any serious landmines. At this point, we can't turn away any Allies, even if I find the entire thing a little fishy. So I shut up and listen, content to probe between descriptions.

***

Hours later—more hours than we should have spent with any one group— we're finally out of the compound and on our way to the next group. We obviously agreed to the alliance, after Lana and Ali checked the terms and came up with nothing too troubling. A few probing questions got us a little more information about their thinking too.

"Did you notice that we never got to meet more of their people? Not even their main team. And I get the feeling they're still holding a bit to the old corporate bureaucracy," Lana says, finishing my unvoiced thought.

"Aye."

"They are a corporation. Soul sucking bastards that they are," Ingrid says, shaking her head. "But the way I understand it, their main team are still below our Levels."

"Huh." I grimace. "Well, at least we know our Levels are one of the reasons they want to help."

"I'm not sure I like that," Lana says, lips thin. "Killing, killing sentients, for experience—"

"Is efficient. Them saying that bothers you?" Ali chimes in. "Even if it's true?"

"Yes." Lana's lips thin again. "It's like most of the ones we met see this as a game. The way they kept going on about our 'prestige' Classes, builds, and how to 'game' their Advancement."

"They might," Ingrid says, "but their leaders don't. From what my friends say, part of it is they're angling for better relations with their government. There's talk about making the campus an academy for Mages. I think they're still thinking about profits, really."

"Academy?" I ask, curious if it has more meanings. Or what, if any, bonuses the System might offer.

"System-registered dedicated learning institution. You get bonuses for learning and research. It requires, well, Credits and land and a few other things," Ali says. "They can't do it right now. It's like a Tier II building."

"So, they need help building upwards," I say slowly. And of course, being the largest and most developed settlement around, having us as allies is probably useful for them. It might even be part of their requirements to get an Academy in place. I make a note to check on that later, but at least now I have a better feel for the group. Idealistic gamers on the bottom end, fast-moving sharks on the top. So, perhaps not the best kind of allies, but probably reliable until things go completely to hell.

"Who's next?" I call, deciding to put this issue aside for now. Whatever the case, getting more help is the goal.

"The Baristas."

***

"You want to start a chain," I say slowly and carefully.

"Exactly. We get land for free. We'll do the buildup ourselves. We operate tax-free and train your people in your settlements. One per Shop," Kaylee, the pink-haired, punk-rock-styled girl, says with an impish grin.

"Leased. And taxed," Lana says, leaning in.

"No way. We own the place and twenty years tax-free."

"Leased. Tax- and rent-free for ten years."

I roll my eyes, sitting back and letting the pair argue. At least this is reasonable. As I sip on a latte, I can't help but think that we're getting the better part of the deal.

***

"We're mercenaries. We get paid for our help."

"I see," I say slowly, while thinking that they really, really aren't. A ragtag group of ex-weekend warriors, gang members, and thieves is what I'd guess. Capstan and his people, the Major, they're mercenaries. These guys are wannabes. "What are your rates?"

"Well now, that'd depend on how many of our people you want and at what Levels."

I grunt, sighing. "Got a rate sheet? And a frequent user reward card?"

"No… but we could look into that," Laila, the African American woman with the big, big hair says uncertainly, not entirely sure if I'm kidding or not.

Truth be told, I'm not sure either.

***

"I hear you'll be fighting more of those aliens," Desmond, the greying, bearded man, says before spitting to the side. He's in charge of a group that formed from one of the suburbs, a mixed group of upper-middle-class folk. His group isn't the strongest, but being far enough from the front lines means they've managed to survive and prosper.

"That's the plan. Freeing the cities and pushing them back," I say.

"And what do you plan for the alien crafters, the non-fighters?"

"They're called Artisans. Galaxy-wide, that is," I say, curious where he's going with this.

"Artisans then."

"Well, I haven't really considered it much yet," I say, frowning. "We didn't have many to deal with in Vancouver."

"And the few you did? Those aliens?"

"Most aren't Sect members, so they've been allowed to stay."

"I see. And if they were part of the Sect?"

"We've been leaving the Artisans alone. They've mostly shipped out anyway. The few who stick around, we've restricted their movements and dealings, but they are unharmed."

"And prisoners?"

"We had none," I say, grimacing. The Sect fought to the last man in Kamloops. The needless deaths soured my emotions, reducing what little patience I have for all this politicking. "Why don't we stop dancing around? Tell me what you're asking."

"I understand that they made our people Serfs in Vancouver. Seems like a good, profitable solution. We certainly could use higher Level Artisans," Desmond says.

Rather than answer him—not that I physically could with the way the anger chokes up my voice—I stand and walk out. Asshole.

"Mr. Lee—" he cuts off as Lana shoots him a disgusted look, the pets growling in unison to her change in emotions.

If I had to listen to him speak further, I might do something he'd regret.

***

Meetings after meetings, that's our next few days as we make our way through the groups willing to talk. Everyone wants something. Assurances, alliances—informal or formal—or even the right to immigrate. Trade deals and training, it's all there. And while I work over the ones who indicated earlier that they were willing to talk, Lana's on the others, the ones who refused, working her Charisma and charm.

All because we want to help them out. Gods, sometimes I hate people.

Chapter 5

I survey my friends, my teammates, my fellow dungeon delvers one last time as Sabre slides into place over my body. Mikito is already fully armed and armored in her own PAV, while Lana finishes checking over the harnesses on her pets. The harnesses are for the mini portable shield generators which will act as additional armor for the pets. Instead of a single generator, Lana commissioned a custom harness with each generator, providing a smaller area of overlapping coverage. It's basically the force field equivalent of scale armor, but projected an inch or so above the pets' bodies. The shields themselves are ablative protections, meant to absorb a small amount of damage before failing and restarting.

Behind Lana, Sam's doing his own last-minute fixes. All around him are dozens of drones. Rather than a few larger drones, Sam has decided to test out a new theory, chaining together multiple small drones via a "hive" mind process, giving him more flexibility but with lower damage output individually. Theoretically, they've got a higher overall damage output but are significantly more vulnerable. As the man put it, it's a bit of an experiment. Still, having dozens of skittering, spider-like drones with a variety of weapons makes the older gentleman look just a touch scary.

Ingrid is Ingrid. The assassin sits quietly, buffing her fingernails while waiting for the rest of the team to get ready. She's clad in her usual getup of light armored jumpsuit, a pair of emergency portable shields on her hips, knives and a blaster awaiting use. The First Nations woman looks perfectly calm, waiting for us to get moving.

"We ready?" I ask, my gaze finally falling on the last and latest addition to the team.

The Latino object of my regard grimaces as he swigs down another potion. A series of small vials is strapped across his body in bandoliers and belts, making him look like a weird mixture of Danny Trejo and a glassmaker. Propped against his feet is a weapon that looks like a slender grenade launcher.

Carlos Garcia (Level 48 Apprentice Alchemist)

HP: 380/380

MP: 1780/1780

Conditions: Stoneskin, Aura of Flame, HP Regeneration Buffed, MP Regeneration Buffed, Perception Buffed, Strength Buffed, … (more)

"I've a few potions for everyone," Carlos says, waving at the green and grey vials that are hand-labeled and propped up on the ground in front of him. His Mexican accent is mixed with American after the years he's spent in Seattle. "Stoneskin is grey. Gives you a little increase in your armor rating. The green is Eagle Eye; it's a Perception buff. They're my best potions, outside of the healing ones. Ingrid said that I should just sell the rest…"

"A few more minutes," Lana calls back as she works on the straps. We'd help, but our helping is what caused the initial delay as Lana fixes our mistakes.

While I wait, I pick up the Stoneskin potion and eye it for a second before downing it.

Stoneskin Buff Gained

+23 Armor Rating

Duration: 6 hours 18 Minutes and 4 Seconds

Thirty Levels ago, this would have been amazing. Twenty Levels and it'd have been a nice boost. Now, it's a small drop in the bucket. Still, a small drop is better than nothing. Mikito picks up the potions, tossing them underhanded to Ingrid and Sam, the last almost fumbling the second catch. Carlos winces at the casual abuse of his work.

"Good choice," I say. If these are his best, then I can understand why Ingrid got Carlos to sell his other work. Until Carlos can get his skill—and Skill—higher, his support potions aren't that useful. "So your Health potions are better?"

"Of course—387 Health each," Carlos says proudly.

"That's not bad. Why the difference?" I ask.

"It's complicated," Carlos says, looking uncertain.

Before he can attempt to explain it, Ali pops into existence, snorting. "Let me simplify it for the boy-o. You know how making items works right, boy-o? Artisans get Skill Trees just like you, but the Skill Trees are a bit more complex. On one branch, you've got production Skills—making things faster, cheaper, or just replicating. Then you've got the assessment or analysis Skills—things that let the Artisan get better at what they're doing. Lastly, you've got the actual product Skills, which dictate what you can produce. Within each of those product Skills, you might have classes of items or tiers which can improve how well you produce items of that sort."

I note how more than a few people look at Ali as he explains things.

"That's right. I've got—"

"Hush, noob. I'm talking," Ali says, running right over Carlos. "Now, when noob over there produces a potion, he's going to be limited to some extent by the materials he uses. There's only so much you can do if your materials suck. After that, his skill and experience at making the most out of the material comes into play. The more experience, the better he is, the more he can use the materials to their utmost. And then, you layer his Class Skills on top of that, boosting whatever he makes by his Skill. Master craftsmen can easily triple or quadruple the effects of even a low Level item due to their Skills."

"Shortbus is correct," Carlos says, nodding. "I've focused most of my Skills on Healing and Mana potions, so my support potions aren't that powerful. But they'll improve as my production Skills get better and I get more experience. Right now, I've got a thirty-eight percent efficiency with producing support potions."

"Shortbus!" Ali starts up.

I send him a glare, shutting the Spirit down.

"Thank you," I say to Carlos before glancing at Ingrid, who has returned to buffing her nails.

I grunt, wondering what she meant by dragging the man back with her and dropping him into our party with a single sentence as an introduction. "Meet our Healer." Sometimes, that woman…

"So are you ready for this?" I ask him.

"I've been in dungeons before," Carlos says firmly. "However, it'd be nice to know what the plan is."

"We're going to port in. Ingrid scouts ahead, finding traps and dealing with single Scouts. Everyone needs to have a shield up at all times—otherwise, the Yurk Scouts will poison you—and we clear the dungeon. Mikito and I are the front-line fighters, Lana and her pets are the flankers, and Sam fills in with his drones. You stay behind with Sam, healing as we need it," I say, shrugging. "Pretty simple. It's not that tough a dungeon."

Carlos stares at me for a second, a faint look of disbelief on his face. That's when Lana calls out she's ready and impatient to get going, so I cast my Portal. Ingrid darts forward, the nail file stowed away in a flash. Roland and Shadow, not to be outdone, race through the Portal, followed by Mikito and Sam's drones. Within seconds, the group is streaming through while Carlos stares at me, dumbfounded by my brilliance.

"You can heal, right?" I say as I gently pull him by his elbow across the Portal before snapping it shut.

"Sort of. I don't have inherent Class Skills, but I've put most of my profits into buying Healing Spells and Skills. Most of my Class Skills are more suited for use outside the dungeon," Carlos says.

"Good. Try to keep up then," I say, looking around the university square.

It's not really a square, more of a rectangle flanked by a squat faculty building to the right with an overhang farther down and elevated walkways to the left. Stairs lead down into the rectangle itself, the light brown squares dirty and overgrown with weeds.

Unlike our first time, there's no large gathering of monsters, no grouping of nastiness. Sam's drones are laying down mines and traps under his direction while others take off into the mist-enshrouded darkness to give us a better view. The digging drones are fast, laying out a mine field in minutes. I briefly wonder if we could use him to help build / rebuild some locations in town but dismiss it. Not the right time. Clearing the dungeon is a sideshow to our main objectives.

"Incoming," Ingrid's voice cackles softly over the communicator.

I'm grateful that Galactic tech comes with "smart" tech, transmitting messages to the correct recipient automatically. The more we use them, the "smarter" the tech gets.

On Ingrid's warning, Lana falls back toward us, Anna and Howard taking stations a bit ahead, while Mikito stands as the spear of the group. No surprise that Roland and Shadow are nowhere to be seen. I step forward, joining the Samurai, while Sam crouches, deploying a portable shield around himself and Carlos as he controls his drones.

On my minimap, I watch the monsters streaming down roads and out of buildings, forming up, seemingly able to see or sense one another through the mists. Groups appear and disappear as Sam's drones move around or, in some cases, get shot down. A few Scouts try to get close, but Ingrid and the pets strike and kill the Scouts long before they reach us to get a decent view. Luckily, we're not near the forest or else it'd be more of a problem.

When they're two-thirds of the way to us, Sam pulls his diggers back or hides them in the ground in an attempt to preserve the element of surprise. I finish my buffs, having tossed Soul Shield on myself, Lana, and Sam. I figured Carlos has enough buffs to keep himself alive. And if he doesn't… well, we'll find out.

At first, it's just one or two Yurks, seen through the parting of the mists. They become more visible, more stable as they near us. Singular Yurks transform into groups moving in lockstep. Shield-bearing Yurks in the front, bow-wielding Yurks behind, and Yurks over twelve feet tall are scattered throughout. They march forward slowly, getting closer and closer to where our traps are set, then they stop as they shake out their lines.

"Boss…" Sam mutters, eyeing the group, obviously uncomfortable with their actions.

"Wai—"

My words are cut off as the Yurk mages make their appearance. Or at least, make their presence known. Lightning bolts reach down, striking the earth in front of the reptile-frogs with booms of fury, electricity dancing in the air and destroying our carefully laid traps. I wonder why they didn't call the strikes down on us. Unfortunately, I thought too soon—that's when the lightning rolls forward, bringing electrical death.

"Hell..." I say, hunching slightly unconsciously as the lightning bathes us.

Electric fire reaches from the heavens, striking all of us as quick as a little dog's temper tantrum, and just as quickly, it's gone. Twisting around, I spot Carlos looking a little worse for the wear, steam rising from his cracked and burnt flesh. Even as I watch, his health creeps above half, but that's not enough, so I throw a Soul Shield on him. He looks relieved, overloaded nerves in his body slowly recovering as he downs another potion. After a second, he stands straighter, burnt and smoking skin healing before my eyes. I absently wonder how he's able to keep consuming so many potions without suffering from potion poisoning, but that's probably a Skill.

"Damn. Your shield is down," Lana says to me, running a hand along her long hair and fixing her ponytail. "And I'm going to have to see a hairdresser after this."

I stare at the young lady, my mind splitting for a second as I realize I haven't actually seen one in the past year. Outside of my hair growing slightly longer, I haven't had to deal with it. For a moment, I wonder how the hell that works—before the plink of arrows hitting Sabre's shield brings me back to the present. Deal with that question later. Later.

The rocking boom of Lana's shotgun, the shrill whistling sound of gauss projectiles fired from Sam's drones, the grunt of exertion as Carlos fires his potions down range anchors me to the moment. Ahead of us, our assault on the Yurks leads to death and fire, clouds of gas and shrapnel raining around us. Mikito absently swings her polearm, cutting arrows from the sky, the clearest traces of her movements the shattered shards of wood and bone.

I raise my hand, unleashing projectiles from Sabre's rifle, each shot drilling into the Yurks. Anna pitches in a few seconds later as the army closes again, tendrils of flame whipping along glistening shells. A thudding boom, a change in rhythm, and the army charges even as the drums shift once more.

Musical Fear Effect Resisted

Without breaking step, Mikito counter-charges the group. I grunt, taking off after the insane woman, eyeing the range estimator in my helmet. Five meters later, I trigger the mini-missiles, the tiny explosives flying forward to tear and disrupt their ranks. A step later, Mikito shines, ghostly armor layering on top of her PAV, her body speeding up and becoming a living spear. The shock of her clash with the already disrupted vanguard throws back the front ranks of the army, the unlucky couple directly in front of her exploding apart from the transferred kinetic force of her attack.

Layered over the explosive meeting of lines, the howls and growls of the puppies reverberate in my chest and hearten our group. I trigger my Sonic Blaster a second later, layering confusion on top of shock before terror arrives in the form of the pets and Ingrid. Some appear from the flanks, others charging into the gap Mikito has created. And then I'm there too, swords dancing in my hands as limbs and bodies separate.

"Holy shit!" Carlos breathes over the communicator.

"Yeah, it takes getting used to," Sam says with a chuckle. "Don't worry, you get used to it. Sort of."

Lana's chuckle runs across the comms, reaching straight down my spine and making my lower body clench. The distraction is unfortunate, the attack from a Yurk behemoth catching me across my body and lifting Sabre off the ground and throwing me into the air. Before I can twist away, another attack slams me into the ground. My landing is only barely reduced by the body of an unfortunate Yurk Warrior.

My protective shields shattered, the next club attack is enough to dent Sabre's armor and leave bruises all along my body. I stagger upward, spinning to send aside the Yurk Warriors who have crowded around me. Mecha-assisted strength and agility combined with my own attributes and my slender grasp of System physics provides me a moment of respite. Even as I stop spinning, the behemoth is before me again, its club approaching at a speed I'm unable to dodge. Thankfully, I'm not alone. A bladed polearm stabs forward, shifting the trajectory of the club.

"No lying down!" Mikito says, darting through a gap and leaving a surprised Yurk Warrior tottering on one foot as she continues her attack, dancing deeper into the army.

I snarl, staring at the Yurk behemoth retracting its giant club, readying for its next attack. Bunching my feet, I hop, feet slamming into the side of the club before I launch myself off it. Not directly at the behemoth as it expects but past it. When I'm half past its body, I twist, slamming my sword into its shoulder to alter my momentum. My shoulder aches, my sword slides and twists as it cuts, but it's enough. A moment later, I swing my other hand, sword in it, into its neck.

As I ride the Yurk down, I raise my hand and unleash a fireball into another behemoth's face, the attack partly deflected as a Warrior tackles me in the middle of my casting. Strong as I am, physics still has some say in this world and I'm shifted sideways, feet skidding on the blood-slick floor. Before I can recover to finish the behemoth, a fast-moving set of vials flies into the roaring monster's mouth. Pink and purple smoke explodes as the vials shatter, the creature grabbing at its throat as it goes on a mad rampage, heedless of friend or foe.

"What the hell?" Lana says.

"Poison, capsaicin, and a hallucinogenic," Carlos says. "Forces an enraged status while dealing damage over time."

I'd add my two bits, but having dealt with one of their leaders, I'm getting swarmed by Yurk Berserkers.

Yurk Berserker (Level 41)

HP: 3287/3483

MP: 230/247

Conditions: Enraged, Pain to Blood, Acidic Form

These guys don't seem to care what kind of damage I deal to them, happy to trade damage for damage. And when I cripple one by lopping off both its arms, it throws itself at me then blows itself up, coating me in unmentionables. Without my shields and the time to replenish them, Sabre's taking a beating and myself within it, swords and axes punching through metal armor even as the nanites do quick repairs.

"It might be time to heal John," Sam says, his voice absentminded as he controls his swarm.

"Right. Sorry!" Carlos replies.

A second later, I'm bathed in white light. My health stabilizes and starts rising. I'm only about a third down, Sabre's armor and my own regeneration more than sufficient for most purposes. Then again, losing a third of my Health would have been enough to kill most Casters. So everything's relative. But now that I've got healing support, I make Sabre disappear, content to let the mecha fix itself while I wade in, ready to deal a little damage face-to-face.

"How's Mikito?" I growl over the radio. I could probably check on my party screen, but I trust her. Hell, while she might not have as much health as me, she's got a decent buffer.

"Fine," Mikito calls, her breathing and voice only slightly short from exertion. A white light flashes as her blade extends, chopping downward and sweeping multiple opponents aside.

After that… well, after that, it's just mop up work.

***

"Not bad," I say to Carlos, stretching out my muscles.

We've been at this dungeon for six hours, and we have finally figured out where the Boss is likely to be. Once we dealt with the main army, the numbers we faced were significantly smaller. It's been annoying, going through classroom after classroom, laboratory after laboratory to deal with the Yurks. They keep switching tactics, going from stand-up battles to traps to ambushes to constant harrying attacks. The numbers and Levels have gotten steadily higher as we figure out the layout of the dungeon and attack the higher Level buildings. And through it all, Carlos has been healing and buffing us.

"Thanks. You guys…" Carlos shakes his head. "I've seen Advanced Classes fight before in Seattle, even joined a few other teams, but…"

"But…?"

"But nothing like you guys," Carlos says, walking alongside us.

"We've all got somewhat rare Classes. It gives us a bit of an advantage," I say.

"It's more than that," Carlos says. "It's more your style…"

"You guys might have been fighting the Sect, but we've been fighting monsters all along," Ingrid says, appearing right behind Carlos and making him jump.

"Gah!"

"Fighting aliens is easy. Most of them only have two hands and two legs. Makes their attack combinations easier to predict. Monsters swarm, come in different sizes and shapes. And they have a much wider range of Skills to use," Ingrid says almost proudly. "The Sect members might have been higher Level, but they weren't as savage. They want to live just as much as you do. Monsters, they don't seem to care. Also, you guys might have been out-Leveled at times, but in Whitehorse, we were always out-Leveled."

I shrug, not entirely sure I agree with Ingrid's explanation. I think the rarity of our Classes makes a bigger difference. More stats per Level, better Skills, hell, better equipment makes a difference. Over the course of fifty Levels, even a single extra attribute point adds up. The difference between someone at Strength 60 and Strength 10 is night and day.

"Enough talk. Sam, how're your drones?" Lana says as we approach the final building—the chemistry labs. Says something about chemistry students when the dungeon Boss decides to hole up in their faculty.

"About half left. I'm out of reserves too. Not sure I'm liking this. Feels like I'm standing around burning Credits like a gangster on a coke high," Sam grouses.

"But effective," I point out.

Compared to previously, Sam's been a lot more useful. I'll admit, the crew-served weapon was great for the war, but in a dungeon, it's limited. Now, his drones can and do a little of everything. Hell, he even had a few dedicated shield drones whose only job was to block attacks.

"That too."

"All right, any last words?" I say as I walk up to the doors.

"Phrasing!" Ali calls out, his statement followed by chuckles but not much else.

***

"Well, this might get interesting. I'm staying intangible," Ali says as we step into the laboratory.

The System's warped the space within, the last laboratory having expanded to the size of a soccer field. All down the way, tables are filled with beakers and Bunsen burners, all of them boiling, distilling, and condensing a variety of liquids and solids, none of which I recognize.

"Take me with you?" Carlos entreats Ali, his eyes darting side to side. "None of this makes sense, but my Skills are saying it's all explosive."

"Figured," I say. "Think it'll regenerate like the other labs?"

"Obviously," Lana says dryly.

Ingrid doesn't answer, slipping forward through the shadows while Roland and Shadow follow on a parallel path. At the end of the laboratory is the Yurk Boss, clad in a laboratory coat of all things, his Enforcers and Bodyguards flanking him. Those, at least, seem to follow the "medieval warfare" theme.

"So. Frigging. Weird," Sam says, his drones scurrying forward. One accidentally knocks over a beaker, and the resulting explosion consumes it and two of its friends. "Sorry!"

"Be careful," I say, watching as the Boss group turns toward us where we stand at the entrance.

They aren't moving, which means they're likely waiting for reinforcements. That's the way they've played it so far. Judging that Ingrid and company have gotten ahead far enough, we move forward, Lana leaving Anna and Howard to guard our backs. One uses heat; the other is the size of a pony. Neither of which works in such confined, volatile spaces. Shadow at least seems to have a weird ability to partly phase through things, occasionally seeming to blend with its own, sentient shadow. Roland, while huge, is scarily agile.

Making a decision, I jog forward, calling for Ingrid and the pets to slow down. Already, I can see the beaker that the drone tipped over back in place, the room magically having "healed" the location. A quick check shows my Soul Shield is at full strength, as is Sabre. Considering what we're facing, I'm dressed fully, even if Sabre is showing signs of damage.

Our enemies don't waste time once we get moving. Yurk Enforcers stand in front while the Bodyguards stay to the side, using atlatls to send spears arcing toward me, missing the fluorescent-lit drop-ceiling by inches. I dodge to the side, but I realize a moment later it doesn't matter—they were never aiming at me. The ensuing explosions take me off my feet, throwing me sideways as the Enforcers seem to almost teleport to my sprawled form.

My shields soak up the initial explosions, the Enforcers swarming me. Axes and swords stab into my body, sparking against the shields. Dodged blows, backhands, and missed strikes set off more explosions as the Enforcers push me around the lab, none of the explosions seeming to harm the Enforcers much.

Yurk Enforcer (Level 48)
HP: 1287/1383
MP: 839/1042
Conditions: Lab Assistant, Shared Pool

"Ali!" I snarl, blocking a shot with my left hand while pumping projectiles into the Yurk's face with the other. A crunch in my side comes from an attack that manages to pierce my shield, its trailing glow an indicator of a Skill.

"Shit. The Boss is giving all the Yurks near immunity to damage from the Lab through a Buff. And that Shared Pool means all your damage is getting shared around them," Ali says, his eyes roving.

"Help please!" I snarl, stepping deep into one Enforcer's attack and grabbing its arm.

I could Blink Step away, but as the tank, my job is to keep them busy. It pulls, its slimy, smooth skin slipping out of my grip before I can throw it into its friend. A Yurk steps up, ready to impale me, and stumbles away, smashing a vial that sends another wash of flame over us as Mikito's naginata pulls out of its body.

"Go. I have them," Mikito says confidently.

I'm not sure she's right, but we need the Boss dead. I Blink Step the rest of the way, appearing next to the Boss with only its pair of Bodyguards now. That was the point of my initial rush, drawing them out to deal with each group in pieces. My sword swings downward, intent on cutting the damn Yurk Boss apart, only to be blocked by a Bodyguard. Pushed backward, I find myself dueling the pair of Bodyguards, unable to get past them to the Boss. The Boss ignores the entire thing, instead mixing together vials. Each time it's done, it tosses the vials away to shatter on the floor. Colored smoke soon surrounds us, a variety of Status effects appearing.

You are Poisoned!
-13 HP per second. Effect partially resisted

You are Slowed!
-8% Agility. Effect partially resisted

You are Hallucinating!

-4% Perception. Effect partially resisted

Again and again, clouds of smoke erupt, affecting us all. Even through Sabre's fully enclosed environmental system, I'm being affected, which doesn't make sense. But then again, it's the System and when has it ever made sense? I do know I'm only taking a portion of the effects, between my Class's innate Resistances and the additional Resistances from Sabre. But as I skip backward and twist to dodge an attack, my friends aren't as lucky.

Howard, Anna, Lana, and Mikito are fighting the half-dozen Enforcers in a chaotic skirmish. Lab tables and equipment are destroyed unceasingly, glass and wood shrapnel flying through the air to impale and injure while the System visibly regrows the set pieces, only for them to be destroyed again a moment later. Lana's bleeding from a cut across her neck, shotgun held low as she feeds more shells into it while being protected by Anna. Shadow explodes from the side, shadow and real mouth taking hold of an Enforcer limb and pulling as if to tear it apart. But none of the monsters have fallen, and at least one, if not more, of the clouds has a regenerative effect.

I coat my sword with Frost Blade, hoping to slow the monsters down. That forces me to trade a cut across my body, which shatters the last of my shields, for the time taken to cast the spell. It also means I can't dismiss the blade anymore, not without the spell losing its effect, but slowing these guys down is important. I fall back again and again.

"Down!" Sam snaps.

I duck, almost impaling myself on a sword before realizing the command wasn't for me. A moment later, criss-crossing beams of fire light up behind me, baking my back even through Sabre. The resulting secondary explosion punches me deeper into the floor, jarring the Bodyguards and Boss above me.

"What the hell was that?" Lana shouts over the radio.

"Tier III Skill, All Hell Breaks Loose. I'm out of drones!" Sam says.

"Explain later. Kill now!" Mikito snarls.

As much as I want to look behind me, I'm busy batting aside swords, slamming my blade into any visible body part. Which, in most cases, is a hand or arm. Within four strikes, I can see the Bodyguards slowing, their hands frozen as the spell takes effect. But I pay for it. Sabre's working overtime to deal with cuts and stabs, applying bandages and patching worn armor. A pale blue cloud reaches me, and a new notification appears.

Antidote applied! Poison Debuff Removed

"Urrrkk…" the Boss gurgles, Ingrid finally making her presence known.

Blades shoved into his kidneys and then withdrawn to cut the Boss's throat, she saws away as she attempts to end this. Backstab and other Skill multipliers notwithstanding, this is a Boss and his health is unnaturally bolstered.

Antidote applied! Perception debuff removed

A Bodyguard teleports beside Ingrid and swings his sword down while she's got her arms full. Before it can connect, Roland appears from the shadows, jaws clamping around the arm, the skill Massive Bite triggering. How something so big and terrifying can hide in this starkly illuminated space is terrifying and puzzling. I'm just glad he's on our side.

Without a distraction, Ingrid focuses her attacks on the Boss, disrupting his ability to create more potions. Even a last-minute explosion which throws her backward doesn't save him, the poison her blade's coated in slowly ripping him apart.

After that, it's mop up time. Carlos continues to throw out potions, some actively destroying the clouds, others just removing debuffs or buffing us in the other direction. With only one Bodyguard to fight, I kill him quickly and return to the fight with the Enforcers, all of whom are suffering from burns and reeling from the damage. Even then, I can tell that Mikito and Lana are the worse for wear.

Congratulations! Dungeon Cleared
_+5,000 XP_

First Clear Bonus
Having cleared the bonus for the first time, you have been rewarded an additional +5,000XP +1,000 Credits.

"Well, that was fun." I grunt, sitting on the floor.

With the Boss defeated, the formerly volatile mixtures seem to have stabilized, letting Carlos and Sam join us as we sprawl on the floor.

"Jesus Christ," Carlos says, shaking his head. "What are your pain resistances? That must have hurt!"

"Pretty high," I say, not wanting to point out my Class came with an innate resistance to pain.

Mikito nods while Lana snorts as she adjusts her clothing futilely. After a moment, she mutters something about going to get changed, her pets following her out the door. Mikito turns bright red, realizing the state of her clothes and the amount of skin she's showing, and Hastes out of the room after Lana.

"I've seen high. Worked with someone with resistances over 40% and he still didn't want to tank. Said it still sucked," Carlos says.

"Ah…" I frown, considering how to answer that.

"Well, boy-o's insane," Ali answers with a knowing grin.

"And I try not to get hurt," Ingrid says with a smirk.

"Never mind all that, what have we got for loot?" Sam interjects, pointing at the Boss's body.

We all pause then grin, spreading out to loot our kills. A few minutes later, with Lana and Mikito back, we share the information on our murder-happy gains.

+28,385 Credits

Tier III Hallucinogenic Recipe Gained

Tier II Potion of Strength Recipe Gained

Those are the interesting items. I'm particularly impressed we got Credits, since that almost never happens. One of the few advantages of fighting something sentient. Of course, the recipes go to Carlos while the miscellaneous monster parts and mildly interesting weapons get packed away for sale. Neither Mikito nor I need their melee weapons and the others don't fight in close quarters, so they're Shop fodder.

"Now what?" Carlos says, looking around.

I shrug. "Now we do it again in a few days when the dungeon resets. And we write up a guide for our people so that they can do it too. Once we clear it enough, the System should have dispersed enough Mana that the dungeon will stop coming back." I mentally send a request to Ali to get an estimate on how many times. "In the meantime, the UBC dungeon needs more checking, which I'm going to leave to you guys."

"Oh…" Carlos frowns, looking about as everyone else nods, Sam looking sad as he picks up the pieces of his drones. I guess that last Skill destroyed his drones. "And you?"

"I've got a trip to plan."

Chapter 6

As much as I'd love to get on Sabre and go, there are things I need to settle. Perhaps most importantly, I need to speak with the Guilds. The first meeting—a video call, aided by the System since we still don't have our communication array up—is to Labashi.

"Major," I say when he finally appears.

"Redeemer. I hope this call is good news," Labashi says.

"It is. I'm willing to offer your Mercenary Company a base. It won't be in Vancouver, but in Burnaby," I say.

"Really. I do not believe that location is able to host our base," Labashi says.

"Not yet. But the ownership requirements aren't too far away. There's a university where a dungeon is formed. We just cleared it; it's easily doable. From what Ali says, we've got about three clears left before it dissipates," I say. "We're willing to let you purchase the land in its entirety."

"Purchase?" Labashi says slowly, rubbing his chin.

It's a much better offer than normal—most contracts are only set up to be leased for a specific number of years. It's one of the important parts about the System now that we're fully integrated—by keeping everything on a lease basis, the chances of a settlement being taken over is reduced. That we were able to purchase land outright during the set up period was one of the few advantages that we, being on Earth, had.

"That is reasonable. After all, we are putting the Credits down for it. And it is a significant amount of land."

I snort, and Labashi flashes me a grin, knowing that his attempt at negotiation isn't getting him anywhere. While he has a point that picking up all that land will help the city, it's still not worth the permanent removal of the land from our control. With the initial probing done, we get down to the brass tacks and negotiating.

We're working on broad strokes of course. Katherine, Lana, Kim, and the rest of them will get the details hammered down later. But at the end, we have an agreement of sorts.

Labashi nods, scanning the notification in front of him as he summarizes our long discussion. "Our headquarters will be in your university, this SFU. In return, we provide a permanent guard for the city and will, on attack of the Lower Mainland, deploy all available forces from our base. In addition, we will provide a company's worth of help twice in assaults. Or an equivalent number of aid split across multiple assaults or defenses. These assaults or additional defenses will take no longer than a month in total of deployment. We do, of course, reserve the right to refuse such attacks as per our usual agreements." Which, from what I recall, mostly amount to "we don't do suicidal attacks." "In return, we will have the land in perpetuity and two years' worth of rent waived."

"And miscellaneous additions about training, resale of your equipment, and on-going use of your engineering division for upgrade," I add. "But that's for the eggheads."

"Egg. Heads?" Labashi raises an eyebrow.

"Never mind. Human terminology. Don't worry about it."

"IT IS DEMEANING TO BE COMPARED TO A NASCENT ORGANIC LIFEFORM."

"Sorry, Kim. Does it help that I'm technically an egghead?"

"NO."

"Redeemer?" Labashi says as I have my quick side conversation.

"If we're agreed, I've got another call," I say, well aware of how expensive this entire conversation is.

"We will let the eggheads finish this agreement. In the meantime, I will begin the process of arranging our presence in your city," Labashi says with a smile. "I look forward to working with you once again."

"Thanks." I watch Labashi fade away before I glance at Katherine. "Who's next?"

"The Crystal Clans," Katherine says with a smile. "Their representative is waiting."

"Sorry, took longer than I expected."

"It is fine. I arranged for a crafting station to be moved in."

"Umm…" I consider then shrug. Ah hell, it worked, didn't it? "Send them in."

***

This negotiation, thankfully, is a lot simpler. The Crystal Clans are mostly an Artisan Guild, so beyond getting a small force added to the rotation for safeguarding the city of Kelowna, we just need to work out their rent, training, and the percentage discount for purchases from the settlement. They aren't looking for anything special and we don't need anything special—just help and a place that's willing to farm out quests on a regular basis. With a transportation system in place and Kim handling the administration, we could even extend some of their quests to people in other settlements.

"Next," I say to Katherine when the door closes.

"That, I believe, would be me," a voice calls from the door.

I look up, blinking as I see a very pretty elf. Long blond hair is swept backward to uncover pointed ears, startlingly blue eyes, and an easy smile.

Lean and thin, he lounges against the door in a relaxed manner. Boy next door charm crossed with male model looks.

"And who are you?" As if I couldn't guess.

"Wynn a Maro. I represent the Burning Leaves," Wynn says with a bow, smiling slightly. "I hope I'm not intruding by entering."

"No." I wave him forward. I could get grumpy about him coming in before we asked for it, but that kind of pettiness isn't my thing. Anyway, I've got enough reasons to be grumpy with the Burning Leaves, including the use of an aura the last time round.

Wynn a Maro, Spider Slayer (Level 38 Fell Ranger)
HP: 2110/2110
MP: 2080/2080
Conditions: None

"That's an Advanced Class, isn't it?" I send to Ali.

"Yup. Be careful, boy-o. I don't think he's here to kill you, but he hasn't talked to you yet."

"Funny."

"Good. Otherwise I'd have to get another present as an apology," Wynn says as he walks forward then stops, a hand twitching as he pulls something from his inventory.

A moment later, he's holding a simple, silver-looking box with a crest made of stylized glyphs I can't read. The glyphs are closer to Egyptian hierographics than Arabic letters, which makes it all kinds of pretty and unintelligible. The sudden, indrawn breath from Ali, on the other hand, is quite interesting.

"What's that?" I say, eyes narrow. Automatic manners have me standing up since he's neared me, which also means I'm more mobile in case that case is something dangerous.

"An apology for my predecessor's actions," Wynn says, bowing his head slightly.

"Take it."

I use both hands to take hold of the gift, flip it open with a thumb, and am surprised to see a simple chain necklace inside. On closer inspection, each ring on the chain seems to be inscribed with many of the same glyphs as the box. Frowning, I pick up the necklace and wait for Ali to provide me the information.

Brumwell Necklace of Shadow Intent

The Brumwell necklace of shadow intent is the hallmark item of the Brumwell Clan. Enchanted by a Master Crafter, this necklace layers shadowy intents over your actions, ensuring that information about your actions is more difficult to ascertain. Ownership of such an item is both a necessity and a mark of prestige among settlement owners and other individuals of power.

Effect: Persistent effect of Shadow Intent (Level 4) results in significantly increased cost of purchasing information from the System about wearer. Effect is persistent for all actions taken while necklace is worn.

"*Those things are rare. We're talking tens of millions of Credits to purchase one, and this is a Level 4 enchantment. Not the rarest, but not cheap.*"

"Thank you," I say. Even if Wynn says this is a gift of apology, I know there are strings attached to such an expensive and overt gift. But like the elf—sorry, the Movana—probably knew, this is a gift I can't turn down.

"Not at all. My predecessor's actions were unaccountably rude. To use his abilities in a negotiation is not how our Guild would want this matter handled," Wynn says.

"True. Why was he allowed to conduct such discussions anyway?" I ask.

"Ah. Politics. His family has certain pull in our Guild."

"Har. And you?"

"I'm one too. But I'm competent," Wynn says, eyes dancing with humor.

"Even so. This is an expensive gift," I say as I close the box. As much as I want to put it on now, I can wait till I have it properly identified by the Shop. He might seem nice, but I won't trust him off the bat just because he's tall and pretty. Also, I'd like to see if I can get it altered so that I don't have to wear a necklace. I hate having things around my neck. "Seems a little much for a Guild building in a small town."

"How much do you know of my Guild?" Wynn asks instead of answering my unasked question.

"Not much."

"Well then, perhaps I can be allowed to enlighten you a bit," Wynn says whilst inclining his head toward the chairs.

I take the hint and sit down, gesturing for him to do so. Once we're comfortably seated, he continues while Katherine goes to get us a fresh pot of tea.

"The Burning Leaves are a Tier II guild. While we accept most applications to join the Guild, we started and are mainly based in Movana territory. In fact, many of our members are closely related to members within the Movana royalty," Wynn says.

"Good for you," I mutter, still unsure what's the point of this discussion.

"At the same time, your previous dealings and relationship with the Truinnar are known. Few have fought the Weapon Master and lived to tell the tale," Wynn continues. "But it is in consideration of those matters that we are interested in yourself."

"Like your stories, the Truinnar and Movana are differing portions of the same race, split when the groups left for the stars. The actual shade of skin of the Truinnar is due to a genetic modification to separate themselves from their cousins. Earth itself is in Truinnar space, which is the larger of the pair of empires," Ali fills in for me.

"Let me get this straight. You gave me a really nice gift because you want to establish relations with me. Because you're jealous of Roxley?" I frown. Such a line of reasoning seems just short of insane to me. Which is why I'm probably missing the point.

"Not jealousy. A maneuver to curtail Truinnar influence on this world. Your lands are the closest to the Duchess's, which makes them strategically important. And then there's you, Redeemer. Or is it Monster Bane? Or Duelist?" I frown again, and Wynn smiles. "Few have managed to gain so many titles without a higher Class. Even fewer are thrice-titled, especially in such a short timeframe."

I grunt, shaking my head. A lot of my titles—Monster Bane and Duelist—are cheats. Since I was still progressing from one tier to the next, the System registered me as only having forty-three Levels, instead of what should be about double that. It means that those titles, while earned through blood, are nowhere as "true" as someone else's. But I'm sure Wynn knows that, which makes his interest puzzling in a way.

"If you're looking at hindering the Truinnar, won't owning settlements be better?" I ask.

"Ugh, you're embarrassing me, boy-o."

"THERE ARE CURRENTLY TWENTY-THREE MOVANA SETTLEMENTS IN AFRICA, CENTERED AROUND EAST AFRICA. A MAP OF SUCH SETTLEMENTS HAS BEEN UPLOADED TO YOUR DATA FILES."

"Well, the Guild is not part of the Kingdom," Wynn says. "And as you know, we are not allowed to own settlements."

"But you're allowed to have Guild Buildings in other settlements," I say slowly, realizing what he is alluding to. The Guild is as "independent" as a twenty-year-old who still lives at home and doesn't pay rent to his parents. They're still going to dictate a portion of his life, whether he likes it or not. So accepting the Guild into my settlements is a double-edged sword. It'll piss off Roxley and the Truinnar, but potentially put me in the good graces of the Movanna. Or at the least, give them a direct and obvious way to spy on me. I tap the box after a second. "I take it your Guild didn't pay for this then."

"No."

"Ah…" I sigh, tapping the gift. Then there are a lot more strings to this gift than I assumed. "Why tell me all this?"

"Because I feel it's better to be clear about our objectives before we begin negotiation."

"Don't think it'd help your cause to hide it?"

"Not in the long run. And I—we—wish to ensure that this is a long-term relationship."

I grunt, leaning back. Ah hell. For all the potential problems, they're the only Tier II guild to make an offer, one that has significant enough reserves to make full use of our dungeon. We need them—their people, their Credits. If we can get a good deal…

"All right, talk."

***

"Are you certain that Ms. Pearson and the AI will be sufficient for this negotiation?" Katherine says when we've shown Wynn out.

"Lana will be fine. They've got a framework of what we want in place." In fact, I've mentioned to Lana that I'm willing to let them have both North Vancouver and Kamloops, if the price is right. "Who's next?"

"Damian."

"Show him in." I sigh. This should be fun.

"You know, boy-o, you've gotten nearly as boring as my former Companion. And all he did was sit around reading all day."

"Trust me, I'm not impressed either."

Our mutual bitching about my life of meetings and talking comes to an end as Damian walks in. The ex-scavenger, ex-rebel, now bureaucrat leader like me seems slightly more harried than the last time I saw him. After a few quick greetings and pleasantries, we get down to business.

"My people are growing concerned about their safety. They've been having to deal with more and more monster attacks recently," Damian says. "They're also complaining about a significant drop in their income."

"THOSE EARMARKED AS SCAVENGERS HAVE SEEN A TOTAL LOSS OF REVENUE OF 9% IN THE LAST MONTH WITH AN AVERAGE DECREASE OF 318.64 CREDITS PER INDIVIDUAL. THIS IS BASED OFF A DECREASE IN TRANSACTION VOLUME OF 2.81%."

I stare at the notification, processing the data. "And what do you want from me?"

"More guards. We also want a timeline of when we can expect the other suburbs to be transformed into full-fledged towns."

"Well…" I shake my head. I'm so not answering that one since I don't have a good idea myself. "From the information I've got, it doesn't look like it's an issue of monsters or what you're bringing back so much as a drop in your selling prices." As Damian opens his mouth, I raise my hand. "Let me see if I have this right. Your men—sorry, people—are bringing in the same number of items, but demand's fallen off. At the same time, they've had to go farther and farther out because nearby residences have all been hit."

Damian shuts his mouth before nodding slightly.

"Right. Well, here's the thing. You guys are either going to have accept it or change your occupation," I say. "As more and more people Level and get Credits through their Skills and occupations, the demand for scavenged items is going to continue dropping. It won't take long before inter-galactic tradeliners arrive, and then your market is really going to crash. Change now or change later, but you're in a losing game."

"Did you tell me and my people to suck it up and deal?" Damian's eyes bulge, a little heat appearing in his voice.

"Yes," I say, then consider. "What we can do is provide career counseling and advice. Purchasing the AI with the skills necessary to do the analysis isn't that expensive. If we pick out a few buildings, we can spread the locations around the city."

"Job retraining," Damian says, disgust in his voice.

"Counseling. No one's going to hold their hands," I say, leaning forward. "Your people aren't cowards, but they've gotten used to an easy way of life, of low risk and a decent amount of Credits. But things change, and they're going to have to change."

"And that's it? That's what you want me to go back to them with?" Damian says, anger thrumming through his voice.

"Yes. They can either change now and be ready for the future, or we can prop them up for a few months, maybe a year or two, and then have it all pulled out from under them. This world of Levels, it gives us a ton of options. But you have to be willing to take them."

"So you want them to fight? Be like your Hakarta and Yerrick friends? Run your dungeon like everyone else?"

I sigh, shaking my head. "I don't want anything from them. I'm just telling you how things are. They can decide to delve or change their Classes or hell, keep doing what they're doing. It's up to them. I'm just saying we're not going to subsidize them or provide anything else."

"This is unacceptable."

"Okay," I say, nodding. "Anything else?"

"We're not done speaking about this yet!" Damian almost shouts, fist hammering into the table so hard he cracks it.

"Yes, we are. Now you can move on to another topic or you can leave."

When Damian gets out a short while later, Katherine is giving me the stink-eye.

"Do you think I'm wrong?"

"In what you said? No. In how you said it? Definitely," Katherine says.

"It was the truth. A necessary truth."

"But you could have been kinder."

A feeling of déjà vu, a memory of a previous conversation. One between myself and my father, Katherine taking my place as I find myself echoing my father as he explained my lack of talent while I decried his tone.

"If I was kinder, he might refuse the truth of my words, holding himself to the tone rather than the intent. He can hate me, but at least he'll have heard me."

There's something in her eyes when I say that, something I can't understand. For a moment, I wonder if she knows why I said what I did, but then I dismiss the thought. Women can't read minds—that's just a fallacy.

"I'll have Lana speak with him later then," Katherine says instead.

I open my mouth to protest but decide against it. Having Lana soften the blow a little while reminding him of the truth is probably the best of both worlds. Good cop, bad cop at its best. "Who's next?"

"We have the delvers."

I groan, knowing what they want. I'm surprised they're coming together, but at least their topic of conversation is known. They'll want to discuss the Guild spot, their concerns about being pushed out, and of course, push for some benefits for themselves. It's annoying, because the Guild could do us a ton of good, with quests and a ready market for our goods, but they'll complain and bitch as if they don't know all that just to get a little leeway. And even if I can push most of this to Lana and Kim as the negotiating parties, they still want to make sure I get my share of it too.

And sadly, I can't tell them to bugger off. Because as much as it is politics, they might actually have a point somewhere in there that I haven't thought of. Thankfully, today's the last of my meeting days. After today, I'll be mostly ready for my trip.

"Then let's get this over with."

***

"John," Lana says softly after pulling away from the kiss the next morning.

"Mmmm…?" I say as I try to re-engage my brain. That was one heck of a goodbye kiss…

"Port me to Vancouver?" Lana says.

"Oh. Right." I blink, waving to open the Portal.

The moment it does, Roland slips in, the only one to accompany us to Kamloops last night.

"And, John, stay safe," Lana says, giving me one last hug before stepping away.

I watch her departing figure, sighing before shutting the inky blackness. "Now then, what next?"

"Mr. Lee!" a voice calls so loudly that it pierces the walls of the house we're in.

When I turn, I blink and stare at KC through the living room windows, the Gunsmith struggling down the walkway with a pair of large metal boxes.

"KC." I nod to the lady, glancing at the boxes as I open the front door.

"Ammo! I finally… ummm… worked through the… well, blueprints. Mostly have them in solid casings, but I, uh… well. I finished these two last night. Hollow points," KC says, flushing under scrutiny and holding up the cases.

"Oh. Thank you!" I blink, taking them from her and storing them in my Altered Space. Before I can say anything further, KC's pulling out even more cases from her inventory, dumping case after case on the ground. "How many did you make?"

"I, uhhh… lost track," KC says ashamedly. "I was, ummm… Leveling so much that well…"

"You got carried away," I finish for her, and she nods. "Well, no matter. I'm sure I can use it. Did you get the rest… ah, I see they're here." I nod, staring at the various other boxes, each carefully labeled. Boxes of explosives, marked and stored, make their appearance. "Just send me the bill. I'll get it paid now."

KC bobs her head quickly, and a moment later, a small notification pops up. I don't even bother looking at the details, just glancing at the final amount and sending the Credits over, letting Kim handle the inventory issues. While he (it? her?) won't be useful once we leave the settlement, for small tasks like these, he's even faster than Ali.

"INVENTORY IS MISSING TWO HIGH-EXPLOSIVE MINES AND CURRENTLY HAS ONE EXTRA WHITE PHOSPHOROUS INCENDIARY GRENADE. ALSO, THERE IS A PACKAGE THAT IS LABELED TO YOU DIRECTLY. I HAVE ASSESSED THAT THERE IS A LOW THREAT RISK AND HAVE NOT INVESTIGATED ITS CONTENTS."

"Let her know by notification. No biggies."

"Thanks again. You and your people," I say. "Anything I should know?"

"Ummm… no… We've had a few visits from Artisans from other cities—villages? Towns?—uhh…"

"Cities is fine. I understand what you mean,"

"Right. Ummm… so, yes. They've been interested in… well, us… it's been fun. One of the, umm… visitors was an… interior designer. Upped our efficiency by 1.6%!"

"That's good." I nod. "Nice speaking with you, KC."

With one last nod, I pop open another Portal and step through. Time to get to work.

***

Since I can only open Portals to places I've visited—and only within a range of a 1,000 KM of me—I have a bit of a journey to make. While we debated having some of the team accompany me, between Sabre and my ability to

Blink Step and open Portals, I should be relatively safe. Of course, I promised to drag my friends to me if things look dangerous and I was still in range, but none of us expect that. At least till Edmonton.

British Columbia during the height of summer is alternately beautiful sunshine and occasional days of rain. Up north where we're going, the rainforest gives way to more desert-like terrain before changing again. Lucky for me, it's mostly sunshine right now, which means traveling along the weather-beaten roads is satisfactory. It does make me wonder what we should do about upkeep—now that I own a bunch of settlements in the province, trade between settlements is slowly picking up. Outside of the main towns, I've avoided taking control of settlements unless it's been requested, just because I don't want the additional responsibility. Surprisingly, that's happened more than once, especially since we have started regular patrols. As much as I might not want to be the local government, we seem to be falling into that role more and more.

Right now, between the lack of on-going transportation and the monster problems, trade caravans are done in an unscheduled, slipshod matter. And while the nitpicky part of me wants to get involved, the lazy part of me points out that this is what the capitalist economy is meant for. Let someone else who wants to earn the Credits organize things.

However, the roads are my problem. That's what the government is for, after all—dealing with resources and projects that make no sense for an individual to undertake. That's why we had governments in the first place—from the mayor of a village, who decided who and when people got to use the common grounds for breeding, to the United Nations, which had helped reduce world hunger and diseases. Still, like any government, I'll admit, that last part is a bit shaky since the UN isn't really a government technically, but whatever. The point is, we organise because we need to.

Unfortunately, I have to contend with that most limiting of factors—scarce resources. Putting Credits and manpower into building the roads and warding them meant I couldn't buy land in the Villages. Focus on upgrading individual Villages and I'd miss the opportunity of upgrading Vancouver from Town to Large Town. Not purchasing specialized buildings means we aren't taking advantage or encouraging specific economies. In Whitehorse, the introduction of the Arborator had provided employment and Credits for a ton of people, increasing our efficiency further. Could I afford to shift our focus from things like that to work on something like roads? Then again, could I neglect trade?

Thoughts like this carry me from Grand Prairie to Edmonton. I could have gone north and east from Kamloops, but that would have put me through a provincial park. And those, from experience, are a tough row to hoe. Not that I shouldn't visit one, but right now, speed is more important than Levels.

Still, for all my desire for speed, I make the time to pop open Portals for those who need it. Small towns. Individuals unlucky enough to be caught in the middle of nowhere and yet lucky enough to still be alive. Groups of survivors swept up and thrown back into civilization. I have to admit, there's a certain satisfaction in helping them all, even if it slows me down.

In time, forests and rolling hills—and a few mountains—give way to flat prairies. The sky opens up, making me both relax from the ease of picking out dangers and tense from being so exposed. No more mountains, no more shade, just the eye in the sky and the rolling plains that were once part of some farmer's land. By the time I hit the prairies proper, the number of individuals I find diminishes to nothing, the survivors most likely having made their way to Edmonton.

Like most prairie cities, Edmonton doesn't really "start" with a fixed boundary; you just find yourself rolling in where more and more buildings make themselves known. Abandoned, discarded, broken down, and bloody, residences and strip malls merge into office buildings. And then there's a wall made of grey concrete and cinder blocks, built by Skill and Credits. And towers that host beam turrets and, perhaps most startling of all, a single man waiting for me.

"Howdy, stranger," the man calls, cowboy hat, plaid shirt, and cowboy boots set against a pair of guns slung low on his hips and a shotgun cradled in his arms. "That's about far enough."

"*Howdy? Goblin's arse. I didn't get any tobacco!*" Ali chimes in, shifting his clothing to mock the stranger.

I'm too busy to answer the Spirit though, as I study the man before me.

Blair Kendall, the Rock of Edmonton (Level 28 Battle Seer)
HP: 3680/3680
MP: 2110/2110
Conditions: None

Holy shit. That's an Advanced Level. He literally has the highest Level I've seen on a human. While he isn't the highest Level human on Earth—I checked, and there's some cheat Level character at Advanced 38—he's the highest in Canada as far as I know. And probably explains why Edmonton has managed to stay independent.

"Afternoon," I say while getting off Sabre slowly. I keep my hands well in sight, not wanting him to get any ideas.

"Nice ride there. Mind telling us why you're visiting this little town of ours? Don't get many strangers these days," Blair says, a hand coming up to absently rub at a close-cut, curly beard.

"Passing through. Maybe a little scouting. Maybe a little chat with the people in charge."

"Really. You're pretty well stocked and armed for someone just passing through. Redeemer of the Dead," Blair says.

I sigh. I really, really, hate that title sometimes. "Well, colour me surprised to have the Rock of Edmonton greet me. Now, if we're done measuring each other, perhaps you can show me where an inn or empty residence is? Preferably one with a working hot shower? Cleanse spells work, but well, I've been on the road for a bit now."

"We aren't done," Blair says. "I'm not letting a potential threat into my city."

"Your city?" I raise an eyebrow, mentally prodding Ali.

"Can't tell, boy-o. You can infer ownership, but you can't actually tell. It's one of the rules instituted by the Council in... blah blah blah year after owners kept getting assassinated. You can buy the events around a transfer, but they don't show up on Status screens anymore."

Ah. That's useful. For me. Somewhat. Maybe.

"Fine. What do you want from me?"

Quest Received—Clear the Plains

A new plains dungeon has appeared near the city of Edmonton. You have been tasked with clearing the dungeon and destroying the Boss. Doing so will gain the favor of the Rock of Edmonton.

Reward: Entry to the town of Edmonton

Accept (Y/N)

"Really?" I grumble, staring at the quest information and the resulting marker.

"Yes." Without another word, Blair walks back through the open gates, which shut behind him. Someone has the flair for the dramatic.

"Scout ahead, will you? Let's get this garbage done."

Nice thing about having access to an entire armory's worth of explosives is that when you're feeling particularly lazy, it's a simple enough matter to overuse them. Since all the explosives were made by individual crafters, all of them are System-registered. With the help of my drones and a liberal application of explosives, clearing the dungeon doesn't even require me to crawl through the tunnels.

I do wonder how he would have expected me to handle this if I hadn't had my drones. After all, the tunnels themselves were barely larger than a man's torso in most points. At times, they were significantly smaller. The only regret I have—and it's a mild regret—is that I won't get any Loot from all this. Even with the sheer volume of explosives, I could have looted the scattered remains if I had been willing to crawl in.

As it stands, the only loot I received were the hides of the dungeon Boss and his minions when they swarmed up and out of the earth at my continued provocations. Sitting at just above Level 30, the dungeon Boss didn't take much to deal with, though his trick of sinking me halfway into the earth was interesting. Having an evolved gopher with shark teeth trying to eat my face from inches away was a new and unpleasant experience. It said something about my life that that didn't even make it into the top hundred nightmares.

When I get the quest update notification, I make my way to the town as fast as I can. Maybe I should research a lava flow or napalm spell, something I could use to flood passageways next time.

The Rock of Edmonton is waiting for me again when I roll up to the wall as twilight falls.

"All done then, are we?" Blair drawls.

"Yes. Now can I go in for a bath?"

"Follow me," Blair says, leading the way into the city. Within the city, a horse waits for him, which he straddles with practiced ease.

"Really?" I say, shaking my head. "A bit on the nose, isn't it?"

"How did you get around, right after the change?" Blair says caustically.

I think back to my mad scramble down the mountain and shut up. Horses are practical and fast and this one at least looks as though its achieved some form of symbiosis with the System. Or else it's just naturally a really pretty horse. I'll admit, I've become inured to big animals after hanging out with Lana.

You have entered the Town of Edmonton
This is a safe zone. Contains:

- *A Shop*
- *City Center*
- *Armory*
- *Adventurer's Guild*
- *More…*

"You have a Guild already?" I say, an eyebrow rising. That was fast. I mean, sure, Carcross had one before Whitehorse, but I'm still surprised they've achieved so much so fast.

All around us, the buildings slowly transform, growing higher as we make our way downtown on PAV and horse.

"Yup. They've been real helpful, they have," Blair drawls. "I hear you just struck a deal with a crafter group for one of your settlements."

"My…" My eyes tighten before I snort. "You were using the time the quest bought you to look me up."

"*I thought that necklace made things harder for people to buy information on me?*" I ask Ali.

"*For previous actions. And it doesn't count if the Guild puts out a press release.*"

"*They did what!?!*"

"*Recruiting material, boy-o.*" I can hear the exasperation in Ali's mental voice.

"Seemed fair. There's quite a bit of information out there on you, for cheap, Redeemer. At least until a few months ago. Then, the information gets a lot more expensive. Be curious to hear how you did that."

"Har." I shake my head, somewhat embarrassed at being called out on it directly. It's not a time that I like to think about directly. Still, of all my titles, that one I earned fair and square, doing something few would have done. Not during the aftermath of an apocalypse at least. It's a strange title, I'll admit, and I'm still uncertain why the System gave it to me. Not the why of the action, but the greater why of how it chose. "Looks like you owe me a story then. Rock."

"Not much to tell, not to someone like you. It came to me probably the same way you earned your other titles," Blair says. "In blood and tears, in front of a smoking gun, over the corpses of friends and foes alike."

"Where we going? And are you going to let anyone else speak to me?" I say, having yet to see a single person since the gate guards.

"Not yet," Blair says with a matter-of-fact honesty. "You'll be staying with me until I decide you're safe enough. Hard to trust people like you."

I would say something about his confidence in dealing with me alone, but I knew that ever since the gate, we'd been shadowed by four individuals, all of them with Advanced Classes. Not as high as Blair, but considering Edmonton must have a finite number of Advanced Classers, I was rather flattered. Hell, even Vancouver didn't have that many—though that was as much the Sect's fault as anything.

A few more gambits at drawing a conversation out of Blair gets me nowhere, so I give up and content myself to being led to his house. When we arrive, I'm somehow not surprised to find that it's a modest duplex. I am surprised by how slovenly the place is—while it's clean, clothing and other bric-a-brac are strewn about everywhere.

"Bathroom's upstairs, around the corner at the end of the hallway."

I grunt in acknowledgement before heading up, sending Ali to keep an eye on Sabre. Soon enough, I'm downstairs again, greeted by a carnivore's dream of a meal. Conversation at dinner is nearly non-existent, consisting of a lot of gurgled beer, moans of pleasure, and chewing. Without the ladies around, I find myself returning to my more slovenly eating habits, including licking my fingers with gusto. When we're done, feet up and beers in hand, we get around to the real talk.

"You're here to set up that Portal of yours, aren't you?"

"Setting some waypoints, yes," I say, clarifying matters a little. "Also to make sure you guys are doing okay. We're in the midst of improving our own towns, and part of that is figuring out what kind of friends we might have."

"And you think we're friends?" Blair sips his beer, tilting his head to the side as he looks at me. Without his hat, he looks much less like a caricature and more like a very tired man.

"I think we could be."

"Even if you're in a state of war?"

"And you kicking out the Grey Company was all kinds of amiable? Way I read it, your fight was a close thing," I say. "And you've got a lot fewer people now."

"Not much for mincing words, are you? Thought you people were all kinds of polite."

"If your town council wanted a diplomatic response, they wouldn't have sent you," I point out. Even if my Chinese origins are mostly gone physically after the gene therapy, he knows my background. And that you people was a damn dig if I had ever heard one. Strangely enough, I find myself not that angry – getting another redneck being casually racist was so far beneath my list of worries, it wouldn't show up even in a thousand years. "And just as an FYI, I grew up in Vancouver."

"Not Richmond? Hear it's a little Asia there."

"Not anymore."

"Ah…" The not-so-subtle reminder of the apocalypse shuts him down. "We aren't ready to cozy up to you, but we're willing to talk."

I grunt, leaning back and nodding. "Fair enough. But I'm only planning to be here for a few days. After that, well, I've got a city to visit."

"Calgary."

"Yes."

Silence descends while we savor the beer and our slowly settling stomachs.

In time, Blair tilts his head, his voice a relaxed drawl. "Might be there are a few interested in helping out. Unofficial-like."

"We'll take any help we can. Unofficial-like."

Silence returns, and this time, it doesn't leave. I find myself relaxing, content to just sit, knowing there's nothing more for me to do. Tomorrow, I'll be talking to politicians and bureaucrats, finding out about the city and trying to put a good face on things. But today… well, today, I get to sit in silence and that's fine enough with me. Blair might be tough, but he's a bit of a racist dick.

Chapter 7

"Sure you won't stay a little longer? I figure you almost have them," Blair drawls, leaning over the saddle horn of his horse as I straddle Sabre.

It's been three days since I've arrived in Edmonton, and while I'm still restricted in where I'm allowed to go, I've made some progress. It probably helped that we got hit by a swarm on the second day. The display of controlled violence I put on was particularly well received. But still…

"People are weird," I say, shaking my head. "And I'm on a timetable."

Blair snorts but nods agreeably. A moment later, a five-foot, two-seventy-something man rides up on his bicycle, a rifle slung over his shoulder, a bicycle helmet on his head.

"Rufus," I greet the man, who flashes me a grin.

"He'll get you as deep as he safely can. But the rest is up to you," Blair says, rubbing his chin. "I still ain't sure about this plan…"

"Good thing it's not up to you then." I flash Blair a grin.

He shakes his head and waves us off.

The journey south from Edmonton is simple enough to handle, especially with a Messenger as my guide. I find it slightly amusing when Rufus explains that he used to be a postal worker, which resulted in him receiving the Class. Thank god I didn't get a class called "Website Designer" or I'd really be screwed.

Rufus does his job well, leading me to Calgary with nary a problem that can't be solved with a liberal application of violence. From there, he guides me to the current headquarters of the humans in the city—an abandoned furniture warehouse. Since I have his company, we get through their security checkpoints with a minimum of trouble, which is nice, since I played that game already in Edmonton.

That's the thing I should have realized—Edmonton and Calgary have been working together for the last little while. It's a partial explanation of why both parties have managed to hold out as long as they have—in fact, Edmonton's state is partly due to the sacrifice of a number of Calgarians according to Rufus.

"Yo, this is John Lee. He's from BC and just bounced from Edmonton, where he stayed with Blair. Blair says, and I quote, he's 'an okay sort for a slit-eyed fucker,'" Rufus says, looking somewhat uncomfortable saying those words. Truth be told, I'm not sure if it's the swearing or the racial slur.

On the other hand, at least the introduction has the trio in the command room give me somewhat favorable nods. One is a First Nations man in his fifties with close-cropped hair and wearing Adventurer chic—an armored jumpsuit and holsters for pistols and knives. The second is a twenty-something weedy man who looks as if he needs a meal or three and a pair of glasses to go with his shirt and pants ensemble. The last is a Nordic blonde of the older persuasion. Her extremely tight blouse, artfully undone one button too much across an ample bosom, screams cougar. It doesn't help that she certainly has the Charisma for it. Committed as I am to Lana, I can't help but check her out.

"Mr. Lee, you're from Vancouver then?" Trevor Badger, the First Nations elder, says after we exchange quick greetings.

"Among other settlements, yes." I nod to him, a part of me wondering which tribe he's a part of. After a moment, I dismiss that thought as unimportant to our current situation. Anyway, it's not as if I'd remember a fact like that. I'd be lucky to remember any of their names by the end of this meeting, if not for Ali and the Status screens.

"Are you here to lend us help?" Donna Luff murmurs. I have to admit, her "Rachel" haircut suits her, but the way she's smiling has my guard up.

That and her occupation of Lawyer. Having dealt with Labashi, I'm not a fan of the Contract Skill she most likely has.

"Pretty much. Sorry it took so long. We've had our own things to handle," I say, grabbing a seat without asking. "Now, I've got some ideas, but perhaps you'd care to fill me in. It's been a little over a week and a half since I've had access to a Shop."

"You didn't…" Donna says, trailing off since the answer was obvious. No, Edmonton didn't give me access to their Shops. All of them were connected to City Cores. "Well, we can certainly fix that. But maybe, Charles?"

Charles grunts, leaning forward, his voice as weedy and thin as him. "Well, I can give a wide overview, but of course details will take more time. Here's where we are…"

Calgary has a total of three City Cores, areas that demarcate the portions of the city and give control of the city itself. Unlike Vancouver or Seattle, which spread its population across numerous adjoining cities, Calgary concentrated most of its population in its main city area. That means they have significantly fewer City Cores to deal with. Initially, humanity had all three Cores under their somewhat fractured control, but with the coming of the aliens, they lost two of the Cores at the cost of quite a few people.

The Kingdom of Peswin currently control a City Core in the southwest of Calgary, beneath the bow river, while the Uvrik are east of the river and humanity has the northwest. Of the three, the Uvrik corporation is in the most tenuous position, having to deal with the brunt of the fighting with humanity, while the halflings sit back and watch from the sidelines.

Those are the basics. The rest is a rundown on the kind of problems the Calgarians are facing. The Peswin currently had the lowest number of Advanced Classes in the city—about twenty or so, all low-Leveled—but had a much larger number of Basic Combat Classers. Uvrik went the other direction, having eleven very high Level Advanced Classers, about a hundred ten Basic Combat Classers, and a very, very large army of drones.

Most importantly for my plans, I got some information about our enemies' current defenses. While everyone had settlement shields set up to stop simple probes, everyone conducted on-going attacks, which meant those shields dropped constantly. Unfortunately, that means that everyone has put a decent amount of funds into upgraded sensors. Still, for all that, everyone was on-board with the first part of my plan. Sneaking in and getting the lay of the land, especially with my ability, was uncontestably a good idea.

It was part two that got them riled up.

"You want to what?" Charles shouts, his reedy voice almost breaking as he squeaks his outrage.

"Talk to them," I say. "Negotiate an alliance. Preferably with both but at least one."

"Are you insane?"

"No. There're either eleven really high Level Advanced Classers or twenty low Level Advanced Classers of the combat persuasion we have to fight. That'd be doable individually, but what happens if the other side hits us right after the fight?" I say.

"We know. Why do you think we're holding off?" Donna says.

"That's what we expect you and your men to help us on," Trevor says pointedly. "Or are you just talk?"

"I can bring a bunch of fighters, enough that we'll have a decent advantage and most likely won't lose too many in a single fight. But not many doesn't mean no one. I'm tired of digging graves and cremating bodies. Aren't you?" When no one replies, I continue. "If we can find some common ground, maybe make an alliance, why don't we?"

"Because they've killed our people!"

"It's our land," Trevor says.

"And how'd that argument work for you guys?" I say pointedly. When I see Trevor bristle, I hold up a hand, my brain catching up with my words. "Sorry. Too far. But getting an ally from another power is a winning strategy, if I recall my Canadian history."

Trevor grunts, obviously still unhappy. I wonder if offering him a chocolate will help.

"What makes you think they'll talk to us?" Donna says when the silence gets uncomfortable, leaning forward and giving me an eyeful.

"I don't. But if we don't try, we won't know."

"And if they try to kill us?"

"Then we'll have their answer," I say with a slight smile. "But I figure we could write up a contract to get a diplomatic talk going."

Donna makes a face, while Charles gets ready to raise another point of contention. I sigh, settling in to continue the argument. We need allies not just for this fight but for all the upcoming fights. We can't keep pissing off the entire Galactic System. I just hope that we aren't embroiling ourselves too much into Galactic politics by creating these alliances.

***

Convincing them took hours, but eventually I received an agreement—after promising to scout out their lands and get moving on preparations for a knock-down, drag-out fight. I'm less than enthused by the idea of that, but between the help we can get from Seattle and BC, we should be able to win. We might even be able to do so without losing too many people, even if we get attacked by both sides. Thankfully, neither group in Calgary seem to be into the entire slavery or random torture business, which means we only have to overcome the basic prejudices and hurt feelings from fighting a constant skirmish for the last few months. Only.

I wish I could say scouting is more difficult, but the fact is, slipping in and causing havoc is just the kind of thing the groups have been doing for the last few months. Joining a skirmishing group when the shields fall is a simple matter, and after that, I limit my attacks. Mostly though, the group of us just run around, making sure I get as much land under my feet as possible.

The next day, we head straight into the Uvrik's territory for a repeat. Unfortunately, a few hours in, we get caught.

The Uvrik have a somewhat different method of dealing with intruders. Their flying drones blanket the sky, dozens of them swooshing over our heads as they triangulate on our position. Much like Sam's smaller drones, none of these do much damage individually, but together, they could easily become a problem. More importantly, these ones are focused on slowing us down, hitting us with oil slicks, insta-concrete canisters, and foam barriers. Area effect spells like Lightning Strike and Fireball sweep the skies, but they just keep coming.

"Move, we can't keep staying here," Iris, the titular leader of our group, screams.

The African Canadian woman matches actions to words even as she looses an arrow at a coming swarm. The arrow shimmers, becoming a dozen. Each ignites and accelerates into the sky, tearing apart the drones. The rest of us are right on her heels.

As we turn the corner of the next block, the four of us find ourselves faced by a wall of steel. Squat robots have shields held in front of their bodies, and the barrels of their beam weapons sticking out gleam in the summer sky, moments before they fire. The portable shield generator around my waist flares white, soaking up the damage as it teeters on the edge of failing.

"Shit!" A thin, young man ducks away as the ends of his long hair catch on fire. The ends burn away as he ducks and rolls. "You assholes! That cost me a hundred Credits to get fixed!"

"Told you you should have gotten the nanoweave!" his friend, Louise, cackles as she stands in the middle of the road, beams aimed at her seeming to bend as they near her form. The twisted flares of light strike the ground, buildings, and drones as she Warps Space.

I admit, I have to grin. It's time for me to test out a few new spells I purchased just before we left. While I'm not earning as much these days—not having that much time to go hunting has put a crimp on my looting and experience gain—I can give myself a salary as the settlement owner. I'm not particularly clear about the formula used—it has something to do with the type of government, the on-going revenue generation, tax base and tax rate amount and duration—but it's enough to replenish my empty wallet. It's a pity I can't use the settlement funds directly for myself, but if I could, royalty and other settlement owners would be truly broken.

"My turn," I whisper to myself and raise my hand. A molten bar of fire shoots from my hand, melting the steel and punching into the robot behind the shield. I swing my hand sideways, lopping the creature and its neighbor in half before the attack fades. Even as the after-images of my strike fade, I dodge aside.

"What was that?" Iris pants as she draws a breath, her own attack punching a hole in a robot next to the ones I attacked.

Ali tosses her a description, since he has little to do in this fight, his orders being to stay hidden and undetectable.

Inferno Beam

A beam of heat raised to the levels of an inferno, able to melt steel and liquefy earth on contact! The perfect spell for those looking to do a lot of damage in a short period of time.
Effect: Does 150 Points of Heat Damage
Cost: 125 Mana

"Move," I snap without thinking, dodging forward and sweeping my hands sideways as my next spell forms. Mud Walls rise from the ground, stretching to the sky before sweeping forward in a V formation, pushing and submerging the attacking robots as the walls create a pathway for us.

Mud Walls

Unlike its more common counterpart Earthen Walls, Mud Walls deals slow, suffocating damage and restricts movement on the battlefield.
Effect: Does 20 Points of Suffocating Damage. -30% Movement Speed
Duration: 2 Minutes
Cost: 75 Mana

Reacting to the tone of my voice, the group charges alongside me. Mana Darts form in my hand to attack more mini drones that block our way. I keep the pace down, making sure the team can catch up, spinning around after a hundred meters to lash out with another Inferno Beam as some of the robots get out of the mud.

'Mana consumption, boy-o. Remember, we don't want to look too powerful," Ali reminds me.

I grunt, pulling the beam rifle from my shoulder. With the team caught up, we get back to running, arrows, projectiles, and spells blowing away any obstructions as we try to get back to "our" part of town.

Luckily for us, our situation has been transmitted to the other teams, and after another couple of minutes of running away, we receive an order over the tactical net.

"Drop and roll in 3. 2. 1. Now!"

Some of my new friends do exactly as the voice commands, but Louise and I take the liberty to interpret the orders, hitting the ground in a long slide. We're both angling to see what's coming, and the extra effort—and a few road burns—is worth the effort. Prepared spells lash out, beams of purple, green, and yellow light that cut through drones are mixed with tiny homing missiles and the deep and continuous boom of a minigun. In seconds, the air behind us is clear of drones, the last lucky few pulling back to stem losses.

I grunt, standing, road rash mostly faded away as my System-assisted healing kicks in. It's weird that I even got it, considering how much health I have, but I've noticed that the System likes to make us hurt. Higher health doesn't mean an inability to take damage—just less. A lot less. Staring at the remnants of my armored jumpsuit, I sigh, making mental note to pick up a few more sets when we get back. Sometimes, I feel like these armor sets are like what pantyhose must have been for women—better to buy cheap and disposable than expensive and nice. Because you never know when the next damn thing is going to leave a tear in it.

We run back to the safety of our lines. It doesn't take long now that we don't have to worry about fighting through masses of drones. A part of me wonders how much all that cost the Uvrik, but I decide against asking. I'm not sure if I'd laugh or cry at the answer.

"You're wanted," Iris says once we've made it safely back.

I nod, turning to head to see the council members. That's the only people they could mean.

"And John? I run the team."

My step hitches slightly from a flare of anger, but I push it down. She's right—I might have been a fraction of a second faster, but it didn't matter. Not at that point. I should have let her give the command rather than do it myself. Having multiple leaders could cause trouble. I wave goodbye in acknowledgement before I leave, Sabre finding me soon after.

"Did you get far enough?" Trevor asks when I walk in.

I'd be annoyed at his abruptness, but it's not like I knocked when I entered. "Good enough for government work." I pause, struck by a thought. "We're the actual government now, aren't we? Crap."

Donna snorts before she taps a projected holographic image. Ali floats over, waving his hand over the image and updating it with our path, a red line charting our progress through the city.

"Now, we ready to chat?" I ask when I realize the three, perched over the map, won't be saying anything soon.

"We've made the requests," Donna says. "We've yet to hear from them."

I frown, considering if they're telling the truth. In the end, I decide not to question them. Better to believe in them than not. "Anything you need from me?"

"The Kingdom's been putting some pressure on us here," Trevor says, pointing at a portion of the map. "They didn't like us picking up those buildings. Our men could use some help, especially with that sensing Skill of yours."

I grunt, nodding. While I'm still limited—as is Ali—by my Levels to pick up anything truly Skilled, that doesn't mean we can't be of help. Our very presence along that line will force the Kingdom to deploy more stealth-oriented teams, reducing the pressure those teams can bring elsewhere along the border. And since I've got nothing better to do, I head off. The only pity is that I'm limited in how much experience I can gain since killing too many of their people before we engage in "peace" talks is probably a bad idea.

***

Two days later, we get our first meeting. You'd think the Uvrik corporation would get on it faster, but hey, who cares about thousands of Credits destroyed, a little blood spilled, and a few worthless lives lost? It's all part of the balance sheet of taking over a city, isn't it?

I'm pacing in a circle, waiting for word of how the meeting went. It's been hours since my presence was restricted to this room near the rest of the Council members. Within it are members of the fast-acting reserve team we've designed, ready to act if things go to hell. Most of them are lounging, reading, playing with weapons.

Hours of pacing, chewing on chocolates, and occasionally attempting to read. It's frustrating, being stuck back here and waiting, but having me there would give away too many of our cards. I could calm myself, instill control over my emotions, suppress them so I can do something "productive," but sometimes, it's important to actually feel what you're feeling, to deal with your emotions rather than suppress them. Or so I'm told.

When I'm finally called into the meeting room, I find Donna with the pair of aides who went along with her, all three relaxing over a big bottle of apocalypse ale.

"John," Trevor greets me, his greeting followed soon after by everyone else's.

"So?" I ask.

"They're willing to talk. But they want you there for the next meeting," Donna says. I blink, raising an eyebrow before she shrugs. "No, I don't know how they figured you were in town."

"Do you think the Kingdom…?" I ask, frowning.

"They still haven't answered any of our missives," Charles says, shaking his head.

"What do they want with me?" I frown, not understanding the request for my presence. I'm just a helper here, an over-powered troop carrier.

"The Manager I was speaking to didn't know. Or wouldn't say," Donna says before looking at the other two. "But they've signed a Contract binding their corporation to a ceasefire to take effect in twenty-four hours. And guaranteeing us safe passage to meet with them. In their headquarters."

"With me?" I say, my eyes wide. That's insane. They can't not know of my ability if they made that call. Unless they're planning a double-cross. Which might make some sense. Crap.

"It's a trap! Maybe."

Trevor leans forward. "We have to do this. Even if it's nothing more than to get John in…"

"They can block my Skills," I say, holding up a hand. There are Skills, Settlement Upgrades, and even spells that can block my Portal Skill. While doing it for the entire town is expensive, for a single headquarters? That's more than reasonable. Hell, I did it for each of the City Cores under my control.

"Still, that close…"

"And if they betray us?" Charles says, shaking his head. "No. Not at their headquarters. It's too dangerous."

Trevor turns to Charles, beginning a loud argument about strategic necessity. All the while, I stare at Donna, who's spinning the empty beer bottle in a circle.

"What do you think?" I ask her softly.

"I think we should go," Donna says. "You were right."

"I like hearing that, but about what?"

"They're willing to talk. Almost eager." After a moment, Donna raises her voice. "We're going."

That leads to another round of arguments, but it's good enough for me. I leave it to the trio, slipping out of the room. Guarantee or not, I've got preparations to make.

***

Our initial meeting place is in a small park, just next to a pair of residential apartments and some office buildings, nearly right between the shifting borders of our settlements. Theoretically, these borders were fixed in the settlement screens and maps, but in wars and battles, locations that are tactically and strategically sound to hold don't hold to the vagaries of the System. Even with settlement shields that regenerate, having an irritating burr of an enemy team can make a huge difference. And so here we are, standing among summer green grass, overgrown and unkempt with last fall's withered leaves because no one has time to care for such trivialities, waiting.

"What makes you think they won't just kill us?" Donna says again, looking around as she sweeps a hand through her hair. Nanowoven, color-shifted to a dirty blond that suits her slim, carefully dressed business-formal figure. Even now, she's chosen something somewhat impractical—a tightly woven suit to show off her figure, combined with dark blue high heels.

"Well, we did get a Contract. And you've got a pair of shields on you. You should be fine," I say, shaking my head. "I'm still curious why it's you and not anyone else."

"Why the woman?"

"Why the Lawyer?"

"Ah, because of my Skills. Contract, Detect Motive, Detect Truth, Confidentiality Agreement, Binding Oath," Donna chants. "All potentially of use in a discussion like this."

"Way I understand the way these things go, there's rarely an agreement on the first meeting," I counter.

She bobs her head. "True. But this is the second one. And I did volunteer."

"Oh?" I raise an eyebrow, surprised.

"I can assess usefulness as much as anyone. Charles is needed for the planning, administration, and running. He also has the greatest support from the Artisans," she stumbles a little at the last word, unused to the term I've introduced. "And Trevor manages our defense. I fill the gaps. This. This is a gap."

"I'd hope we are more than that," a voice calls out before I can answer her. The voice is low and growly, holding a trembling timbre that a human voice might get after a twenty-pack-a-day habit. The speaker is just as much a surprise—a humanoid-looking foxhound walking on two feet toward us in a single-breasted tunic that extends to his knees in gold and brown.

Stafin (Level 34 Adjunct)

HP: 270/270

MP: 1080/1080

Condition: None

"Stafin," I say, inclining my head, at the same time sending a thought to Ali while Donna makes her own introduction. *"A single name?"*

"Common among his people for commoners. They get another name for each notable clan that accepts them into their inner pack, or if they do something worthy among his people," Ali explains.

"I have been requested to guide you forthwith. If you will…" Stafin gestures, big, soulful eyes fixed on us.

We glance at one another then nod, walking forward. After much discussion, we've kept our party small. If they do attack us, keeping Donna alive will be hard enough, never mind anyone else.

As we head deeper, I take the time to study the changes the Uvrik corporation has made to their side of the city. While their drones cluster around us, none of them seem particularly aggressive, most docked in the numerous charging stations added to buildings. In addition, I note that a number of the buildings have widened windows, glass removed and allowing the ever-present winds to blow through. Though I do note the slightest shimmer in front of those windows, which speaks of a secondary environmental shielding system to keep out rain and debris.

"Uvrik corp—are they all shifters like Stafin?" I ask Ali, realizing I never did check. Never really thought about it, since the fighters we deal with are, as usual, a wide-ranging mixture of Galactic races. And shifters are part of our culture, so they're likely sources of bad Mana translation too.

"They aren't shifters. They only have one form—and not all of them have the same form. The people you've been fighting, most of them are from the same planet. The Uvrik originate from the planet of Izu, where genetic modification is the norm. They've been mixing and matching genes, altering their base code such that if it wasn't for the System, they probably couldn't even reproduce normally," Ali says, shaking his head. *"That's why they've got so many different forms."*

"Weird. What's with the lack of glass?"

While I hold my mental conversation, Donna is engaging Stafin in a war of words, fishing for knowledge. It's not a bad try, and listening to the pair verbally spar, I realize how damn far behind I am in some areas. But hey, I can punch out an elephant these days, so we all have our strengths.

"They've got all the enhanced senses and enhanced musculature that extensive gene alterations give you. Without the glass, they get to smell and hear more, giving them better awareness through the city."

I can see that. Lana, for example, has extended senses over and above what an increase in Perception would offer. I've more than once noted her using those senses to spot monsters or unexpected guests early, saving us from injury or embarrassment in equal measure. Having no fixed address might seem free and easy and fun, but it also means that we catch our private time when we can.

"So how come you decided to chat with us? Thus far, the Kingdom has been a little on the slow side," I ask in a break during the conversation between Donna and Stafin. My bluntness gets a look from Donna, but she keeps quiet.

"They will not answer," Stafin says, shaking his head.

"Oh…?" Donna steps in, arching an eyebrow.

I'm sure she's wondering, like me, why he'd feed us such valuable information. Or perhaps it's a lie, but if so, it's a stupid lie. Then again, if he's right, it's possible that that information doesn't have any real value since we'll learn of it soon enough.

"We attempted to speak with them concerning the city when they first arrived," Stafin says.

"And you didn't try to talk to us?" Donna says softly, though I can tell there's a bit of an edge to it.

"At that time, the consensus was that it was unnecessary," Stafin says, tilting his head toward me. "The appearance of the Redeemer in the last few days has altered the strategic environment."

Well, that partly explains things. Not that we hadn't figured it was something like that. Or that they'll probably want to end up negotiating some form of access to my settlements. If they're playing fair. On the other hand, it's possible they've got other considerations. Thoughts about the potential reasons why I'm coming along and what our negotiation options are in light of this information keep me occupied till we're led onto the roof of a parking garage.

What used to be a parking lot has been partly enclosed with force shields, all the vehicles removed, and the grey concrete cleared and replaced with white marble. What used to be dark and dingy sparkles with mana-imbued lighting that provides an open-air feeling. Only a few things—like the entrances and the sloping ramps—give a hint of what the building used to be used for.

The entirety of the roof of the parking lot has been transformed into an open air meeting area with green grass, small shrubbery, and comfortable lounging chairs. The grass itself looks familiar but subtly different, enough that I spend a moment assessing it. Seated in three of the seats are the heads of the Uvrik corporation in Calgary. The first is another dog-like variation, a weird mixture of beagle and huskie with long, drooping ears and an elegant pointed face. The second looks like one of those fish from the deep crossed with a particularly hairy caterpillar—a creature of angles, fangs, and nightmarish bristles with hands. And the third is the most "human," if you ignored the extra pair of mammaries, the swivelling antenna, and the cascading greenish-purple hair.

Donna halts—and I admit, so do I—at the sight of the trio, our poor human brains attempting to process the peculiarity before us. Whether it's due to a higher exposure to weirdness or just a higher Willpower, I find myself striding forward and extending a hand. For the first time, I kind of regret that the aliens have to, by common Galactic courtesy, use our greeting methods—I'm not looking forward to touching the spider-fish thing.

"John Lee," I say, shaking hands as I'm introduced around.

Donna approaches and greets them as well, failing to suppress a shudder as she touches the creature of oceanic nightmares.

Rikard (Level 46 Urban Planner)
HP: 370/370
MP: 1280//1280
Condition: Trimark Link

Uwa Bima, Lord of the Sixty Third Chase of Balump (Level 17 Barrister)
HP: 670/670
MP: 1780//1780
Condition: Trimark Link

Quatta (Level 3 Security Consultant)

HP: 820/820

MP: 930//930

Condition: Trimark Link

"Trimark Link?"

"Similar to your Two are One. Except shared across multiple individuals. They're all hooked up to two others."

Smart. I'm actually happy to note they took such actions. It means they're taking us seriously.

"Redeemer. Ms. Luff. Thank you for coming to speak with us. Do you care for refreshments?" Uwa the fish-spider takes the lead, a small thing I absently note.

Pity I didn't have much time to study their culture and whether his taking the lead means they're taking this seriously or if it's just the way things work for them. After all, even on Earth, in certain cultures, the boss doesn't speak much, working through their assistants for all but the most important bits. We quickly decline their hospitality, not just because of potential poison but because their idea of snacks is eclectic. Wasabi peas, dried shrimp, and raw, unsliced cucumbers aren't exactly business meeting food.

"Lord Bima or Lord Uwa?" I send to Ali, unsure of how to answer him.

"Neither. Just Uwa. That's not a noble name, just a title."

"Well, I'm sure you've all read the offer," Donna says now that the initial pleasantries are over. Among the earlier correspondence passed was our one-page ceasefire offer.

"Yes. I believe you Americans prefer a blunt answer?" Before we can correct him, Uwa's already continuing. "A peace settlement on your terms is unacceptable. The City Core we hold has already cost us a significant amount of resources."

"But that cost is a sunk cost," Donna says, leaning forward on the lounging chair. "Continued war will increase such cost, with little return."

"But the cost to you is high as well. In addition, control of a City Core provides significant non-Credit advantages," Uwa retorts.

I watch the pair spar, arguing for a few more minutes about what, to me, seems an obvious conclusion. They're willing to do this, or else there's no point in dragging us out here. Irritated, I fiddle with my inventory, pulling out some chocolate. I pop a piece into my mouth, only to get a slight smile from Rikard.

"Did our food not suit your needs?" Rikard asks, drawing the attention of the other three.

I swallow the chocolate, refusing to look at Donna's glare. "Nothing like that. Call it a bad habit for when I get bored."

"Bored?" Quatta breathes, her voice high and pitchy.

"Yeah. I'm not a big fan of arguing over what seems to be a given. You guys are willing to sue for peace. The question is, what do you want? Just tell us, rather than talking in circles."

"But we are negotiating…" Uwa pauses, eyes focused a few feet in front of him. "Ah. I see. You are even more blunt than expected. I shall have to update our protocols."

Donna hisses, waving her hands slightly while shooting me a glare. "Please, Mr. Uwa, don't base your protocols on John. He is unusual even for us humans."

I grunt, refusing to apologize or back down from my initial question. "So?"

"Very well. We are willing to stop aggressive actions against you. The corporation is not willing to expand hostilities with the Kingdom, and as such, we do not agree to aid you in attacking them. We will give up the City Core, giving you majority control of the city, but require adequate compensation. That includes land in your settlements, Redeemer," Uwa says.

"How much land?"

"Well, that is a matter to be negotiated." Uwa seems to straighten in his chair, frills and hair tucking closer to his body.

"Arse," I mutter but don't protest any further, gesturing for Donna to take over. Even I'm not dumb enough to think that we won't have to talk about this a bit. Still, being the dumb, impatient hick means that this entire conversation had sped up more than I could have reasonably expected.

The negotiation continues between Uwa and Donna, the pair starting with the number of settlements then switching to specific settlements, lot sizes, building types, addresses, and more. Even I can tell that there are details that will need more time, more research to be completed. The fact that a good portion of this discussion includes my settlements also means that my people will need to get involved.

The conversation takes hours, and in the meantime, I'm giving Rikard and Quatta a lesson in proper meeting foods. Cheese, crackers, a wide variety of chocolates, and pork rinds appear as we talk.

Uwa and Donna call it as the day gets closer to the end. There are too many details to finish by themselves, but at least for now, a broad agreement has reached. As such, the trio leads us to the exit.

That's when I grab my chance to ask a question that has been bugging me. "Why did you agree?"

"A simple calculation about the return on investment across the options provided. With your current settlements, especially Vancouver with its dungeon, we expect to see a significant return in the future for much lower on-going expenses if we can reach an agreement. If this agreement is successful, upper management has indicated that we might be willing to negotiate for additional locations," Uwa says. "Obviously, that would depend on your continued expansion and success."

"Of course."

"Careful there, boy-o. That's how the Yerrick lost. They kept giving out land, and they eventually found themselves bought out of their own cities."

"I remember," I say while smiling and saying goodbye. After all, there's no guarantee that that is what the Uvrik corporation is actually considering. And pigs may fly.

Chapter 8

You'd think that something already agreed upon in principle would be fast to negotiate. Even with everyone's earnest desire to get this done, the final peace treaty took weeks to complete. And that's with significant cribbing by Kim and Ali from other Galactic agreements and Donna's 24/7 work ethic. The woman even Leveled twice during the entire process. But in the end, we had a signed and vetted agreement that covered timing, penalties, land trades, Credit payments, tax exemptions, and more. Frankly, if we hadn't used the Shop to get the entire thing vetted by a third-party Galactic Barrister, I'd have been afraid to sign it.

During this entire time, the Kingdom refused to talk to us. In fact, the little goblin-asses picked up the tempo of their attacks, forcing us to deploy even more people to their border. Since the damn halflings are refusing to talk to us and the Uvrik already know about me, there's little reason for me to stay hidden any further. It's even likely they've bought enough information from the Shop that they know I'm here. Finally, the council let me loose. That, of course, brought its own problems, including a couple of targeted ambushes. All those attacks were beginning to feel a little personal, but at the same time, it's kind of hard to get really angry at people who are, like, three and a half feet tall. But trust me, they sure do try.

Which of course leads us to today and the attack we've planned. Now that we have a peace agreement in place with the Uvrik and no contact with the Kingdom, it's time for us to finish this. Which leaves me on this blasted street, fighting off another damn swarm of halflings.

"Get. Off. Me," I snarl, kicking and punting the halfling through the air.

I send a burst of projectile fire after the spinning body, and the impacts of the explosive projectiles throw the body on a new, bloody trajectory. Even as my attacker falls away, another little bastard charges me with a tiny serrated knife and plunges it into Sabre's beleaguered thigh armor.

"Chain Fireball," a voice intones behind me, all the warning I get before a sphere twice the size of a basketball flashes past me and splits into five smaller spheres which head off in different directions and explode. The explosion throws me and the swarm of halflings apart, making Sabre's damage board flash red all over.

"Arse," I snap, dragging the poor mecha back into my inventory with a thought.

Two hours into our attack on the Kingdom and my trusty mecha has seen better days. A part of me notes that it'll likely come back with additional resistances against edged and fire damage, while another points out that there's a reason why the previous version of the PAV had easily replaceable armor parts. It's going to be weeks before Sabre is back in action.

"You good?" Chetan says, his Indian accent coming through even more clearly under stress, his fingers shifting as he hand-casts a healing spell on me.

Dealing with the Mages from Seattle is frustrating, since none of us are coordinated in our actions or decisions. I hate fighting with new people, but they've been assigned to me since they're a decent stopgap while my team provides heavier firepower.

"Warning first, damn it!" I snarl.

When Chetan taps his ear, I realize the helmet is too damaged to transmit and I do a quick swap with another copy before repeating my angry answer.

Chetan Patel (Level 8 Life Mage)

HP: 301/340

MP: 1733/2830

Conditions: Gaia's Embrace, Anaerobic Surplus, Mana Drip

"Sorry about that," Daniel says as he walks up.

I glance back at the Vietnamese-born mage who—thanks to the gene editing purchase—stands shoulder-to-shoulder with me. Swirling around him are small fire elementals. I've seen those fire elementals flash forward and intercept beam attacks and rubble, absorbing attacks and leaving Daniel untouched.

"We needed them clear," Daniel says. "The colonel has new orders for us. We're needed at 45 St and 8th Ave. Southwest for both."

Daniel Nguyen (Level 11 Fire Conjurer)

HP: 237/280

MP: 2803/3400

Conditions: Embrace of the Sun, Mana Drip, Roving Flames

"That's right across the city!" I grumble, my map updating with the new directions. Our scouts, who've backtracked since we got held up by this ambush, wave us forward, and we comply. "Which idiot decided to name everything using numbers and compass directions?"

I get a shrug from the two Mages who match my pace. Thankfully for them, we're forced to keep to a slower pace as our scouts try to get us around the fiercest of the fights. That, according to the damn colonel, isn't my job. No, I'm just a giant transportation machine. Pulling a beam rifle from my inventory after a thought, I keep my eyes swivelling left and right in search of threats the scouts might have missed—or who, like the ambush party, moved in our direction since they left.

"We getting reinforcement for our team?" Chetan pants, his Stamina obviously not up to snuff. Running and fighting as much as we have done has obviously taught him to sink more points into Constitution the next time he Levels.

"No idea. Why don't you ask?" Daniel suggests sweetly.

Chetan grimaces, knowing that he'd get another "we're working on it" answer. "We're Mages damn it, not tanks. We're DPS at best, long-range support. They could have at least given us Mike."

I grin, recalling the overweight programmer who had classed in as a Druid. The first time we released him, Mike had been in his dire bear form, a minibus-sized transformation that smashed its way through the Kingdom's hardest strong point via brute strength.

"How's your Mana?" Lancer 3's voice cackles in my ear.

I admit, I had to giggle a little internally when he was first introduced to me as my point of contact. I'll admit it's juvenile, but calling the soldiers by Lancer 6 or Lancer 3 or the like just made me smile. "Okay."

"Numbers."

"Five eighty-seven and increasing."

"Get it up to at 750 at least. We need you to open the Portal at 14 and 33rd, then we'll need another Portal to the Saddledome from Westbrook Mall once the teams have done mop-up there. Coordinates are being updated on your map."

I nod, reaching to my Mana Bracer and pulling out another fifty or so Mana. That should easily put me in the range they need before we reach them. Unfortunately, I'm realizing just how little an additional three hundred Mana is in such a long battle. "Do we join the mop-up?"

"If it's not complete yet, yes. We need those troops over at the Saddledome."

"And me?"

The Saddledome is where nearly half of our imported forces are. The high Level Basics and any Advanced fighters we brought are locked into a battle to free the dome and the City Core from the Kingdom. Unfortunately, the Kingdom seems to have dumped a ton of money into defenses on those buildings—never mind how big they are naturally—and our people have been bogged down.

"We'll let you know. Over," Lancer 3 says curtly.

"That—" I begin, then realize he's already left. If he was talking to me directly, things must be urgent. A quick mental switch and I'm on the team's frequency. "Let's pick up the pace."

***

We come in on 13th Ave to see Westbrook Mall wreathed in flames, the northern half crushed and mostly rubble. Explosions, gouts of flame, and a cyclone of debris greet us, the roar of spells, Skills, and explosives drowning out most of the screams as we hit 37th St. Most.

"Where's the team?" Chetan asks, panting a little as we come to a stop.

"Get your asses under cover." Wride fades in from the shadows near the corner, his crossbow held loosely in his arms, green army fatigues somehow blending in even in the grey concrete. We scramble to take cover, reminded to do so now that we aren't running headlong, as he says, "Our targets are inside. The damn halfies are fighting inside the mall and blowing it up as our people push them back."

Elliot Wride (Level 44 Apprentice Ranger)

HP: 1788/2300

MP: 450/450

Conditions: Urban Spirit, System Shadow, Eagle Eye

I crane my neck around, getting a hiss from Wride, but I ignore him. Anyone who wants to take a potshot at me will have to get through my restored Soul Shield. Still, I don't hang my head out too long.

"We've got to get to them," I say.

"Jess is scouting it now," Wride says. A moment later, our maps update, new route markers appearing. I frown, staring at them, which makes Wride stop from moving off. "What?"

"We're going around," I say.

"Yes. We're going to flank the halfies," Wride says as he tilts his head to stare directly at me. "Is that a problem?"

Dots move on my minimap, red and blue, enemies and friendlies. I can see the force concentrations, the numbers. Hell, I can even see where the damn halflings are on the map. A few explosives into the wall, Lightning Strike, Chain Fireballs, and then a Blink Step in would finish this, with less of our people down. I could finish this fight in a minute. But then I'd have blown half of my remaining Mana and probably lose my Soul Shield, which would require me to refresh it, which would put me well below what Wier needs me for.

"Nothing." I grit my teeth, shaking my head.

It pisses me off, not being able to help more. I feel helplessness as I condemn some of the fighters within to death just so that we can throw the survivors into the grinder again a few seconds later.

Miners nods then pops up, checking out the surroundings before he takes off, slipping from cover to cover in full view of us. I know he's doing it to let us know where to move, annoying as it might be to be schooled like this. But he's the expert. I just kill things.

****

By the time we get to the mall's southern entrance, Jess has disarmed the traps laid across the entrance, dealt with the pair of watchers they kept out, and found us an entrance. Even as we slip in, I have to admire the Advanced Level Ranger and his effectiveness. The man might not be as tough in a stand-up fight as I am, but damn is he good at his job.

Together, Miners and Jess move ahead of us even as the sound of battle approaches. Within seconds, we're in our ambush spots, the pair highlighting our positions in our maps. Not a moment too soon since the first of the halflings appear a moment later. Jess has us hold our fire even as the halflings take position a bare twenty meters ahead of us.

Absently, I twist the beam rifle in my hand, debating which spells I could use as I eye my designated zone of fire. The journey takes just over three minutes, returning another three hundred or so Mana to me. That's good enough for a Blink Step in close and then Blade Strikes. Or an Inferno Beam into the biggest cluster. They're too spread out for Lightning Strike to be particularly cost effective. I could Mud Wall them, but that'd be hard to move through later, so I nix that idea.

My thoughts are interrupted as the halflings lay down covering fire, another group rushing toward their prepared positions. I grin, knowing that Chetan's spell and Kelly's Skill are still hiding us from their own sensors.

"Now!" Jess snaps over the comms.

There's just over fifteen halflings in front of us, most having barely gotten themselves under cover before we let loose. A beam of white-hot fire flies from my hands as Wride holds down the trigger on his crossbow, bolts slamming through the bodies of the halflings and piercing their defenses. Jess uses a more traditional assault rifle, System-registered bullets tearing into their backs. In his corner, Daniel goes for something a little more cinematic, an elemental fire wyrm that comes to life and whips around to lay waste to the halflings.

The initial shock sees us add a few of the injured to our kill count, but the halflings react well. They spin about, taking cover and returning fire, only to find that their initial attackers are charging them. After a moment, I realize that Jess probably warned the other team too, letting them coordinate with us. Rather than stand and fight, the halflings break, charging us in a mad scramble that our combined firepower is insufficient to stem. A few harried minutes later, with me resorting to my blade as the last couple manage to get into melee distance, we're done.

The rescued team has barely caught their breath before I've got the Portal open to send them to their next fight. Ten seconds after that, we're on the road again, feet slapping asphalt as we head to our next objective.

It's not the kind of fight I like. But as I glance at the ground we've gained and the kill count Ali has been quietly updating, I realize it might be the kind of fight we need.

***

"All right, Redeemer," Lancer 3's voice comes an hour and a half later as I get ready to open another Portal for a group of weary fighters. I'd have done it already, but they needed a moment to sort themselves out. "You're cleared to follow the squad."

"To the Saddledome?" I say slightly incredulously. Finally!

"Yes. There's an obstacle your particular Skills are needed for," Lancer 3 says. I make a mental note to look at his Status and get his name next time. "You will be briefed when you arrive."

"Got it," I say, waving to the group around me.

A quick briefing and a shuddering passage through the Portal later, we're a block and a half away from the Saddledome. The other team starts down a side street with their own orders while we follow the updated map details on ours.

The Saddledome is huge, a multi-hall complex that hosted the Calgary Stampede and other giant conventions. It's not a single building, though the largest one has multiple halls that are joined together, allowing access internally. Even so, when we get through the entrance and spend ten minutes jogging, I'm pretty sure it's never been this big.

"What the hell? This place wasn't this big at FanExpo!" Chetan mutters.

"FanExpo?"

"Stan Lee signing."

"Nerd," Ali crows before he waves. "It's a City Center building that's been modified with a minor pocket dimension."

"A pocket dimension?" Daniel squeaks.

"A minor one. Relax," Ali says nonchalantly. "Come on, you think my team wouldn't be able to blast our way through your tiny building by now?"

Chetan grunts, saving his breath while Jess and Wride wave us onward. Our passage through the empty, gaping hallways is only marked by the appearance of corpses, combat damage, and the occasional unexploded trap.

Oh yeah, traps. There are a lot of them. Everything from the classic pitfall to chaos mines, walls filled with high-explosives and ball-bearings and automated laser turrets. Most of them are destroyed, but a few have reset by now, which we either avoid or just destroy again. It's annoying and occasionally painful, but it doesn't take too long before we catch up with the vanguard.

The army boys make up the majority of the fighters here, most of them split up into groups of four and hanging together in a squad of two teams. Or in some cases, what's left of two teams. The non-military personnel are more loosely organized, but even then, they mostly hang out in their parties.

"Miss me?" I say, sliding into the space next to a familiar redhead resting against a wall around the corner from the fight.

She cracks open an eye then grins weakly. Next to her, Anna lies, fur singed and missing two legs. I frown, eyeing the fox with mild concern. Anna was pretty old when she was first picked up by Lana, and the last year has added streaks of white to her light red fur.

"John." Lana's voice is filled with relief and exhaustion at the same time. She hands me a thermos filled with coffee, which I swig quickly after dropping my helmet, the Skill-produced nectar of the gods automatically adding a small Stamina and Mana buff.

"Thanks."

"About time," Sam grumbles from his spot a short distance away. He's leaning up against the wall, fiddling with a drone in his hands as he attempts to fix it. He seems completely oblivious to the fact that they've been stuck in the same spot for the last twenty minutes.

"Mikito?" I say as I search for the diminutive Japanese woman. On the other hand, I do spot Laila with her afro and her team.

"Down the other hallway with Carlos," Lana says. "They've got this menagerie there which has a never-ending supply of monsters, it seems. They're desperate for healers."

"Oh, I don't get an inquiry?" Ingrid says.

I jump slightly, adrenaline from hours of fighting leaving my nerves slightly overstrung. It's only a small portion of my lizard brain that remembers she's a friend, allowing me not to put my fist through her smirking face.

"Gotcha," Ingrid adds.

"Funny. And that's why I didn't ask," I say. "So I hear you need me?"

"I do. If you're done with catching up with your friends," Captain Angus Tyrell says sarcastically from a few feet down, hunched over clear air with his aides. Of course, I know they're actually staring at a shared display, one I'm not privy to.

I flash the captain a smile as I walk over, eyeing soldier-boy and noting the damage on his suit. Good, not someone who leads from the back. "What can I do for you?"

"There's a chasm in the other room. There used to be a bridge, but they destroyed it when we arrived. Attempts at fording the bridge have met stiff resistance. We need you to cause a disruption while opening a Portal for our men," Captain Tyrell says while indicating exactly where he'd like that Portal on the 3D map he's shared with me. "We'll be supporting you the best we can, but you'll need to handle most of the fighting yourself to begin with."

I grimace, eyeing the thirty or so dots. A quick thought and Ali highlights the Advanced Class fighters in the group, flashing me their details. I'm a bit grateful he's removed their names for now, those details not something I require.

Gale Mage (Level 17)

HP: 303/320

MP: 2103/2480

Conditions: Shield of Air, Wind Blades, Mana Drip

Medjay Warrior (Level 29)

HP: 2868/3110

MP: 983/1080

Conditions: Body of Stone, Millicent's Ever Healing Remedy, Sense of Shifting Sands

Tagma Rider (Level 7)

HP: 1455/1480

MP: 988/1070

Conditions: Linked Mount, Health of the Many

3rd Bone Ranger (Level 6)

HP: 1577/1680

MP: 781/990

Conditions: Dimensional Sight, Air Sense, Mana Drip, Wqq's Blessing

Four Advanced Fighters. None of their Conditions are particularly surprising, mostly buffs for their abilities, regeneration or defensive spells or Skills. Nothing extraordinary, but there are four of them. Three of which are melee fighters. I exhale then blink as first green, then purple light washes over me, my own conditions updating as the nearby spellcasters throw buffs on me too.

Haste

Mana Drip

Yeller's Patented Kinetic to Blood Regeneration

Plot Armor

…

The buffs keep coming, but after a while, I stop looking at them and focus on the way the changes make me feel while keeping an eye on my Mana. I'm nearly topped up and my health has never been better. Other than a quick swap of armor, I'm about as ready as I can be. I could spend the time assessing if the spellcasters are coordinating properly or just trust that they aren't clashing their buffs, canceling each other out. After all, certain types of Skills and spells actually clash in their properties and it isn't always the "better" Skill that stays in effect.

As I exhale and pop my head around the corner again, the conversation with Ali pops back into mind.

"No such thing as infinite buffs, boy-o. On average, you can get about three buffs for each of your secondary attributes, like Mana or Health. The first ups the related attribute, the second the regeneration, and the last the actual value. Spells or castable Skills that try to affect the same thing will often conflict unless the spellcaster is good. Or the Skill's particularly unique.

'That doesn't include passives of course. So your skill Body's Resolve won't clash with another regeneration spell, but a second spell of the same kind could if it was an active type. Of course, if you tried to get a second passive Skill, chances are you'd definitely clash. If you want, there's a bunch of research on it, including the specific combinable Spells and Skills. But you ain't a real spellcaster and…"

A hand slips into mine, pulling me back from my memories. I turn to see Lana holding it, giving it a gentle squeeze.

"Worried?" she asks.

"Nope." A single raised eyebrow and I chuckle softly. "Fine. Just a bit. It's been a while since..."

"Yeah." Lana nods. She understands. It's been a while since I did something this stupid. But there's no one else, is there? And so, what is is. She kisses my helmet on the side before she drops down again. "You're wasting your buffs. Boy-o."

I chuckle softly and take the gentle ribbing as the encouragement it is before nodding to the captain to indicate I'm ready. A second later, my backup opens up. Sam's drones sweep out first, laying down smoke and beam weapon fire. A few seconds later, the rifle squads who have been hunkering down and trading potshots open up, tearing into their opponents, soon joined by the spellcasters who have been conserving Mana. We stream into the cavern, taking cover under the portable shields and mobile armor that litter our side of the chasm. For a moment, I take it all in, the metallic floor and walls, the cavernous drop-off with its ill-lit bottom, and the defenders on the opposite side, a bare two hundred meters away. Then I act.

Blink Step. Maximum range, five hundred meters. An easy flicker, especially as Ali has swung high to give me an even better vantage point, one not obscured by the growing wall of smoke. My first target would be the Mage, but an anti-teleport formation that Ali spots makes that impossible. So I pop into being right behind the Bone Ranger crouched over a metallic wall and firing his repeating beam rifle. It's a simple thing to extend a foot into his bottom and let physics take over. The Ranger's yelp of surprise makes me grin even as he flails and falls into the cavern. I doubt he'll die, but out of the fight is just as good a result for now.

A polearm flashes, a blade cleaving through my Soul Shield to be stopped an inch into my shoulder. My eyes wide, I jerk aside even as my attacker rips the weapon away, his hands burning from a damage reflection buff. I keep dodging, my Soul Shield forming around the torn hole even as the pair of Advanced Fighters close in on me. The Medjay is tall, nearly our size, with a pair of javelins in hand and long, sweeping hair. The Tagma is a stocky halfling female wielding a beam-pistol-and-sabre combo.

A hand twists as my eyes lock on the empty point of space the captain requested. A moment later, a tear in space appears, a black hole that offers nothing. Before I can rejoice, I'm grabbed by invisible hands and thrown into the sky. A moment later, a javelin is thrown at me, smashing into my Soul Shield, then it defies common sense as it hangs suspended in air, spinning and drilling into my Soul Shield.

"Lightning Strike, boy-o!" Ali cries as he swoops forward in front of my hands.

Hands slammed together, I call forth my spell, electricity playing along the crowd, attacking the Kingdom's men even as Ali channels his own Affinity through it, upgrading the damage. We sweep the attack across the ground before finding our angle of attack changing abruptly. A moment later, vertigo.

"What the…?" I snarl then realize that the air grip has thrown me over the chasm before releasing me. Before I lose sight of the Portal, I trigger Blink Step to pop back into the air and get ready to re-engage.

Left alone by himself, Ali floats, exposed. Already, spells arc toward the Spirit, who is dodging into the chasm while attempting to fade out of existence.

As gravity takes me back down, I land in a crouch, feet flexing as I soak up my initial momentum, knees aching from the impact. The Soul Shield lasts for a fraction of a second longer before another beam rips into it. A javelin pierces my chest a moment later. I fall backward even as the javelin tears through my body and exits, flying back into the Medjay Warrior's hand. Before he can attack me again, a pair of halflings dogpile my crouching form, blocking his attack.

Since I lost sight of my Portal, it snaps closed to the accompaniment of a loud scream. Even as I roll and buck off my little assailants as they stab me with poison and frost-coated weapons, I'm calling forth the Mana needed to open a second Portal. A twist and flip gets me to my feet, one of the halflings behind my back.

A bone-shuddering thud from behind is accompanied by a flash of orange and black. Roland at least made it through, and the halfling's body crunches under his massive teeth. A second later, the second Portal snaps open, just to the side of where a Marine crouches, firing his repeating beam rifle as he bleeds from the stumps of his feet.

"Chain Fireball!"

The screamed warning has me throwing myself forward, ending up behind the Portal as the flaming sphere traverses the chasm. Insane or not, more of our people throw themselves through the Portal into the middle of the exploding flames. Entire rifle teams exit and take station, the few healers—or designated healers—doing their best to buff the front-line fighters. Ingrid appears from the shadows, wreathed in fire, to tackle the Medjay Warrior while Jess and Miners bully the Tagma Rider. I take a moment to recover from getting cooked. Again.

"Keep the Portal up. We're nearly done," the captain's voice cackles over the communicator.

I grit my teeth and nod, layering a newly generated Soul Shield over my form while taking potshots with my beam rifle. I can't afford to take my eyes off the Portal again, so I keep my help to the minimum. But the team doesn't need it. Lana and puppies charge out of the Portal to smash apart the last resistance at the hallway exit. With our people inside their lines, the tide of battle turns. More and more of our men stream in, the Kingdom personnel unable to slow us down. And just like that, the fight is pretty much over, support personnel streaming in seconds later through the Portal.

"So, magic school bus, how you doing?" Ali says over our mental connection.

"Magic school bus?"

"What? You're yellow and transport children around."

I pause, considering if I should be insulted or proud to be compared to a classic children's book. Wait. No. Insulted. Very much so. "Go roll in some Goblin shit."

"That's my boy-o." Ali chuckles, floating up from the chasm. He's literally smoking, damage from spells having pulled his Mana-imbued form apart.

"Why all the racist shit lately?" I say, stretching.

"No reason." Ali flashes me a smile. There's something in it that I don't understand but nags at my intuition. For all that he's an annoyance, his sense of humor tends toward the bizarre and perverted, not racist and hurtful. Which makes his recent actions weird.

"Mr. Lee," Angus speaks a moment later, making me look up. "Colonel Wier says you may continue to work with us or proceed with the additional deployment of our troops."

"He's giving me a choice?" I say.

Lana snorts, walking over to me as she stares at the hole in my chest armor, the skin beneath already patched up. "The colonel knows you need to Level too."

"Ah." I consider the offer. "I'll stay with you guys. If there's nothing else, I'll join the vanguard."

"That—" Angus shuts up, deciding not to protest further.

Dangerous or not, the vanguard is where the experience is. Flashing him a grin, I trot forward, Lana following me, flanked by the puppies.

Time to finish this then.

Chapter 9

"Where to next?" Lana asks a day later.

We're curled up on a couch in a newly purchased building in Calgary, one that we picked up from our earnings in the fight. Down the hallway, Ingrid and Mikito each have their own apartments while Sam's taken over the caretaker's place and the parking lot beneath for his drones. Last I saw, the older man was muttering something about upgrading Mikito's PAV further.

"Mmmm… I'm not sure," I say softly. "Things have cooled down for the Americans in Washington. Or heated up. There's a new entrant and it's messing up everyone. So Wier's been ordered to take things a bit slower." I let that topic die before I continue. "How're our settlements?"

"Your settlements," Lana says, prodding me in the short ribs.

"Yeah, yeah. We've got a rough outline for a government. I'll get Ali to send it to you. Basically, a constitutional monarchy, with a steward, captain of guard, generals, and the rest. The administration of cities will be left to the self-elected city councils, with those under me as a check against them. There'll be a series of individuals, roaming judges if you will, who can override decisions and mete justice out too. But we'll mostly let the cities do their thing. And once all this is done…"

"You'll give it up?"

"Yup." My lips twist in a half-smile. "Any other form is much harder to dissolve."

"You're asking people to trust you to give it back," Lana says softly, eyes fixed on me.

"And you know what they say about power…" Ali cackles from his corner where he's watching his latest binge TV show. As far as I know, he's currently on a *Dr. Who* binge—including the lost seasons. I'm a bit confused about what those are, but really, that confusion is the least of my problems.

"I know," I say. "We're working on options to give you people a way around this. But I don't think it'll matter in time."

"Oh…?" Lana arches an eyebrow.

I kiss her, just because she looks so damn good that way.

When I pull away, she murmurs, "Stop changing the subject."

"Just a premonition about the future."

When I refuse to elaborate, Lana drops the topic and answers my original question. "Vancouver's doing well. We're well on the way to meeting the Large Town requirements. The land purchase requirement is the problem. We're trying to balance it with development in Burnaby to get it up to a Town level, but it's still only at eighty-three percent right now. The parks are a tough nut to crack, but we're getting there. New West, Richmond, and Surrey are next up, though Surrey seems like they're going to get there by themselves.

"As for Kamloops and Kelowna, they're both Towns, as you know. No real chance of them becoming Large Towns, not without a larger population…" Lana sighs and I nod. That isn't possible until we can direct more people to them. With a minimum of twenty thousand population and a ninety-eight percent land purchase requirement, the Large Town status isn't even worth considering.

"Sounds like things are in hand," I say softly. "And the scattered other settlements?"

"We've pulled everyone who is willing to come out. There are still holdouts but…" Lana shrugs, and I have to agree with her. There's not much we can do about those.

"What are we doing with the production spot for Vancouver?"

"Who knows? The damn Artisans keep arguing among themselves, so nothing's happening. If I hear how 'innovation is the only way forward' one more time," Lana growls softly. "Why do you think I made my way out here?"

I chuckle, giving the woman a squeeze. "Thank you."

"You're welcome. So. Where next?"

I sigh, rubbing my face. My heart says to swing by and clear the prairies and keep going till I hit the Atlantic. Hopefully by that time, there'll be enough people who can help that they'll be able to free the Maritimes. Sense says dealing with the larger, more geographically close cities in the US is a better use of my time. We can free more people faster. Logic… well, hell. I haven't actually looked at the information we have on the cities lately, so focused am I on Calgary and our potential alliances.

"Onward. Always onward."

***

Later that evening, when Lana's finally asleep, I have time to review my status updates. I have to smile slightly at the newly increased Levels, a smile that is wiped away when I recall why exactly I've gained these Levels. I exhale, pushing aside the mild guilt once more. Survivor's guilt, that feeling of not being good enough, of not having sacrificed enough. It's been more than a year now and still it lingers. For all my attempts at being more in touch with my emotions, I have a feeling certain things might continue to exist forever.

Glancing over my Status Screen, I note I've got another free Class Skill Point and nine free attributes to allocate. That's a decent amount for upgrading, which means I should probably spend it. It's strange, but at this point, those nine free points aren't that huge a deal. That last battle was painful and once again showcased the need for more Mana and more Mana

Regeneration. It's one of the many reasons why I avoid picking up more passive Skills—too many of them harm my Mana Regeneration.

That being the case, Intelligence and Willpower seem to be the best bets. Dumping three more points into Intelligence, four into Willpower, and one each into Luck and Perception makes me happy. Now that we've got a larger sample size, I'm pretty sure that increases in Luck increase at the very least the number of Credits I get to take from those I kill. And money is good.

After that, I have to decide what to buy with my last Class Skill Point. And that's a difficult choice. I'm not going to get many more from now on, so rather than make the decision, I put it on hold. Never know what I might need in the future.

Status Screen			
Name	John Lee	Class	Erethran Honor Guard
Race	Human (Male)	Level	46
Titles			
Monster's Bane, Redeemer of the Dead, Duelist			
Health	2120	Stamina	2120
Mana	1660	Mana Regeneration	129/ minute*
Attributes			
Strength	112	Agility	199
Constitution	212	Perception	63
Intelligence	166	Willpower	164
Charisma	18	Luck	33

Class Skills			
Mana Imbue	2	Blade Strike	2
Thousand Steps	1	Altered Space	2
Two are One	1	The Body's Resolve	3
Greater Detection	1	A Thousand blades	1
Soul Shield	2	Blink Step	2
Portal	3	Army of One	1
Sanctum	1	Instantaneous Inventory*	1
Cleave*	2	Frenzy*	1
Elemental Strike*	1 (Ice)	Shrunken Footprints*	1
Tech Link*	2		

Combat Spells	
Improved Minor Healing (II)	Greater Regeneration
Greater Healing	Mana Drip
Improved Mana Dart (IV)	Enhanced Lightning Strike
Fireball	Polar Zone
Freezing Blade	Inferno Strike
Mud Walls	

As dawn breaks, Mikito and I have just finished a round of sparring. Ingrid's on breakfast duty thankfully, while Sam continues to work on replacing his drones. Lana walks out of our bedroom, dressed but distracted as she swings her hand and mutters, working on one of her many projects. As hard as I work on building my combat skills, Lana probably does twice that in handling the various business and settlement interests she's been given.

"What's for breakfast?" Mikito asks, sliding into a seat. She eyes the stacks of omelets and the jars of honey, real butter, and jam, along with links of sausages and bacon. "Oooh, bannock!"

Everyone looks up, realizing what Mikito said. All eyes but Ingrid's alight on the floury goodness on the table, our hands and bodies darting forward. Triggering Blink Step, I snatch four pieces of bannock before popping back to my seat, smirking at Sam, who is only just beginning to go for the fast shrinking pile. My smirk is wiped away a second later when Lana casually takes half of my share directly from my plate. When I move to protest, Lana cheats and uses big, puppy dog eyes on me.

"Thanks," I mutter to Ingrid, eyeing the pot of boiling oil to see if she's making any more. I'm not the only one.

"There's no more," Ingrid answers our unasked question. "You know I have to make these by hand. The Shop's just isn't right."

I grunt, offering her a nod. Personally, I think it's more of a matter of her personal skill at making it rather than the ingredients offered not being up to par. But as I stuff my face, I have to concede that I'm not exactly the expert on this.

"Portaling us back to BC today?" Sam asks when we're all on our second—or in Lana's case, third—plate.

"That's the plan. Most of the fighters need to be back," I say. "Kamloops first, then individual Portals everywhere else."

"You ever going to do the Vancouver dungeon?" Mikito asks.

I grimace with regret. It's rather stupid that I have a dungeon of my own and I haven't even stepped foot into it. "Not yet."

"Well, keep this up and we'll catch up with you," Mikito says, shaking her head. "Not helping anyone if you aren't Leveling. Even another couple of Levels would allow you to extend your Portal range."

"I know," I snap then hold a hand up in apology. I could point out I could extend my Portal range right now, but I want to save that Skill Point like a squirrel with a nut.

Lana quietly pushes some coffee over while I get my irritation back under control. My temper's getting better, but I have to admit, the stress of finding time to do everything is a bit of a killer.

"Nice one," Ingrid says sarcastically, digging a dagger into my emotional vulnerability.

"Sorry, Mikito. Everyone," I say, which gets Ingrid's nod. A sip of coffee—plain coffee, not the magical brew from the Baristas—helps calm me down a little more. "I know I'm letting you guys down. Being the only one with the Skill is a bit stressful. The colonel keeps reminding me not to take risks, but at the same time, I need to be out charting new waypoints and leveling."

"Why can't you buy it for anyone else?" Sam asks, frowning.

"System limit," Ali chimes in, happy to play the know-it-all. "You already know you can't buy a Skill above your Class Skill tier, right? Well, Portal and a lot of the equivalent long-distance teleportation Skills are Advanced Class final tier. Even the spells including the teleportation rituals require at least Advanced Class casters.

"Even if you could get to that Level, you also have the problem of cost. John gets a huge discount because it's his Class—just like you would in yours—but for others, they'd have to pay through the nose. Firstly, because it's an Advanced Class Skill. Then again because it's from a rare Class. Then for the Tier. We're talking hundreds of thousands of Credits."

"But John…?"

"Is a cheat character," Ingrid says, quoting an old friend. "According to the System, he's only at Level 43 Basic, even if he has access to his Advanced Class Skills."

"That's so unfair," Sam mutters, shaking his head.

"Oh please, Mr. Swarm-of-Drones," I say. "You barely get shot at because your drones do the work. And you get more assist experience than anyone I know."

"It is rather useful, isn't it?" Sam says with a smirk.

Before we can start another round of ribbing, a knock on the apartment door interrupts us.

"Come in."

"Mr. Lee." A young man strides in wearing an army uniform, greeting me when I turn to regard him. "Colonel Wier sends his greetings and requests your presence in his office. As soon as possible."

"Is it something urgent?" I frown, tilting my head toward the window.

Lana shakes her head in my peripheral vision, indicating that she hasn't picked out any sign of any large-scale fighting.

"No significant problems from the sensor net."

"Yes, sir. He did mention ASAP," the private says firmly.

I sigh, deciding I won't be getting a third breakfast plate then. I'll survive. "One second."

I turned toward the group and glance at Mikito, who has grown quiet. I make a note to talk to her when I can, just to make sure we're good. Sometimes it's hard to tell, with how quiet she is.

Realizing I've forgotten what I meant to say and can't recall it, I shrug and wave goodbye, using the same gesture to open a Portal. "I'll see you all later."

A moment later, I'm a couple of kilometers away from my apartment, the private dashing through the Portal as Ali snickers and follows. When the Portal snaps closed, I realize no one's in the colonel's office.

"Huh." I frown, opening the office door and striding out.

The private scrambles after me, looking confused. We run into the colonel walking back with a cup of coffee and a breakfast plate balanced in his hands.

"Ah, that was fast. Well done, Private Keel. You're dismissed."

Keel doesn't waste a second, leaving after saluting.

"I take it you Portalled into my command post?" Wier says.

"You did say it was urgent," I say, not at all apologetic.

"Yes. It was. Is," Wier says, gesturing for me to take a seat. "We have news that the Sons of Odin and a few other groups banded together and launched an attack on the Mages' base. They were repulsed, but not without losses. Sit down. The fight has been over for over a day already."

I grunt, sitting while guilt claws at me. I dragged the Mages to Calgary to help us, the entire group being one of the few willing volunteers. Now their people lay dead because those who should have been guarding them were helping me.

"We've already informed the Mages and hastened all preparations for our return to Seattle. However…" The colonel eyes me. "I cannot act against them."

"Why?"

"Politics," Wier says bitterly. "We're not to act against US citizens except in self-defense. The Secretary, the acting president, has issued an order barring direct action against US civilians. My hands are tied."

I grunt, my lips curling in distaste. Stupid orders, at least from my perspective. Except I can see how the Secretary might not want to set the precedent. Still, stupid. "You want me to help."

"I cannot, officially, ask for aid from a foreign power," Wier says softly. "But if my allies were to appear in Seattle and decide to do some scouting ahead of freeing up additional US cities, it would not be inappropriate for them to defend themselves or act humanely if they came across criminal behavior."

Damn weaselly words. But for all that, Wier's sticking his neck out a bit, telling us this and asking for help, albeit obliquely, while indicating he won't act against us. Not that I'd say no to the Mages anyway.

"Fine. But you should have asked my team to come too," I say, standing and waving to create a Portal.

Seconds later, I'm back in my apartment building, to the surprise of my team. Seeing their faces, I brace myself to explain what has happened.

"Right, who wants to go on a road trip?"

***

Staring at the blasted ruins that surround us, pockmarked earthen craters and the burnt remnants of trees and shrubbery, the desperation and scale of the battle fought here is clear. With System-assisted reconstruction, the extent that's still damaged shows that there was even greater destruction before.

"Thanks, John. We'll see you!" Chetan says as he scrambles away.

His reminder of social niceties gets a chorus of agreements and repetitions from the other Mages as they nearly sprint into the buildings, concern written across their faces.

"You're not going?" Carlos says to Daniel, who is still standing with us.

"No. I'll get a report later," Daniel says, his face impassive. "You're our guests, so someone has to show you around."

"That's not necessary," Lana says, shaking her head. "You should be checking on your friends."

"They will be fine. Or not. In either case, it's too late," Daniel explains. "Shall I show you to your quarters?"

"Uhh…" Lana's obviously perturbed.

"Har! Between you and John, we could get a skit going." Ingrid snorts and prods him with her elbow. "Show us the way, Mr. Robot."

"I'm not a robot. I just don't see the fuss about crying over spilt milk," Daniel protests.

When I hear Ingrid tease him again, I tune out the words while gesturing for Mikito to fall to the back with me. Sam, seeing the two of us moving to have a private chat, swings away from the group even as he releases some scouting drones.

"Yes?" Mikito asks.

"Just wanted to apologize again. About snapping," I say, rubbing my nose.

Mikito wrinkles her nose slightly. "It is okay."

She's obviously uncomfortable with me tackling my social faux pas directly. Sometimes, it's hard to navigate the damn cultural channels—when should I not talk about feelings, when should I?

"Right. Good." I nod.

Mikito speeds up, but just before she leaves easy speaking range, she adds, "I'll take it out of you tomorrow morning."

I blink at the tiny Japanese woman and feel a thread of fear run through me. Perhaps her hanging out with Lana and Ingrid is a bad idea.

***

We're in a large meeting room. Charles, Chetan, Daniel, and the rest of the Mages are all clustered around a paper map of the city. On it, pins are placed for all the City Cores, and small, finely painted pewter miniatures indicate the various parties involved.

"A bit old school here, aren't we?" Sam says, eyeing the map.

"You're complaining about how we choose to display our information?" Charles says, staring at Sam.

"You guys are the tech geeks, aren't you? I'd have expected, I don't know, holographic maps. Didn't think you'd be a bunch of luddites," Sam rebuts.

"Hey! We have that in our real—" Chetan says and gets glared down by Charles. Mocha-colored skin flushing, he subsides with an embarrassed grin.

While Chetan is explaining that we're not being allowed into their main conference room, I'm busy picking up some of the miniatures and admiring the paint job. Some are obvious—the infantry trooper for the US Army, the horned Viking helmet for the Sons of Odin, and the chainmail bikini warrior for the women-only group. Others require a little more thought, like the bardic figurine with a lute for the Baristas. Luckily, they've got a little note on the board indicating which piece is what.

"Boys." Lana rolls her eyes. "Are we done yet? What are your plans, Charles?"

Charles nods, tapping the board. "All the figures with a red base belong to an enemy group that we know attacked us. The yellows are those we believe might be supporting these groups, but we aren't sure. Greens are friendlies, of course—"

"Wait, why are greens friendlies? I thought blue was for friendlies?" a portly mage interrupts.

"We agreed on green for friendlies and blue for allies, Steven," Charles says exasperatedly.

"Well, we've got no blues on the board, so we should use blue for friendlies—"

"Steven," Charles says softly, anger tinging his voice. Daniel, beside Steven, elbows the portly man, who finally shuts up. Charles turns to us. "Sorry."

"What do we know about our opponents?" I say while tapping the little Viking figurine.

"Actually, we thought we'd have you talk with this group," Charles says, pointing at a smaller figurine.

I frown, staring at the location before looking at their helpful note. Oh, the suburban group with Desmond. "We can do that."

"Problem?" Charles asks, hearing the uncertainty in my voice.

"Just not used to planning to kill other humans. Well, not much," I say, recalling a few times when I'd done that. But the circumstances were different. Sort of. Maybe it's just that we're looking at a larger group, a bunch of people who used to be plain old middle-class suburban residents.

"If it's too much…"

"No. We're allies," I cut him off but find myself shooting a glance at my team.

Mikito is impassive as ever. Ingrid and Carlos look slightly angry, while Sam is giving his usual stoic expression. By now, I know that's his version of "I'm unhappy, but I understand we're doing this." It's only Lana who looks as uncomfortable as I feel, but Lana gives me a firm nod. For all her empathy, the redhead knows how to push it aside. As for our healer, he just stays silent.

"We're good," I say.

"Thank you. Now, Daniel, your group is going to hit Ethan's group," Charles says.

With our marching orders given, I can keep quiet and watch, remembering the potential areas and stewing in my thoughts. Thoughts which revolve around having to kill humans. When they deserve it or not, I hate this.

"Now remember, we're taking prisoners if we can, but don't risk yourself. Attack only those on the list. A lot of these groups have non-combatants, just like we do, so be careful," Charles says sternly. "I'm leaving it to you all on how to engage your groups, but do your best to keep the casualties down. But don't risk yourself."

A chorus of agreement meets his pronouncement, after which there are a few last things to sort out. The final thing is, of course, the registration of everyone who attacked the Mages on a bounty list, adding them as a potential Quest reward for turning in these attackers. With the Mages' mysterious leadership team going after the strongest group—the Sons of Odin—cleanup of everyone else should be simple enough. When we finally split up, the final "go" time is still to be determined. Just in case our opponents are trying to get that information from the System.

***

"You going to be okay with this?" I ask Sam while Carlos and I lend a helping hand to the Technomancer.

Carlos tilts his head when he hears me speak but doesn't say anything. Unlike us, Carlos has been fighting humanoid sentients for the majority of last year and is also a native, so he's a little more invested.

"I'll survive," Sam grunts. "Higher please."

I comply, lifting the covering of the larger drone higher. "Thought you were going for smaller drones?"

"Just doing some work for their mechanics. My drones are ready," Sam said, rubbing his nose. "There's a Skill called 'Optimization' that I can use if I work on a piece of advanced technology. Keeps the drone running at a seven percent efficiency increase for the next six hours."

"Ah." I nod. "You know, you can skip out on this if it's an issue."

"No. They attacked our allies. We have to hit them. And my drones will provide us more coverage and control of the non-combatants," Sam says. "I'm not happy about this. But it needs to be done."

"They're assholes anyway." At the looks he gets from us, Carlos clarifies. "My friends and I, we were part of Desmond's group for a bit. We quickly found ourselves doing all their dirty jobs—night patrols, corpse cleanup, harvesting. Somehow, the whiter team that joined at the same time never got the same share of work."

"They just assigned you guys?" Sam says.

"Nah. There's always an excuse, you know? Why the schedule changed. Why the other team couldn't do it. Someone got hurt. Somehow we're more suited to harvesting than the others," Carlos says bitterly.

Sam winces and murmurs some consoling words while I keep quiet, caught in my thoughts.

"Was this why you're being a bit of a dick? Getting my walls up?"

"A bit. You're a bit of a softie at times. And let's just say that I picked up some chatter lately."

It's no real surprise. Even in Vancouver, I've seen some of the old prejudices rise up, though little of it was directed at me. Being insulated by position, wealth, and power means that I don't have to deal with the same level of bullshit as before. But people like Carlos and his friends—who, I absently note, he's only now mentioned—probably had it worse. Add the fact that the lines are drawn clearer down here, and well…

"Drop it. I don't need your pop psychology. Been dealing with that shit my whole life. And from what Lana tells me, we're going to have to deal with it more when we deal with the Galactics once we're out of Earth."

"You can lower it," Sam repeats, and I comply, dropping the drone's top as requested.

"Do you think Mikito will be fine with this?" Carlos says hesitantly.

"Mikito?" I say with a frown.

"Yes. She was so, umm… cold," Carlos ventures.

"Ah. Yes, she is." I lean back to consider my friend's reaction. I'd just taken her lack of objection as acceptance, the young woman's willingness to jump into our violent confrontations a given in my mind. "Mikito should be fine. She's done this before."

"Yes, but is she okay?" Carlos stresses the last word, trying to get his point across.

After peering at Carlos for a moment, Sam snorts while I frown, unsure of why the man is so insistent on that point.

"*Oy, inventory of rocks. He likes her.*" Ali's mental thought is filled with exasperation, obviously cluing in on my lack of a clue. "And you, lover-boy, just talk to her."

"Me? No, I didn't. I'm not—" Carlos splutters a bit. We all chuckle, making the Latino flush. When we're finally done laughing, he sets us off again with his next question. "Do you think she'd be okay with that?"

"Outside of Carlos's interest, we actually got a plan for this?" Sam says, having pulled out various pieces of another drone to put together.

"Sort of. I was thinking of asking them real nice…"

A buzz precedes an announcement in my ear that notifies us it's time to get moving. The attack is on.

***

"I get it now." Mikito laughs behind her hand as she surveys the golf course grounds and clubhouse.

We all look at her askance, most of us having understood the barbarian with the club figurine used and not finding the hilarity in it that she does. All but Carlos, who laughs a little too hard.

"Are you sure this is a good idea?" Sam mutters.

Since we still have to journey south to the actual city core after the attack announcement is made, I have more than enough time to brief the team on the "plan." Calling it a plan is rather generous, but we out-Level these fellows enough that it shouldn't matter. It's part of the reason we've all got our helmets down, showcasing our faces. On the other hand, Lana's pets are all farther behind, hidden behind invisibility potions and ready to back us up.

"It'll be fine," I say. "If we don't take their City Core, we'd be forced to hunt their fighters down anyway. This way, they'll do all the work for us by gathering here. We won't even need to hunt them down."

"And if they refuse to fight?" Lana asks as she cranes her neck and surveys the slowly gathering teams of enemy combatants.

Most of the fighters are streaming in from the various houses dotting the golf course, luxurious residences that once overlooked carefully manicured, pesticide-ridden grounds. Someone had actually spent the Credits to ensure the grounds were still manicured and cut, managed by the System rather than underpaid groundskeepers.

"Then they lose their Core. And the Mages can figure out who they want to kick out," I say.

I have no intention of taking the City Core here. I have more than enough on my hands, dealing with the politics and development of the settlements in BC. There's no need to invite even more trouble by getting involved in the US. Not yet at least.

"Mr. Lee, Mr. Turner." Desmond walks to the forefront of the group, hand resting on the butt of his pistol. "What's the purpose of your visit?"

"Your Core," I say. "We're here to take it from you. And there are a few people we've got a bounty to collect on. *Ali.*"

A moment later, the list of wanted personnel appears as a System notification for everyone present. Ali's even been nice enough to sort the ones in this group to the top and highlight them for easy reading. He's considerate that way.

"You're just going to take a quest from those Mages? Do their bidding? I thought you were independent!" Desmond sputters.

"Well, it's nice experience," I drawl before I drop the act and let him see some of the anger in my eyes. "And you guys attacked first."

"It has nothing to do with you!"

"Except they're our allies. And you're assholes," I say then gesture to the team to walk forward.

We cross the space between us, Carlos and Sam tapping their helmets, the hardware shifting around their neck and forming around their face as asphalt crunches under our feet. Our opponents shift and ready weapons. I hear spells being chanted and buffs being added, but I don't break eye contact with Desmond.

"You think you can beat us? There's only five of you!" Desmond snarls, his pistol drawn.

From a hundred feet, we're down to fifty, the slow, rhythmic thread of our steps not stopping. They have numerous spells held ready, but thus far, no one has attacked.

"Five?" Lana whispers.

"Ingrid's gone again," Sam mutters, his voice carrying to us via the communicator.

Without a word, Lana triggers her Aura of the Red Queen, her hair darkening into a blood red, her features growing slightly shadowed, her pale skin lightening. The beautiful redhead becomes so much more intimidating, the fear effect that the Aura triggers causing indrawn breaths and a few involuntary steps back.

"Tell me," I call, raising my voice to carry to everyone around us. "Are you all willing to die for Desmond and his friends? Because the first person to shoot dies. I don't know if you all agreed on the attack, but for those of you on the list, we're not going to kill you. Neither are the Mages."

"What... what are you going to do with us?" a voice shouts.

I chuckle softly. "I hear you guys are fans of serfdom—"

I never get to finish my sentence because Desmond opens up, the melee fighter with the sword and tower shield behind him moving next to him whilst glowing a purple color. Smoothly, another of his allies drops to her knees, brown hair billowing as she fires her plasma rifle. A mage snaps off a spell, and steel birds appear around the group, razor-sharp wings extended. All around us, a few of Desmond's people open fire while others hesitate at the sudden onset of violence.

"Sam, Lana, crowd control!" I snarl, my sword appearing in my hand and cutting the plasma beam.

Of course physics doesn't work that way and the beam, aided by a Skill, melts my sword partly and slams into my chest anyway, a fraction of a second before Desmond's second shot manages to hit me. Even as my armor smokes and my skin bubbles, a soothing green light washes over me as Carlos gets to work. Rather than take another shot, I cast Soul Shield. I'd purposely left it off since I didn't want to come in too hard—but perhaps I could have worded our earlier entrance better.

Damn Charisma.

Mikito, under her Haste Skill, ducks the majority of the birds as she runs to Desmond, only to be blocked by the wannabe-legionnaire. The pair exchange attacks, Mikito's longer weapon leaving her mostly safe from the legionnaire's gladius. However, each attack that he blocks seems to cast a red glow that drops Mikito's health a little while the swooping metal birds force her to duck and dodge while fighting.

While everyone's distracted by Mikito, Ingrid makes her appearance, her knives sliding into the steel mage's back. His back arches and he gurgles in pain as she yanks the blades from his kidneys and restabs him in the shoulder blades. He sinks to his knees. Finally free to choose my target, I Blink Step above Desmond.

"Time to die," I snarl, my sword dismissed and recalled to give it back its edge.

Even as I drop, I activate Cleave and Elemental Strike—Ice. I don't even need my additional blades as my cut tears into Desmond, the blade sliding through his body with garish ease. Blood, bone, and muscle part, frosting over. Desmond chokes, his lungs compromised as he attempts to wheeze out a protest. He falls backward, ripping the blade from his body.

A moment later, the blood that escaped from the frozen flesh stops running, growing grey and firm. In a flash, the rest of Desmond's body is covered in the same greyness and his mouth splits into a grin as he drops his pistols and launches himself from his feet with an uppercut.

"Got you," Desmond snarls.

With a casual twist of my hands, I bring my sword across my body to block the attack. Rather than cut through his fist fully, it only sinks in a few centimeters before the surface of his newly hardened body punches through my defense and pushes me back.

Class Skill: Blood to Stone (Level 3)

Transforms lost hit points into defensive armor, increasing the defense of the user. Blood to Stone increases armor at a ratio of 1.2:1 for each health loss.

Cost: 200 Mana

Duration: 3 minutes

"Dream on," I snarl, cutting at Desmond with my sword the moment I rush back to him.

He might have a better defense, but I've got a Soul Shield, so even when he does manage to actually hit me, it does no damage. Again and again we clash, blade against fist, and wounds open across Desmond's body. A faked cross turns into a front kick which turns into a spinning backhand by Desmond, his attacks shattering my Soul Shield. In return, I duck under and cut his leg, slicing a line of grey damage. But even as I watch, his wounds slowly knit together, his chest wound nearly entirely healed.

"Lana, I'm marking his healers!" Ali sends over the party chat.

In a few moments, his healers are glowing. We've been avoiding attacking them since they aren't direct damage dealers, but since it's gotten this far, the gloves are off. At this rate, his defense is just going to keep creeping up, making my attacks almost utterly useless.

Shattered glass draws my attention and I'm forced to jerk my head back just a little too late. Gnarly, rough knuckles graze my jaw, tearing open surface wounds. From the shattered vials, smoke pours out, covering the battlefield.

-31 Poison Damage Taken (Poison Resisted)

The notification flashes in the corner of my eyes even as I find the poison burning my skin and exposed flesh. I would swear, but it's the right call. The healing from Desmond's friends drops as they lose sight of him. Forced to rely on his own regeneration and armor, he backpedals but continues to laugh softly as I keep hitting him, trying to drag down his health. He's mostly on the defense for the moment, taking damage and dishing a little out before a fully drawn shoulder cut across his chest leaves just a white line across his skin.

"Thousand hells," I swear.

"My Skill stacks, stupid." Desmond laughs maniacally as he throws himself forward, disregarding defense at all.

I'm forced to backpedal, blocking, dodging, and occasionally eating a shot. Cleave should work, but only a little longer—his damage resistance keeps going up. I can slow him down with Freezing Blade, but it won't kill him… slow him down…

I chuckle, catching a cut, then grab him, spin him around, and slam him into the ground. He's good, but he has nowhere near my agility. And while he might have had some hand-to-hand training in the past, I've spent the last year and a half training with Mikito. My shift in tactics puts him down, his arm stretched across my chest and locked at the elbow and shoulder while I press his face into the ground.

"You can't stop me!" Desmond chokes out, pushing upward for a second.

I know if he's really willing to do it, he could dislocate his arm and get out, so I cast before he gets the idea. In the few seconds my spell requires to conjure, I look around to survey the situation.

A body falling from a rooftop shows Ingrid is dealing with some of our ranged attackers, her Shadow Form giving her the maneuverability required. Carlos is hunkered low with Sam and Lana in our original position, a series of defensive shield drones offering support as the group fights off a pair of attackers. The puppies are dealing with a cluster of ranged fighters on the left, Anna and Roland intimidating another cluster of surrendered combatants to the right. Mikito, having dealt with her attacker, is finishing off the female rifle-bearer.

That's all the time I have before my spell forms. Shoving down hard, I jump and Blink Step away even as the Mud Walls form, slamming together to cover Desmond.

"Carlos, Ice!" I snap even as I cast Polar Zone on the Mud Walls.

A couple of potions—twinkling, periwinkle blue bottles of liquid—crash against the liquified earth, releasing their sub-zero contents and completing the freezing process. The sudden emergence of the mud and the entombment of their leader freezes our assailants, their ace in the hole neutralized. Hopefully.

"Is he dead?" Carlos says, staring at the newly created frozen, brown hill.

Just in case, I make a note to cast Polar Zone again once the cooldown is off.

"Nope. He might suffocate in a few hours, but his Constitution is high enough to keep him alive for a bit," Ali says, peering at his screens.

"But he's taking damage…" Sam says. Even from there, he can feel the unnatural cold radiating from the hill. "A bit cruel, no?"

I shrug, keeping my face impassive. Best to play cruel and uncaring. Truth be told, while I might have been able to kill the son of a bitch eventually, it'd have been a slog. Better to leave him stuck until the Mages come by and drag him away. His Skill was a nasty, overpowered one.

"Are we done?" I ask threateningly, letting my gaze slide over our shocked opponents. There are a few quick nods, a few faces turned away in shame. "Good."

I wave, using up a large chunk of my remaining Mana and dragging a headache with it to open a Portal. The Mage team that's been waiting steps through and heads into the building to take over the Core while Lana, under her Aura and with Ali's help, sorts out the wanted figures. No surprise, not all of them decide to come peacefully once we lay hands on them. A few with stealth abilities even attempt to run away. Luckily, we have Ali and the pets around to corral the majority of those, though a few manage to get away during the fight or perhaps were never around. They're a problem for later.

Five minutes later, as the Mage team comes back out of the building, an explosion attracts everyone's attention. At this distance, all we hear is a low rumbling sound, but all eyes turn in that direction. Lana's eyes narrow as a large plume of smoke rises from the downtown core.

"What is it?" Carlos says.

"Space Needle," Lana says slowly, her eyes brimming with unshed tears. "It's where the Sons of Odin had their headquarters."

"The Mage leaders?" Mikito asks quietly.

"Yes," Ali answers for Lana. "They decided to make a show of it and blew up the entire building."

"Civilians?" I say with a frown.

Ali shrugs. He has a little more information than we do, but it isn't as if he's omniscient. I make a mental note to have a conversation with our "friends" later about that. If the Sons of Odin were anything like this group, there might have been some innocents in there. Then again, there might not have been. Better not to jump to conclusions before I tear out someone's throat. Still, this display puts another mark in the column of "don't necessarily trust the Mages" portion of my brain.

An hour later, when the Mages have sent enough people to keep the peace and the crowd has dispersed, my team gathers again in front of the Core to be ported back.

"Are we really going to let them make them slaves?" Sam asks, looking at the bound and guarded group of prisoners awaiting transportation.

"Not exactly," Lana says softly, shaking her head. "There's going to be trial. Those who were just ancillary, they'll be jailed for a bit then released with a Contract forced on them. Only be the ones who killed or took direct part will be made serfs and put under guard. And even then, there's a time limit—well, a Credit limit."

"What's to stop them from adding fines and charging more?" Ingrid asks, eyes narrowed. "There's a lot of loopholes in that system."

"Because we won't allow it," Ali says firmly, meeting Ingrid's eyes. "Lana, Katherine, Kim, and I have all gone through their documents. And we're keeping an eye on it."

"And they let us?" Sam says with surprise.

"Well, let's just say that there's more than one faction in play," Lana says with a slight smile.

I blink, curious how the lady managed to get all this done. I mean, we've barely had a few hours all in.

The team reluctantly let the topic drop. It's not real justice, but in this world, it's the best we can do. For all that we might dislike the concept of slavery, they did start the damn fight. And tossing people, no matter how self-serving, arrogant, and idiotic, into prison would be a waste of resources when we desperately need all hands on deck. Prison would not just cost us the prisoners, but we'd need prison guards too. Better to use the System controls to get them to work for us. And who knows, maybe a little punishment might smarten them up.

And leeches might fly.

***

Later that evening, Lana and I are seated on the couch overlooking the large backyard in Lana's house in Richmond in the Lower Mainland. Rather than sticking around the town, I Portalled us back to the large ex-farmland that Lana had purchased in the suburb for her use. The ample fenced grounds offer a convenient place for the puppies to stretch their legs. Considering their husky breeds, that's a necessity.

"This is for you," I say, waving slightly to pull the small cardboard box from my Altered Space.

Lana frowns, staring at the box before she opens it to reveal the small paper charm with words of unknown origin on them. "This is…?" Lana frowns.

"Pick it up," I say.

When she complies, the item information appears.

Talisman of Teleportation (Tier III)

Upon use, the talisman will either transport user to anchored location or to a random, safe teleportation location within 5km of the user's origin.

"How…?"

"Loot from Calgary," I reply. "Congratulations, Beast Master."

"Oh!" Lana flushes, smiling slightly. "I didn't think you'd noticed."

Lana Pearson (Beast Master Level 1)

HP: 420/420

MP: 620/620

Conditions: Bestial Senses, Linked x 4

"I did. Just didn't have much time to congratulate you during the fight," I say. "I take it you've switched the experience gain to something more balanced?" Lana nods, confirming my guess. "What're the Skills like?"

"Different. Sort of," Lana says with a shrug. "Three trees. The first buffs me—the usual but better increases to my personal Skills and survivability. There's even an option to take control of swarms or hives in there. The other two options are divergent in their needs. I guess you could say the first is an evolutionary option. Here…”

Forced Evolution (Level 0)

Forcibly causes a pet to undergo an evolution. Evolution will (generally) be beneficial to the pet. Reduces Mana Regeneration by 5 permanently

“Not much explanation,” I mutter, dismissing the notice. “And the other?”

Biological Overdrive

Increases biology of pet by 300%. Attack, speed, defense, and damage values will increase during overdrive period. Pets will suffer a negative exhaustion effect after overdrive duration is complete.

Duration: 10 Minutes

Cost: 250 Mana per pet

“Is that title correct?” I frown, staring at the Skill's title.

“Translation issues, boy-o,” Ali says, shaking his head. By this point, both of us have gotten used to the damn Spirit randomly floating in when he feels like it. Thankfully, after forcibly banishing the Spirit twice for intruding when he shouldn't, he's stopped coming in while we're otherwise intimately engaged. “Not everyone has me cleaning up their UI.”

“The other Skills are similar,” Lana says, ignoring the byplay between us. “Basically, I can push my pets to be more powerful for a short period or chance evolutions and other changes on them, giving them longer-term effects. But they don't seem to be as powerful.”

"Mostly," Ali agrees. "It's an option between long-lasting effects or guaranteed hard-hitters. Though you sometimes get a little of the second with the evolutions. They can get weird."

I grunt. Considering some of the strange and less-than-successful evolutions we've seen—more often as corpses—I have to agree with Ali on that. Still, considering how much Mana and the number of evolutions that happened, the ratio of "good" to "bad" mutations is incredibly favorable. The fact that these evolutions don't seem entirely random has generated a significant amount of discussion in my books, some of which I'd gained a few upgrades to my System Quest by reading. The general consensus is that either the Mana or the System self-selects for successful mutations, which lends to the belief of intelligent design behind these actions. A cruel intelligence though. There seems to be a small but significant number of random mutations that are neither beneficial nor benign but just weird.

"What did you choose?"

"I haven't," Lana says softly, doubt creeping into her voice. When I stay silent, Lana is forced to fill in. "I don't want to hurt them. But..."

"But the evolutions could do that too," I say, and she nods. Even now, the woman still visits the little girl we left Elsa with, when she can convince me to Portal her up. It's touching, if a little worrying. Sometimes, I wonder how much more pain that big heart of hers can take.

"Yes," Lana says, leaning her head against me again. "What should I do?"

I don't answer, just giving her a squeeze. Even if I want to talk, to advise, I've learned my lesson and bite my tongue. Literally. Sometimes, women just want to talk.

It's into that comfortable, if morose, silence that Kim's notification appears.

"REQUESTING AUTHORIZATION TO USE FUNDS TO ASCERTAIN ALTERATIONS IN SETTLEMENT MARKETPLACE."

"What?" I say out loud.

"REQUESTING AUTHORIZATION TO USE FUNDS TO ASCERTAIN ALTERATIONS IN SETTLEMENT MARKETPLACE."

"I got that," I snarl then draw a breath, forcing down my irritation. No point getting angry. It's a machine. Sort of. "I meant, what alterations?"

"UNKNOWN. REQUISITION FUNDS TO…"

"We got that, bits-for-brains. Boy-o wants to know what alterations you're seeing," Ali says.

"RECENT PRICE FLUCTUATIONS IN QUANTUM STABILIZERS AND ANTI-TELEPORTATION SHIELDS," Kim says.

A moment later, a graph pops up with so many lines on it, my eyes blur trying to read it.

"We got it, bits-for-brains. Authorized," Ali says.

"UNABLE TO ACCEPT AUTHORIZATION FROM LOWER ELEMENTAL FORM."

"I'll give you lower—"

"Ali." I cut him off before I say slowly, "Why are you tracking this? I thought you were limited to the settlement?"

"A REQUEST FOR INFORMATION FROM THE LOWER ELEMENTAL FORM WAS DEEMED TO OFFER AN ACCEPTABLE RETURN ON THE RESOURCES DEDICATED TO SUCH TRACKING," Kim says. "REQUESTING AUTHORIZATION TO UTILISE SETTLEMENT FUNDS."

Once I parse the answer, I shrug. "Do it." Then I turn to Ali. "Explain?"

"Not much to explain, boy-o. You know what anti-teleportation shields are. Quantum stabilizers do the same, but they include things like your

Quantum State Manipulator. There're a bunch of variations of course, from single-activation stabilizers to on-going fields," Ali says. "I figured since you've purchased the QSM again and are waiting for its delivery, and with your Skills, it'd be a good idea to make sure the cities we're going into aren't utilizing it. Don't want to jump into a place that is quantum locked. It'd be real painful. Or deadly."

"We can tell that from this…?" I say, frowning at the graph that hasn't disappeared.

"No idea about the graph. I just bought some information on the next few cities," Ali says. "Looks like bits-for-brains took it a step further."

"DATA CONFIRMED. ASSESSMENT IS THAT SETTLEMENTS WITHIN NORTH AMERICA HAVE SEEN A SIGNIFICANT INCREASE IN PURCHASES OF ANTI-TELEPORTATION AND QUANTUM STABILIZERS."

"John?" Lana says, frowning as she reads the information Kim and Ali have so kindly shared to her.

"It's like this, Lana," Ali says. "They're taking steps to stop John from bouncing around inside their cities or dropping an army on their doorsteps. Skills that involve spatial distortions, like his Blink Step and Portal, are going to be seriously degraded. Depending on the level of interference, it's either going to be impossible, seriously curtailed, or just painful to use."

"Painful?"

"Certain quantum stabilizers only react on use of the Skill. They disrupt the actual teleportation, damaging those transported."

"Nasty," I say with a wince.

"Yup. They're also the most common," Ali says. "Cheaper to purchase an occasional trigger piece than a whole anti-teleport field, you know?"

"Yeah," I say, rubbing my chin. This isn't good news. Not at all. It looks like our actions have caught some attention. "How much damage are we talking?"

"Depends on the field. Anything from a couple of hundred health points to a few thousand."

"So, no jumping."

"No jumping."

"We need to tell the colonel," Lana says softly.

I nod. Ah hell, I bet he's going to make me do the US next. Still, maybe Voodoo Donuts survived…

***

Wier takes the news with equanimity. Seated in his office alone, his table is bare but for a cup of coffee when we arrive. Soon afterward, his aide comes in to take notes while we inform him of the bad news. Since Sam had promised to work with the army's mechanics on a new project, he tagged along when we went down, leaving Mikito and Ingrid to their solo adventuring efforts.

"I have news of my own," Wier says after he digests the information. "Fort Irwin and Camp Pendleton both survived the System changeover and have contacted us. We have begun further coordination, though contact is via messenger. Forces around these bases have joined together, including the remnants of the Edwards air force detachment, the Marines of 29 Palms, and various navy services. Unfortunately, the navy were the hardest hit among our men, with significant losses in equipment and personnel. They are currently in battle with the local alien forces known as the Zarrie.

"In addition, our efforts at aiding Portland have resulted in significant progress at whittling down the enemy's forces. We—I—expect to see a significant increase in pressure on the resistance in the next few weeks."

"You want me to go down and tag their land, don't you?" I state.

"Yes."

"It seems like we're reacting more than planning recently," Lana says, frowning. "We did Edmonton and Calgary because John wanted to free them and they were close. You helped us because that was part of the agreement, our Skills and men in trade for yours. But now, instead of continuing down south from there or farther east, we came to deal with Seattle. Now we're going down to Portland?"

"The battlefield is fluid, Ms. Pearson," Wier says calmly.

"Maybe, but I'd think you would have more of a plan," Lana says, an unspoken accusation in her voice.

"You are perceptive, Ms. Pearson," Wier says then raises a hand to make a call.

In a few minutes, Captain Angus Tyrell joins us and the table hosts a projection of the map of North America. Friendly settlements are coded green, hostile settlements are red, and those currently contested are yellow. Pretty much the entirety of the eastern seaboard is red with dashes of yellow, while the Midwest is a mixture of reds and yellows. The western seaboard is obviously what we're dealing with, and it's a mixture of reds, yellows, and of course, our greens. Overall, the greens are extremely rare, with most of those located in smaller towns and one large clump in the southern USA.

Silence descends as Wier lets us peruse the map, and I spot some interesting notes. Woodbridge, Virginia, yellow. Ashland, Oregon—a weird half-green, half-red coloration. A quick perusal shows it's Galactic-owned and neutral to humans. Meeker, Oklahoma, green. Hardin, Illinois, red.

"As you can see, most of our country—and yours—is held by others. Of these settlements, even fewer have an active resistance. You'll note that Los Angeles and southern USA have the highest number of such resistance cells," Wier says, waving his fingers down the map.

"Not exactly true," Sam says, pointing upward to our Midwest, where many places glow yellow.

"Yes, but those settlements have smaller populations. Very small," Wier says. "In addition, many of these locations with resistance are backed up by members of our armed forces, the national guard, and members of the police and security services." A slight pause before a half-smile. "As much as there might be complaints about our armed forces and the militarization of our police force, in instances like this, it is particularly useful."

"You want us to go through Portland, LA, and then back up to each of these resistance cities?" I say softly, flicking my gaze along them.

Sam is right, there are a few towns and settlements—including a few greens—that we could free in Regina and Manitoba. But their numbers don't compare at all. If we punch east from LA, we could link up with a bunch of greens and yellows, rather than the frightening bloc of red farther north. I absently note that more than a few places in the middle of the States seem to host some really nasty monsters.

"We have more people. And well-trained ones. We can't afford to wait. Our enemies are already reacting to our growing strength," Wier says. "The faster we are able to grow, the safer we all will be."

"And how about what's happening in Ontario?" Sam asks.

"Ontario?" I mutter while Lana's face grows fixed.

"It is tragic, but this is the most efficient use of our resources," Angus answers.

"Efficient? Do you know what they're doing? The Galactics in Ontario are worse than the Thirteen Moon Sect. At least those assholes played nice. These guys are just shipping people wholesale to other planets and importing their own instead. If we keep this up, in less than a year, they'll have gotten rid of the majority of the population!" Sam snaps.

"And in Italy, the aliens are shooting anyone who tries to hide in their cities," Angus says. "In Kenya, for fighting back, they sold the settlement keys so that there are no more safe zones at all, other than a few Galactic-owned ones. In Borneo, there's less than 0.1% of the population left because the entire jungle has mutated into a Level 200+ location. What's your point?"

I twitch, listening to the list of calamities. For all the good that we do, it's a drop in the ocean. Ever since people got a little more funds, they've been picking up information about our world—real information, not rumors—and learning about the tragedies that await us. It's something I've tried to avoid myself—an ostrich's choice to keep myself sane. There's nothing I can do about most of it, so I can only soldier on.

"We can save Ontario, unlike those places," Sam says. "That's my point."

"And linking up with our men around Los Angeles will allow us to act on multiple cities at once. Right now, we have to stop and reinforce each city with nearly all of our men until things stabilize because we do not have enough. With more units, we can continue to our attacks," Wier repeats.

"LA also has a large economy," Lana pipes up. "If we can get access to their funds, we can divert some of it to building defenses in other cities, just like we're doing in BC. We could even set up teleportation gates between each city, giving us a way to reinforce them that doesn't rely on John."

I grunt, knowing that'd be useful. It'd fix the issue about bad roads and logistics, though the upfront cost involved is staggering. Rebuilding the defenses, upgrading each city, and making sure the settlements work is important. While fixed defenses will never be as important or as good as trained personnel, that's no excuse for leaving the gates open either. Especially in a Dungeon World.

"Fine," Sam says, sitting back and crossing his arms.

I'm slightly amused, though I do my best to hide it. For all of Sam's protests, it's not as if this was his choice. I'm the idiot who has to drive everywhere to get the Portals set up. Still, I'm glad to see he's passionate.

"Then we're agreed. Portland is next," Wier says with finality. "We'll make sure you get briefed on the city and the others further below. I'm particularly concerned about the Zarrie in LA. They're one of the worse groups from what we gather."

"Thank you," I say softly. Information is good. If we're going to liberate this continent, the more information we can gather, the better. So yeah, Portland is next.

Chapter 10

It says something about humanity that we went through an apocalypse in which our libraries and schools burned down and our government institutions were trampled and lost, but this building that provides deep-fried, sugary goodness is the first thing we rebuilt. Biting into the mocha-covered donut of heaven, I survey the battlefield.

The fight for Portland was less of a grind than what we faced in Calgary. Rather than fight a running urban battle, the Movana clan that owned the city had focused their forces at each of the City Cores. So while each fight had been more brutal, with a higher number of losses than in Calgary, they had been more contained and gone faster. Once we managed to knock down a good portion of their forces, most of the Movana gave up. It helped, I think, that Ali and Kim had started sharing our serf-of-war conditions, stating the conditions and prices for buyback. Wier had muttered something about Italy and condottieri when he heard about it, but hadn't directly objected.

"Are you going to share?" Colonel Wier asks then promptly helps himself to the box of donuts on the picnic table that someone dragged all the way here. The greying older man looks around for a chair and, finding none, settles himself into a standing relaxed posture.

Behind Wier, his bodyguards glance at the donuts longingly but don't make a move.

"Looks like I don't have to," I say.

"Good. Because I wasn't going to ask," a jovial voice calls. A moment later, a delicate black hand grabs a donut before it's slid into large, luscious lips. "If anyone makes a joke, I'll personally beat them till they're bleeding from all their holes."

"Firstly, pretty sure you just made the joke yourself, Chief. And secondly, isn't that police brutality?" I say, grinning at the uniformed officer of the law.

"I'll put the report in myself. Pretty sure the DA will get around to it in a few decades."

The chief grins and I snort, regarding the woman and her blood-splattered, burnt, and gooey uniform. It still fits her quite well, emphasizing the decent-sized bust and toned waistline. Considering it's unlikely she got it fitted since the System, she must have been pretty fit even before the System added its cosmetic changes. Her hair woven into a series of braids, the African American chief seems to be reveling in the sugary goodness, even going so far as to lick the cream off her fingers.

After a moment, I cast Cleanse on her uniform, wiping away the blood and grime at least.

Danielle Fuller (Sergeant of the Guard Level 7)
HP: 1230/1230
MP: 1380/1380
Conditions: Sense of the City

"Got to get that spell," Danielle says with a smile, shaking her head. "Got to get the department the spell. Do those slackers some good."

"Well, we are hoping that there's a lot less of this," I say, glancing around the city. There's not much damage from our battles, but the on-going guerilla warfare that Danielle and her people conducted shows in the shattered buildings all around us.

"I've been dying to ask. Why are you all wearing your uniforms?" Ali says, shaking his head. "I mean, sure, Ingrid told you when we'd do this, but it's not exactly useful."

"Why shouldn't we? We've been hiding who and what we are for the last year. I'll be damned if I let my people hide a day longer. We're not thieves. We're the police," Danielle says with sudden heat, making Ali blink and float backward.

After a moment, he raises his finger and points at the box of donuts. "You definitely need more sugar."

I smack myself on the forehead, realizing that after spending all this time with me, Ali might have a warped notion of why humans get angry. "Ali, not every problem can be solved by the addition of sugar…"

"Just yours," Lana says sweetly as she snags a donut.

I growl at her without any heat. "Out of curiosity, if we're all here, who's running the war?" I cock my head to the side to see if I can hear any additional explosions.

"That's what I have subordinates for," Danielle says with a sniff before she regains her seriousness. "It's all mop-up right now. The elves aren't even trying to fight back anymore. We just have to find them before they get away."

"Good to know," I say with a nod. Considering I've not been asked to shuttle anyone for the last half hour, I figured it was something like that. "What's the butcher's bill?"

"Within acceptable limits," Wier says and, with a slight twitch of his eyes, indicates the surroundings and our audience.

Oops. Perhaps I'll wait for the actual report later. Or just ask Ali. Part of hanging out and joking is to improve morale, to let people know that things are returning to normal. Either that or they really wanted the donuts.

An older, portly gentleman coughs to draw our attention before flicking his gaze to the box of donuts. "And mine's twenty Credits."

"Dear, I forgot my wallet…" Lana says.

I roll my eyes, mentally triggering the command to send the Credits over. Well, that's another city down at least.

***

Hours later, we're in a meeting room that's been cleaned and cleared. Scorch marks and gaping holes are filling in at a rate that if you looked away and back after a little while, the change would be noticeable. Around the table, Lana, Sam, and myself are seated. On the opposite side, there's the colonel, Captain Tyrell, and their aides, as well as a new addition—Romeo, a Combat Engineer. From what I recall, it was their people and their fortifications, along with Danielle's core of officers, that kept the resistance in Portland alive. Danielle is here too, as the third spoke in the wheel, along with Portland's current civil leader, an ex-deputy mayor. He's dressed in Adventurer chic, auburn hair buzzed cut and eyes hard and weary from the battle. He was the one who was willing to lead from the frontlines, something I have to admire somewhat. Up in the Mages' portion of the table, Charles sits silently by himself, content to listen for now.

"Did you have to destroy the shield generators and the quantum stabilizers?" Philip, the ex-deputy mayor, complains. "It's going to cost us nearly as much to fix them as to buy them new!"

"Your techies were taking too long," Wier says. "The entire plan hinged on our ability to shift our forces around swiftly."

"But if we'd had another five minutes, we'd have finished!"

"Your people said that five minutes earlier. I made a military decision, as is my right," Wier states, making Philip flush a bit. "Now, I believe we're here to discuss our next steps?"

"We need you here for a few weeks more at least. Even if we do set up deals with a Guild, like you suggest, it'll take them time to send their people over. And if the elves hit us again…" Danielle shakes her head. "We don't have enough people, not alone, to handle them."

"We can give you a few days. My men need to rest and refit," Wier says. "But we need to continue our push. While my men can handle the smaller towns without significantly degrading our forces and the addition of Romeo's sappers has been good, we need more trained men. Do you have any further leads about the armed forces?"

"Hey! Boy-o here can still kick any of your men's butts," Ali says challengingly.

"Mr. Lee is an exception. While we are still adapting our tactics to the System, trained soldiers can and will win against undisciplined warriors," Angus replies for Wier, meeting the spirit's gaze challengingly.

I groan silently as the pair start up again. Ever since they had a chance to actually talk, they've been like oil and water. "Ali…"

"Captain."

The pair shut up before they can get truly started.

"Well, it'll take me a few days to continue my sweep anyway. I'm assuming we're still looking to link up with the bases and cities down south?" I say, looking at Wier.

"Yes. Any luck on expanding your radius?" Wier asks, leaning forward.

"It's possible, but I'm leery of dedicating it right now," I say with a shrug.

Wier purses his lips but doesn't push it. After all, Skill point distribution is a private matter and something that has already developed a series of social taboos. Not pushing people into allocation is a big one.

"And purchasing it?" Angus asks.

"It's viable," I say.

In truth, it's a lot more than viable. Since the System allows me to purchase the Advanced Skill because it's part of my Class but still registers my Levels on the "basic" status, the pricing is infinitely cheaper for me than for anyone else. Truth is, I was getting it cheap if I bought the Skill. Relatively speaking. A mere sixty-five thousand Credits for the next Level and another seventy for the one after that.

"But you haven't picked it up yet?" Wier asks with a frown.

"No," I say. "None of your jumps have required it as yet, and we're pretty sure information about my Status has been purchased a few times already."

Picking up the next Level would give me a range of around five thousand kilometers, while the fifth Level would let me open a Portal anywhere on Earth with a range of over twenty-five thousand kilometers. After that, the numbers get even more ridiculous. My only concern is those anti-teleportation devices—the farther away the Portal, the easier it is to destabilize the transmission. There's a formula that lets you figure out the potential additional cost of holding a stable Portal open against interference, but it's the kind of math that they give to PhD students, not ex-web programmers.

"Then when will you be able to continue, Mr. Lee?" Wier says.

I find myself grimacing, knowing that what he's asking is when can I get to the army bases in California so that he can set up some reliable and immediate communication. They can still run their people out the old-fashioned way, especially since my Skill is no longer hidden, but in terms of easy, fast communication and responsiveness, I'm the go-to guy.

"Give me a day," I say after a moment. Ah hell, I always wanted to see San Francisco.

***

Of course, getting to San Francisco wasn't a straight drive. There were a few cities on the way, places that I had to deal with. Salem was a battleground as the remaining Galactic holdouts from Portland pushed back against our people. Neither party was willing to throw down completely, so everyone took potshots at each other and called it a day. Rather than get too involved, I stayed to the outskirts, and even then, I got shot at.

For the next few towns, I do much the same, swinging inward enough to get the notification that I've entered their territory but never getting too close. Eugene is weird, run by an advisory council with a strange, peaceful mixture of about six different Galactic groups and three human factions. The Galactics are a group of crustacean-like creatures with pincer or pincer-like hands and shell coverings and a sponge monster. Two of their species can't survive in the open air, using a mixture of technology and magic to keep themselves wet and alive. Luckily for me, the first group I meet in Eugene has a mixture of humans and Galactics, ensuring that we don't start our relations in a violent manner. Once they work out that I'm not a threat, they make some introductions between the town administrators and me before leaving me with a short, bottle-blond twenty-year-old.

"And you're okay with all this?" I say, glancing around the quiet restaurant we've taken over.

"Definitely. Portland might have problems, but Im'in'ee are cool. They be refugees from the third Dungeon World. They're scrappers and runners. We be a good place to settle and chill, you know?" Oz says as he rubs his hands together, pleading with me to understand.

"Sounds like the Yerrick," I say softly.

With all my anger against the Galactics and the System, it's easy to forget that others have been crushed under the System's relentless expansion, its heartless judgment of worth without a shred of mercy. We are all playthings under the System, cogs in a machine.

"The who?"

"Yerrick. Alien minotaurs," I answer with a half-smile. "Nice, honorable group. If weird."

"Don't know about honor, but the Immies are real," Oz says with a firm nod, almost daring me to contradict him.

"I get it," I say, bowing my head to him. "But I'm just a messenger. I'll open a Portal, let you speak with the ones you really have to convince."

"Fair," Oz says. "You got any deetz on them?"

"Just tell it like it is," I say.

Not long after that, I make my way back to report on matters and pop open a Portal so that Lana and others can get involved. Even Katherine makes an appearance, my personal pair of eyes and ears and a precious note-taker in the upcoming negotiations.

***

Leaving others to deal with the negotiations, I keep driving south. There's no real rush, but sitting around a conference table and chatting is my version of hell. I'm more than happy to leave it to others while I take the time to deal with any monsters and dungeons I run into. There's no point in going fast, especially since my backup teams aren't ready. Not yet.

After that, my journey is a passage of small town after small town, most of them feeder settlements for the bigger cities. Whether it's the higher density of people that brought about the monsters or just bad luck, most of these settlements are worse for the wear. Many of the towns are abandoned, and those that aren't are filled to the brim with refugees from other locations. Only a couple are actual Villages, their City Cores owned and managed by others.

Where there are no City Cores, I find myself opening up my Portal and sending the survivors to Seattle. We're dumping them into the football stadium, a spot specially designated and upgraded to take newcomers. Wier even made me go all the way to Harbor Island in Seattle so that I'd have a place to Portal in unwanted guests if I'm ever forced to. He had a group of his people take the time to set up a minefield on the island, along with using Benjamin's Architect abilities to create a sturdy, reinforced wall. All in all, it's an idea that I had Ben steal for the rest of our settlements.

Since my goal is mostly to make my way south to give the colonel and his people more choices in their attacks, I'm trying to avoid getting into full-out fights. As such, while I'm not happy about locating a number of settlements owned by Galactics, I don't necessarily step up to deal with them. Wier and his people will eventually take them, with or without my help.

When I'm passing near another tiny town whose name I can't even be bothered to remember, I get jumped. A group of Pooskeens, nasty little dog-like creatures, dogpile me a mile out of the settlement. I find myself fighting for my stuff, Sabre doing donuts and firing the Inlin under my mental command while I alternately punch, kick, and stab at the small, furred monsters. For all their lack of size, their teeth are sharp and their knives even sharper.

"Hit me!" I snarl, fed up as I throw away one Pooskeen to just have another two jump on me.

Ali doesn't even hesitate—that little asshole—before he throws a bolt of electricity at me. And keeps throwing it. With my Class resistances and my increased resistance from my Elemental Affinity, it hurts enough to make me scream rather than being the teeth-clenching, nerve destroying event it should be. Once I can focus, I Blink Step straight into the air and spin around to lob a fireball at the space where I used to be. Sabre cooks, but its flame resistance has gone up enough that it's a minor thing.

After that violent introduction to the Pooskeens, I call Wier's people and my team together and we conduct a little clean-up. There's no quarter given or asked—the stripped bare bones and metal cages filled with humans hanging around town drive away anyone's desire for such mercy. The soldiers and Carlos are left to keep the survivors safe while the rest of the team go hunting. We go through the town quick and violent, the swarm of defensive drones hacked and destroyed by Sam.

"John, southwest corner of the map," Ali says to me as we finish with our latest batch of annoying rugrats.

"I see it," I say, frowning. A half-dozen dots moving very fast.

"If I'm not wrong, that's the settlement owner. High-Level Advanced fighter, a Pooskeen Red Fur and his people," Ali continues.

The others tilt their head toward him, listening to our conversation.

"They're running away?" I frown.

"Got it in one. You need to choose—take him and his people on or take the city."

"Why can't we do both?" Sam growls.

"Two reasons. You'll need everyone to stand a good chance of winning. And the Red Fur's set the power generators and shield to overheat. I figure you've got about three minutes to get to the City Core and fix it," Ali says, grimacing. "But I wouldn't trust my numbers. I'm not exactly the tech guy."

"The city," I say without hesitation. "Ali, can you highlight where Sam needs to go? Maybe he can fix the power generators directly. I'm assuming that'll cause the most damage."

"Oh yeah, send me to get cooked immediately," Sam mutters softly. "I'm too old for this shit."

"Probably," Ali says, though he doesn't sound confident. Still, a new glowing dot appears on the minimap while a second, less bright one appears on nearly the opposite side of the town. "Second one is the shield generators."

"Sam, Ingrid, and Lana. You're on the power generators," I order.

There's no wasted time as the pair and the puppies peel off while I hope that Ingrid is following. If not, I'm sure she's off doing something useful. For a moment, my mind offers the image of Ingrid lazing around on a rooftop with martinis and a beach umbrella while we fight, making pithy comments, before I shove away the irrelevant thought. "Mikito, we're going to speed things up."

"Yes," Mikito's agreement trails along behind her as she takes off running, headed straight for the City Core.

I have to speed up to catch up with the Japanese woman punching her way through the weak resistance with ease. Even then, with my Thousand Steps and occasional Blink Steps helping cover ground, we're nearly too late.

"Eleven seconds," I say, shuddering.

Whether it was because the asshole Pooskeen has not read the Evil Overlord list or he is just a sadistic bastard, there is a giant countdown timer when we finally make it to the City Core. Luckily, actually deactivating the self-destruct sequence is easy. I just have to stand there with my hand on the City Core until it finishes registering my new ownership, then I cancel the orders.

"Eh, it wouldn't be that bad," Ali starts.

"THE SPIRIT IS CORRECT. THE DAMAGE DONE TO YOU WOULD ONLY BE SUFFICIENT TO REQUIRE A WEEK OF REPAIRS FOR SABRE. YOUR ALLIES WOULD LIKELY ALL SURVIVE."

"And the human survivors?"

"COLLATERAL DAMAGE." Kim answers.

"So how is it that you're down here?" I decide to change the subject before anyone else picks up on it. While the notifications can normally only be seen by me and anyone else Kim decides to show them to, there's no guarantee his notifications can't be intercepted. While Kim can fake empathy, its occasional lapses can be jarring.

"UPGRADES AUTHORIZED BY BENJAMIN, THE COUNCIL, AND LANA TO YOUR SETTLEMENTS HAS INCREASED MY OPERATING CAPACITY AND LIMITS. WITHIN NORTH AMERICA, I AM ABLE TO ACCESS OWNED SETTLEMENTS AND AID IN THEIR DEVELOPMENT."

"Nice," I say. "Okay, well, start putting together a list of what we should upgrade here. I'm thinking the usual beam turrets, drones, and maybe a wall. Keep it within budget. I don't want to be throwing my Credits into a pit."

"CONFIRMED."

"You know, they might not want to stay," Ali says.

I grunt in understanding. Whatever, Kim's a computer—it probably would only take a few minutes for him to get that information together.

"John. We need to get the survivors out. Now," Carlos calls to me on the radio, his voice filled with rage and shock.

"I'll be there in a bit. Just settling the city—"

"No. Portal here and create another for them. We're getting them out immediately."

"What's going on?" I ask.

"They're shell-shocked and on the verge of a complete breakdown. They don't believe they're safe," Carlos replies. "And I don't blame them. The survivors in the cage… they were being penned until they signed a Serfdom contract. Those who died from hunger or the beatings were eaten."

"Eighteen hells," I swear. That's frightening. I stare at the City Core for a moment, wishing I had just sold it. "On my way."

We spend the rest of the day cleaning up, stealing everything the Pooskeens left that's useable and selling everything that isn't. We aren't going to leave anything here, even if we don't have the time to deal with them properly. Lana and the council have begun organizing a trauma team that can help survivors deal with their problems. They even have a triage process that highlights those who are dangerously unstable for immediate treatment via the Shop. The worst cases I bring along with me, my access to a better and more immediate Shop critical.

***

"John?" The voice is liquid chocolate to my ears, my body clenching down below as my breath shortens. Damn it.

"Roxley." I turn from staring at the doorway the child was taken through, too catatonic to move himself, and face the Truinnar.

The Shop has my tab, and Ali's in the corner, negotiating with his friend for a group discount as we usher in more and more people. I can feel my Credits draining, but I can't regret it, not really.

"You look well," Roxley says with a purr, his eyes gliding over my body.

I admit, I check out that tall hunk of blackness for a second, admiring his form. I might still be angry with him over his betrayal in Whitehorse, but that doesn't alter the fact that he's pretty. Really pretty.

"What's this about? You didn't just turn up here by chance," I say tightly.

One of the reasons why I rarely see other shoppers is because the time-space laws in this Shop have been messed with. A conversation about it with Foxy the salesperson left my head hurting, but he indicated that while it might seem that time moves differently here, it's just them adjusting the timelines for when I arrive and leave. It helps keep things exclusive. And thus makes it nearly impossible for there to be a coincidental run-in.

"No." Roxley takes a seat, staring at me and waiting.

Eventually, I walk over and sit in the lounging chairs across from him.

"I came to speak to you about your actions. And the Zarrie."

"My actions?"

"You're no longer a single fighter. You're the owner of a large number of strategic settlements. It will not be long before your lands draw additional attention," Roxley says softly.

"And…?" It's not as if I didn't know that. Part of the planning for the city includes building out the Tier I & II military / adventurer buildings to add security forces to the important settlements. As the other settlements upgrade to Towns and more, we'll be adding additional buildings. On top of that, we've already started specializing the cities to some extent. Places like

Kelowna are focusing on production, while Vancouver itself is fast becoming a hippy, urban dungeon delving / military town.

"And you're seeking to begin a battle with a new Empire," Roxley says, leaning forward. "One that is closely allied to the Movana. Your new allies."

"My new allies?" I say with an eyebrow raise.

"Please. Do not act as if you do not know what your actions with the Burning Leaves meant."

"And…?"

As I keep playing dumb, I see the flash of irritation in Roxley's eyes, gone so fast that only someone who has spent so much time with him would notice. Time having dinner, talking, sparring, kissi… actually, not that last part. Dragging my mind back to matters at hand, I pay attention to the dark elf. A part of me wonders why I'm daydreaming so much, another says that it's because it's been a bit since Lana and I had some time together, and with the death I've seen… well, it's a normal reaction to my hormones.

"You know that Earth is in the Truinnar's sphere of influence. What you might not understand is how close you are to our borders. It is disputable if Earth lies with us or the Movana. That dispute was put to rest in the courts, and we were meant to take your planet when the System came online. But…" Roxley waves as if to encompass everything that has happened in the last year and a half.

"That didn't happen. You suggesting the Movana did something?"

"I would not defame them in such a manner," Roxley states primly. "My point is that as a Dungeon World, your planet is considered a neutral ground. All races, all species from the Galaxy may enter it. Of course, those whose borders lie close to your world are the most interested."

"The Movana and Truinnar," I say, nodding. "You're still not explaining what this has to do with me."

"You are beginning to swim in deeper waters, John, and your actions can have wider consequences," Roxley says exasperatedly. "The Zarrie are traditionally allies of the Movana as their planet lies within the Movana's sphere of influence. Acting against them sets you—and your settlements—at odds. It is unlikely to escalate to a full-out war, but your actions will have consequences. Trade blockades, assassinations, and yes, wars have been fought for less."

"So I should what? Stop?" I say. "It's interesting that you're talking to me about it when the Movana haven't."

"I cannot speak for them. I can only recommend that you seek allies before it is too late," Roxley says. "If you intend to act against the Movana, ally yourself with us."

"Us. You. The Duchess."

"My kingdom," Roxley says, nodding. "We—I—have shown that while we might not be your ideal choices, we are significantly better than some alternatives." Roxley pointedly looks at the door, making me grunt in acknowledgement. Roxley and the Duchess never went this far. The worse they ever did was set-up Serf contracts, and while I'm not a fan of them, they can be at least be somewhat fair. For all the harm and financial finagling the Duchess did, even her Serf contracts at least played fair. "You cannot, your people cannot, continue to do this alone."

"You expect me to trust you. After what happened," I say.

"I did what was best for the city, and I will not apologize for that."

I grunt. Rather than answer Roxley, I walk toward the exit.

"John…"

"I'll think about it. But for now, I've got work to do."

I open the door without turning around, feeling the anger boil inside me. Because while he might not have a reason to apologize for his actions, there's no reason why he shouldn't have apologized to me. But perhaps I'm being petty.

That's the problem with dealing with Roxley. I can never tell where I stand or what I feel. And so rather than deal with it right now, I walk out. Because I am telling the truth. There's work to do. There's always work to do.

****

As bad as that day was, it has nothing on the next town a few days later. I find myself calling for help, bouncing the call through the limited use communicators we've purchased from the Shop rather than opening a Portal. The town of Clinton isn't even on the No. 5 highway, but I'd seen the map and figured swinging out of my way by twenty minutes would make it easier for the teams when they arrive.

My first hint of something being wrong is the crucified bodies of Galactics dotting the fields and road in. Whoever did it was insistent that crucifixion was the way to go, ripping, tearing, and otherwise forcibly positioning bodies that had more than—or less than—four limbs into the appropriate poses. Worse, a few unlucky bastards were still alive, clamped still and constantly, unwillingly healing from damage as the System "helped" them survive.

"Goblin's ass. This is wrong," Ali says as he observes a bug-eyed creature involuntarily flap its wing and click in pain.

"No shit."

"No, I mean, this is really wrong. Continuous torture without removing an individual from the System's automatic healing is considered a Class A felony," Ali says.

"And…?"

"It's the kind of felony that gets you put on Galactic bounty hunter lists," Ali says.

Even as he speaks, I'm directing Sabre to the cross and using the anti-gravity plates to get closer to the alien. When it clicks and snaps at me, I ignore it, focusing on the nails driven into its body and wings to hold it aloft. After a moment of hesitation, I conjure my sword and cut and pry the creature free.

More clicks. More trembles.

"What's it saying?" I grunt, yanking stick-thin feet free.

"Don't know," Ali says with a shrug.

"I thought you could translate everything?"

"I'm old, not omnipotent," Ali snaps. "Also, it's not as if these guys are all that common."

"These guys?" I say with a smirk while I pry the nails from creature's arms, letting myself revel in the fact that Ali is stumped rather than focus on the gruesome task.

Each motion, each removed nail elicits more clicks and occasional whistles. Unfortunately, the poor creature has multiple nails driven through it, probably due to its higher-than-normal Strength factor.

Bent over the creature's body, I can smell its dry, dusty, and acrid scent, a mix of desert air and sulphur that assaults my nostrils. Each nail I grip is sticky with black blood, stubborn in its refusal to exit without extracting another pound of flesh. Each movement brings forth another series of high-pitched chirps, but even with its arms and wings free, it makes no move to stop me. When I'm done, the creature falls to the ground and lies prone, body shivering as aftershocks ripple through it.

"How many left?" I ask, glancing around the forest of stakes.

"Two more of the bugs. There's a Hakarta that's barely hanging on—"

"Just the numbers, Ali," I say, not wishing to hear a list filled with sorrow.

"Seven."

Out of maybe fifty crosses. I wonder how they found so many Galactics, how they captured them all and did this. But it's a small matter, unnecessary information.

I reach out my hand, calling forth streams of Mana and weaving it into the universe, tearing a hole that links one location to another. Moments after the Portal solidifies, a soldier exits, rifle held in guard as he scans for threats. I see his tension increase when he sees where I brought him, the rifle coming up further as he readies himself for trouble.

"Get the teams out here. We've got people to save and people to kill," I order the soldier.

He nods and heads back into the Portal, disappearing within seconds. Rather than keep the Portal open, I close it and let the teams gather while I wait. A quick check with Ali indicates that none of the survivors are about to expire in the next hour, which gives us more than enough time.

"Incoming, boy-o," Ali announces, and I look to where the Spirit points.

In the distance, a group of five are walking toward me, weapons out and ready for use. They don't seem to be in particular hurry, but they aren't lollygagging either.

"Levels?" I ask Ali. I could try to review each of them individually, but I'd rather stay focused. There's no guarantee they don't have their own little tricks.

"Mostly Combat Classers, all in the late thirties and early forties. Two Bandits, one Soldier, a Channeller, and a Biochemist."

"Channeller and Biochemist?" I frown, hoping for more information. Problem with Classes that are too obtuse is it's hard to tell what they might come up with.

"Magic user with continual cast specialization. Watch out for explosives and poisons from the Biochemist."

The bug finally pulls itself together, its wounds closed, though it occasionally still twitches. Though I'm not entirely sure if that is due to the torture or just a facet of its biology. After a moment, the bug dresses itself using a slap-on, liquid-like fabric and pulls a small extending baton from its System inventory. Its thin hands extend again and it loops a string around its neck, the material a flexible plastic-like substance that glows once the final loop is attached.

"Thanks to be given, Savior of the Fallen," the creature buzzes and clicks before being translated.

"Oh, you're up. Good. Stay back," I say quietly.

"Choice sub-optimal, Savior. One desires vengeance."

I grunt, looking at the bug's status again.

Ox'imm'qq (Level 31 Merchant)
HP: 593/1080
MP: 780/780
Conditions: Feared, Enraged

"Fine. But don't get in my way," I say with a sigh, then I raise my hand as the group ahead of us gets within twenty meters. "You can stop there."

"I don't think so," the salt-and-pepper bearded man with the ball cap replies, his friends spreading out to give each of them a clear shot. They don't even break step at my warning. "What are you doing damaging our stuff?"

"Did you just call him—it—stuff?" I say incredulously, watching as the two Bandits keep coming.

The leader has a rusted, spiked club in hand. The other Bandit wields a pair of knives that glisten with a greenish tint. The only Soldier drops to a knee, cradling his rifle against his shoulder. The Channeller stops as well, and with my Mana Sight, I can see energy gathering around his arms. Only the Biochemist follows the front line, staying a few steps behind the Bandits.

"You're one of those alien lovers, aren't you?" Beardface sniffs and spits to the side, grinning. "Well, don't worry. We don't kill humans. We're just going to teach you not to touch what's not yours."

"Could you people be any more stereotypical?" I reply, keeping my hands out to my sides and empty. "And this doesn't have to end in violence…"

Rather than answer me, Beardface dashes forward in a full-out sprint. As he does, his and his friends' bodies blur, losing definition in their edges. He covers the distance between us in seconds, followed by his friend, who is only a few steps behind him. It'd be impressive if I didn't spar with Mikito on a regular basis. I drop into a reverse lunge, left leg thrust out behind me as I summon my sword to catch the club on my guard. It's not as effective as you'd think since the club is conical and spiked. The edges of a spike punch into the lightly armored bracers of my arm. On the other hand, the momentum of his sprint drives him fully onto my sword, the blade sliding through his ribs with ease.

I grin, twisting at my hips as I conjure a Blade Strike and rip my sword out of his body, sending an arc of power tearing through his body. His friend appears by his side, thrusting daggers at my exposed body. Out of the corner of my eyes, I watch as the bug launches itself at Beardface, floating through the air as its crackling baton swings toward the Bandit's head.

Rather than take the hit, I tap into Ali's viewpoint. A thought later and I Blink Step toward the Soldier, my blade plunging into his body as I fall. As I land, my free hand snaps out sideways and the Portal opens right behind the Channeller. Too focused on his spell, the mage doesn't see the Portal, his hands clapping as a black shroud falls over my body, trapping me within. It squeezes, attempting to crush me while robbing me of oxygen and my senses at the same time.

Seconds, maybe ten, maybe a hundred, within the inky blackness. It's hard to tell how much time passes objectively, the only indicator the glow of defunct notifications in my helmet and the beating of my heart. Even my connection to Ali is muted, a buzz at the back of my mind that has fallen to a whisper. As suddenly as the spell took effect, it shatters, bringing too-bright light and the roar of battle.

Miraculously, my Portal is still open, the connection to it somehow having survived the spell. The Channeller is on the ground, bleeding from multiple gunshot and beam rifle wounds as Jess bayonets him. The asshole enemy Soldier I attacked is falling back, firing as two members of Jess's squad hound him. Meanwhile, Roland and Howard tear into the Bandits and the Biochemist. Mikito and Shadow are crouched over the bug, teeth bared but not attacking as Ali hovers over them protectively.

"Up and at 'em," Sam says as he hauls me to my feet. Around him, his drones circle in a spiralling pattern, not taking part in the fight yet. "I'm already picking up activity in the town."

"Keep an eye on them," I say, glancing at the soldiers, including Jess, who has made his way to me. "Get your men on taking down the Galactics. Ali will mark those alive for you."

"Copy that," Jess says, assigning his men to the job immediately.

Others are sent to set up a perimeter for the incoming forces. Wride is among the perimeter scouts, jogging forward in an easy trot. Lana walks up to me, making a face.

"What are you guys doing here?" I mutter softly. I'm surprised to see the entire team here, since I figured most of them had better things to do than wait around for me to contact them.

"Luck. We were having lunch after Mikito's and my meeting with Wier," Lana says as if she's afraid to raise her voice. "John, those bodies…"

"Yeah. We'll deal with it. And them." I nod toward the settlement where the gates have reopened.

From the gates, a small group of fighters step forward, armed to the teeth. Around me, the soldiers and my team regroup, ready for another fight.

***

Maybe it was the fact that we were just too angry, but the resulting battle was a lot simpler than I had expected. Once their main group fell to a combination of concentrated rifle fire and area effect spells, the town itself was devoid of any real threat, the few remaining high Level Combat Classers giving up the moment we stepped through the sundered walls. It's only later, when we take control of the city, that we realize that the settlement owner and a few of his close allies had already absconded under the shadows of a Skill. This is fast becoming a thing. I make a mental note to get Wier and Lana to look into creating a team to help us deal with that. Until Ali and I upgrade our Skills, we definitely need someone who can pierce these concealment Skills more reliably.

Cleaning up the city, freeing the few rattled and some angry citizens is a simple enough matter. With only a couple thousand survivors, it's a real question if we should keep the place at all. Between the kind of people involved and the settlement being located in this Level 30 zone that's hours away from any real help, it's a decent question. It doesn't help that even I can tell our presence is resented. After some consideration, I make the smart decision and lob the entire problem over to Jess to hand to Wier, making him the settlement owner for now.

It doesn't help that we find, in nearly the center of town, this.

"Are you sure the System will fix the damage?" Sam asks Ali for the umpteenth time as he carefully moves the rods into the newly created lead container.

"Yup. Radiation is a low-grade damage over time effect. Your natural regeneration is more than sufficient to fix it. You'd really only need to worry about kids and maybe some real suckers with no points in Constitution," Ali reassures Sam. "And even then, a swig of Carlos's potions should fix it."

"Well, that'd also explain the lack of safety equipment," I say helpfully.

"Stupidity also does the same," Sam grouses, looking around the Alchemist's lab. "Who the hell makes plutonium?"

"Someone wanting their own nuclear warhead," Lieutenant Marco Sprouse says as he stands by, watching the entire operation diligently.

Outside, his rather relieved team is keeping an eye on the lab and ensuring we're not interrupted. The Lieutenant was dragged out here from Portland, one of the combat engineers sent to "help" us contain radioactive material. I still find it amusing that Sam's the one managing said radioactive material though.

"I thought it was pretty difficult to build nukes?" I say, frowning. I mean, didn't it take the entire brainpower of the States to figure out how to do it in the first place?

"Well, as you've pointed out to the Colonel numerous times, everything is for sale," Marco says and lets me draw the obvious conclusions.

I do, soon enough, my eyes widening. "Shit…" I look at the nonchalant-looking Spirit. "What? What am I missing?"

"Everything important," drawls Ali. When my eyes narrow, he snorts. "You're carrying a particle beam rifle over your shoulder, driving on an anti-gravity-driven Personal Assault Vehicle, and regularly throw around lightning while teleporting hundreds of feet. What makes you think a small nuclear explosion is that important?"

"Because they're nukes?" Sam says as he finishes screwing the container closed.

"It'd destroy most non-System-registered buildings, but even a mildly reinforced System building should be able to stand up to the explosion if the nuke wasn't System-registered. Most of what you've got are the equivalent of Tier IV weapons, dangerous for non-Combatants and Basic Classes—but that's the same as most of your spells and Skills. I'll admit, if you built the bomb from scratch and used your Skills, it'd have a little more of a kick—but nothing a good settlement Shield couldn't stop," Ali says. "At best, it'd be considered a Tier II weapon."

There's a long silence as our worldview takes a beating. The idea that a nuke—a weapon of mass destruction—isn't really all that powerful in this new world takes some getting used to. Maybe a little more widespread in its basic destructive potential, but a single high Level Advanced Classer could probably tank the damage and dish out more damage over the longer run. Still…

"What happened to the US's nukes?" I ask the Lieutenant, curiosity burning me.

"I'm not privy to such information," Marco replies stoically.

"Would you tell me if you knew?" I ask.

"You would not be cleared for that information either," Marco replies, which leads to an annoyed grunt from me.

Still, the non-answer leads me to believe that not only has the colonel learnt what has happened to most of the US's nukes, it's also well in hand. I can't see him refusing to direct me to one of those earlier if that wasn't the case.

"We're going to have to track down the Alchemist who did this," I say, changing the subject.

"I believe the colonel will agree with your assessment. I've requested that Sam use his drones to continue searching for our escapees."

"I wouldn't worry about that," Sam says grimly. "We've got a few Bounty Hunters and Trackers who'll make finding these asses easy. And the military boys have their own police squad. We'll find them, even if we have to issue a quest."

"Just make sure they bring enough friends," I mutter and get a nod.

Now that the radioactive material is safely stored away, the Lieutenant calls in his people to cart it through the newly opened Portal. Within seconds, people are streaming in to help settle the city as well. Getting all this settled will take a while, and for the time being, my presence is needed. It's just another damn delay on the way south.

Chapter 11

Life never takes you to where you expect it to. After our last disturbing settlement, I've reached the Six Rivers, Klamath national forest reserves. Being drawn once more into the leafy embrace of tall, mutated trees is actually comforting. The few settlements that either border or are located within the forest reserves are mostly empty, the few survivors more than grateful to be Portalled somewhere safer.

I could almost believe that the rest of the trip down would be that simple. After all, the settlements nearest a big city get emptied as the survivors flock to the city for mutual support and safety.

It's at Williams, California, a tiny little crossroads town hours away from Sacramento, that things change once again. The town itself is empty, abandoned buildings and broken-down vehicles telling the usual tale of the apocalypse. No bodies this time though. Not even the rotted remains we expect to find occasionally.

No, what I get is a real, live Galactic sitting in the middle of the crossroads, one with red skin, horns, pointed ears, and a tail. The fact that he doesn't reach for a gun and is lounging on a bright red, bullet-shaped hovering vehicle clues me in that this will be a more social kind of confrontation. Unsurprisingly, that puts me even more on guard.

"Greetings, Redeemer."

Dylan Pratma, Grandmaster of the Forge (Level 8 Executive Diplomat)

HP: 2830/2830

MP: 8940/8940

Conditions: Aura of Benevolence, Tier II Pheromones, Shield of the Stars

"Grandmaster?"

"Just a title. He is a Master Class though," Ali says warningly.

"Greetings, Grandmaster Pratma," I say with a smile, pulling Sabre to a stop and bringing my helmet down with practiced motions. "I'm going to assume your presence here is not a coincidence."

"Forsooth, that is the truth of such matters," Pratma says with a grin, running a hand along the silver-grey suit he wears. Seeing my glance at his clothing, Pratma smiles again. "The dress, the cloth that drapes across your kind's bodies, speaks to the petals of my vanity, the dressings of success and opulence that man revels in."

"That's one of us," I mutter.

I hate suits. It's why I worked for a tech company. And what the hell is up with his speech pattern? I almost want to ask him, but I'm not entirely sure what the etiquette is with regard to botched language downloads.

"In this time of darkness, a moment of light is required, a time to speak and perchance come to an agreement of minds. We seek to speak with yourself under the greater aegis of the System and a bond of peace," Pratma continues, his voice becoming almost rote.

"A… what?"

"Bond of peace. Exactly as it sounds like, boy-o," Ali explains. "You both promise not to injure one another while you talk. Generally has a duration and other terms and conditions… ah, here it comes."

I get a notification, one that makes my eyes glaze over. When I shoot Ali a helpless look, the Spirit laughs.

"Boy-o here hates reading. Something simpler would be best."

I growl softly at Ali over the besmirchment of my good name, but he is effective. The next notification is much shorter, a simple agreement that promises that we'll talk and not harm each other nor allow each other to come to harm during this conversation and an hour afterward. I agree to it, curiosity driving the decision more than anything else.

"How come the Uvrik didn't use this for our meeting?"

"What did you think the Contract was? It's all just variations on the same thing."

"Gratitude is given to the Redeemer, he who sets to rest those who have fallen, who resolves the wishes of the forsaken and lost. We speak now, if the slayer of beasts will allow, about the peace that reigns in our fair cities and the coming clouds of war, of those who might be lost and those who might be saved," Pratma says.

I stare at the devil again before coughing and waving for Pratma to continue.

"I come from the city by the bay, the settlement of golden gates, the abode of the fog children and the city of the blessed ritual in the hopes of peace, of an agreement between our two empires."

"You're from San Francisco and Sacramento," I say. Memory of my briefings about the owners of the settlements come back to me, sparse as the details might be. The pair of neighboring cities had been taken and controlled by the same organization, another damn corporation. "You're part of the Golden Water Corporation's upper management, aren't you?"

"In the manner of decisions, in the choices of the actions that the business of the golden liquid might take, it might be said I have some say. Some, those touched by the green-eyed beast, might say that I have more than some, but it is not for one to speak about such minor things. Such words are a hateful bile that erupts from my throat and wipes away all sweet words."

"Okay…" I wave him on, wondering if we'll ever get to the point.

"In the time since the coming of the System, since the approach of those starborn, the glimmering dihydrogen monoxide has laid claim to the lands of the golden gate and the blessed ritual. We have provided a shield against the night, a sword against the rapacious. We have given greatly and taken fairly, provided succor for the frail and training for the strong.

"But the clouds of time drift ever onward and the System comes fully birthed, extending its tendrils through all facets. Now, other starborn come in greater numbers, some with needs and desires that encompass all that they see, hear, and smell, seeking to only take from the wealth that flows from the blood of the Mana-evolved. And those native-born to your fair land strike back, seeking safety in numbers and under the glowing barrels of your guns. But it will be insufficient. For the starborn are numerous, like the kelp in the sea, the eggs of the kooma. If there is only blood and death in your path toward peace, only blood and death will you find."

"And what does that have to do with you?" I say.

"A meeting of minds, an agreement among those more rational. We seek to show you our fine and fair intentions while swearing upon our good names and under the aegis of the System an alliance, one born from fair intentions and future Credits," Pratma says with a smile, hands spreading to show them open and inviting.

I fall silent, considering what Pratma said. He's not wrong—we can't fight everyone. It's why I pushed for us to talk with the Uvrik corporation in Calgary, why we have tried to come to some agreement with Galactics when we can. I know that the Americans aren't happy with that, there being a very clear desire to "win" back their land, but Wier seems to understand the strategic implications of an all-out war. Even if we could beat the first wave—and that's a big if—the second, third, and all the subsequent waves would win out eventually. There're so many more of them than us that engaging in a constant acceleration of violence can only end in the devastation of our population. At the same time, we can't afford not to take action, not to push back and acquire our cities.

What Pratma offers, what Roxley has in the North, is a potential solution. My biggest hesitation is the same one that afflicts me in BC right now—the various webs of Galactic politics being unknowable for us. The Movana and Truinnar, the Yerrick, Hakarta, and more. All of them have alliances and deals, and any one such deal we make could draw us into fights we want nothing to do with. Yet we need our people to deal with the real monsters out there. A memory of the previous human-run settlement comes to mind unbeckoned, disheveled survivors and starving children reminding me that the monsters aren't just among the Galactics.

"This isn't going to be an easy conversation, you understand? And I'm not likely to be the man you'll want to speak with," I say. "But I'll pass your recommendation up the chain."

"In the pursuit of peace, admonishments, anger, and abuse are but minor inconveniences. Among the dross and vitriol of words spoken in anger and overflowing emotions, one can find true orichalcum."

"Ali, what are you doing?" I send to the spirit.

He's staring at Pratma, hands held up in a small rectangle formation in front of his face. *"Recording. This guy's incredible."*

I roll my eyes at Ali's answer but nod to Pratma, content to give him a non-verbal answer, partly in fear that he'll start up again. With a gesture, a Portal appears next to me and I step through it to report on the latest change, Sabre following me. I'm sure someone has plans for this. In either case, having me do the negotiations is probably the worse idea possible.

*****

"John…"

"Yes, dear?" I say with a smile later that evening, when we're alone and picking through the remnants of our dinner. Mmm, barbecued mammoth creature slathered with Yurk butter.

"Why didn't you warn us about him?" Lana says, just the slightest edge to her voice.

I can't help but flash her a shit-eating grin, which gets me a pinch. Twisting away, I regret provoking the woman—and that Pratma insisted I stay, at least till a minimal agreement had been made. Something about my ability being a potential danger.

"Didn't think it was relevant. He's understandable." *Mostly.*

"And the fact that he sounds like he's from a badly written sixteenth-century play?"

"Is amusing. I'm kind of sad that the agreements are so…"

"Business like?" Lana snorts, shaking her head. "Imprecise, flowery language is not something you want in your alliance agreements. Even if they make for more fun reading."

"Yeah…" I give her a hug. "Thanks for coming."

"You're welcome. It made sense to ensure we had some oversight on this. Wier is nice enough, but his people are kind of like you."

"Except that diplomat."

"Peter? Yes. We're lucky he survived. And kept his Class," Lana says, smiling. "That Skill of his is quite useful."

"Diplomatic Immunity?" I say. "Complete immunity to damage, targeting, and spells? It's a bit broken, as Jason would say. If it lasted for longer than a few seconds, it'd be really broken."

"Do you think we'll get an agreement?" Lana says, a slightly wistful note in her voice. "It'd be nice to have a couple of big cities on our side, ones that we don't have to protect. After the Uvrik gave up their portion of Calgary, we've mostly been taking over smaller settlements owned by the Galactics. If we can get what they promise—that the humans can help us if they want—we'll receive a lot of of help without the cost."

"Aye. San Jose's going to be problematic though," I say with a grimace.

"Do you think it'll throw off the negotiations?"

San Jose is technically a contested city, one that exists in an uneasy cold war with Pratma's people. Whether we would give it up—if we even have a right to make that decision—is something that would be a sticking point in the negotiations.

"Maybe. Depends on how stubborn everybody is. If the Pratma give up on San Jose, it'd be great. Otherwise, they might have to learn to live with them. If it was just Wier, I'd be more optimistic." I shrug. "But he's in contact with his bosses now and I don't know them. And there's a lot of pressure to not give up any 'American' soil."

At the last few words, Lana grimaced. We've both heard such sentiments more than once, sometimes with the American changed to Canadian. It's no surprise really. No one wants to consider themselves conquered, but perhaps because we lived for over a year with Roxley as the "owner" of Whitehorse, it's something we can accept. Needs must when the devil drives, and the devil's on a German autobahn.

"Keep an ear out on this?" I finally say to break the silence and get a nod from Lana.

After a moment, to distract us from the conversation, I kiss her with my hands on her hips, a hand sliding along her waist. In short order, we're not worrying about the state of the world anymore, our focus on much more immediate and intimate matters.

***

A week passes in a flash. The first three days I spend stuck in the meetings, forced to listen as they negotiate a basic agreement between all parties. Since I was there, I even signed it, putting the settlements I owned up north into the document. City and myself, all bound by a simple acknowledgement. Once again I shivered at that level of power, that ability to control the lives of so many with so little.

After that, I was allowed to roam while they hammered down more concrete details, like when the first trade caravan could come in, when the first group could visit the cities. Mostly, I spent my time driving around, finding the few last human holdouts, and Portalling them to bigger settlements. There were a few nice surprises. A First Nations—wait, Native American—tribe that had managed to survive by holing up in their casino, along with a bunch of their workers and high-rollers. It highly amused me that the casino was a "Gambling Fort" with some truly strange, chance-based defensive measures. There was a church whose preacher had sacrificed his own Class and Perk to register the building in the System, allowing it to become a sanctuary against the violence and saving the town that had grown up around it. His actions had saved hundreds of people, the megachurch more than sufficient to accommodate them all.

I even spent a day back in BC, taking the time to review my settlements and work with Katherine about new developments. Richmond and Burnaby were now full-fledged Towns, the outlying suburbs a short hop away. With two more Towns, I had the option of joining them into one major Settlement to ease administrative burdens. Of course, I would also lose out slightly on the option of having more ancillary buildings, but the loss wasn't as great as I feared. Rather than having three, I'd only have two, which meant I couldn't add another Adventurers Guild till we had at least one more suburb, as Labashi already had his Mercenary Corp in place. Still, after some consideration, I decided to push ahead with it, joining the City Cores of both of those suburbs with Vancouver's.

Partly, that was to help the City Dungeon grow. Simply put, the City Dungeon fed off the ambient Mana of the settlement it was connected to, allowing refresh rates and size to be dictated by these changes. Since I'd now tripled the size of the settlement, the Dungeon had a much larger area to draw upon and would thus grow faster. There were other ways to develop the Dungeon of course—including dedicating more Mana to it directly—but this was the "cheapest" way to do so in the short-term. The requirements to get more ambient Mana from a fixed location were quite wide-ranging, including Credits, technology, and of course, more Mana. Since actual Credits were a crucial shortfall for our settlements, with a large portion of our on-going income dedicated to rebuilding basic infrastructure, this was the best option.

After that, I had to deal with a few interest groups and the various city councils when they realized what I had done. I let them argue for an hour in the conference room before telling them to suck it up and work out who was going to be in charge of what before I left. It wasn't particularly nice but I didn't need to be nice—I just needed it to be effective. In the long-term, it could cause trouble, but really, I wasn't exactly planning to run the city in the long-term. Owning the settlements was a short-term solution, one that met my own goals but at some point, someone more competent and who actually gave a damn about running it would need to take over.

Visiting Kamloops was a lot more relaxed. Ben and the rest of the council had the city well in hand, and the smaller population meant that there were a lot fewer egos to stroke. While Ben's current Class only gave him abilities to alter existing buildings and provide short-term boosts, he indicated that his Advanced Class would be able to permanently alter and boost buildings or potentially an entire settlement, depending on which way he went. After some discussion, we ended up assigning him as the Mayor of the Town in a bid to increase his experience gain, as well as potentially open up even more interesting Classes.

As for Kelowna—well, it was doing okay. The farmlands were doing well, and the Adventurer's Guild had, as promised, provided a significant security force. Mostly, Kelowna was in the development stage, with the focus on clearing out monsters and reclaiming lands, so there was little to report.

The last thing I decided to deal with was a visit to the Shop. The fox was, as usual, attentive to my needs, even if most of what I was picking up was the usual. I did, however, take the time to purchase the upgrades for my Portal Skill and a few others. Doing that took out a large portion of my personal Credits, but considering I was getting further and further away from my settlements, it was a necessary expense. Since I was still waiting for the Quantum State Manipulator to arrive, the Class Skills were more important than picking up a few more toys. A quick glance at the Portal Skill once purchased reaffirmed my decision.

Portal (Level 5)

Effect: Creates a 5-meter by 5-meter portal which can connect to a previously traveled location by user. May be used by others. Maximum distance range of portals is 25,000 kilometers.

Cost: 250 Mana + 100 Mana per minute (minimum cost 350 Mana)

My last meeting of importance in Vancouver was with Wynn. The Burning Leaves guild master had invited me out for dinner, an offer that Katherine made sure I couldn't refuse. If you've never had sushi made by a Sushi Chef with System-mutated ingredients, you are missing out. For most of the dinner, our conversation was benign, revolving around recent Guild-authorized quests and equipment sales. It was only toward the end that Wynn brought up the topic I had been dreading.

"Is there no way for there to be a peaceful resolution to your disagreement with the Zarrie?" Wynn says softly.

"Not the right person to ask. I'm just a hired hand."

Wynn's flat stare made me grin weakly. My threadbare excuse was as worthless as a teddy bear without a soul.

"Redeemer, you must understand, the royal family have traditionally been allied with the Zarrie. While the mutual defense agreements do not apply on a Dungeon World, there are consequences to such action."

"You guys leaving?" I ask bluntly.

"No. The Guild is independent, as you know," Wynn replies. "But unwarranted aggression against our allies does cast a bad light on your settlements."

"Unwarranted." I grunt, shaking my head. "The Zarrie are asses and you know it. They're petty tyrants, and while they might not be doing the entire System slavery thing, they're more than happy to beat, blackmail, and kill as they wish. They're bullies."

"Political realities often dictate distasteful bedfellows."

"Good thing I'm not a politician then." Before Wynn can say anything else, I hold my hand up and stare at the man. "We'll work with those who are willing to work with us. Who are willing to conduct themselves with grace. Everyone else can burn."

"And that is the stance of your settlements?"

"I guess it is."

"Very well." Wynn falls silent before he points at a purplish slice of sashimi streaked with dark yellow. "Have you tried the Quem fish? I was surprised to find that they are thriving in your English Bay. They are considered a Galactic delicacy…"

And with that, the topic is dropped. I still am not sure what, if any, the effects our attack on the Zarrie in LA will have, but in the end, it doesn't matter. I am not going to back down. I'd rather have a few good, reliable allies than a bunch of political flakes. Even if a part of me considers that entire statement a naïve belief.

After all that, when the agreement with Pratma is finally signed, I am finally allowed to leave the town—under escort—to travel through the outskirts of Sacramento and head farther south. Lana and the rest of the small diplomatic team actually get to visit the settlement itself, with additional visits to San Francisco planned for later on. The goal, of course, is to verify the information we've purchased from the System. There's nothing like actually seeing things with your own two eyes—especially when it's possible to have the System "lie" for you with certain Skills. Admittedly, that is a rarer Skill, but it is possible.

Traveling with a pair of guards is interesting. Both have low Level Advanced Classes, but for the actual fighting of the various monsters we encounter, I am on my own. I kind of guess what they are up to, so I keep the use of my Skills to the minimum. Still, when Ali locates a new dungeon, the potential gain from clearing it outweighs any security concerns and I make sure to clear it, Blink Stepping and Inferno Striking through its interior.

At the end of the smoking ruins, amid the stench of burnt fur and cooked flesh, I am truly grateful I don't have to explain the canine and leonine corpses to Lana.

Once I am far enough away from San Jose, my silent companions leave me, allowing me to complete the rest of the trip by myself. The remainder of the trip is routine, filled with wandering monsters, displaced refugees, and the occasional enterprising bandit. Even the big cities like Fresno and Bakersfield are rote exercises in travel and rescue by now.

Thanks to Ali adjusting my Status, I don't have much trouble entering the city itself. Fresno is interesting in that they aren't exactly oppressing the humans, but there are more than a few signs of bias shown toward Galactics. Recalling my discussion with Wynn, I make a note of what I see before popping a Portal open for Ingrid and a friend of hers to do some reconnaissance. We'll decide how far to take it once we have more details.

Bakersfield is more cut-and-dry, another one of those cities that need a helping hand dealing with a bunch of Galactic asses. Rather than fight for a settlement we can't hold, I just pop open the Portal, drag a few fire teams through, and round up everyone we can before we leave. We leave a single team to stick around and round up anyone else with a short-range communication device to let me know when they need a pick-up. Interestingly enough, the Galactics don't even try to really obstruct us, sending a few token drones and enforcers while we're busy pulling people out. It is almost as if they are relieved to get rid of the stinky humans.

All these boring, easy trips change when I turn east and make my way to Fort Irwin.

Chapter 12

I have to admit, I was surprised to learn that Fort Irwin had been both an actual military base and a training center. That means that they'd had on-site housing and a fluctuating number of members on base at any time. Luckily for the base, a number of units had been undergoing training when the System hit, so they'd had a large number of trained personnel on-hand to deal with the monsters, even if our guns aren't half as effective as they used to be. Unfortunately, they also got unlucky enough to get targeted with a monster drop. A couple of high Level sand worms were teleported around their base. For all that, the general in charge had managed to keep the majority of civilians and base households secure.

While Fort Irwin has nowhere near the numbers that Camp Pendleton does, it has the benefit of being nearby and fully staffed. In addition, they're desperately in need of a restock. As a System-designated Fort, they've got a significant advantage over most random buildings, especially since the designation includes the entirety of the base. From what Wier says, they've even been able to gain limited access to the Shop through a few Quartermasters' Class Skills. But access or not, they've been seriously limited in their ability to develop, which is where I come in.

For all that, you'd think I'd be greeted with open arms. Instead, first I get stopped and interrogated by a roving patrol in the 45° Celsius weather. If it isn't for the fact that I'm mostly resistant to minor changes in temperature like this, I'd be pissed. As it stands, once they finish their not-so-subtle interrogation, I'm escorted onto base under armed guard.

The base itself is an interesting place. They've obviously laid out numerous mines around their shelter, the walls replaced and increased to nearly thirty feet high. Watchtowers made of reinforced concrete sit above the walls, beam turrets and rocket launchers arranged to cover the approaches. I absently note the shield that opens as we near the walls, the gate that rolls open soundlessly, and the armed guards that patrol the walls. It is, for want of a better word, a military fortification.

It doesn't take long for them to bring me to meet the general in charge. He's got a close-cut hairstyle, salt-and-pepper hair on a too-tanned face that emphasizes the wrinkles he's not gotten rid of and a steely glare that dictates respect. The only thing that detracts from the professional look is the fact he probably should have shaved this morning. Or he might just be unlucky enough to need to shave more than once a day.

Richard Miller (Officer Level 16)

_HP: 880/880_

_MP: 1290/1290_

Conditions: Aura of Command

Mental Influence Resisted

"Mr. Lee," General Richard Miller says as he stands and offers me his hand. I absently note the notification that pushes aside the aura, the briefest flare as my resistances and stubborn will engage and beat aside his low Level Class skill. "General Richard Miller, Commander of Fort Irwin."

"General Miller," I say, casting a quick glance at the others in the room.

I get quick introductions when my interest is shown, though I promptly forget their names as I'm interrupted by a floating, invisible Spirit.

"Isn't that a drink?"

"Not now!"

"Thank you for coming. Colonel Wier informed me that we could be expecting you within the week. You've made good time," Miller says with a smile.

"Not too bad," I agree, tilting my head. "You know, if you pointed me at a suitable location, we could continue this talk while you get resupplied."

"All in good time, Mr. Lee. I wished to speak with you before we began such an operation," the general says with a smile. "Communication with the colonel has been somewhat difficult, our conversations limited. I was hoping you could perhaps detail a little about the situation in Seattle and your own settlements."

I return Miller's frank stare before nodding. At first, I start with talking about Seattle, but Miller's incisive questions have me jumping backward again and again as I detail my own settlements, the Galactics I've come across, and the basic System knowledge we've gained. He's particularly interested in Trasher's little book, so I send the survival guide to him and his aides with a thought. Through the entire conversation, notes are taken, and before I know it, nearly half the day has passed.

"Well, that's all been fascinating. But you're right, we should really open the Portal to the colonel. I'm sure he can brief me himself," Miller says as he stands, one hand sweeping low to beckon an aide closer. "Major Alvarez will show you where you can set up the Portal."

"So I've passed?"

"Passed?" Miller says, playing dumb.

"Your assessment," I say bluntly. Out of the corner of my eyes, I note that the soldiers who were clustered around the office have slowly dispersed.

"Yes." Miller doesn't apologize, which I can understand. Without access to the full Shop to verify how truthful I am, he's only got Class Skills and his own intuition. Which, probably, is good enough, but probably doesn't cut it when you're in charge of so many lives. "If you'll follow the major, we do look forward to getting our supplies."

"Got it." I offer him a wave, walking out of the door, followed by the major soon afterward.

Out of the corner of my eyes, I see the general bending his head and falling into a deeper conversation with his people.

"This way, sir." Alvarez waves a tanned hand.

I follow along, almost wanting to whistle a jaunty tune to break the seriousness they all seem to carry. Then again, they've been surviving in the arse-end of nowhere for nearly a year, fighting Level 40 plus monsters and hemmed in by even higher Level zones and Galactics. I'd be tense too.

***

Watching Wier and his posse of uniformed aides walk away to talk with the general, I release the Portal before it drains me completely. A moment later, I'm seated on a lounge chair pulled from my Altered Space, a bar of chocolate in hand while I wait for my Mana to recover. Alvarez stares at me for a second but chooses not to comment. Instead, we spend the time watching the small group of assigned personnel move the various pieces of equipment that were brought over during the few minutes the Portal was open, distributing them as needed.

Shifting goods via the Portal is weird—a large group from this side jumps through in a bid to make purchases at the Shop while another stream of individuals comes in from Seattle, all of them toting boxes double to triple their size and even more stored in their System inventory. The sheer volume moved is significantly higher than what it seems, especially since a few of those have Class Skills that let them carry more in their inventory than you'd guess. The ability to overstack slots in a System inventory is a bit of a cheat.

"What's in the boxes?" I ask Alvarez after I finish my first bar of chocolate.

"Non-System-generated items we need," Alvarez replies. When I glare at him, the man relents, probably deciding that replying is better than annoying me enough to stop opening Portals. "Fresh vegetables and supplements, new clothing, toilet paper, and umm… other sanitary equipment."

"Pads?"

"It's been an issue," Alvarez says stiffly.

I chuckle softly, though I do recall more than one time when the young ladies in the team disappeared into houses and stores before stuffing said items into my Altered Space. I once asked why they just didn't get their genes changed or something else and received a blistering earful from Ingrid about how the System cheats and reverts such changes quickly. At a guess, it's a by-product of the entire damn "get everyone pregnant" directive.

"So what are the men requesting?" I'm rather curious to see what it is they, being stuck without the basics, might be after.

"Nothing they can't live without," Alvarez replies then relents. "Beer. Smokes. Deodorant is high on the list too. Disposable razors. System-registered knives."

I chuckle and decide not to comment further. I'm sure there are other less savory requests, but considering the major is handling most of this in an official capacity, fulfilling those is likely to be done via less official channels.

"Fair enough." I glance at my Mana gauge. "Another five minutes and I should be good to go."

Alvarez nods. Upon spotting the still-lingering boxes, he strides away to have a quiet chat with the poor lieutenant in charge of storing the products.

Rather than watch them, I lean back and chill for now. It's going to be a long night of shuttling people back and forth as my Mana regenerates.

***

The next morning, I'm called into the newly restructured situation room, a place now filled with paper maps, floating blue System notification screens, projected maps of the surroundings, and more esoteric lines of information. A few people are in here, working and watching the screens, but I'm led straight to the main table where the general and Wier stand.

"Morning, gents," I greet the tired-looking pair and their surrounding aides.

"Mr. Lee," Miller says, inclining his head slightly in greeting. Wier follows with his own greeting. "We received some disturbing news late last night."

"Oh…?"

"The Zarrie Kingdom in LA has received a large batch of reinforcements of Jaracks. Current estimates put it at a full brigade, but we're still verifying data," Miller informs me.

"*Jarack?*"

"*You humans have them translated as were-jackals. Which is weird because they don't actually transform,*" Ali clarifies.

"What's their force composition now of Advanced and Master Classes?" I say with a frown.

"Total combat Classes show three low Level Master Classes and forty-three Advanced Classes spread between Los Angeles and its surroundings," Miller replies. "As you know, they had just over two-thirds of their numbers deployed against Camp Pendleton. That allowed the other resistance cells in

Los Angeles to continue fighting. But with the reinforcements, we expect the balance of power to change drastically."

The Marines in Camp Pendleton and the various other members of the armed forces have done a stellar job—out-Leveled as they've been, they've refused to back down and have kept up a string of harassing attacks. Once they Leveled up enough, they even managed to get a few of their old toys, like their tanks and artillery, back in action. So much so that the Zarrie have had to keep a significant armed presence near their borders to contain the Marines.

While a Master Class is powerful—scarily so—I'm given to understand that the Marines have shown a willingness to trade a lot of lives for a kill. It's that willingness that allowed them to chalk up a Master Class kill and just over a dozen Advanced Classers. Swarm tactics aren't uncommon—it's why I didn't get a world first for killing a Master Class individual on Earth. It's also why most Advanced and Master Class individuals have escape Skills and spells on hand, but surprise and arrogance can often disarm even the best prepared. Levels help ensure that there's a significant weight to the entire quality argument, but quantity still has a quality of its own. And no Kingdom is willing to lose a Master Class just to kill a few hundred Basics.

"Sounds like time's running out," I say, staring at the map and the small markers on the board. Amusingly enough, I think I understood the Seattle mages' map better than this more "professional" one. But in the end, the truth they impart is the same. "You need me to speed up and head south now."

"Yes," Miller says, his head coming up. "Once you provide them the settings for our communication formation, we'll be able to support one another with greater ease. We should also be able to achieve real-time communication between our two bases."

"Are we changing the plan then? Go wide to reach Pendleton rather than through the city to create waypoints?" I ask. That was the initial plan. Between my stealth skills and the new Shrunken Footprints Skill, I should be able to sneak into the city itself. Due to the constant fighting, the areas around LA don't have stable settlement shields that I have to concern myself about.

"Yes." Wier traces a path south, elaborating on the challenges I can expect to face as best as they know.

I settle in to listen and ask some questions, though as always, I'll make my own decisions when it gets right down to it. Being the man on the bike, that's my responsibility. Still, in the back of my mind, I worry that all this talking means more lives are being lost.

***

"Major." I greet Alvarez when he walks up, followed by a squad—I hope that's the right term. A bunch of soldiers anyway—in a squat military machine with a big cannon on it seen in way too many Hollywood movies.

"Mr. Lee." Alvarez nods to me. "The members of Staff Sergeant Johnson's squad will be following you. Their orders are to ensure that you make it to Camp Pendleton and to aid in the verification of your identity. That is, of course, secondary to the verification documents and passphrases you've been provided with."

I grunt, recalling the rather specific talk Alvarez had with me after this morning's meeting. He'd been particularly pedantic about it, ensuring that I recalled everything word for word and in the right order before he let me go. Luckily, a stupidly high Intelligence meant that when and if I concentrated, small things like that were easy to memorize. And I have to admit, I cheated and recorded the information in my helmet just in case.

"That going to last? Things are going to get rough," I say, glancing at the vehicle. Even if they've changed out the engines to make it run, the fact stands that most vehicles made pre-System aren't strong enough to take a solid whacking. Heck, I recall a particularly exuberant five-year-old putting a dent in an abandoned vehicle back in Whitehorse.

"This particular vehicle has been rebuilt entirely by our Machinists," Alvarez answers, glancing at the vehicle with some pride before looking at me. "It will suffice. Staff Sergeant Johnson and his team have most recently traveled the road you're on, so please make sure to listen to them."

"All right, let's go," I say and twist Sabre's throttle. The bike slides forward without a sound, rolling out of the gates.

It's only a few minutes later that I realize I forgot to actually talk to the sergeant. Oops…

***

On the shorter route, it's just under two hundred miles from Fort Irwin to Camp Pendleton. On a good day, that'd be a three hour or so drive, maybe less depending on traffic. Now, with monsters, destroyed roads, hostile settlements, and insane environmental factors, that three-hour drive could easily take a whole day. And we're taking the long way around, cutting away from Los Angeles to swing by Joshua Tree National Park, Palm Springs, and the Cleveland National Forest. Any of those areas could easily force us to take much longer than a single day if we wanted to do this quietly.

Unfortunately, the option of doing things quietly has gone the way of the Zarrie reinforcements, and so we're just going to do it fast. In a short period after we leave the base, the Humvee overtakes me to take point, kicking up dust while a pair of tiny drones fly overhead to provide overwatch. Neither of those are anywhere as good as Ali, but I don't tell them that. Wouldn't want to hurt their feelings.

We swing off the highway more than once, often because there isn't a highway left, the pavement destroyed by fights or just the movement of a monster. In one case, the footprints are so large and reptilian that it seems as if the Midwest is about to be hit by a herd of immigrating kaiju. Off-road, we have to slow down, rolling up and over barren hills, dealing with sudden bogs and hidden monsters.

Palm Springs was once a resort town for the big Hollywood elites, a place where you could commonly see withered, old rich folk and Hollywood starlets within the same day. It had been pretentious, brown, and filled with marble, an oasis of rich snobbery and transplanted plants.

"Five hundred Credits per person." The green-polo-shirt, white-shorts-wearing tanned Golfer grins at us, his titular clubs slung across his shoulder.

He and his friends found us as we tried to swing around the settlement, not wanting to stop at a human-owned place. A quick glance at their Levels shows that they're a mix of mid 40s to low 30s, a weird assortment of Classes ranging from pure combat to well, Golfers.

I lipread Polo Shirt's words as I stay behind the Humvee, Johnson having indicated that he's in charge of this negotiation.

"We letting them shake us down?" I mutter to the soldier sent to babysit me.

He's got his head on a swivel, checking behind us for potential problems, trusting his friends to do the same in their own zones of responsibility. I'm doing the same too, sort of. Ali is double-checking and verifying information on the sensor maps while I look around with my own eyes.

"We have an agreement with the settlement," the soldier says out of the corner of his mouth. "We pay them for passage; they leave us alone."

"They that tough to take down?"

"Not in my experience," he says. "But I just follow orders."

I grunt, watching as Johnson pays for our passage and gets a briefing on the most recent movements by our mutual enemies. Patrol routes, schedules, and sightings of new enemies are all part of the report. I have to admit, the information is useful, even if I'm not thrilled by the idea of being extorted. When we get back on the road, I find myself asking Johnson about the situation.

"The owner of Palm Springs is not particularly friendly with us. We've come to an agreement that allows us passage through their areas, but it's tenuous."

"Why do you let them stay?" I frown, considering the distances between Palm Springs and the base. It'd certainly give the base access to a Shop, which I know they badly need.

"They're an American settlement," Johnson says with a grunt. "Our job is to protect them, not forcibly conscript their lands."

"Ah... politics," I say.

I'm not entirely sure I agree with the general's decision, but then again, I'm not a soldier. Living your whole life believing you need to keep the very people who are being piss-ass annoyances alive must create some kind of mental dissonance. It doesn't help that these citizens can and probably will do significant damage in any fight. In the end, I'm just a helpful visitor here. While I like to think of myself as a citizen of the world, that's less likely to be a viewpoint that's agreed upon by the Americans. So all I can do is keep quiet and take it for what is.

***

The last few hours of our trip are a slow, agonizing process. Under the cover of Ali's abilities and the Skills of a pair of the soldiers, we sneak in past the fluid battle lines surrounding Camp Pendleton. With such a large area to cover, the Zarrie can only use roving patrols, droids, and fixed sensor grids to keep watch. Unfortunately for them, all of those can easily be subverted, given enough time, patience, and Skill.

The Zarrie patrols are a mixture of desert-themed creatures. The Jarack reinforcements are jackal-faced humanoids with fur on their bodies and equipped with a mixture of high-tech and melee weapons. They act as the main frontline of the Zarrie while being covered by large, carapace-laden heavies who tote around oversized beam weapons and physical shields. Mixed in among that group are smaller, dog-sized creatures with a shiny, sac-like back that can spit out an acidic-poisonous mixture. Lastly, each patrol has a metallic, vehicular aid—whether airborne or ground—to provide AI-driven help. From what Ali tells me, they're not the greatest help, but if you need to cart around corpses or scout out potential new problems, the drones did the job.

Mostly we try to avoid even seeing them, but while the information we've received is useful, it's not complete, so we find ourselves hiding, trusting in our Skills and abilities as we sneak closer to our objective. Killing the patrols would be simple, but that would give away our position and if they decided to purchase more information, they'd know what we're up to. In this case, secrecy is our shield. So we traverse mutated forests, destroyed roads, and deal with numerous bush fires, either trusting in our armor and Skills to keep us alive or swinging wide. It's a hard call to make—sometimes those wild fires are fueled by Mana and System-enhanced plants, making them a danger even to me.

Again and again, we have to stop and start, our "short" journey lengthening as we swing around System-enhanced problems and the occasional firefight. Finally Johnson decides we're close enough and makes contact with the base itself. After that, it's just more waiting before we're met by the Marines and led in at a breakneck speed.

As we cross the barbed wire fences that surround the buildings, I find myself relaxing. Even if we're still under guard, being surrounded by humans and the mostly theoretical safety of the walls is comforting. Johnson and his men relax too, especially as we cross deeper into the base itself. Though we've all heard of the fierce fighting that has occurred, there's little on the base to indicate that, all the buildings in pristine condition due to the System. Nothing to indicate a problem, except the way the soldiers move and the edge they all hold. They're like live weapons, ready to explode into action at any time. The obvious presence of the military police as we head deeper shows that this state of constant battle readiness has taken its toll on the personnel.

Once we're in, I'm led to a secure bunker where I'm interrogated— nicely—by the guards. As check after check is passed, I find my tension ratcheting up once again. Soon, I'll be meeting the man in charge and opening a Portal for Wier and Miller. And then we'll really begin.

***

"Thank you, Mr. Lee. For allowing us to have this conversation," Sanchez says, the Puerto Rican marine colonel offering me a smile. There's an edge to the marine, a hardness and a lurking pain in his eyes and a coldness to his smile that reminds me not to underestimate the man.

"You're welcome," I answer before glancing toward Wier and Miller.

They too offer their thanks before we get down to the meat of the meeting. The uniformed men aren't the only individuals present at this meeting. The usual suspects like the mages from Seattle, the Baristas, and of course Lana and Mikito, are all present. In addition, Labashi and a few members of the Adventurers Guilds we've begun to work with are here too. In Labashi's case, he's here to fill a contract with Wier. The Guilds are here to set up Quests for their members once we've decided upon a plan.

"Thank you for coming," Miller states once everyone's settled. In the center of the meeting room is a projection of California. "As you know, we must finish this fight before the Zarrie can reinforce further. Of the seventeen City Cores highlighted here, we must take seven for the first phase to be considered complete.

"Due to the significant amount of scrutiny placed upon our forces by the Zarrie, our plans of operations cannot be discussed in any detail. What we are here to discuss is the timeframe the attacks will be conducted under, the requirements that each force has to be ready, the chain of command, and what, if any, concerns you might have about the attack and your group's involvement."

It's kind of amusing, listening to all this. I was in on the earlier conversation between the three, the long talk that Miller had with the other two army officers, along with my interjections, about the System and the

Shop's ability to extract information. Wier, having had more interactions with the Shop itself, was able to provide further information and even shared a few of the documents and books he'd purchased detailing military tactics formed in the presence of the System. The meeting we're having now is the result of that earlier conversation. However, a bold statement like that, among us civilians, obviously doesn't garner many points for Miller.

"You're not telling us the plan?" Charles says, an edge to his voice.

"We're just civilians, you know." Kaylee, the Barista, shifts her tone to one parodying the military, almost barking her next words. "We aren't trusted with things like planning or thinking. Civilians would just mess it up."

"Har. We've cleared more cities than these army boys!"

Labashi watches, his lips pursed. He's obviously clear on the why, while the Guilds don't seem too perturbed. In fact, I catch a few smiles. Because of the vagueness of the plans, the resulting quests' expenses will be high.

"You prefer they tell you the plan now and change it midway?" Lana says, the voice of reason as always. "Because if General Miller is right, and I'll bet that he is, any plans he actually articulates, puts into writing, or otherwise communicates is open to purchasing. Now, there are Skills and technology to make it harder or at least more expensive to buy that information, but that's more expensive, not impossible. So being kept in the dark is the best way forward."

"And if General Miller is assassinated?" Laila asks from her chair. I'm amused that she's in a sleeveless pantsuit, one that shows off her tightly toned arms.

She looks almost as delicious as the dark-chocolate aide who sits by her side, his arms shown off in a sleeveless vest. For a moment, I wonder if it's just coincidence or a case of well-designed uniforms before I pull my attention back to Miller.

"The chain of command passes from General Miller to myself to Colonel Wier to Mr. Lee," Sanchez answers, waving his fingers and flicking over a document. In it is the new chain of command.

I'm surprised to note Lana's and Sam's names on it and relatively high, though we go through a couple more military personnel before it seriously switches around to non-military personnel.

"Why's John so high up?" Kaylee asks, prodding the paper. "He military too?"

"No. Mr. Lee's special Skills dictate his position in the chain of command. If he is still able to function at that point, he will be in the best position to ascertain the next steps for our attack," Miller replies.

"Ah, he gets to decide if we run away?" Daniel asks, stating the obvious.

There's more than a few frowns at the mage, but he ignores them all. Whether it's a case of the programmer being entirely oblivious or not caring, he seems more than happy to annoy everyone.

"Or press the attack," Miller says. "Our troops have been so informed. Now, we have much to discuss and not much time."

The grumbling stills, at least for the moment, as we turn toward the minutiae of battle prep. It amuses me slightly since my own portion of this is done. I've got Sabre, Ali, and my sword. Everything else... well, that's for others to handle. My people are in good hands. Once again, I'm the damn transport hub.

***

"You were pretty quiet in there," Sam says to me later that evening where our team has gathered in the house we've been allocated.

Everyone's here, including Carlos and Ingrid, which is a nice change of pace from the recent norm. Perhaps it's because we've all lost our families that voluntary gatherings like this are all the more important, familiar bonds reestablished to offer comfort and succor.

"Didn't have much to contribute," I say with a shrug. "You and Lana have a better idea of what our men are like these days. Though I'm surprised you weren't there." I say that to Mikito, who sighs.

"Training. We're closing in on clearing the fiftieth level zone of your dungeon," Mikito says with a slight bite.

"Ah, right." I blink and duck my head, recalling that I was the one who had mentioned we should try to clear the dungeon ourselves. We never got around to it, mostly because I'm too busy running errands. Truthfully, outside of pulling the team in for the occasional clearance of a newly found, uncleared dungeon on my route, we haven't had much fighting time together recently.

"Leave him alone, Miki," Carlos says. "He's busy doing hero stuff. We've got the dungeons covered."

"*Miki...?*" I do my best to hide my astonishment at the lack of naginata protruding from Carlos's body at the use of a nickname.

"Lazing around and road-tripping," Mikito mutters grumpily, though mostly good-naturedly.

"That does raise the question—when are we taking the rest of Canada?" Ingrid says, leaning forward. "Not that helping the Americans isn't important, but you know..."

"National pride," I say with a half-smile. "After this. I'll be porting up to Calgary and heading east once the battle here is over and things have settled. Wier has promised more help from his people. With the Marines clear, they'll have enough people to make an actual push of it by themselves once they settle LA. Calgary's pretty secure now and Edmonton is raring to go, so we're next on the agenda."

"Good," Sam grunts.

I glance at the older man, recalling his concerns over Ontario.

"We're pretty settled up in BC too. The mountains farther north are an issue, but things are beginning to settle. The negotiations with the sirens in Vancouver Island are nearly over," Lana adds, shaking her curly red hair. "Though I'm not entirely sure we'll get many immigrants from there."

"Men," Ingrid says with a snort.

"Good," Carlos says happily, returning to the initial topic. "Don't get me wrong, I don't mind helping them but…"

"It'll be good to get started," I say, nodding. "Any news on the Rockies?"

A few faces are made at that question.

Ingrid answers without hesitation. "Level 80 to 120 depending on the zone. No survivors. Our scouts have indicated a series of flying monsters ranging from gargoyles, griffins, and drakes to elemental rock hounds and creatures we don't even have names for. And that's at the edges."

"Sounds like the passes up north are the way to go, unless there're a few lower Level zones down south," I say.

It's frustrating, but we're also lucky. As the latest Dungeon World, we're still considered "new," and while certain zones have a higher level of ambient Mana than others, we're nowhere close to the levels of older Dungeon Worlds. Over time—measured in years and decades, thankfully—the amount of ambient Mana on Earth will rise too. In fact, the introduction of Earth as a Dungeon World has helped the other Dungeon Worlds significantly, slowing down the Mana saturation in their worlds. The continual increase in zones and Levels in older Dungeon Worlds is what makes City Dungeons so damn popular. The City Dungeons themselves are much more controlled and it's why we haven't seen a rush of new Galactic Adventurers. While the rewards in experience and loot is better in a Dungeon World, City Dungeons are just safer and more accessible for those at the lower end of the scale. It's like travelling to a new country to take a degree – sure, technically possible but it's expensive and risky. Of course, not a rush is relative. When you're talking populations of hundreds of billions, fractions are still huge.

"The scouts are working that route right now, but it's slow going. Between the Galactics streaming in, the need to locate and work with survivors, and the lack of a base, I don't expect there to be any major developments," Ingrid says. "They've asked for funds to build up a Fort they located, but it's pretty broken right now."

"Done. Talk to Kim. He'll arrange for the Credits." I trust the assassin to know and vet the scouts. While she isn't directly in charge of their operations—it's a tad too much responsibility for the lady—I know she's interested in the process. It's almost like stepping into a new world each time you explore a new region these days. "The Americans giving them a hard time?"

With the border down, there's little to separate our countries except an imaginary state of mind—certainly, we don't have a giant wall to demarcate the difference. But the walls we build in our minds can be harder to break than even a diamond-studded wall in reality.

"Not too much. Many of them are happy to see just about anyone. The few who aren't... well, our scouts are some of our highest Level Combat Classers," Ingrid says. "Anyone who objects too pointedly gets the point."

"Badoom-Krash!" Ali shouts, playing imaginary drums to go alongside the sound effect.

"And that's enough of that. On another note, there's been talk about reclaiming some of the other settlements," Lana says. "Some of the survivors have indicated a desire to head back home. Others just want to explore. We've been able to keep it in check mostly, or at least redirect them to one of our smaller Villages in BC, but it's not just us. Alberta's indicated the same thing—people want to go home. Even if that home is now owned by a seventeen-foot-tall green man."

"That's an oddly specific example," Carlos says.

"It is, isn't it?" Lana says sweetly.

"What do you want me to do about it?" I say with a frown.

"Nothing. There's nothing you can do, but you remember how the System called us NPCs? Like we were just background to their lives?" Lana says, and I nod. "Well, I wonder if that's because it's true. Once we start populating the other settlements, we'll need the Galactics to help keep order. To keep them settled. We don't have the population anymore to keep all our cities going."

"You think they knew. That they planned for this." At her nod, I glance at Ali. The Spirit nods and I sigh. Time to let the team know the truth I've already read. "They did. It's common practice for the Galactics. We're not the first, the second, or the hundredth world to be taken over. The only reason they've only got twelve Dungeon Worlds is because at a certain point, most Dungeon Worlds self-destruct. The ambient Mana pushes the monsters to a point where it's impossible for all but the most Legendary individuals to visit. Many of the core worlds among the Galactics aren't very different from those Dungeon Worlds by now."

My words make the group blink—not at the words themselves but at the Quest Notification they receive. For the first time, Carlos gets introduced to my private obsession—the System Quest. All of them receive a little experience as they uncover another secret of the System. And as always, there's no way to tell why or how this piece of knowledge and not another is important enough that the System will award us.

"Thanks for the experience. I think," Carlos says, his brow furrowed as he reads the quest log.

"Don't worry about it. John's obsessed with it. He even reads books," Ingrid says the last mostly teasingly but with just a hint of derision in her voice.

"Enough of picking on John," Lana says, frowning. "His book reading is actually useful. If we know what they're planning, maybe we can do something about it."

"Like what? Not die?" Ingrid says with a snort. "The problem is we don't have enough people. And I'm not sacrificing my body to put more babes in the cradle."

Sam snorts, almost choking on the drink he was sipping. Ingrid grins evilly, making it clear that was on purpose.

Even if she doesn't, the number of babies that have popped out and that are due is staggering. Probably a quarter of the female population is expecting or will be expecting. It's not natural, but from the conversations I've lipread, the pregnancies are all going extremely well—much better than previous experiences. No morning sickness, no cramps or swollen feet or overheating. It's a dream pregnancy, if it weren't for the fact that in many cases it's a surprise.

"I'm not sure how," Lana says, not bothering to rise to Ingrid's bait. It's never worth it with her. "But at least we know the Galactics are pushing us to work with them. So maybe we have more of a bargaining position than we thought."

Ingrid snorts but doesn't rebut Lana. I nod, content to let the redhead work on this problem too now that I've put the bug in her ear. I have my own thoughts on the matter, but as always, they diverge somewhat.

As Lana falls silent, Sam takes it upon himself to switch topics to something lighter, a recounting of finding some old rock band that survived the apocalypse in their retreat and is having an upcoming concert. Even in the worst of times, there's always a silver lining.

Chapter 13

Six days. It takes six days for preparations to be complete before the first major steps are taken. Of course, with my Skill, I'm privy to the majority of the changes, including the process of transporting hundreds of Marines to Fort Irwin. By the end of that week, I am sick of the often-repeated snarky comments and gloating by the Marines about how they were all "Marines," unlike the other non-Classed generic soldiers. The Marines are just the start, of course. After that, I port over fighters from settlements all across the country.

Six days. And in those six days, I manage to catch up with Lana, Mikito, and Sam and even get to know Carlos a little better. The Hispanic man is an interesting mix of confidence and sudden attacks of doubt, at times certain of his place in all this and other times completely out of his depth. Then again, perhaps he's just easier to read than most. Six days and we even manage to sneak in a full day of dungeoning, making a speed run through the majority of the buildings in Vancouver's City Dungeon to grab loot and experience. It played out well, with some modest loot that sells for good Credits and very decent experience gains.

Six days to get all our preparations sorted. At that thought, I pull out my character sheet, staring at the screen and the latest series of upgrades I've made. Upgrades. So weird to think of myself like a computer that gets its RAM switched out, my hard disk defragged, or new peripherals added.

Status Screen			
Name	John Lee	Class	Erethran Honor Guard
Race	Human (Male)	Level	48
Titles			
Monster's Bane, Redeemer of the Dead, Duelist			
Health	2240	Stamina	2240
Mana	1740	Mana Regeneration	135 / minute
Attributes			
Strength	116	Agility	207
Constitution	224	Perception	63
Intelligence	174	Willpower	170
Charisma	18	Luck	33
Class Skills			
Mana Imbue	3*	Blade Strike*	3
Thousand Steps	1	Altered Space	2
Two are One	1	The Body's Resolve	3
Greater Detection	1	A Thousand blades*	3
Soul Shield	2	Blink Step	2
Portal*	5	Army of One	2
Sanctum	2	Instantaneous	1

		Inventory*	
Cleave*	2	Frenzy*	1
Elemental Strike*	1 (Ice)	Shrunken Footprints*	1
Tech Link*	2		
Combat Spells			
Improved Minor Healing (II)		Greater Regeneration	
Greater Healing		Mana Drip	
Improved Mana Dart (IV)		Enhanced Lightning Strike	
Fireball		Polar Zone	
Freezing Blade		Inferno Strike	
Mud Walls			

Having gotten over my hesitation about "buying" Skill Levels, I spent my most recent earnings on upgrading Thousand Blades twice, adding two new blades to my arsenal. Luckily, the Skill increases also let me set how many new blades I call forth, since actually wielding five swords, four of them free-floating, is rather difficult, especially with my butchered Erethran Honor Guard style of appearing / disappearing blades. It was only after playing with them a bit that I realized I desperately needed to increase my Perception to help aid my sense of where those blades are.

I also upgraded Mana Imbue and Blade Strike with the last of my funds, increasing my attack power in my stalwart combat Skills.

Mana Imbue (Level 3)

Soulbound weapon now permanently imbued with mana to deal more damage on each hit. +20 Base Damage (Mana). Will ignore armor and resistances. Mana regeneration reduced by 10 Mana per minute permanently.

Blade Strike (Level 3)

By projecting additional Mana and stamina into a strike, the Erethran Honor Guard's Soulbound weapon may project a strike up to 30 feet away.
Cost: 30 Stamina + 30 Mana

The decrease in my Mana regeneration sucked, but the increase in base damage helped. Over time, I've realized how powerful this unresistible increase in base damage can be. Sure, it might seem small when compared to the thousands of hit points an enemy might have, but it's base damage. That damage is multiplied by where and how well you hit the individual, after which of course armor, dodging, and other passive skills take effect. In the end, a few points increase in base damage can make a big difference, especially when that amount isn't reduced by resistances.

All this is, of course, a minor addition when stacked up against the huge gain in my attack power when it's multiplied by Army of One. As tempting as it was to use both of my free Skill points to upgrade it again, I instead purchased another point in Sanctum. Surviving takes precedence, no matter how much fun it is to kick ass. Having an ace in the hole, an "ignore all attacks" card is something I can't ignore.

Sanctum (Level 2)

An Erethran Honor Guard's ultimate trump card in safeguarding their target, Sanctum creates a flexible shield that blocks all incoming attacks, hostile teleportations, and Skills. At this Level of Skill, the user must specify dimensions of the Sanctum upon use of the Skill. The Sanctum cannot be moved while the Skill is activated.

Dimensions: Maximum 15 cubic meters.

Cost: 1,000 Mana

Duration: 2 minute and 7 seconds

The upgrade for Army of One, on the other hand, was slightly disappointing. For another point, I somehow expected a little more.

Army of One (Level 2)

The Honor Guard's feared penultimate combat ability, Army of One builds upon previous Skills, allowing the user to unleash an awe-inspiring attack to deal with their enemies. Attack may now be guided around minor obstacles.

*Effect: Army of One allows the projection of (Number of Thousand Blades conjured weapons * 3) Blade Strike attacks up to 300 meters away from user. Each attack deals 3 * Blade Strike Level damage (inclusive of Mana Imbue and Soulbound weapon bonus)*

Cost: 750 Mana

Overall satisfied with the upgrades and the way I had spent my accumulated Credits, I flicked over to my sparse equipment sets. The Mana bracer is fully filled, which gives me a nice Mana battery to reach for. Even after all this time fighting other sentients, I've yet to find a better ring. Since multiple rings can cancel each other out, I'm stuck with someone's engagement ring. It's a bit morbid, but considering they were here to enslave and kill us, I'm mostly over the ethical issues.

I'm still wielding the same beam pistol and rifle, along with Sabre, as when I first started. Most equipment that we've found is only marginally better, and marginal increases aren't worth it. I've come across a few rifles that would have been better quality if they hadn't been destroyed, but unfortunately, my fighting style has a tendency to leave a lot of things in pieces. And while I could have bought myself a better rifle, spending the Credits on such a thing rather than say, a Skill, just seems wrong. Equipment can be wrecked or changed eventually. Skills stay forever.

The biggest upgrade I have is actually a small technical module that takes a slot on my Neural Link. It's taken a little bit of time to get used to it, so I haven't seen its effects well until our most recent dungeon dive, but now, it feels right.

Perceptive Filter

The perceptive filter interacts with the user's senses to highlight specific sensory inputs. While unable to expand the range of the user's senses, the perception filter is able to note specific, potentially useful, sensory inputs that the user has ignored and highlight them for the user to note.

Effect: Variable. Currently provides a +4 to Perception

Requires: One Neural Link Slot

It's a weird little technological upgrade, but in the dungeon, twice it highlighted a hidden doorway that we nearly missed. The first time was due to a slight scarring on the floor which had flashed red in my vision, the second via increasing the smell of the monster lurking behind the door. Overall, I'm quite pleased by the little find, and it made yanking the neural link out of the Galactic's head worthwhile. It went a small way to rebalancing my Perception requirements at least.

Six days. I've been brought into a few more strategy meetings, gleaned a little more from the casual talk among our people and the way men have been distributed or the locations I've been led to to set up Portal locations.

As much as we try to keep such information compartmentalized, some of it is easy enough to grasp, even for one as untrained in the art of war as I am.

Three Master Class enemies need a counter. They're walking tank divisions, powerful enough to turn the tide of battle in any location. You can kill them if you throw enough Basic Classes at them, if you're willing to stuff people down the exhaust pipes till the tracks are gummed up and they can't move or see. Or you can counter strength with strength.

Seven teams, each rated to take out a single Master Class Galactic. I know the goal is to use a minimum of two teams for each Master Class. They're all situated in the back of the line, waiting for me to Portal them in. Lana and company are one such team. Two Hakarta teams of eight men apiece, a pair of Special Forces teams from Fort Lewis, and two squads of Marines make up the remainder of the Master-Class killers.

Throughout the main fighting force, smaller elite groups are scattered. Our non-military fighters have naturally broken themselves into fighting parties, people they know and trust. Adventuring parties mixed with infantry fire teams, all of them backing each other up with appropriate allocations of Skills and spells. Each squad has been graded and ranked, ranging from the Basic to Master Class killers, some teams larger than others. Within each combat rank are additional grades. And based off these grades, the Officers, Commanders, and Tacticians can allocate help as needed to tackle threats.

Six days to break down, calculate, and tag each group. And during that time, the few resistance groups doing battle with the Zarrie continue to die, without news, without hope, without aid. Knowing that we could do more for them and yet we aren't guts me. We can't, not without letting the Zarrie know that we're making a move, that we're getting closer. That's one of the lessons from Wier's books. You can't fight a war as if the enemy knows all your moves, but you can't afford to discount it either. And so we leave them to fight and die, battling over neighborhood blocks that hold no meaning and City Cores that change every few weeks.

Six days, and finally, we're ready.

***

The sight the next morning is something to behold. Soldiers and Marines, civilians and police officers, Galactics and humans in all shapes and sizes exit Fort Irwin. I watch as the myriad of figures, transported on everything from pony-sized puppies to futuristic armored personnel carriers, upgraded tanks, and Bradleys trek forward, an army of mish-mashed individuals with one will, and I marvel at the weirdness of the System once more.

Our first step is to take the cities that lie between Fort Irwin and Los Angeles. While I can Portal people directly into combat, I'm still one man with a limited window on my Portal. There're only so many people I can safely and quickly transport.

Barstow is our first stop, followed by the urban sprawl that makes up Hesperia, Victorville, and the rest. After that, we'll probably skip the Angeles National Forest and its myriad Level 80 monsters and clear part of the way through San Bernardino. Luckily for us, the entire San Bernardino county is a battle-ridden ground filled with pissed off Californians and Galactics in equal measure. San Bernardino itself seems to have done really well, with nearly half of its City Cores held by its residents. I guess living in a crime-ridden, poverty-stricken city has some benefits when the apocalypse comes. Fact is, they'd have done even better if they weren't so busy fighting each other and selling one another out, but that's humans for you.

Those are the easy marching orders to discern, even if no one has said as much. Still, for now, it's Hesperia and on coming battles while we wait to see if and when the Zarrie react.

***

While the core zones of LA and its surrounding areas have settlement shields in place, the various towns and cities that encompass the San Bernardino valley have none of those defenses. Most of their City Cores and regions remain blasted ruins, areas that have suffered from the initial apocalypse, the monsters that have grown up in the city, and later, the sneak attacks by the Marines and the army.

As settlements have a strict financial management policy—otherwise, settlement owners would be tossing Credits in and drawing them out willy-nilly—the lack of development isn't surprising. I actually do need to do more research on why these Credit management policies in settlements are in place, but that's something for future John to do.

Idle thoughts I'm able to have because, like the Master Class-rated teams, I'm benched from the fight around Hesperia. The less our enemies know of my presence, the better off we are. That's about the biggest drawback to purchasing information from the store—it's always a time-specific purchase. I can tell where someone is at the moment I purchase their location, but it offers no System-guaranteed tracking. It means for someone with the innate mobility I have, they can only rely on technology and Skills to keep track of me.

Staring out of the window of the In-n-Out burger shack that's been taken over by the Master Class teams, I watch the smoke rise from the sprawling cities and try to convince myself that the smell of burnt flesh and overheated metal is coming from the kitchen. Sam and a couple others have the grill fired up, tossing hamburgers and making fries as they cheat physics and entropy to make the mundane cooking equipment work once more. It's a good distraction and a better use of time than my own brooding.

"And that's the last Core," Major Alvarez informs me as he walks over from the small command post he and his fellow minders have set up in one corner.

"Good." Seeing that that's all Alvarez has to say, I realize I still don't have any marching orders. "Losses?"

"Minimal. Six Basic teams, one Advanced-ranked team were complete losses. Two Advanced teams have lost significant numbers and have been combined," Alvarez replies.

Considering an Advanced Class team of Galactics was holding each of the Cores, I'm pleasantly surprised.

"Mr. Lee, I have a question if you have a moment," Alvarez says. "For you and your Spirit."

"He's got a name you know. Ali. Like the boxer," Ali says with a snort.

"Go ahead," I say, ignoring Ali, who is floating beside me and pulling together strands of data.

I almost wish Kim was here, but since I don't own any of these settlements, he (it?) is currently out of reach. Still, the AI's data processing capability is better than Ali's and would be useful, even if he doesn't have the right knowledge sets.

"Like us, most Galactics seem to adventure and do battle in teams. Thus, the numerous teams of Advanced Class fighters we've met," Alvarez says. "But we've yet to meet any Master Class teams."

"What? You want to meet some?" Ali says tauntingly. "I'm sure that can be arranged."

"Why ask me?" I ask.

"Your propensity for reading is well known. And you've got certain advantages in acquiring additional knowledge." Alvarez says the last part while shooting a glance at Ali.

"Less than you'd think," I say with a smile.

"Hey!"

"But to answer your question, there are. In fact, there are more Master Class teams than solo adventurers who ascend to that level. However, the teams rarely stay together after that," I say, shooting Alvarez a glance. Seeing that he's still listening, I continue. "You understand how the experience requirements keep rising each stage, right? Thus, it costs you roughly fifty thousand experience points to go from Level 1 to 2 when you're an Advanced Class. By the time you hit Level 41, you need roughly two hundred fifty thousand points. Now, double that again when you're starting out as a Master Class. You see the problem?"

Alvarez blinks, his jaw working. He's doing the math quietly, thinking of his experience gains recently, his eyes slowly widening.

"That's right. Group experience distribution rules while killing monsters means there's less total experience distributed than if you fought solo. When you need that much experience to go up a single Level, you can't adventure with your team. In fact, adventuring and 'grinding' for experience isn't even that smart anymore."

"Then what is?"

"Quests. We don't see a lot of it here, mostly because we don't have the set up, but in properly established Galactic worlds, there are numerous quests available." I shrug. "It's also why you don't see many Master Classes running around here. They're too busy Leveling to bother with things like this. Of course…"

"Of course…?"

"Well, not everyone wants to Level after they reach that point," I say. "It's why the ones we find are normally lower Leveled."

"Ah, except couldn't protecting the settlements be part of their quests?" Alvarez asks.

"Yup. It probably is too." I pause, considering how to answer simply. "Quests, well, they gain in experience as the need and duration they aren't completed increases. So say a quest to pull a tooth from a live dragon isn't completed in a year. The experience it gives goes up every day, and by the end of the year, the experience gain from completion is probably worth double what it was. A 'protect' quest like this, well, it isn't particularly old, so it probably isn't very good experience. Not for a Master Class."

"Oh…" Alvarez nods in thanks. Before he can ask a follow-up question, he stills, his eyes glazing over as he listens and reads a notification only he can see.

Without saying goodbye, the major walks off, muttering to himself. I could listen in, but I don't, willfully ignoring the man.

"Not going to point out that you're a giant cheater?" Ali sends.

I snort quietly. No, I'm definitely not going to point out how, because of me skipping an entire Class Level, I need significantly less experience to Level than what I just described. Even if, right now, it means my last few Levels have been a grind.

"Animal style?" Carlos asks, holding a platter of burgers in front of me. I stare at him uncomprehendingly, wondering if we've switched to talking about fighting techniques. "Animal style burgers? You know what, never mind. Just eat it."

I shake my head, grabbing the tray and putting it on the table next to me. Americans are weird. In a moment, Lana joins me, snatching a stuffed burger with cheese melting off the definitely-not-beef patties, and I push the thought aside, starting in on my meal before it all disappears.

***

San Bernardino itself is a trickier nut to crack. By the time we get to it a half day later, the damn city and most of its surroundings are on fire. The constant battles and the lack of upgrades to the county and its surroundings have all but guaranteed that wild fires are a constant danger. It doesn't help that the System replaces the burnt-out brush within days each time. This wildfire seems to have really gotten out of hand though.

"Bet you it's some mage who's gotten hold of a new fire spell," Sam mutters as he directs drones to dump more fire retardant on the smoking hillside.

"No chance. Fire mages are smarter than that. It's probably one of you non-mages," Chetan says with a bite. He weaves his hand slightly, guiding a whip of flame to cut into the earth and burn the grass on it to create a firebreak. Either that or he's just looking for the chance to burn something.

"We need a temperature drop over here," Ingrid's voice cackles over the communicators.

"Got it," I say.

I almost pop open a Portal by reflex before remembering I'm not supposed to and Blink Step my way over to the lady. Mostly, I'm thankful that I don't have to listen to Sam and Chetan's argument, since it's one that I've heard numerous times. Stuck as we are on the surrounding hills, we can barely even see San Bernardino. But at least this time, we get to do something.

"Isn't this kind of pointless?" Ingrid says to me when I'm done casting Polar Zone over the area, the assassin standing with one leg cocked and relaxed.

"Aren't you working? And what do you mean?" I say.

"The System regrows everything super-fast anyway. So all this, it'll just regrow in what? A week? And I'm waiting for my spell cooldown to come off. It's not as if I have that many useful spells, you know," Ingrid says.

"Sure, it's a waste of time," Ali answers Ingrid with a smile.

"Stop smiling at me. It makes me worried when you do, you pervert," Ingrid says while raising her hand to cast a cone of cold at another piece of ground. A few seconds later, she throws a rain cloud over another spot.

"Rain?" I say.

"Soothing rain. Mana regeneration and a mild healing regeneration increase," Ingrid answers. "It's from a ring."

"Huh…"

"I'm waiting, Spirit."

"What? There's nothing to worry about. Let it burn. Let it burn again. After a while, you'll just get fire-resistant grass, fire elementals, explosive plants, and other creatures that either thrive on the burning and promote it or, you know, creatures that can just ignore it," Ali says with a shrug. "It's all good."

"Explosive plants?" I say.

"Sure. What better way to promote fires?" Ali says.

"Right. More water." Ingrid nods firmly.

The desert is already tough enough, with the Mana-enhanced sandstorms, crazy-ass winds, and mutated animals. We don't need even nastier forms of plants and creatures coming along.

***

The conquest of San Bernardino was messy, destructive, and ultimately, successful. Luckily, we only lost a few Advanced Class team members, the majority of our losses being focused around our Basic Classes. There, we lost a lot more, including the complete wipe of five teams. It was a painful loss that left our people reeling. Rather than push ahead, Miller called for a break. Various scout groups kept moving ahead while the logistics and backend helpers came along to shore up the city's defenses.

The Zarrie hit us the next morning as we near LA. They let our scouting parties past, the main body of our fighting force stretched out as we deal with a giant, shifting canyon that moves without rhyme or reason, creating caverns and gaps. It doesn't help that ginormous beetles crawl from the ground at random intervals, launching themselves at our teams and attempting to drag them into the earthen gaps.

I'm working my way through the canyon, using my beam rifle to pick off threatening beetles while sitting safely on the floating PAV. The Zarrie attack hits us from the northwest, to the right of the broken-up road and canyon, as the latest attack from the beetles recedes.

The Zarrie lob the System-equivalent of artillery shells at us—high explosive high-tech weaponry, kinetic impact spells, traditional chemical explosive shells, and spell-enchanted weapons. Amongst all the explosive destruction comes waves of poisonous gas and quick-solidifying chemicals, the enchanted smoke obscuring our vision.

Long hours of combat and in some cases, training, kicks in after the initial shock. Teams pull in close and tight, hunkering down and guarding each other as they trigger additional static defenses. Unfortunately, the screams that reverberate through the canyon speak to the futility of that defense.

"Ali, go high."

"On it."

The spirit must have been moving already because within moments, I get a secondary feed from his vision, a slightly disorienting moment as I "see" through his eyes. It's not a clear vision, partly because my mind still struggles to parse both visions at the same time and partly because our link isn't that powerful. Yet. It's still more than enough for what I need. In the relative safety of the shields I've already conjured, I have a few moments to assess the battlefield in peace.

In the northeast, there are no friendly dots left. All our scouts, all the men tasked with keeping that flank safe are gone. Even the dots that were there before have disappeared, some replaced with red and others gone as if they were never there. Now, the ridge is filled with Galactics shooting into the obscuring smoke, laying down suppressive fire as another group rushes in to engage us in melee combat. As Ali spins around, I spot the teams that haven't been caught in the initial trap blocked off, walled away from the fight by a Skill that creates a towering, translucent wall that constantly shifts in size, sending out spikes to lash out at our men.

"Boy-o…" Ali highlights one particular figure on the cliff, flashing him in a rainbow outline repeatedly.

The distance is a bit too far to make out details beyond its raised hands that just look wrong and a tail. One thing I do note is that next to him is a team of spellcasters forming a ritual circle.

"Master Class?"

"Either that or he's got one hell of a spell. That wall is his," Ali states.

As he speaks, I watch a spike erupt from the wall, punching through the chest of the female melee fighter who's been whaling on it with her mace. A moment later the spike enlarges, tearing the woman apart in a shower of gore, splattering all those around with her innards.

"Asshole," I snarl. With a thought, Sabre transforms around me even as I traverse the smoke-filled terrain. *"Jump lines, Blink, Portal,"* I mentally command my helmet, the software over-layering cylindrical domes ahead of me to indicate the max distances for my Skills. It's a minor adjustment that I came up with since Calgary, a little advantage to help my spells. Before I trigger either of my Skills, I check that both shields are fully activated.

Once ready, I use Ali's viewpoint to Blink Step into the air above the smoke, giving me a moment to view the battle fully. As I fall, I thrust out a hand and launch a fireball into an approaching team of Galactics, Ali swooping past me as he attempts to close the distance to skip ahead again. Not that I need it—the Galactics are barely a few hundred meters away.

An icon flashes on my helmet—a lock and a figure stepping through a doorway. Before I can consciously understand what it means, I've triggered Blink Step to put me close to the cliff face. It's a mistake. As I use Blink Step, a molecular grater is taken to every cell in my body, leaving tiny tears all over my prone form.

"Quantum lo... never mind." Ali's warning is just as late as my own realization.

My body curls up in shock while nerves scream and limbs twitch.

"Redeemer, we've identified a Master Class individual on the field. Details have been forwarded," Alvarez's voice cackles over the communicator too late. Not that he's slow—it's only been a short while since this has started.

I have no time to complain about my codename or explain my side of the story, the flicking danger signal showing that the Galactics haven't ignored my mistake. Spells and explosions slam into me again and again, and with a force of will, I roll and twist to get away.

"Kill him!" The roar from above tells me I'm definitely targeted.

"*Time to go, boy-o,*" Ali mutters.

"Trying…" I grunt, then trigger the sonic pulser and a quartet of mini-missiles.

Those missiles don't get far, the barrage of explosives tearing them apart. Luckily, they're loaded with one of Carlos's concoctions, a mixture of alchemical poison and high-density, signal-retardant smoke. Scrambling aside, I trigger Thousand Steps, boosting my movement speed for a few precious seconds.

"Redeemer, I have reports that you're under attack. Help is on the way. Teams one and four are waiting on the Portal," Alvarez's voice cackles over the communicator again.

"Can't," I growl, scanning the notification as I scramble away while laying down my own covering fire and refreshing my Soul Shield. "Quantum lock. Spell. Advanced Class team."

"Copy. Artillery is ranging. Brace for splash in five. Over," Alvarez says, entirely too calm.

While I'm not a soldier, I can understand what he means by context and I'm not happy. On the other hand, the Galactics are significantly less, so when our men recover from the sudden attack, they return fire with our own version of artillery. Which in some cases is actual artillery and mortar shells.

The rippling explosion throws me backward, putting me into a backward roll that is aided by the spherical shield surrounding me. Sabre's shield is down, only the newly refreshed Soul Shield saving me from further injury.

Even under the protection of the sound dampeners in my helmet and the Soul Shield, my ear rings and my body throbs in sympathy with the explosions. For all that, the quantum lock continues to hold.

"Redeemer. Results? Over."

"Lock is still on."

"Teams two and five are en route to your position. We have released eight Advanced Class teams to deal with the surprise attack. Communication and visual surveillance of the vanguard has been compromised. Do you have further updates?" Alvarez calls.

In the corner of my mind, I'm sure Wier and Miller are dealing with the rest of the military forces, but I'm a touch busy to tune in there.

"Ali…"

"Updates are all routing to you and Sabre. But their smoke is throwing up some real interference. All I can say is, hurry!"

"I'm feeding you what I can. Ali says the information's unreliable. Just hurry," I say, dancing backward as I spot three teams braving the still-falling artillery to advance on my position. "Got to dance. I'll Portal people in once I can."

"Understood. Out."

Watching the three teams rush me, spells, projectiles, and other killing attacks reaching for me, I make a quick decision. With my higher Agility, Thousand Steps, and Sabre's anti-gravity plates and jets, I could stay away from the teams and pull them apart by letting the faster fellows chase me while I blast them. Kite and kill. Except they've got healers and I don't and their range damage dealers could probably do some real damage if I let this go on too long. And let's face the facts. Running away just isn't what I do.

Rushing my attackers, I open up with more mini-missiles, watching my stock of pre-loaded missiles drop again. Still, the explosives do their job, throwing the group into disarray as they dodge, close their eyes, and overall attempt to ride out the blast. Two steps to the right leaves me bypassing the lead group, dodging between the trio while I drop a couple of grenades behind me. Chaos grenades sow salt water taffy, a gremlin, and a block of solidified magma in my wake.

Then I'm among the other pair of teams, dancing through them and firing the Inlin whenever I can while swinging my sword. The first Jarack dodges then breaks into a wide grin as it realizes my diagonal cut will miss him. What he doesn't realize till too late is that the four blades trailing along behind all have his name on them. Even a last-minute dodge is insufficient for him to escape damage.

In the midst of the group, I dance, blades appearing and disappearing as I cut and twist, leaving a trailing array of flying blades behind me. Spells and Skills are triggered as fast as I can, Cleave cutting apart a spellcaster and sending it flying into its friends. Fireballs targeted at the epicenter of the group wash over me and them, dealing pain and confusion in equal amounts.

The teams I'm fighting are dangerous, high Level Basic fighters that chip and damage Sabre. I have to pull the mecha back after a while, scared that the PAV will be wrecked before we start the real war. In my armored skinsuit, I fight, Blink Stepping and calling forth Lightning Bolts even as the teams attempt to kill me. I'm constantly throwing up my Soul Shield as it shatters, drawing upon the Mana Battery recklessly while I fight.

And all along, I get glimpses of the larger battle. The smoke from the initial attack is slowly dissipating, reinforcements shattering a hole in the transparent wall and additional Skills holding it apart. The Zarrie pull back as the tide of battle turns against them while ranged spells fall against their prepared position. Another ritual spell is enacted when the majority of our enemies have fallen back, the spell completed a second after the quantum lock is released. And then our attackers are gone.

At that point, the remainder of the team I'm fighting throws down their weapons, as do the rest of those left behind. Their surrender leaves us with no outlet for our wrath as the mangled remains of our friends remind us that this time, we lost.

Chapter 14

Hours after the attack, we pull the army together and get moving. We change the way we do things, with the scouts on our flanks significantly increased and more frequent check-ins. In addition, each team is now able to watch each other, the zones they're scouting reduced to allow this to happen. And there are more changes, drones and Skills put into place while we recover from the attack that took out nearly a third of the vanguard. Too many damn teams, too many people.

For all that, when Miller makes the call, I'm not surprised. The Portal back to have the conversation in person is quick.

"General," I greet Miller, who is bent over the System-generated map, muttering orders to his people.

"Mr. Lee. Thank you for coming," Miller says as he walks over to me. "It looks like the next step of the operation must begin earlier than we expected."

"Sounds good," I say, flashing him a grim smile. "If I knew what it was."

"Ah, yes." Miller shrugs unapologetically and waves me over to look at the map. "We'll need you to leave the teams for now. For the next step, you'll need both your team and Sergeant Johnson's."

"I thought they were part of the Master Class kill groups."

"They were," Miller says. "Now, you'll need them to help you get into LA itself. The following route is what we'd recommend…"

"Miller…" I say warningly, unhappy about how obtuse he's being. I understand the need for it, but he's asking me to bring my friends into the middle of the lions' den. And as we have learned, they are more than ready to deal with my Skills.

"Mr. Lee, you are skilled. High Leveled. A veritable god of war on the battlefield from what my men say," Miller says, meeting my eyes. "But right now, you're a soldier. Now, you can decide to be an officer, to make the decisions and run this battle. And if you do, I'll step aside." I see more than a few of his men shift, obviously uncomfortable with his words. "Because there can't be more than one commander, not at this time. But you chose to step aside earlier, and I cannot, will not, have more of my men risk their lives if you are going to change your mind in the middle of the operation."

I grit my teeth, my temper flaring as he calls me to the carpet. A part of me wonders why he didn't do it somewhere else, somewhere more private. But mostly, I'm thinking. Thinking of what he said, of the decisions I've made. Miller's right. Stepping aside to let the army personnel run the fight was a deliberate choice, one based on the belief that they know what they're doing better than I do. Now, we're bloodied and hurt and our people have died. And maybe I could have done something better, and maybe I couldn't have. But here I am, jostling his elbow because now he's putting the people I care about in danger. Now, I've got to risk more than my life, and I realize that doubt is eating away at me. Not knowing, not understanding is making me question when I shouldn't.

I can either accept that he's in charge or I can take over. What is is. Choose or not, but I can't keep coming back to it. Once again, I go over the reasons why I stepped aside. My lack of training. My lack of people skills. My lack of knowledge of the Skills and people involved. The crushing responsibility and guilt for all the lives that will be lost. And perhaps most importantly of all, my final goals. Running the war, running each battle in the USA is not important. Not for me.

I exhale raggedly, pushing aside the anger and the petty jealousy. The desire to be the one in charge. The doubt that we're being hung out to dry. My personal doubts about authority. There's a war to fight and me questioning Miller is not helping. "Sorry. Tell me what needs to be done."

"Good," Miller says.

He gestures to one of the aides, who hurries out of the room, before he turns back to the table, a glowing green line appearing at his gesture. The line charts where he wants me to go, the locations I need to hit. While I upload the data into my HUD and memorize the route, I also spend time assessing it, making mental notes for areas of particular interest. A hill here, a tall building there, a dam another place.

Before I can ask any questions, I'm interrupted by the presence of three new individuals. They're all entertainers—two Actors and a Performer, I realize. I frown, curious, but Miller shakes his head.

"Give them your hand, Mr. Lee."

I grunt and do so, watching as the first touches it. I feel a surge of Mana wash over me, one that is mostly benign in nature. Rather than resist it, I let it penetrate me, knowing that Miller must have a reason. One after the other, the entertainers touch me, step back, and nod to Miller before they are dismissed.

"I'm not getting an explanation, am I?"

"No."

"Figured," I grumble slightly, intrigued but silent for now.

***

You'd think that a single settlement shield, a piece of technology that lays a wall of force across the entirety of a region, would be sufficient to stop stealthy incursions. If you did—and I did—you'd be wrong. After all, why bother with sense when the System is in play?

"Move," Johnson hisses at me.

I jolt forward, ducking through the glowing hole in the settlement shield that one of his soldiers has created. I'm not even sure what kind of spell it is that can breach a settlement shield without alerting anyone, but I make note to find out. And to perhaps institute regular in-settlement patrols on our own settlements.

As I duck through, I skitter out of the way of the window, being careful of where I place my feet on the unsteady floor while the quantum lock notification appears in my HUD. The settlement shield was generated in a sphere, one that cares not for minor non-System-developed features like commercial buildings. As such, we're breaching the settlement shield from the second floor of a squat commercial building that once housed a clothing store below and a dental office above. I'm somewhat amused that the ladies took the seconds to shove a few particularly pretty handbags into my hands for storage and that the settlement shield bisected the entire store neatly in the middle. Even so, the building seems to be mostly intact, which is why it was chosen.

You Have Entered the Village of Pasadena

Mana flows in this area are stabilized. No monster spawning will happen.
This Safe Space includes:

- *Village of Pasadena City Center*
- *The Shop*
- *Tier IV Settlement Shield*

The team streams in after me, the puppies the only ones who have trouble squeezing through the opening. Once through, the hole slowly shrinks, leaving us trapped with hundreds of our enemies. Of course, if we do end up fighting them, we're doing something wrong.

Ingrid and another soldier disappear after a moment, the pair heading out to scout, while Johnson sits with us, his own Skill—Shadow Cloak—hiding us from technological and Skill scrutiny. Or so we're forced to assume. With nothing to do and unable to tap into our Skills or spells, we're forced to wait in tense silence. Even speaking is discouraged, since the possibility of an individual with enhanced senses is a major concern.

Seated next to the air filter, I find myself leaning against the wall and thinking about the progress of the war, Lana leaning against me and working on her businesses in her own System windows. Even though I know this is how she's dealing with the stress, I almost feel guilty about not checking up on my settlements. Almost. But first things first, we've got to survive this war.

We're a couple of settlements ahead of the main fighting force from Fort Irwin, and if the plan goes well, we'll be sneaking through this suburb into the next, making our way slowly into LA itself. Cutting through the Angeles National Forest and its higher Level monsters gave us a way to sneak in that would be much more difficult for the larger army. Over the following few days, the Fort Irwin army will take over the settlements in the way, going on a slow and steady route rather than a blitzkrieg approach. That should reduce the likelihood that the Zarrie ambushes succeed, even if we give them more opportunities to do so. At the same time, I know that Camp Pendleton will step up their own attacks, pushing the Zarrie in the south and threatening their settlements there, forcing them to fight a battle on two fronts.

There's a danger to that of course—the Zarrie could easily concentrate their forces and hit us hard, a term that I believe is defeat in detail. But that's where the other aspect of the plan lies, the one that I've begun to realize is Miller's goal. If we can get in deep enough, we can cause real trouble for the

Zarrie while their men are busy. They've shown the ability to teleport large numbers of their men, more than we can. But it seems to require a significant number of individuals and cast time, something that we don't need. If they can teleport in, we can teleport out. Or better, teleport our people in to where they expect to be safe.

And that's what I think we might actually be going for, a location where the Master Classes will be. It's why we're trekking all over with Johnson's people, checking out different spots. Because it's not enough to take over the City Cores—those are, at best, temporary victories. While controlling them ensures that last-minute reinforcements via teleportation pads and instantaneous System-assisted communication is removed, it isn't a guarantee of victory.

No, what we need to do to win is to destroy their ability to fight back. Their forces. And in that sense, the three Master Class Combat Classers are the main targets. Taking them out will reduce the Zarrie's ability to wage an effective war, leaving them with only their non-Combat Master Classers within Los Angeles itself. A group that we can defeat as we take the City Cores.

In the world of the System, wars aren't about land or resources. Or perhaps people are the resources of import. A single Master Class individual can change the face of a battle with a single Skill.

Which is why we're moving in deeper than ever. We've already crossed most of the areas where the army will fight, close enough that I can wield my Portal Skill to put us there if a Master Class appears and I'm ordered to do so. Of course, we'd have to break the quantum lock that the shield has in place, but I'm certain that if I'm called, those will go down. But...

But meeting the Master Class individuals in battle, in a time and place that they know of, is a bad idea. They haven't gotten this far by being stupid, and not having at least a few modes of retreat would be the definition of foolish. No. We need to hit them where they don't expect it, which is why we're sneaking in deep. If we can hit them when they're not expecting it, when they've retreated or are resting, we might just have a chance.

Of course, the fact that I'm not at the various battle grounds might be a bit of a tip-off. Which is where the entertainers come in. Really, it didn't take a genius to realize what they were for once I actually took the time to think about it. Hopefully though, since none of them had a conversation with me nor did Miller discuss matters directly, the actual plan to use them hasn't been compromised. Once again, we're relying on the exactness of information gathering in the System to launch our sneak attack.

Exhaling slowly, I find Lana looking at me with a cocked eyebrow. I shake my head, unable to tell her my thoughts and uncertain of what to say really. It is what it is. Either this gamble works, or we're going to get stuck fighting in close quarters against more people than I'd like. Rather than answer me verbally, Lana flashes me a smile and hands me a bar of chocolate before turning back to her interface.

***

Tension mounts as one day turns into another. Cut off from any news, we can only move forward, sneaking from building to building, hiding from patrols and civilians in equal measure, working our way in deeper. We rely on a mixture of our scouts' abilities, Sam's drones, and the pets enhanced senses to give us warning. Even then, it's slow going.

As I hunker behind an abandoned dumpster, its contents well past ripe and moving into that rarified sphere of rancid, I find myself holding my breath as an unanticipated Jarack Bounty Hunter saunters down the street, his black furred head turning side to side. The brown stripe running across its face gives it a weird, patchy look. Occasionally, the Jarack cocks its head to the side, sniffing loudly as it attempts to catch new scents.

Across the street, holding on to the wall by his fingertips, is Sam, his face red with the physical strain and his held breath. He's barely ten feet off the ground, a vertical jump that took him out of the direct line of sight of the Jarack, but he's vulnerable to the creature's nose, even under the effects of Carlos's scentless potion. Our scents have been diminished, not erased. It doesn't help that I'm certain that the damn Jarack has a Skill that expands its senses.

Again the Jarack snuffles, its head tilted before it takes a few steps forward. Then it stops, cocking its head and sniffing again. I almost growl in frustration. A sudden crackle of sound from its communicator, set to speak softly but so loud in the silence around us, almost makes me jump. The Jarack growls and whines, its language translated in text for me by Ali.

"At Y 45, Z 38. Smelled something. New smell. Human. Not native. Beam weaponry. Old blood. No. No trace. Yes. I hunt runners. Six hundred Credits. No. Six. Five. Yes. No. I no want. Four five. Okay. Deposit half."

The creature seems to smirk, its lips widening, then it looks around once more. It speaks after a moment, this time in English. "Lucky prey. New job pay more than stragglers. I have scent. I come back later. Best run. Run fast…"

Cackling to itself and us, its half-laugh half-howl setting our hairs on edge, the Jarack drops to its hands and lopes off. I blink, not having seen any others do that. Then again, this particular Jarack seemed more animalistic than others.

"Gods," Mikito whispers next to me after the Galactic has been gone for five minutes, making me jump.

I stare at her, wondering when she managed to creep up on me. I must have been too focused on the damn monster.

"Johnson says move. No more daydreaming."

Grunting, I scan the buildings one last time, an action that makes Mikito almost prod me in the back before I skitter forward. By this time, Sam's already dropped down and disappeared down the alleyway, moving to the next point.

***

A day later, Ingrid comes back in the evening, armored jumpsuit torn and a slightly wide look in her eyes.

"Time to go."

"Ingrid?" I say with a frown, already crossing to her.

Carlos beats me to it, a healing spell washing over her form, it's tell-tale colors muted as Carlos pays the extra Mana to hide the illumination.

"Caught the bounty hunter sneaking up on us. He'd already caught Malik when I got there."

"Malik?" Johnson asks concernedly.

"He's fine. Watching the exit. We used Carlos's goop potion on the body too," Ingrid clarifies.

Johnson nods, relief flashing across his face. Without a further word, Ingrid steps aside, and the rest of the team crosses to the door toward our exit route. By now, this is all routine.

Chapter 15

Days of sneaking, creeping from one block to another. Our progress is agonizingly slow, our scouts forced to divert around clusters or, in some cases, push us through them at a run. And all the time, we make our way deeper, following the roughly mapped route.

Now, we all can see why. A simple piece of information, bought from the Shop. Because all that knowledge that can be bought cuts both ways.

After days, even if all the other areas we've been to haven't panned out, we're here. Overlooking the former mansion, now refurbished and upgraded to suit Galactic tastes. Plants that none of us recognize lie around the well-kept lawns, the only visible defensive measure. Gold and brown, its walls reflect the desert sunlight while misters keep the inside cool. A weird mixture of high-tech and low, but who am I to complain?

My first sight of two of the Master Classes comes a few hours later. First is a Jarack, a staggering nine-foot-tall monster, its fur doing little to hide the rippling muscles that make up its animalistic form. It walks out of the house and lounges on a chair, a haunch of barely cooked meat in its hand. After the haunch is mostly done, the creature tosses the meat to one of the cactus-like plants that lunges forward, its spiky body opening to clamp shut on the bone.

W'mee of the Three Sands, Heretic of the Dawn, Slayer of Grayak Scorpions and Master of the Yellow Pit (Level 18 Singer of the Thrice-Dipped Blades)

HP: 4280/4280

MP: 1780/1780

Conditions: Skin of Basalt, The Sands Blessing

"Sands Blessing?" I send to Ali, getting a mental shrug back. I almost want to growl at him, but without a direct connection to the Shop, Ali's a little more limited in his research possibilities.

Still, after a moment he sends more information. *"Probably an overall damage reduction buff."*

A thin, obsidian-skinned female clad in nothing but her birthday suit walks out soon after. A moment's view and I realize that she doesn't look dark, she literally is dark—a creature made of fleshy stone that shifts unnaturally as she walks. It's almost as if she doesn't have a skeleton. Standing next to W'mee, the woman speaks in the Jarack's language. We're too far away for Ali to hear and translate, so I can only consider the creature before me.

Km, Mistress of the Purple Pit, Slayer of Goblins, Hakarta, Jarack, Minaa and Griffons (Level 8 Obsidian Oracle)
HP: 980/980
MP: 7830/7830
Conditions: Skin of Obsidian, Earthen Link, The Stone's Memory

We watch in silence for a time. Km returns to the residence before W'mee does an hour later. Without anything further to hold our attention, most of us fall back, leaving a single scout to watch and report. As much as we'd like to attack, we have to wait to give the others time to get in position.

"Correct me if I'm wrong," Johnson says, his voice soft, "but you only get Slayer titles when you've killed a large number of individuals, right?"

"Yes," Ali answers, frowning. "Total numbers vary depending on the creature—after all, otherwise it'd be real easy to get a Slayer of Ants or Goblins—but we're looking at thousands at the minimum."

"Balls…" curses one of the soldiers, his hair closely cut in an attempt to hide his balding top spot. Ian something. Redford. A quick glance at his name confirms it. "She's a stone-cold killer, that one."

Groans erupt. Somehow, the image of a cursing, punning soldier never made its way into collective media. Probably for the best.

"We're thinking close combat build for the jackal?" Johnson says, pulling our attention back to business. At the nods and words of agreement, Johnson continues. "We'll need teams three and five on him then. In the short term, Ms. Pearson—"

"Lana," Lana reminds Johnson, who shrugs.

"Km looks to be specced as a Mage. She should be our first target," I say, rubbing my chin. "I don't like that Earthen Link—it could be a damage reduction or damage shifting Skill. If that's the case, she'll probably be a lot harder to kill than her health actually indicates."

"If you boys open up on her, I'll finish off the job," Ingrid says from her position against the wall, where she's carefully cleaning her nails with a knife.

"Not a bad plan," I say. "We still got the last Master Class to handle."

"The Bastion, right? Defensive caster?" Mikito says.

"Closer to Mike," Ali corrects. "A Paladin-like build—good healing, good area control, and high defense."

"Teams One and Four then?" Johnson says musingly.

"Four to six," I reply. That'll put one Hakarta team and the Marines on him, which means mostly long-range fire and overwhelming explosions. It should, with care, at least push the Bastion to stay on the defensive and out of helping his teammates, allowing us to finish the fight.

"And you, Mr. Lee?" Johnson asks, his head tilted.

"I'll throw in where I'm needed, but I'll start on the mage once everyone is Ported here," I say after some consideration.

Better to finish her than to wait. Johnson and his team, while strong, aren't really suited for the all-out combat we can expect. It's why we're going to be pushing his people to the outskirts to guard against reinforcements when this finally kicks off.

After that, we sketch out the battle plans a bit more. There's no guarantee we'll fight all three of them at once, even if that is our goal. We have no concern about being overheard—after all, if they know enough to ask those kinds of questions, they know enough to find and end us.

***

Two days pass. Two days because there was no good way to estimate how long it'd have taken us to get in, so we're working on an estimated timeline for everyone else to get into place. And so we find ourselves watching the Master Classers. It's rare for all three of them to hang out at the same time in the same building. I would have expected them to stay by themselves, but whether it's because they're an old team, forced to work together, or some other form of politics, they're all sticking to the same residence. That makes our life easier, since we know where they are. Theoretically. Problem is, they're rarely home.

That fast becomes the major concern. That one day when the two Master Classers were together was an anomaly. Often, the mansion is empty of them all; other times, only a single Master Classer is around. It's no surprise—the armies must be pushing forward, and the Master Classers are their most powerful weapons. While it's not a good idea for them to always be on the front—and I understand the politics involved mean that they aren't likely to follow orders that closely anyway—they probably have other, closer, resting areas. When they do come back to the mansion, we get to see some of the after-effects of the fights—a scorched tail here, a slightly different body configuration on Km there. And still, we wait.

This morning sees the return of Km, the mage looking as though she's been put through the grinder. Instead of smooth, shiny skin, its scratched and marred, pieces chipped away and some dark fluid leaking out. The damage is surprising, since injuries under the aegis of the System heal within ten minutes mostly. I squint, calling up her Status.

Km (Level 8 Obsidian Oracle, Mistress of the Purple Pit, Slayer of Goblins, Hakarta, Jarack, Minaa, Griffons)
HP: 631/980
MP: 7830/7830
*Conditions: Skin of Obsidian, Earthen Link (Disrupted), The Stone's Memory (Corrupted), Chipped * 3*

"Chipped?"

"Like it? I figured that's the closest explanation I could find. It's the Ez's equivalent of losing a… hmmm… finger? Fingers? Since they're fluid in their construction, damage for them is a bit longer lasting. She'll need to rest to heal, but she will heal."

"They did good," I mutter softly, my voice muffled by the helmet.

Once she's gone, we settle back into our usual routine of waiting. For a moment, I regard my friends, wondering if any of them will fall today. Ingrid's in her corner, playing with her knife and a System-generated screen game. I still can't see her Level and I'm fast believing that I never will. Still, I'm pretty sure from conversations I've overheard that she's at least over Level 10 in her Advanced Class.

Mikito's downstairs, going through her forms with a pair of soldiers, training as always. Between her constant training and dungeon delving, she's the highest Leveled of our team at Level 17. Lana, on the other hand, is the lowest, barely crossing Level 4 now that she's stopped splitting her experience. She's busy on her screen, reading for pleasure now that she's caught up on all her paperwork. When I asked Lana earlier what she was reading, she showed me the cover of a bodice ripper by someone called Georgette Heyer. Not surprisingly, I backed off pretty fast, though the predatory glint in her eye made me wonder if she was getting the wrong idea.

Both Sam and Carlos have caught up with Lana, having spent more time dedicated to their actual Classes, and are at Level 9 and 10. They've taken over a floor upstairs after having promised to be careful about the kind of experiments they'll do. They've roped in a couple of Johnson's men, when they aren't on watch, to help with their experiments.

Me? I just curled up and got back to reading.

... to work around the low sample size of Master Class subjects, we used a large number of specialized Advanced Classers, many of whom have dedicated their unassigned attributes to enhance assigned attributes. As such, we were able, as you can see in the following graph, to gather a statistically significant sample size of individuals with attributes above 500. This researcher does understand that the limitation of insufficient Master Class subjects might alter the results of this experiment, but believes that, following research done by Re & Makow and the Vuu Institute, such differences will be minimal.

Initial results from the experiment (see attached charts 42, 43, 44) indicate that overall increases in abilities do not progress in a highly correlated fashion. Overall trends do indicate a diminishing return upon reaching attribute levels over 100 (approximately, see additional discussion by Wexq, Fre, and Immik for attribute level progression). However, when examined from the perspective of species traits, a closer direct relationship between levels may be found.

It is advanced in this paper that it is due to some of the inherent features in a+ species that dictate the level progression in attributes for an individual. By understanding and conducting further research on each individual, it might be possible to ascertain the specific increases and alterations that increases in an attribute might create on a physical, mental, and molecular basis.

Hours creep by as I work through the dense scientific paper, jumping from one article to another, following the rabbit hole of information. Sometimes I have to put down a note, as I've yet to purchase those papers or referenced books. Other times, I find myself jotting notes about mistakes or areas I disagree with.

I'm so caught up in what I'm doing, I barely notice the heat of the California sun beating down on the un-air-conditioned room we're in or when Johnson hisses at us. I turn, and he raises a single finger, pointing at the window. It doesn't take me long to see the Bastion sauntering back with a grin. Once again, I reflect on the three-fingered, mildly-scaled figure with its long tail, wondering where exactly they came across the lazy special effects guy to do his makeup. Seriously, how "non-human" he looks is as bad as some old sci-fi TV shows, other than the too-realistic fingers and tail.

S'hu'mma, Defender of The Sixth Oasis (Level 16 Sand Bastion)

HP: 4880/4880

MP: 4190/4190

Conditions: None

A second later, a chirp comes from Johnson's earbud. He stiffens, tilting his head as he listens. My lips press together, knowing that there's only one way he's getting any information—single-use extra-strong communication options from the Shop. They're single-use since Miller bought the best they had. We have no clue how strong the disruption fields the Zarrie have are, so we limited each team to two communications devices.

Johnson listens before he nods and looks up. "Gather up." Within seconds, we're all gathered around the Sergeant. "We're a go for Operation Barracuda. We take the Bastion first, then the Oracle. Redeemer will hold back."

I grunt, eyeing the quantum lock in the corner of my eyes. There's barely a murmur from my friends or the soldiers as they pull back, Lana stopping for a moment to squeeze my shoulder. I notice one of the soldiers exit, obviously to alert the rest of the team.

Within seconds, the group have gathered their belongings and left the building, leaving me alone. I turn back to the windows to watch, unable to do anything as yet. Bastion has stopped moving forward, his head cocked, a readiness through his body that was not there before. Obviously, Johnson's message was noted. From my vantage point, knowing what to look for, I can see my team moving forward, using cover like the pros they've become.

"Come on…" Ali mutters, staring into space.

A flicker in the lock, and a few seconds later, a low rumble from the east. So soft I would never have heard it before the System and the increase in my Perception. For the puppies and Lana though, it's clear as day, from the way they shift and stare before turning away. Bastion obviously hears it, his lips pulling apart, but he makes no move, continuing to stand in the middle of the streets. A flicker of movement in the mansion that holds the Ez is all the indication I get about her. Thankfully, the vast majority of the houses around here are empty, the humans having congregated around the Shops and the Galactics having either done the same or gone out fighting.

I force myself to breathe as my chest tightens, anxiety creeping up on me as time crawls by. Minutes of stasis is broken by Bastion snarling and walking toward the mansion. As he does so, I spot another group approaching. A quick dial-in of my helmet gives me some details. Ali provides more.

"All four Advanced Classes. Three fighters, one spellcaster," Ali says.

Meeting Bastion right outside the mansion, the Advanced Classers jabber and yowl away. I snarl slightly, realizing that our team is running into more trouble than they counted on. But there's nothing I can do.

The battle starts with a barrage of spells, beam discharges, and grenades targeted on Bastion. The first few land on him, unobstructed by any Skill, and he staggers, light cuts running across his body. Within seconds, the barrage stops hitting as a shield forms around the four. The Jarack Advanced Classers spin around—two pulling rifles, another a giant axe, while the healer buffs the group—moments before the close combat fighters attack, exploding from behind the hastily thrown wall.

Ingrid stabs the healer, putting her knife into its throat and ripping sideways. It gurgles, not dead but disabled, clutching at its furred throat. As it falls down, Roland appears from the shadows and pounces on it, jaws clamping on his head and crushing while its feet claw at the body. I know that strike, *Massive Pounce*, and it adds a stun effect, along with massive bonuses to damage. A part of me pities the healer. A very, very small part.

Meanwhile, the puppies target the Bastion. Shadow goes low, ripping into ankle and knee, while Howard goes high, clamping its jaws around a hastily thrown up arm. Strong as the Master Class might be, physics still have a say in this world, and he gets taken down to the ground. As the Bastion struggles, Anna lashes out with her flames at the Jarack Advanced Classers, her attacks reflecting off the remaining shield and cooking them from within.

Caught outside the fast-created shield wall, Mikito and Lana are attacking it with fury, doing their best to wear it down while Carlos stays back, his gun held ready to deal with reinforcements. Without the Master Class controlling it, the shield wall seems to be lacking its offensive abilities, which is good. Redford is working his magic, ripping a slowly growing hole with his magic while the others get ready to scurry in. The tiny hole is sufficient, allowing Sam to send in drones to lay down additional cover fire.

Surprise keeps the Galactics on the backfoot for a few precious seconds, but soon enough, the Galactics recover. The puppies get thrown aside, blasted away by the Bastion with a Skill. The Master Classer stands up, looking only mildly damaged after having been chewed upon. While searching his surroundings, he bats Roland out of the air when the tiger pounces at him. Smartly, the First Nations woman has disappeared already, her job with the healer complete. Unfortunately, the remaining pets aren't as lucky. The Advanced Classers turn their attacks on Anna, who takes a beating, her fires doing little to ward off the blades and beams.

Lana screams, watching as Anna is hurt. Carlos and one of Johnson's men focuses on the fox, doing their best to prop up the pet's health. But it's a losing cause with so many attacks focused against the creature. A final swing sends the fox flying, her body nearly severed in two, limp and bloody. Still, her sacrifice was not for nothing. Johnson and his men spill into the gap, turning the Advanced Classers on them. Mikito darts in soon after, headed straight for the Bastion.

As the Master Classer turns his attention to the assailants outside, a spike erupts from the wall, intent on tearing apart Johnson's shield breaker. Another of his men steps in, holding forth his hands and stopping the spike cold. There's strain on the soldier's face as his Mana shield diverts the attack, but he can do nothing as another plunges into Lana's side, ripping open her shoulder.

A rumble, this time much closer to us, distracts everyone for a moment. At the same time, the teleportation lock disappears and I bare my teeth. Barely a minute has passed since the attack, but already Km is on her way out. I decide to put a stop to that, as well as trigger my side of this desperate plan. I step backward then rush the wall, springing at full speed.

Blink Step. Once. Then again.

Vertigo rushes through me at the sudden shift of space again and again, but it disappears as quickly as it comes, allowing me to use my built-up momentum to slam into the newly emerged Oracle. A part of me notices that she seems to still be slightly damaged, but I'm mostly focused on my sword, the newly formed blade twisting in her body. Surprisingly, it only gets a few inches deep. A moment later, Thousand Blades is activated, blades forming next to my hand as I twist the sword, forcing the newly formed blades to arc toward her body. Surprised or not, she flips backward, gracefully avoiding my attacks while a rock shelf lifts me into the air.

Twisting while airborne, I focus. Not on her, but on the Portal I need, creating it so that the waiting teams can stream in to help, splitting my focus between Ali's and my views. Flying through the air as I am, the hastily cast Portal hangs two feet above the ground and slightly canted, but that doesn't stop the Hakarta who are waiting.

"Teams Two, Three, Five, and Six are scrambling. We need the Portal for four minutes, Redeemer," Alvarez barks over the newly restored communication channel.

Rock wraps around me, quickly engulfing my body. I grunt, feeling my connection to the Portal waver a little, and I'm forced to rely solely on Ali's view and our connection. As the rock constricts me, my concentration wavers before I bite my lip and focus. Armor, meant to stop projectiles and beam weaponry, does nothing to stop the attack as she compresses my body, crushing bone and stealing air from my lungs. My health drops and I realize I have no shield. I curse my carelessness, having paid so much attention to the fight and my friends' situation that I neglected my own preparations.

I focus through the pain, biting my bottom lip as my attention splits. Spells form, boosting my regeneration first. Then healing to fix bones that are slowly being crushed, skin that sizzles as the Oracle adds heat to the liquid rock around me. But still, I stay within her attack, forcing her to concentrate on me as the Portal spits out our friends. Trading pain for people.

Of course, like me, the caster can split her attention. Many of the first Hakarta to jump in are now engulfed in thigh-high mud, trapped. But rather than let it stop them, the Hakarta are grabbing and tossing incomers out of range of the spell, accepting the pain to allow their friends to engage the Oracle. Seeing her attacks failing to stop them, she falls back, a pair of rock elementals flowing up from the ground to slow her attackers.

"Move, move, move," chants one of the Hakarta. Galactics or not, it seem certain words are universal.

In the shield, Mikito and Ingrid are sparring with the Bastion, forcing him to pay attention to them while Roland sneaks in to land his occasional attacks. The puppies and drones have joined forces to harass the Advanced Classers, the drones throwing out beam attacks, napalm, and flash bursts to confuse and hurt, as well as the occasional vertical shield to block attacks and jar bodies. Meanwhile, Johnson and the remnants of his team in the shield are picking off each Advanced Classer, pouring fire and flame while Carlos does his best to heal everyone. Already, the soldier who had guarded the hole opener is on the ground, unmoving.

"Boy-o, she's not channeling anymore," Ali informs me, bringing attention back to my own condition.

I realize he's right—the rock's no longer crushing, just sizzling. I Blink Step and pop up behind the Oracle.

"Boo," I whisper hoarsely. Not that she can hear me, not through my helmet.

Once more, I thrust my sword forward, lunging into full extension. I use Cleave and Elemental Strike at the same time, adding to my attack. The blade, empowered by Skill and physics, plunges through her empowered, buffed body.

Blade Strike. Twisting with my hips, I rip the sword out sideways, the initial edge of my attack burrowing through her body to aid my movement. My blade catches, barely shifting a few inches in her body, but the scream of grating rock and the fresh, oily liquid that flows from her speaks of grievous injury. Even as I recover, a Hakarta in what I can only describe as spiky football armor tackles her away from me. He's closely followed by his entire team, each of them piling onto her, the rubble of her stone elementals a testament to their effectiveness. As I move to join them, a razor cloud of dust and shattered earthen flooring rises, cutting into exposed skin and blinding those within it. Reflexively, I stagger backward.

"Redeemer!" Johnson shouts, dragging my attention back to the shield.

I grunt, surprised to see that the Bastion is not only still standing but managing to float away with little damage, his shield now constricted around his body. Globs of energy form around the shield, shooting forward once in a while to attack the gathered Advanced Class team members, forcing them to block the attacks. He might be mostly unharmed, but not so the Jarack Advanced Classers. Mikito, unable to reach the Master Classer, has thrown herself against the unfortunate Galactics. The last member falls, unable to get his footing under the combined assault of the Samurai and the puppies.

I glance at my Mana, snarling as I assess the fight. Not enough. I will Sabre to activate a Greater Mana Potion and feel the hypodermic needle punch into my skin. The liquid rushes through my body, increasing my Mana. Another thought has me drawing upon the Mana Battery to fill my empty tank. It's a rush, but it makes me shudder slightly too, as it always does. But it's enough, more than enough.

"Foolish. You bugs will not survive," the Bastion hisses, his voice slithery and cold, beady gold eyes glittering with malice. He's confident, safe in the protection of his shield.

"Not today," I say, raising my sword above my head.

I call forth the Skill, stepping forward and cutting as I do so. Around me, twelve ghostly swords appear and repeat my attack, Blade Strikes arcing out from the newly formed swords to smash against the Bastion's shield, each strike thrice the size and intensity of any I've conjured before. It smashes into the Bastion's already weakened shield, shattering it and cutting into his flesh.

Moments later, Carlos fires his little grenade / potion launcher directly at the Master Classer. The Bastion snorts dismissively, seemingly undamaged from that attack, his body already visibly healing. Other attacks from the team bounce off him, but then a look of surprise flashes across his face.

"Ikaaaaaaaaaaaaa?" the Bastion screams as he plunges to the ground, gravity reasserting itself on his floating form.

"He can't use Skills for the next few seconds!" Carlos shouts, alerting us of the opportunity he's given us.

Without coaching, the rest of the long-range attackers open up, throwing Spells and Skills at the prone form. Everyone opens up. Behind me, I hear the continued battle as Teams Two and Three keep the Stone Oracle busy, shattering walls and setting the dried ground on fire as that tempest of rock howls.

I'd help, but reeling from Mana loss, I find myself sitting down. I'm not completely out of Mana, but with barely a hundred left, it's close enough that I feel sick. Mana sickness from overuse and overdrawing of Mana is a major issue for those of us with high Mana levels. It's a weird phenomena since even a year ago, this level of Mana would have been my maximum. The loss of Mana is almost like drug withdrawal, or what I think a drug withdrawal would feel like.

By the time I recover, drawing on my Mana Battery to fill the hungering void in my body, the battle is nearly done. Tough as the Bastion might be, without his protective Skills, his health falls like a waterfall under the combined assault of our teams. Even the close-range fighters like Mikito have long-range attacks which they add to the pile, wiping away the Bastion's health. As I raise my hand to attack, a notification pops up.

Level Up!

You've reached Level 49 as an Erethran Honor Guard. Stat Points automatically distributed. You have 3 Free Attribute Points and 1 Class Skill Point to distribute.

One nice thing about this world is that if you pay attention, the System clues you in when someone is well and truly dead. Small things like experience gains—though just by being part of this war, I'm getting a small trickle of experience constantly—and sometimes, bigger notifications like this one. I push the notification away, looking for the Oracle. Instead, I see the two teams tasked with her attack coming back. Half of them split off to deal with the carnivorous cactus inside the compound.

"Report," Johnson says to one of the other soldiers.

"Sir, the last target is currently engaged southwest with the Marines," the soldier replies. "General Miller informs you that you and the Redeemer are on independent command for now. Forces from Fort Irwin are recovering from the attack conducted by the Oracle and the Bastion."

Johnson's lips tighten, obviously understanding what the soldier's implying. If they're recovering, it means the two Master Classers must have laid on the hurt. Still, there's nothing much to be done about it now, and if there is revenge to be taken, we've certainly done so. The smoking corpse that Ingrid is busy looting is more than testament to that fact.

"We dealt with the Oracle?" I say, frowning as I turn back. A flicker of shame crosses the faces of the teams designated to handle her—at least those not covered by full-face masks. "What happened?"

"She created a series of stone simulacrum. Simulacra? Your English is very imprecise. By the time we destroyed them all, she'd slipped away," one of the Hakarta answers. "Probably an Earth Movement Skill or Spell."

I grimace, hating that we didn't manage to finish off both the Master Classes. That was the point of our attacks after all. Now, we'll have to track her down again. If we can.

"Redeemer. By your leave, I'll take my men and attempt to penetrate the next settlement to remove their shield. This settlement shield still needs to be destroyed and its City Core taken," Johnson says, offering his "recommendation."

"Sure. Team Two, hit the shield generator. Team Three, we need communication back. Johnson, get us a way into the next settlement. The rest of us are going to hit the City Core. We'll keep hitting them until they turn around and hammer us. And remember, we're the distraction now, not the main event," I say, glancing at the teams. I get nods all around, and I find myself smiling grimly. "Good. Move people. We've got work to do."

Chapter 16

Hours later, we've managed to take down the shield generator and take the City Core for the section of town that comprises Alhambra and parts of south Pasadena. A part of me is amused by the first, thinking more of a classic board game than desert-baked avenues.

"Anything?" I ask as we walk out of the Core room, Kim already patched in and feeding me settlement data.

Ali and Kim feed much of the relevant data to the teams still in the settlement, directing them to the last few holdouts we can locate. Luckily, it's something that can be done in the background, leaving me mostly free from the buzz of conversation.

"Nothing," Alvarez says, shaking his head. "General Miller indicates that they've pulled back all forces to the north and south. Both armies are advancing with minimal resistance and casualties. Scouts have yet to ascertain the enemy's gathering point, but it's believed to be somewhere in south Los Angeles."

"You thinking they're looking for a knock-out fight?" I say, frowning.

If they're willing to give up land to concentrate their forces, whichever army they hit will suffer unless we can join forces. Theoretically, once we've got all our people together, we'll have the advantage of numbers. But it doesn't matter if they hammer us to pieces while we're gathering.

"If they're smart, sure," Alvarez replies. "The general is leaning toward that, so the armies are moving to link up in Anaheim."

A few additional words of clarification and a borrowed map gives me an idea. Within the next few hours, the Fort Irwin army should be at south LA, hammering on the settlement shield. The Marines will take longer, possibly as long as a half day since they've got at least two settlements to punch through. Of course, they could go around, but there're dangers in that too.

"We moving to link up?" I say with a frown.

I hate giving back the City Cores, especially after we've paid for them with blood and tears, but as I glance sideways, I note that the soldiers and my team are already interfacing with the local resistance, who've come out of the woodwork. A slightly bitter part of me wonders where they were during the actual fighting. I have to chide myself for that uncharitable thought—the resistance has been conducting hit-and-run tactics for the last year, so it's no wonder they weren't exactly set up for a final push. As it stands, their need to hide has keep their Levels suppressed—which is probably another reason they've survived so far. Still, they're numerous and enthusiastic which, all things considered, is the best we can do.

"Yes. Once everything's settled." Alvarez adds leadingly, "But we don't require you or your team at this time."

"Yeah, yeah. I should get going," I say. "Though communication will be a problem if I leave."

"Here." Alvarez reaches out, a small boxy contraption in his hand.

I take it, my eyes lighting up slightly as I read the notice.

Joola Communication Booster (Tier II)

Military Grade Communication Booster able to deliver your message where and when it needs to be. Joola Tech is the only way to go when what you need to say needs to be heard!

Effect: Disregard all communication interference from shields, communication scramblers, Skills, and Spells below Tier of communication booster. Fifty percent chance of breaking through equivalent tier blockages (chance decreases dependent on proximity to emanating blockage)

Requirements: 1 Hard Point

"Nice…" I stare at the box, unsure of how to use it.

"Slot it into Sabre, boy-o," Ali says.

I sigh, transforming the mecha. That's when I run into the next problem. I'm out of slots. After a moment's hesitation, I extract the Monolam Temporal Cloak, pulling it into my inventory, and slot in the communication booster. There's a little hum, some movement as Sabre alters itself and the box to ensure that it works. If I'm going to be blaring my position away anyway, there's no point using the Temporal Cloak.

A few hasty goodbyes and one much less hasty kiss and I'm on the move, headed to meet up with Johnson and his team. They'll help me breach the necessary shields, hopefully only requiring me to use the damn communication booster once. It's not exactly a good feeling painting a target on your back.

***

"Redeemer," Wier greets me, shaking my hand as I stop outside the impromptu command center set up in the midst of a mall.

"Colonel," I say, looking around at the organized chaos. "What's up?"

"We're entrenching," Wier says, waving to encompass the hurried work. He doesn't lead me in, which makes me frown, but I don't say a thing. I'm not running the war and… "We need you to set waypoints through the line if you can."

I grunt, knowing he was about to say that. It's not hugely surprising, since we own this settlement now. Being set up right across from south LA, where we're pretty certain the Galactics have gathered, we'll need to be ready. Still, before anything else, I pull a Portal open to drag over Lana and company. When the teams are through and the Portal shut, I get back on Sabre, only to be stopped by Lana.

"Where are you going?" Lana says with a frown.

"Got to set some waypoints along the line and through the city."

"Then I'm coming," Lana says. "The boys need a run anyway."

"That's…" I frown, and she glares at me. I shut up, deciding that I could use the company. Or perhaps it's her who could use it.

We take off, Wier having updated my map with his recommended path. At first, we ride in silence, the only sound the soft pad of furred paws, the crunch of walls being torn down, and the distant bark and hiss of firearms.

As the silence grows brittle, I turn my head sideways, speaking to her over the communicator and on a private channel. "How are you doing?"

"I'm healed."

"I mean, well, you know. Emotionally," I say. "Ann—"

"We knew it was a danger. We had to take the healer down first, and none of us could get any closer. It was a calculated risk to get Ingrid enough time," Lana says softly, shaking her head.

"I understand," I say. "But I didn't ask if the plan was good. I'm asking how you're doing."

"I'll survive. After this. After it's all over, I'll make you stop and we'll find a place and I'll cry my eyes out. And you'll hold me. Afterward," Lana says softly, her words almost an order to put an end to this conversation.

I feel my chest constrict, the ache at the raw, suppressed pain making my eyes blur for a second. Damn it.

***

Thankfully, without the infamous Los Angeles traffic in play, the entire process takes only a few hours. I make sure to swing wide, patrolling along both the border and where the teams have dug in and a little behind, letting my "map" for where I can drop people off build. After that, we get directed to a nearby apartment building, the highest vantage point available where the rest of the strike teams have gathered.

Not that we have to wait long. I've barely got my feet out from under me and a second plate of food in my stomach when the call comes. The Zarrie are on their way, and this time, they're not playing around. Once they actually cross their settlement shield, we get a direct feed from the drones.

Galactics, so many of them I can't even count them. It's not as if I ever learned the skill of mass counting, but it has to be hundreds, maybe thousands. The way they move, I'd be surprised if they weren't organized in teams like us, flitting forward across the roads and around the buildings. The Galactics are a mixture, nearly half consisting of Jaracks, but there's Ez, the carapaced fighters, lizard creatures like Bastion, and a scattering of other Galactic types. As always, they're dressed in a mixture of weaponry and armor, from melee weaponry to modern armor, though most lean toward the last. For a long time, I scan, searching among the faces, before I'm interrupted.

"Got you!" Sam crows.

A moment later, the video feeds shift and split. Highlighted in green, in the midst of the crowd, is the Jarack Master Class and the Oracle. I frown, almost wanting to ask if he's sure. I hate to say it, but the Jarack and Ez, most of them look similar to me. If not for Ali's help, I wouldn't be able to tell the difference.

"*Ali…*"

"*Marked.*"

I grunt in thanks, watching as they near. An idle thought of opening a Portal to toss a few spells on top of the Master Classers pops into mind, but I discard the thought just as fast. I doubt we'd kill them. And truthfully, I wouldn't be surprised if the teams next to the Master Classers are there to act as bodyguards. We'll have to deal with them, but surprise won't count in this equation.

Alvarez, as always, is with us, having made his way here by now. He walks over to where we're staring at the main projected screen and squats next to me before he speaks. "We'll be updating your map with where we need the Portals. But your feedback on which Master Class to target first is sought."

"The Ez," I say. "Oracle's a spellcaster or wide-area Skill user. She's more dangerous to more people. She's also shown the ability to run away and the willingness to do so. W'mee's a brick. He'll keep going and going, but he ain't going to be doing much damage overall. Take her down first, focus on containing him."

Alvarez smiles slightly, nodding. "That's what we thought too."

"But—"

"But they're likely going to be expecting that."

"Did you just use me as the dumb man's plan?" I ask slightly. Alvarez, of course, doesn't reply, so I grunt, waving him to continue.

"We've got other plans for the teams," Alvarez says. His hand shifts, my map updating a little before he outlines the updated plan.

I grunt and listen, turning my head to stare at the remaining members of the teams. We've all taken a beating, most teams having at least one member and some more than one. These guys are the cream of the crop, people who have shown not just good Levels but an ability to adapt in combat. And yet, the losses are clear. I cannot help but imagine what it's like for those unlucky enough to be on the frontlines. And a feeling in my gut says that it isn't the end of our losses yet.

***

When the armies clash, we watch. The men from Fort Irwin are as dug in as they can be, but the Marines have yet to make their way up. By the time they do, this will be over.

Initially, it's a series of probes, weapons, and spells lobbed at each other at a distance, artillery—or the System equivalent—lobbed at each line as the Galactics push ahead. Without the Bastion, the Galactics are using a mix of Skills and technology to shield their lines, much like us. The temperature rises as fireballs bloom and beam weapons rip the sky apart in flashes of azure light. Ozone permeates the air, along with the unmistakeable smell of cooked human flesh. Galactics all smell different too, burnt fur biting at the nose and alien blood bringing a fruity smell.

So damn much blood. It doesn't help that the System regenerates it, allowing creatures with legs that have been blown off to crawl forward as they "heal" from the damage. The ground grows soggy, earth churned up under repeated assaults, sewage and other lines exposed to the sky. We can feel it, the searing heat on our flesh, the bitter cold that washes over us as a spell is formed, the wind constantly swirling as different spells take effect.

A woman stands to fire her crossbow and is impaled by a spear. Another mage scrambles forward in front of a fallen friend, his hands crossed as he takes the brunt of an attack, his Mana Shield tearing apart under the stress. A group of Galactics rush the line, the carapaced tank holding forth a shield made up of shield generators and solid Galactic steel. They push forward, fur burning and carapace shattering as area effect attacks hammer them, ivy leaves grasping and tearing. An Advanced Class soldier steps forward, his body glowing, and tears apart the shield with a single exhalation. A moment later, the soldier falls, his shoulder ripped from his body by a whip of flame. All of these moments are but a small portion of the heroics that happen all across the line.

And still, I watch, my stomach clenching as I desire to be out there, doing something.

"Alvarez…" Mikito says softly, asking the major where, when, can we act.

Alvarez shakes his head, his concentration still on the channels and orders he hears.

"This is just the opening," Sam says softly, his eyes hard. Of us all, he's got the most experience, the most time seeing the battles up close and personal with his drones. Mikito and I might have been on the front-lines, but he sees it all from above. "They'll need us when it gets hot. When the Galactics are stuck in. We're the cavalry."

Hate it or not, Sam's right. The vast majority of the army has yet to arrive. No, better for us to wait. Miller has the same clues, the same vision. And when it's time, he'll call on us.

***

"Redeemer. Updating map." Alvarez's voice breaks my focus. "Portals at the green. Team leaders, your maps are updating too."

Affirmatives are voiced all around while I conjure, going by the numbers. I punch out the first Portal as instructed, ten feet above the air so that it can form. No forming Portals inside people or objects. Sort of like appearing in other matter when you shift from one quantum state to another. It hurts. A lot. And sometimes ends in violent explosions. And when I say sometimes, I mean more likely than most. There's an entire Galactic channel dedicated to those who don't take that warning seriously.

I watch the first team rush through the Portal, tossing explosives and potions in before them to clear the way. Seconds later, they're piling through, Skills and spells activating in a flurry as they land on top of the group that has breached our lines, filling the gap and giving the reinforcements time to arrive. No time to watch them though. The Portal slams shut and I focus to open the next.

Again and again, Portals open, depositing teams on the frontlines. Hitting crucial areas to give us an edge. Once a short distance away from the front to reinforce a weakening area. Another time right on top of a group of healers who've been doing a stellar job. Lana and company drop among a team of spellcasters, Mikito and Ingrid tearing into the group while the puppies and Roland corral them and keep back the reinforcements. Sam rolls in right behind in his armored drone, ready to reinforce, his beam cannon firing. Carlos rides behind it, his potion /grenade launcher in hand.

Within minutes, I'm nearly out of Mana and forced to rely on a Greater Mana Potion. Blessings and buffs reinforce my regeneration, but it's not enough, not nearly enough. Alvarez watches me, lips pursed as he waits for me to drop the last couple of teams. I pull a little from the Mana Bracer, but the need isn't crucial yet, so I only take a little. In the meantime, all we can do is watch the screens.

Our reinforcements make a difference, smashing the groups they've targeted and shifting the tide of battle. Lana and company jump on the puppies, riding them through the fray to return to the line, shields flaring as they try and fail to allay the damage. Meanwhile, the Hakarta jump team dealing with the healers have triggered sonic pulsers, stunning those around them as they leapfrog back. Their greater mass lets them pick up and throw their opponents aside when blocked. I even see one particularly large Hakarta pick up a carapaced enemy and use the unlucky bastard as a shield.

"Whoa! And there he goes," Ali exclaims, pointing.

I tilt my head and blink, seeing a twenty-foot-tall creature where W'mee used to be. Though his titular name makes sense now, the creature wielding a flexible, three-bladed whip-sword in one hand. Each strike reaches tens of meters backward, cutting into flesh and armor as though its soggy newspaper, leaving sprays of blood and mashed meat behind.

"What happened?" I growl.

"Mages have been keeping him penned in with multiple disruptive spells. He's been doing some damage, but the line's been falling back and reforming to keep him and his men boxed in. Looks like Pee-Pee decided he'd had enough," Ali explains.

"And…?"

"Transformation Skill. Must be part of his Master Class Skill set. Those things have a limited duration though. If we can keep him penned, once it's gone, he'll be weakened," Ali says.

"How long?" Alvarez asks urgently.

"No idea." Ali shrugs. "Might be ten minutes, might be an hour. Depends on the Skill, the rarity, and of course, how many points he's put in."

Alvarez snorts and relays information. Obviously, I'm not the only one caught by surprise. I absently wonder if they're about to purchase the information from the Shop. If they have the time. Turning my head, I search for and find Km, the rock-creature pushing back the defenders she faces. Luckily, prior experience shows. Instead of facing her directly, the teams have stacked as many shields as they can, along with drones, guardians, and long-range fighters, in front of the Oracle. Only a few elementally resistant fighters stand directly in her way, taking the pounding and being healed constantly by a brace of healers who themselves are supported by others. Behind Km, other Ez are flowing forth, their skin reflecting different types of rock—granite, brick, clay, and others I don't understand. Luckily, they seem content to take their time and follow her. Still, the Ez's advance, while slower, is across a much wider area than the Jarack's.

"Ready," I say, raising my finger.

A few moments later, the next Portal slams shut and we're sitting in silence again. One more team, just another few minutes. But in a battle, a few minutes can be a lifetime and the team I dropped to slow down the Jarack is getting hammered. The tank, a lanky soldier who looks as if he could come apart in a single hit, keeps getting up no matter how many times he's hit. His blood flies as the whip-like blades flick through the air, cutting into the tank and a few brave souls.

"This is bullshit, boy-o," Ali says softly, pointing at the screens. "They're getting their asses creamed. Which is weird to bring food into your posteriors…"

"Never mind that," I say as the Jarack grabs the lanky gentleman and sticks him in his mouth, worrying the shoulder with those powerful jaws. And still, the tank fights on, somehow still alive. Beside the struggling pair, the healer keeps casting spells, pouring in everything he has while the others attack and cut, trying to do their best to hurt the Jarack and failing, forced to dodge as the three blades swirl again. "Enough."

"Redeemer?"

"I'm going in. You guys are going to have get there yourselves. I recommend running." I stand, eyeing the distance.

Ali's already flying forward as fast as he can, understanding what I intend to do. Hopscotching my way there is faster and cheaper for me. A thought and the Mana Battery floods my body, dumping hundreds of Mana points into me for the upcoming fight.

"Redeemer, you can't do this. We need you—" Alvarez says.

"You need me out there," I interrupt, waiting for Ali. "Your men can't take him. I can. Throw the rest at the Oracle. I'll slow him down at the least."

"Your orders—"

I don't answer, instead activating Blink Step when Ali hits the maximum distance. I land and run, Sabre boosting my movement speed as I cover the distance to my target, intent on conserving as much as I can. Four hundred plus Mana right now. Barely enough to do anything.

"Redeemer! You are defying your orders—"

The communicator cuts off with a thought and I Blink Step to get closer. I'm moving as fast as I can. No more worries, no more concerns and half-doubts if I'm doing this right. Just the run, the necessity of battle.

***

The soldier is tossed aside, his body halved but still alive. He's screaming, struggling to crawl back to his body, when the Jarack crosses the distance to the healer and mage. Blood keeps blossoming from the wounds across W'mee's body as bullets tear open wounds, beams burn flesh, and spells cut into him. But it's all surface, nothing going deep. He's torn into our defensive line, well behind where our teams have dug in. The remaining members of the shattered line fire against those who try to take advantage of the gap while W'mee keeps the reinforcements from arriving.

W'mee of the Three Sands, Heretic of the Dawn, Slayer of Grayak Scorpions and Master of the Yellow Pit (Level 18 Singer of the Thrice-Dipped Blades)

_HP: 39403 /42800_

_MP: 283/1780_

Conditions: Skin of Basalt, The Sands Blessing, The Desert's Son (Transformation)

"W'mee!" I roar, punching the volume up on my speakers as I finally arrive.

The Jarack pauses, staring at me as I stride forward, slowing down now that I've gotten his attention.

"Redeemer!" he howls, ignoring the others as his eyes narrow on me. He runs forward, taking my challenge as he laughs in his cackling, insane way.

"I need information on that Sands Blessing."

"On it, boy-o. I'm getting data now, I'll get you my guesses when I can."

Three blades against my one. I could conjure the other five, but I never keep them up for long, the cost on my Mana Regeneration too high. Better to use them and make them disappear, fight in bursts. I need to keep him busy, distracted. I start the dance with the sonic pulser and mini-missiles loaded with grey goo, all meant to slow down my opponent. The pulser makes W'mee growl, the missiles are cut out of the air long before they reach him, and the couple that do land are unable to do much to slow him down.

"All combatants in this area, back off. I don't want to get shot," I snarl over the comms as a couple of shots graze by me, one bouncing off Sabre's shielding.

The shooting slows down, then he's here, blades whistling. My first block is wrong, catching the attack too far from the tip and allowing the whip to wrap over my sword to hammer into the Shield. My shield drops by nearly a third from just that aborted attack. The last blade luckily lands on the ground, missing me and my Shield by inches.

I see his hand swing sideways and I throw myself into a jump, spinning away before I'm wrapped up by the blades or have my foot chopped off. Within seconds, the blades are spinning again, coming back toward me as I land and dash forward. A side of a building is torn apart, the blades ripping through unenhanced stone and steel with casual ease. Even as it does so, W'mee changes the angle of his cut, catching a sniper and killing him.

No time to think, I form blades from my Skill, spinning my arms and setting up their angles, my eyes tight with focus. A calm settles over me. A battle calm, where my mind runs clear and clean, while around it, the raging fires of my temper burn. Clarity, anger, and speed. I grin beneath my helmet, feeling alive as I dance on the edge of oblivion.

The Jarack's blades clash with mine, slithering and twisting as he attempts to cut through my floating ones, his movements hampered by their arcs and their sudden appearance and disappearance. But I can't get close to him either, those blades twisting and turning like a blender blade around his body.

"What is this…?" W'mee howls, flicking his hand.

Three blades ripple, dancing and lashing out like snakes even as fires form and are expelled by their tips. I'm long gone, stepping aside and discarding my summoned weapons. All the while, I'm firing the Inlin and my missiles every moment I can. No grenades though. Nothing that would hide me and take away his focus. That's not my job, not right now.

The Sands Blessing

Effect: Passive Buff. Provides a 11(?) increase in regeneration and 43(?)% increase in resistances while in suitable, desert-like atmospheric conditions.

"I'm barely scratching him," I snarl at Ali.

My biggest gun is gone, my Mana potions unable to be used further to give me a boost. A missed block, a blade sneaking between my wall of swords, and my shield drops by a quarter. I fire the Inlin, armor-piercing bullets digging divots into his flesh. Another cut and yank, my sword ripped from my hand. I let him have it, calling another as I duck forward.

"I'm working on it!" Ali says, his voice tinged with a touch of desperation.

"Redeemer, hold him for one more minute. Reinforcements incoming."

A quick step, one that I didn't anticipate, and W'mee kicks me, throwing me into a building and out. My shield flares, Sabre showing nearly eighty percent loss of shield integrity. I'm good and he's obviously not used to the Honor Guard's fighting methods, but I can't stay on the defensive only. Even as he crashes through the building, playing ugly brown monster to the building's structure, I'm desperately trying to figure out what to do.

"No can do," I grunt, making a decision.

I run forward as he exits the crumbling building, the momentary rush through the structure forcing the Jarack to stop swinging his blades. Just long enough for me to get close as he starts up those metallic shredders.

He snarls, blocking my first swing. Then the second. And the third. I stick close to him, taking clawed attacks on the shield, on Sabre's armor when it fails, as I refuse to let him gain distance. I twist and dodge, stabbing his arm and legs, my blades hovering around me as he keeps attempting to back away. I'm doing little to truly hurt him, but each blow, blocked or successful, leaves a tinge of blue ice.

Freezing Blade, each attack slowing down the asshole. But it's not enough, not by far. Even after ten strikes, he's only a third slower. With a snarl, he glows, heat radiating from his body. Thankfully, the ice along his wounds does not dissipate. Instead, the heat burns Sabre's armor, making me squint and sweat as asphalt liquefies. But it doesn't kill me, doesn't slow me down. Resistances cut both ways, and like him, I can take it. Ali, in the corner of my eyes, shoots straight up as he attempts to avoid the Skill, his Spirit body crisping while less fortunate, less mobile souls burn.

Body of Sun

Effect: Channels the power of the desert sun through the caster's body. Deals 200 base heat damage per second.

Duration: Channeled

Red lights scream as Sabre seizes up, joints and armor melting away. The Jarack bounces back and away, finally free of me, his blades flicking close to lick at the mess that is my PAV. I snarl, making the decision to store the mecha once again. The action, the sudden change, and a twist of my upper body saves my heart, leaving a light wound across the chest. The moment the mecha is gone, along with my helmet, the temperature soars and the accumulated sweat evaporates as my skin blisters. Even as I shield my eyes, his blades plunge into my body, tearing it apart and sending me sprawling.

Thankfully, the Skill cuts off, though the remaining heat is still high enough to cook my flesh as I peel myself off the ground. So few blue dots in my minimap. His Skill might be over, but I'm too far away from him now to attack. I can't hold him, not much longer…

"You did well, Redeemer," W'mee says, cackling. "But you are no match for me."

"No…" I cough, my throat dry, my head pounding as I realize my Mana reserves are barely more than a hundred. "No, I'm not."

W'mee's hand drops, the weapon swinging down, three blades glowing red with fire coming to end me. I can't beat him. I never could. But that was never the point. As the blades whistle through the air, I Blink Step, taken high above by Ali.

Spells and artillery, mortars and potions fall. The combined attacks of dozens of stragglers, of people called from battle all around, splash against his body. I spin, twisting to look down at the fast-approaching body, my sword held out before me.

This fight was never just mine. It couldn't be. No matter how strong a single person can be, a hundred scratches are enough. He knows it. Should have known it. But in the heat of battle, fighting someone who refuses to back down, who refuses to fall, who uses skills and Spells he has never met before, W'mee forgets. Blade plunging through the creature's shoulder, mass and momentum driving it through the monster and sending us to the ground, my shin and arm crack under the sudden pressure. The other conjured blades follow, plunging deep into the monster, one accidentally punching through me and pinning us together.

Pain, as we struggle. The sword pinning us together is dismissed before it tears me apart as the Jarack twists and attempts to scramble away. I hang onto my original blade, stubbornly clinging to it as the creature's high health now works against it, the blade unable to rip free. I keep him pinned, focusing on keeping him still as the attacks fall. Pain. More pain as flesh tears, bones crack, and blood boils. And blessed relief, as healing spells reach me, a never-ending torture as my body seesaws between the two.

Pain, in my body, in my head as I drain my strength, my Mana, my stamina to the extreme. The attack cuts deep, focused within the creature and unable to escape. As it twists, the sword slips and turns, facing away and finally pulling free. No more time, so I take the risk and release one last Blade

Strike, my Mana insufficient and so the Skill takes from my flesh, my body. An explosive blast from another spell tears through me, cutting through my weakened body and throwing me away, my arm severed.

Then the ground, gooey and melted and hot. I skid, body creating a wave of asphalt that sticks and hurts and burns. And then darkness.

Chapter 17

New arms are weird. Having them regrow my lost arm in the Shop was the most expedient way of getting myself fixed after I came to, but it doesn't feel right. Standing to the side of the Shop interface, I roll my shoulders again while I wait for the arm to feel better. Says something about the things the System probably does to us that after a few hours, even a completely new arm is forgotten and accepted.

Fighting the rest of the battle, once I woke up, with one arm was a new and interesting experience. Thankfully, the main fight was over by that point, the Oracle forced to pull back after she was once again severely injured. This time around, she triggered a short-range teleportation, most likely bought from the Shop. It wasn't long after that we learnt that she left the planet. I guess no matter the level of loyalty, watching two other Master Class individuals die was more than a sufficient deterrent.

Once their Master Class support was down, the Zarrie pulled back, intent on fighting again another time. That's when the other portion of Miller's plan kicked in, the resistance fighters, the members of the 1st Special Forces group, and the vanguard of the Marines making their presence known. Pinned between the three forces that were quite happy to rain long-range destruction down on the Zarrie, things got pretty bloody, or so I was told. Rather than risk even more loss of life, Miller let the Zarrie forces call a ceasefire when they sent a banner of truce.

I later learn that the Marines had an even nastier time in their own fights. With the lines drawn for so long, their initial push was through entrenched positions. If it wasn't for the fact that the Marines seemed to have geared their squads for hard and fast fights with specialized melee, ranged, and mage teams, they might not have managed to push through.

For all that we might have disagreements, Miller is a damn professional. It's only after the fight, during the ceasefire, that I learn that the Zarrie had sent more than a few assassins after him and the command structure. Luckily, the one thing California isn't lacking is actors. I'm still not sure I'd have made the call he did, but it certainly allowed him to run the battle without major interference.

One of the few silver linings is the sheer volume of titles being awarded. Ali had a good time telling me about them. Some of the more memorable ones include Mikito's Blood Warden, a couple of Last Stands, a Lord of Guts and Glory, and amusingly, Murphy's Law Incarnated.

Right now, Miller, Wier, and a bunch of other politicians and interest groups are busy talking it up. Since we're just allies, they've declined our participation in these talks, leaving Sam to listen in. Lana's presence was declined, a few groups citing her unfair use of Charisma to influence matters. Rather than kick up a fuss, we stayed out of it. Luckily, Major Ruka has arrived, happy to be paid to play Galactic consultant.

"Still don't see why they wanted a Hakarta and not me," Ali grumbles, staring in the direction where the meeting continues to be held.

"Probably because they could do without your sarcasm." Grunting, I shake my head and stretch, feeling my muscles shift as I marvel at the lack of pain.

In the corner of my eyes, I once more stare at the slowly blinking icon before I decide to acknowledge it.

Congratulations! You've reached Level 50!

Attributes automatically assigned. 3 additional attributes available to be assigned.

You may now choose a Master Class.

Would you like to do so?

(Y/N)

Finally. I'm tempted to look at the list, but doing so will start a process I can't halt. Frustratingly enough, I'm unlikely to have a chance to choose anything really special, anything that will give me an edge, like the Honor Guard Class. But as Ali pointed out, I'm already broken enough as it is.

"John?" Lana calls, reappearing behind me.

She smiles slightly when I turn to face her, somehow having managed to not only change into new clothing but clean up. The simple cream blouse and yoga pants do wonders to show off her voluptuous form, making me drink in the view. It's only the second calling of my name—or maybe third—that I answer her.

"Sorry. What?"

"How's the new arm?" Lana says, wrapping an arm around my waist and sneaking in a kiss before I can answer. There are still shadows under her eyes, a tightness in the hug that speaks of her holding back grief.

"Good. Feels a little strange still, but it's fine." I give her another squeeze.

Still, for how relaxed things are, something feels off. Frowning, I tilt my head from side to side, wondering what's bugging me. Lana's the one to voice the problem first.

"Where're the pups and Roland?" Lana speaks softly, eyebrows drawing together. For a moment she focuses then steps away from me, a hand materializing her shotgun as she opens her mouth to say something.

"Well, I am glad to hear that you are better…" The woman who walks over is seven feet tall, purple hair slicked back in a pixie cut that shows off coral-like ears and slitted yellow eyes. Her nose is almost non-existent, just a pair of nostrils with the slightest almost beak-like overhang.

Ayuri d'Malla of the Dawn, Breaker of the Sixth Legion, Hero of the Sixth Kumma Wars, Mistress of Knives, Bloodflower, Slayer of Kumma, Goblins, Mizza… (Level 42 Erethran Champion)
HP: 9830/9830
MP: 4740/4740
Conditions: Buffs. LOT OF BUFFS.

"*Ali…?*" I note the sudden flash of information above her, the lack of full disclosure as Ali translates the information quickly.

Behind Ayuri comes a pair of *just* normal Erethran Honor Guards, though both are close to hitting the Level cap. A single male and female companion to Ayuri.

"Redeemer of the Dead. What an interesting title," Ayuri says, tapping her lips.

"What did you do to my pets?" Lana growls, stopped from raising her shotgun by my hand on her arm.

We don't stand a chance, not against Ayuri herself and definitely not with two of her friends. Better to play nice. Especially since they don't seem to be directly aggressive. Yet.

"Oh, they're fine. We had to put them in stasis as they refused to let us in," Ayuri says with a smile to Lana, her eyes flicking to the woman before dismissing the redhead as a threat. "We're not interested in your petty squabbles."

"What are you interested in?" I ask, knowing the answer even as I do so. There's only one reason for the Erethran to be here, considering we're nearly at the opposite end of the System Galaxy. Even for a new Dungeon World, they aren't going to send a Champion all the way out here. At least, not *just* for the Dungeon World.

"You, of course, Redeemer. Imagine our surprise when we began to receive updates about how a member of the Honor Guard was gaining titles on the new Dungeon World. Even more so when he kept gaining Levels at an astounding rate. And then of course, he became a settlement owner…" Ayuri shakes her head. "Well, it was such an interesting piece of news. Considering the few we authorized to visit were still on the first ships."

"Well, about that…" I pause as Ayuri's initially benign, if slightly intimidating, visage changes, going flat.

"No need to explain, Redeemer. We know what happened. What we're interested in is what will happen," Ayuri says, closing the distance between us so fast I don't even see her move. Even Mikito with Haste isn't that fast. Androgynous body inches from mine, she looms over me, those tiny pupils judging me. "Were you perhaps considering becoming a Champion? Or an Honor Guard General?"

"*You can't be a Champion, boy-o, but the General is available,*" Ali sends to me urgently.

"I can't be a Champion—" I start.

"Quiet, Spirit. Speak again and we will banish you," Ayuri hisses to where Ali is, flicking a glance backward to one of the Honor Guards. That Guard fixes her gaze on the Spirit, whose mocha skin loses color. "And how are we to believe that, Redeemer? You have already stolen the honor of our Empire once."

"I—"

"Once a thief, always a thief, I say." The voice that emanates from the last Honor Guard member is droll, bored as a Yukon summer day is long and deep.

"Enough," I growl, my temper flaring after getting interrupted so damn often. Interrupted and subtly threatened. "Either let me answer in peace or fight me, because this lack of manners is getting damn tiring."

"He barks." The woman—Unilo—chuckles softly. "Perhaps I shall stop its whistling."

"Whistling?" Lana mutters, uncertain.

"Do your dogs not whistle while they bark?" Unilo says, tilting her head.

"Uhhh, no," Lana says firmly.

"Har. What weird creatures."

Ignoring the pair, Ayuri stares at me till I break and speak. "What?"

"You have not answered my question. What Class do you intend to take now?"

"Well..." I say softly, playing for time as my mind spins. There's something here, something nagging me about this entire encounter. "What does it matter to you?"

"About two moves," Ayuri says with a smile.

"You're threatening me." I state that flatly, my hand to the side as I get ready to call my sword.

"Stating a fact. If you were to choose a Class that besmirches our honor, we would have to resolve the matter. Immediately."

"I see." I give in finally to the lead-in. "And what Class wouldn't?"

"Why, none of them that you have now," Ayuri states. When she gets no reaction from me, she turns toward the man. "Mayaya, you won the bet."

"Yay," Mayaya intones, still in that same bored tone. "I shall drink in pleasure."

"So. Class?" I say again while Ali spins in a circle, obviously aching to speak but unable or unwilling to do so.

Lana looks perturbed, but I shake my head to her and she lets me lead this conversation. For now.

"You understand our position, of course. You cannot be a General. That would compromise too many things. And any Class below that is well, insulting," Ayuri says, shaking her head. "So now we must kill you. Unless…"

"Go on," I growl softly, getting tired of her playing this game and letting my impatience run through my voice. Now that we've been talking for a bit, I can sense her damn glee underneath all the threats. She's having fun, and it's pissing me off. Dangerous as she might be, I've just been through an entire war. Having her continue to play is testing what little patience I have.

"Unless you choose to take up a Class Quest. One that is only open to certain members of the Erethran Empire."

"I see. And the catch is…?" I say.

"It's a good Class Quest. Very powerful. Very popular to try. But somewhat lethal."

"Somewhat?"

"Always!" Ali shouts, shaking his head as he finally can't hold it in anymore. "No one's succeeded in the last two hundred years."

"Two hundred twenty-three years. Galactic standard," Unilo says flatly then waves her hand.

The next moment, Ali disappears with a scream as he's banished. Lana and I stare at Unilo, who shrugs as if that display of power was a minor thing. Which, I guess, for her it is.

"I see." I hold up my hands as if weighing the two options. "So. Death by your hands or an impossible quest."

"Yes," Ayuri says with a wide smile, baring too-sharp teeth.

"John…" Lana says softly, her eyes doing murder arithmetic as she judges the trio.

"It's fine," I say to Lana, holding a finger up to the three while turning to the redhead and giving her a quick kiss. "Looks like I'm going on a trip."

"You're not leaving me."

"Sorry, human, but this is a single-person Quest," Ayuri says.

"I'm not happy about this," Lana says, gripping my shirt tightly. Tears form at her eyes, her fists clenched white. "We can beat them."

"No. No, we can't," I whisper, placing a hand over hers. I meet Lana's violet eyes, which swim with unshed tears, my own vision growing slightly blurry. "And even if we could, we shouldn't. I need to do this."

"Why?" Lana says, her voice heartbroken.

"You know why." As she shakes her head in denial, I continue. "I need more strength. More power. And all the other choices, they aren't good enough. If it's impossible, it's definitely a powerful Class."

"And you could die."

"And that matters?" I shake my head, realizing those are the wrong words. "No. It matters. But I could die here too. I nearly did. This way, I have a chance. A chance…" I can't say the rest. Can't. Won't. Not here, not with them beside me.

"I know," Lana says, burying her face in my shirt as tears flow. "I can't lose you. Not again."

In her voice, I hear all the pain, all the losses she's suffered. Her puppies, Richard, Anna. Friends who fell in Whitehorse and others on the way. It kills me to do this to her, but I have no choice.

"I'll be back. I promise."

She half laughs, half sobs at my answer. Before we can say anything else, Ayuri harrumphs. Bored by our goodbyes, the Champion grabs my shoulder, pulling me away from Lana and leaving the redhead clutching the shreds of my shirt.

"Mayaya!" Ayuri calls, hoisting me up in the air as Mayaya opens a Portal.

Lana steps forward and is blocked by a Soul Shield, one warped to block her movements. "John!"

With a single flick of her hand, Ayuri tosses me through the black oval of space. I spin around in the air, watching the intimidating blackness approach at speed, offering me no clue of what is to come.

"Glad you agreed. Don't die. I bet on you this time!" Ayuri calls as I enter the Portal.

My atoms rip apart, the transition wreathing me in pain I've never experienced before. Even as I land, I hear the last words Ayuri says as the Portal shrinks.

"Right then. Take me to your leaders!"

And then the Portal snaps shut, stranding me in darkness. Alone.

\###

The End

John will be back in

World Unbound (Book 6 of the System Apocalypse)

Author's Note

Thank you for reading Book 5 and I hope you enjoyed it. This book included a lot more interactions with the US military and I have to thank all the beta readers who helped me correct issues. Any errors or issues with the way the military work / talk / interact is entirely my fault. For those who serve, I hope you enjoyed the book and I stayed true to them. I'll admit, we are lacking a large amount of cursing 😊.

If you enjoyed reading the book, please do leave a review and rating. It helps sales and yes, that's the reason I write!

Make sure to follow John's continuing quest in:

- World Unbound (Book 6 of the System Apocalypse)
  https://readerlinks.com/l/729311

In addition, please check out my other series, Adventures on Brad (a more traditional LitRPG fantasy), Hidden Wishes (an urban fantasy GameLit series), and A Thousand Li (a cultivation series inspired by Chinese wuxia and xianxia novels).

To support me directly, please go to my Patreon account:

- https://www.patreon.com/taowong

For more great information about LitRPG series, check out the Facebook groups:

- LitRPG Society
  https://www.facebook.com/groups/LitRPGsociety/
- LitRPG Books
  https://www.facebook.com/groups/LitRPG.books/

About the Author

Tao Wong is an avid fantasy and sci-fi reader who spends his time working and writing in the North of Canada. He's spent way too many years doing martial arts of many forms, and having broken himself too often, he is now an avid fantasy and sci-fi reader who spends his time working and writing in the North of Canada.

For updates on the series and other books written by Tao Wong (and special one-shot stories), please visit the author's website:

http://www.mylifemytao.com

Subscribers to Tao's mailing list will receive exclusive access to short stories in the Thousand Li and System Apocalypse universes:

https://www.subscribepage.com/taowong

Or visit his Facebook Page: https://www.facebook.com/taowongauthor/

About the Publisher

Starlit Publishing is wholly owned and operated by Tao Wong. It is a science fiction and fantasy publisher focused on the LitRPG & cultivation genres. Their focus is on promoting new, upcoming authors in the genre whose writing challenges the existing stereotypes while giving a rip-roaring good read.

For more information on Starlit Publishing, visit their website: https://www.starlitpublishing.com/

You can also join Starlit Publishing's mailing list to learn of new, exciting authors and book releases.

https://starlitpublishing.com/newsletter-signup/

Glossary

Erethran Honor Guard Skill Tree

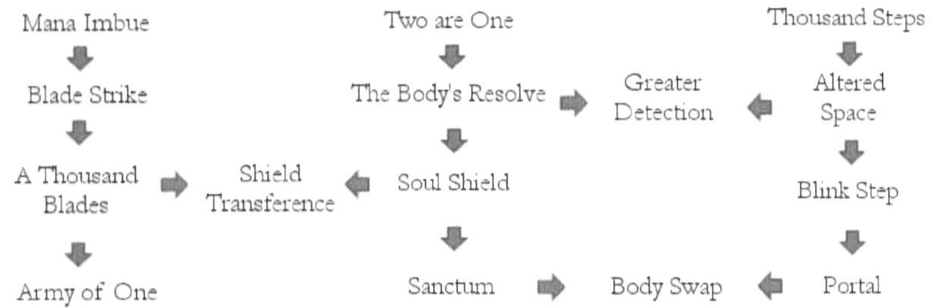

John's Skills

Mana Imbue (Level 3)

Soulbound weapon now permanently imbued with mana to deal more damage on each hit. +20 Base Damage (Mana). Will ignore armor and resistances. Mana regeneration reduced by 10 Mana per minute permanently.

Blade Strike (Level 3)

By projecting additional Mana and stamina into a strike, the Erethran Honor Guard's Soulbound weapon may project a strike up to 30 feet away.

Cost: 30 Stamina + 30 Mana

Thousand Steps (Level 1)

Movement speed for the Honor Guard and allies are increased by 5% while skill is active. This ability is stackable with other movement-related skills.

Cost: 20 Stamina + 20 Mana per minute

Altered Space (Level 2)

The Honor Guard now has access to an extra-dimensional storage location of 30 cubic feet. Items stored must be touched to be willed in and may not include living creatures or items currently affected by auras that are not the Honor Guard's. Mana regeneration reduced by 10 Mana per minute permanently.

Two are One (Level 1)

Effect: Transfer 10% of all damage from Target to Self.

Cost: 5 Mana per second

The Body's Resolve (Level 3)

Effect: Increase natural health regeneration by 35%. On-going health status effects reduced by 33%. Honor Guard may now regenerate lost limbs. Mana regeneration reduced by 15 Mana per minute permanently.

Greater Detection (Level 1)

Effect: User may now detect System creatures up to 1 kilometer away. General information about strength level is provided on detection. Stealth skills, Class skills, and ambient mana density will influence the effectiveness of this skill. Mana regeneration reduced by 5 Mana per minute permanently.

A Thousand Blades (Level 3)

Creates four duplicate copies of the user's designated weapon. Duplicate copies deal base damage of copied items. May be combined with Mana Imbue and Shield Transference. Mana Cost: 3 Mana per second.

Soul Shield (Level 2)

Effect: Creates a manipulable shield to cover the caster's or target's body. Shield has 1,000 Hit Points.

Cost: 250 Mana

Blink Step (Level 2)

Effect: Instantaneous teleportation via line-of-sight. May include Spirit's line of sight. Maximum range—500 meters.

Cost: 100 Mana

Frenzy (Level 1)

Effect: When activated, pain is reduced by 80%, damage increased by 30%, stamina regeneration rate increased by 20%. Mana regeneration rate decreased by 10%.

Frenzy will not deactivate until all enemies have been slain. User may not retreat while Frenzy is active.

Cleave (Level 2)

Effect: Physical attacks deal 60% more base damage. Effect may be combined with other Class Skills.

Cost: 25 Mana

Elemental Strike (Level 1 - Ice)

Effect: Used to imbue a weapon with freezing damage. Adds +5 Base Damage to attacks and a 10% chance of reducing speed by 5% upon contact. Lasts for 30 seconds.

Cost: 50 Mana

Instantaneous Inventory (Maxed)

Allows user to place or remove any System-recognized item from Inventory if space allows. Includes the automatic arrangement of space in the inventory. User must be touching item.

Cost: 5 Mana per item

Portal (Level 5)

Effect: Creates a 5-meter by 5-meter portal which can connect to a previously traveled location by user. May be used by others. Maximum distance range of portals is 25,000 kilometers.

Cost: 250 Mana + 100 Mana per minute (minimum cost 350 Mana)

Army of One (Level 2)

The Honor Guard's feared penultimate combat ability, Army of One builds upon previous Skills, allowing the user to unleash an awe-inspiring attack to deal with their enemies. Attack may now be guided around minor obstacles.

Effect: Army of One allows the projection of (Number of Thousand Blades conjured weapons * 3) Blade Strike attacks up to 300 meters away from user. Each attack deals 3 * Blade Strike Level damage (inclusive of Mana Imbue and Soulbound weapon bonus).

Cost: 750 Mana

Sanctum (Level 2)

An Erethran Honor Guard's ultimate trump card in safeguarding their target, Sanctum creates a flexible shield that blocks all incoming attacks, hostile teleportations and Skills. At this Level of Skill, the user must specify dimensions of the Sanctum upon use of the Skill. The Sanctum cannot be moved while the Skill is activated.

Dimensions: Maximum 15 cubic meters.

Cost: 1,000 Mana

Duration: 2 minute and 7 seconds

Shrunken Footprints (Level 1)

Reduces System presence of user, increasing the chance of the user evading detection of System-assisted sensing Skills and equipment. Also increases cost of information purchased about user. Reduces Mana Regeneration by 5 permanently.

Tech Link (Level 2)

Effect: Tech Link allows user to increase their skill level in using a technological item, increasing input and versatility in usage of said items. Effects vary depending on item. General increase in efficiency of 10%. Mana regeneration rate decreased by 10%.

Designated Technological Items: Neural Link, Sabre

Spells

Improved Minor Healing (III)

Effect: Heals 35 Health per casting. Target must be in contact during healing. Cooldown 60 seconds.

Cost: 20 Mana

Improved Mana Dart (IV)

Effect: Creates four darts out of pure Mana, which can be directed to damage a target. Each dart does 15 damage. Cooldown 10 seconds.

Cost: 25 Mana

Enhanced Lightning Strike

Effect: Call forth the power of the gods, casting lightning. Lightning strike may affect additional targets depending on proximity, charge and other conductive materials on-hand. Does 100 points of electrical damage.

Lightning Strike may be continuously channeled to increase damage for 10 additional damage per second.

Cost: 75 Mana.

Continuous cast cost: 5 Mana / second

Lightning Strike may be enhanced by using the Elemental Affinity of Electromagnetic Force. Damage increased by 20% per level of affinity.

Greater Regeneration

Effect: Increases natural health regeneration of target by 5%. Only single use of spell effective on a target at a time.

Duration: 10 minutes

Cost: 100 Mana

Fireball

Effect: Create an exploding sphere of fire. Deals 150 points of fire damage to those caught within. Sphere of fire expands to 3 meters radius (on average). Cooldown 60 seconds.

Cost: 100 Mana

Polar Zone

Effect: Create a thirty meter diameter blizzard that freezes all targets within one. Does 10 points of freezing damage per minute plus reduces effected individuals speed by 5%. Cooldown 60 seconds.

Cost: 200 Mana

Greater Healing

Effect: Heals 75 Health per casting. Target does not require contact during healing. Cooldown 60 seconds per target.

Cost: 50 Mana

Mana Drip

Effect: Increases natural health regeneration of target by 5%. Only single use of spell effective on a target at a time.

Duration: 10 minutes

Cost: 100 Mana

Freezing Blade

Effect: Enchants weapon with a slowing effect. A 5% slowing effect is applied on a successful strike. This effect is cumulative and lasts for 1 minute. Cooldown 3 minutes

Spell Duration: 1 minute.

Cost: 150 Mana

Inferno Beam

A beam of heat raised to the levels of an inferno, able to melt steel and earth on contact! The perfect spell for those looking to do a lot of damage in a short period of time.

Effect: Does 150 Points of Heat Damage

Cost: 125 Mana

Mud Walls

Unlike its more common counterpart Earthen Walls, Mud Walls focus is more on dealing slow, suffocating damage and restricting movement on the battlefield.

Effect: Does 20 Points of Suffocating Damage. -30% Movement Speed

Duration: 2 Minutes

Cost: 75 Mana

Sabre's Load-Out

Omnitron III Class II Personal Assault Vehicle (Sabre)

Core: Class II Omnitron Mana Engine

CPU: Class D Xylik Core CPU

Armor Rating: Tier IV (Modified with Adaptive Resistance)

Hard Points: 5 (5 Used)

Soft Points: 3 (3 Used)

Requires: Neural Link for Advanced Configuration

Battery Capacity: 120/120

Attribute Bonuses: +35 Strength, +18 Agility, +10 Perception

Inlin Type II Projectile Rifle

Base Damage: N/A (Dependent Upon Ammunition)

Ammo Capacity: 45/45

Available Ammunition: 250 Standard, 150 Armor Piercing, 200 High Explosive, 25 Luminescent

Ares Type II Shield Generator

Base Shielding: 2,000 HP

Regeneration Rate: 50/second unlinked, 200/second linked

Mkylin Type IV Mini-Missile Launchers

Base Damage: N/A (dependent on missiles purchased)

Battery Capacity: 6/6

Reload rate from internal batteries: 10 seconds

Available Ammunition: 12 Standard, 12 High Explosive, 12 Armor Piercing, 4 Napalm

Monolam Temporal Cloak

This Temporal Cloaks splices the user's timeline, adjusting their physical, emotional, and psychic presence to randomly associated times. This allows the user to evade notice from most sensors and individuals. The Monolam Temporal Cloak has multiple settings for a variety of situations, varying the type and level of dispersal of the signal.

Requirements: 1 Hardpoint, Tier IV Mana Engine

Duration: Varies depending on cloaking level

Type II Webbing Mini-Missile

Base Damage: N/A

Effect: Disperses insta-webbing upon impact or on activation. Dispersal covers 3 cubic feet.

Cost: 500 Credits

Shinowa Type II Sonic Pulser

Base Damage: 25 per second

Additional Effect: Disrupts auditory sense of balance on opponent during use. Effects have a small chance of continuing after use.

Joola Communication Booster (Tier II)

Military Grade Communication Booster able to deliver your message where and when it needs to be. Joola Tech is the only way to go when what you need to say needs to be heard!

Effect: Disregard all communication interference from shields, communication scramblers, Skills and Spells below Tier of communication booster. 50% chance of breaking through equivalent tier blockages (chance decreases dependent on proximity to emanating blockage)

Other Equipment

Silversmith Mark II Beam Pistol (Upgradeable)

Base Damage: 18

Battery Capacity: 24/24

Recharge Rate: 2 per hour per GMU

Tier IV Neural Link

Neural link may support up to 5 connections.

Current connections: Omnitron III Class II Personal Assault Vehicle

Software Installed: Rich'lki Firewall Class IV, Omnitron III Class IV Controller

Ferllx Type II Twinned-Beam Rifle (Modified)

Base Damage: 57

Battery Capacity: 17/17

Recharge rate: 1 per hour per GMU (currently 12)

Tier II Sword (Soulbound Personal Weapon of an Erethran Honor Guard)

Base Damage: 98

Durability: N/A (Personal Weapon)

Special Abilities: +20 Mana Damage, Blade Strike

Kryl Ring of Regeneration

Often used as betrothal bands, Kyrl rings are highly sought after and must be ordered months in advance.

Health Regeneration: +30

Stamina Regeneration: +15

Mana Regeneration: +5

Tier III Bracer of Mana Storage

A custom work by an unknown maker, this bracer acts a storage battery for personal Mana. Useful for Mages and other Classes that rely on Mana. Mana storage ratio is 50 to 1.

Mana Capacity: 350/350

Fey-steel Dagger

Fey-steel is not actual steel but an unknown alloy. Normally reserved only for the Sidhe nobility, a small—by Galactic standards—amount of Fey-steel is released for sale each year. Fey-steel takes enchantments extremely well.

Base Damage: 28

Durability: 110/100

Special Abilities: None

Brumwell Necklace of Shadow Intent

The Brumwell necklace of shadow intent is the hallmark item of the Brumwell Clan. Enchanted by a Master Crafter, this necklace layers shadowy intents over your actions, ensuring that information about your actions are more difficult to ascertain. Ownership of such an item is both a necessity and a mark of prestige among settlement owners and other individuals of power.

Effect: Persistent effect of Shadow Intent (Level 4) results in significantly increased cost of purchasing information from the System about wearer. Effect is persistent for all actions taken while necklace is worn.